Long Drives and Lonesome Roads

John Evans

This is a work of fiction. Names, characters, places, and incidents either are the product of the author's imagination or are used fictitiously, and any resemblance to actual persons living or dead, business establishments, events, or locales, is entirely coincidental.

© COPYRIGHT 2026 by John Evans

All rights reserved. No part of this book may be used or reproduced in any manner whatsoever without written permission of the publisher except in the case of brief quotations embodied in critical articles or reviews.

AI was not used to write this book, to create the cover art, or in formatting.

NO AI TRAINING: Without in any way limiting the author's and publisher's exclusive rights under copyright, any use of this publication to "train" generative artificial intelligence (AI) technologies to generate text is expressly prohibited. The author reserves all rights to license uses of this work for genAI training and development of machine learning language models.

Warning: Not intended for persons under the age of 18. May contain coarse language and mature content that may disturb some readers. Reader discretion advised.

Cover Art Design by: Kelly Moran/Rowan Prose Publishing
Photo Credit: Adobe Images/Deposit Photos
First Edition
ISBN: 978-1-961967-76-2
Rowan Prose Publishing, LLC
www.RowanProsePublishing.com
Published in the United States of America

OTHER BOOKS BY JOHN EVANS:

PRAISE FOR JOHN EVANS:

"Quick pacing, this novel goes for the stake, the sword, and the torch to deliver escapism and a new direction of vampire lore. If you want magic, open the yellow pages. You want a badass hunter with a quick joke, call Tobias Halson: Werewolf Hunter."
-Wes Cambron, author of *Unbalanced & Unprepared*

"A significant new voice in the genre."
-Entertainment Monthly

"Immersive and masterful."
-Bestselling Author Boris Bacic

"In this bloody, horrific novel, the action comes swiftly and with unrelenting intensity. It'll keep you on the edge as events unfold and these dreadful secrets are revealed. Nobody is safe and nobody can escape. Once these creatures have their sights on you, there's no place to run that can protect you. I always love a good werewolf book and this one takes that legend and gives it a unique bend, which I always appreciate. I highly recommend it."
-Horror Reads on "Midnight Falls"

"Vampire Hunter is truly a remarkable read that got me out of a months-long reading slump and has made me so excited for more, impatiently counting down the days until the sequel is released."
-Ella Dupuie, author of *Fractures of the Fallen*

"With hard-hitting stories ranging from the unnerving to the macabre to the darkly humorous, Long Drives and Lonesome Roads *is a killer collection that deserves to sit on every shelf."*
-Pedro Iniguez, Bram Stoker Award Winner

Table of Contents

Ghouls Ride Free
The Idol
The Hand
The Basement
The Barn
Rawhead
The Clown
Rest Stop
The Dead Stay Dead
The Why of It All
The Window
Riders Before the Storm
The Balloon
Charlie Wasn't There
In The Valley of the Garden
The Passenger

Foreword by the Author

The primary inspiration behind this collection is road trips. I have traveled a lot in my life. Spending hours driving on roads in the good old U. S. of A. As a kid, my parents would drive us to Florida in the summer on vacation, sometimes to Myrtle Beach, or Gatlinburg. My parents were not big on flying, mainly because my dad was terrified of it. So, long road trips were a family staple. On those long car rides, we would often listen to audiobooks. Mostly, this was for my parents' entertainment. As kids, we had other distractions—namely sleeping, Gameboys, and books. Oh yes, my parents encouraged reading as a way to keep us quiet in the car. It also caused bouts of motion sickness and vomiting.

As we were avid readers, we could also enjoy the audiobooks. Mostly, it was things like Mary Higgins Clark, or 'The Cat Who' series by Lilian Jackson Braun, occasionally Michael Crichton or John Grisham and, eventually, the 'Harry Potter' series. Then, as I got older and it was just my dad and I, we would listen to darker stuff, like King or Koontz, and sometimes Patterson.

The problem with audiobooks and car trips was it always seemed like you had to stop and get out of the car at the good parts. Of course, later, I discovered the perfect pairing for shorter car trips—ones that were not hours long—this was, of course, short story collections. I love a good short story collection. If you really want to see what an author is made of, really see what they're all about, look at their short story collections.

Maintaining that Stephen King's 'Nightshift' and 'Skeleton Crew' are better than any of his novels is a hill I will die on. He tends to waffle when he writes novels. Lord knows I love me some IHOP, but being long-winded is valid criticism some have of his works.

Short stories are harder to write than novels because, well, they are shorter. You don't have time to mess about like with a novel. You can't waste three pages describing a tree. They're punchy. You have to get in to introduce the characters, build the world, set the stage, light the fuse, and skedaddle before the reader can get bored and start calling for your hide.

It's a trick to pull off, and even harder to master. Now, try to imagine doing all that in under the thirty five hundred word limit most literary magazines and anthologies put on submissions. I wasn't able to get a single thing published until I started telling them that they only had to pay me for the word limit. And I know that some union people are gonna get mad at me for that, but the industry is tough, and as a small indie author, you have to do what it takes sometimes.

But there are none of those pesky word limits here. Some are a tad long, while others are brief, but all make for perfect snack size bits for listening to in the car. Maybe you are listening to them in your car right now, in which case...did you remember to check your backseat for serial killers when you got in?

That's what I wanted to create, a series of bite size stories you could enjoy at your own pace. Whether you are reading or listening to them I hope you enjoy them. The subjects, of course, also are to capture that road trip feeling. A lot of them do feature vehicles and driving, mainly because, as I stated before, they are based, in part, on my own trepidation when it comes to traveling. The rest have to do with childhood fears and things like my first job and such.

In addition to exploring my own fears, I use short stories as a means of literary experimentation. I try different ways and methods of telling stories, voices, formats, and structure. So, take these stories for what they are—a young writer's early attempts at learning a very difficult craft.

While I hope some of these do frighten some of you, I truly want you to enjoy yourself. Make sure to turn on all the lights real bright, crawl under the protection of the covers, and read until the sun comes up. After all, the monsters can't get you in daylight.

And if you are listening to this in the car, make sure to check your backseat.

Ghouls Ride Free

The Cavalier's dim lights cut through the dark as the car made its way up Highway 68 on the last leg of its trip. It was an old 1989 model whose paint had been bright red when it was new. Now, it was a washed-out sun-faded orange with a bit of rust on the driver's side rear fender. There was a peeling bumper sticker on the back, beneath the defective turn signal that didn't flash, but stayed on as long as the car was running. The sticker had once read "Girls Ride Free. Guys Have to Pay For It," but with age and a lot of rough miles, it had grown faded and dirty. Time and water had warped it so that it appeared to read "Ghouls Ride Free," with the second half having worn off some time ago.

Shane had been driving for the last three hours and still had about an hour left before making it to Maysville. He didn't live in Maysville, but just across the bridge in Aberdeen, and it would be a relief to finally be home. The drive to Nashville, nearly a month ago, had been hell. He hadn't known if the old car would even make it that far. It was over twenty years old and, at low speeds, had a ferocious rattle in the front end. By some miracle, it still ran. It did take several minutes for the starter to catch, though. Having to sit there and look like an idiot, as the car coughed and sputtered, made him feel like more of a loser.

But that was about to change. He had gone down to Nashville because his dying mother had been in the hospice wing at Saint Thomas. It had been cancer that finally killed her, not the drugs she had been shooting, snorting, and shoving up her ass for over sixty years. God damn cancer, when so many other junkies these days were getting a hot needle and drowning in their own vomit.

It was a horrible way to think about her, but she had not exactly been "Mother of the Year." Having left Shane at home alone, with either a full diaper or an empty stomach, with no food in the house, just so she could go out and score. He practically had to raise himself with her being on the nod most of the time. When she wasn't, she was worse than useless. And there were the empty promises, all the times she vowed to get clean, though she never did. Then there were the times luck happened to throw them a few bucks, and she would promise a real Christmas with presents or a birthday trip out to a restaurant with a real birthday cake, not a little Debbie's with an old birthday candle in it. Of course, that never happened, and the found money would just find its way into her arm through a needle. Unfortunately, not a hot one.

It's no wonder that I turned into a user myself, he thought as he peered through the haze of cigarette smoke. The Cavalier's ashtray was overflowing with butts and ashes. He was overcompensating, which was usual for recovering junkies. They find new habits or double up on others to replace their old addictions. Addicts found other addictions, alcoholics found religion, and smokers found, well, he didn't know what smokers resorted to other than that awful gum and those ridiculous patches.

The car gave a shudder as it reached a speed too fast for its liking. The damn thing would rattle like a coffee can full of loose nails if anyone pushed it up past fifty. You either got used to driving slowly or tried to ignore the sound of the car threatening to tear itself apart. On the positive side, he rarely got pulled over anymore since he didn't have any choice other than to obey the speed limit.

It was just as well. Even though it had been a year since he had stopped slamming junk into his own arm, he still wasn't too keen on cops. They were always looking for a reason to harass people. Especially if you looked like a junkie, because no one loves a junkie more than other junkies. Hypocritical pigs loved them more than anyone 'cause that meant they were probably holding. And why buy your own drugs when you could get them for free off some punk? Besides, what were the junkies gonna do, call the cops? Shane almost made himself laugh at that thought. The car took a sharp swerve to the right and raised hell on the rumble strips.

Quite a racket, you had to give them that, he thought as he pulled the car back onto the road properly. He was blinded temporarily when another car passed. It was one of those cars with bright LED lights that were just as bad as high beams. *Gonna get me one of those,* he thought to himself, *then I'll be the one blinding assholes on the road.* He frowned at the Cavalier's own weak lights. They were a sickly yellow color from age and dimming slightly. You couldn't see more than ten or so feet ahead, but they were better than nothing.

"Not for much longer," he told himself. The one good thing about this whole miserable trip was that the dumb junkie bitch had done him at least one favor in his whole life. After her funeral, a cheap state-funded thing with a featureless casket on state-allotted land for burying the destitute and nameless, which was fitting, he had been approached by an insurance man. The man, in his cheap suit and balding head, had notified him of an insurance policy that had been taken out years ago.

She must have forgotten about it, because if she hadn't, she would have cashed it out and, *poof*, it too would have disappeared into the same place all the birthdays and Christmases had gone. It wasn't anything grand, just a few thousand bucks, but to the terminally broke, it looked like a king's fortune. That small fortune would go to a new car. Shane amused himself with the thought of taking the old Cavalier out back and shooting it like Ol' Yeller. Fun, but not realistic. He would drag the old heap to the local "Cash for Clunkers" program and use the cash for a down payment on a car.

Not a new car, but at least a better car. Something from this decade, at least, instead of a vehicle that was around when

Reagan was in office. He smashed out his butt in the overladen ash box. He would have to make sure it had an ashtray. Most cars nowadays don't have ashtrays, and the newer ones don't even have dashboard lighters. Pussies were making it so you couldn't have fun anywhere anymore.

He tried to turn up the radio as he pushed in the lighter to heat it up for another smoke. The radio was nearly pure static. Faint sounds could be heard buried underneath that blizzard, but he couldn't tell if it was music or ads at this point. He flipped the dial. Nothing. Both the AM and FM bands were static. He hit the button to switch over to the tape deck. There was a high-pitched whine and a disturbing grinding sound, but still no music.

Shane groaned as, at that moment, the first few drops of rain splattered on his windshield. He punched the dash in frustration, causing the tape deck to finally start working. The middle part of "Come Sail Away" came blaring out of the speakers. The Styx tape had been jammed in the tape machine since he had gotten the car. He had tried to pry it out a few times, but never with any luck. His next car would have a CD player, he promised himself, one of those nice six-CD changer ones.

He quickly turned the radio down before switching on the wiper knob. The wiper blades made audible screeching sounds as they traveled back and forth, nearly drowning out the music. "Not much longer," he told himself. "Not much longer." He and the car both just had to tough it out for a little longer, just a few weeks, maybe a month tops. Once the check came in, he wouldn't have to deal with this rust bucket ever again. That was if his luck held out.

God forbid that something else goes awry, but that's how the universe works. It gave you something good, just to kick you in the nuts when you weren't looking. Life was a lot like those Charlie Brown comic strips. The ones where Lucy pretends to hold the football for Charlie Brown to kick, only to pull it away at the last second. Life was a cruel bitch, but we all keep trying to kick that damn football.

It had scared him that the first thing he had thought, upon hearing about his little windfall, was how much heroin he could buy with that. It had been a long time since he had felt the urge to fix, but that had brought the old itch roaring back. He had almost done the old junkie shuffle on the spot.

"Jitter and jive all you want, just don't let them see you do it. Maintain, man, maintain. Can I get an amen? Once a junkie, always a junkie. And being the bastard offspring of a junkie, well, you are right fucked from the start with a genetic craving for the stuff. Can I get an amen?!"

All the old adages from the rehab days were floating back. The long days of group therapy, the longer nights of solitude, and too much thinking. And the whole time needing to fix, fix, fix. A shiver ran down Shane's back, causing him to crank his window up and turn on the heater.

He was not backsliding. He did not want to score or fix. He just wanted to get home, go to sleep, and be done with this nightmare. He worked too hard to get that one-year chip, and he wasn't gonna blow it now, at the first sign of serendipity. He had turned his life around. No more drugs and sketchy "friends." No more lying around stoned at some hooker's house just waiting for some other junkie to knife you for your money or your stash. No more coming to unfamiliar surroundings with no clue where you were or how long you were on the nod.

He was clean now. He had a job, an apartment, and soon a new car that wasn't a reject from *Mad Max*. He was not a junkie anymore. He was not his mother. His mother, lying in the hospital bed, stinking of cancer and shit. A skeleton wasting away to skin and bone, as cancer ate her from the inside out. And the irony of it all, the sick fucking joke, was the IV in her arm. Pumping her full of morphine, the good stuff. She was living the junkie dream with hot and cold running junk on tap and no dealer to cut her off or demand she earn it by sucking his cock. Just a medically prescribed heavenly high.

Shane calmed his mind, as he had learned in the New Beginnings Rehabilitation Facility, and waited for it to pass. *Jitter and jive, jitter and jive, just don't let them see you doing the junkie shuffle. Get that shit under control. Can I get an amen?!* The junkie mantras ran through his mind. These were not taught by the folks at New Beginnings. They wouldn't consider teaching addicts something so crass—or truthful.

No, the good doctors and nurses at rehab were more about meditation, self-improvement, and all those other feel-good lies. No, drug addicts were either self-taught or schooled by other addicts in the ways of the junkie mantras, usually while in custody under the watchful eye of the Popo, or in the late hours when their last fix was far out and there was no knowing when or if the next one was coming. After all the self-loathing, the bargaining with God, and self-harm, they found their way to the nirvana of junkie self-enlightenment.

"Learn to maintain. Fake it till you make it, brother." Shane himself had learned them from a big black man in the New Beginnings facility. He didn't know how long the man had been there, but he was clearly a long-time junkie and repeat rider on the rehab rollercoaster. The two had been roommates, and in the long hours of the night, after the methadone and the puking, he had coached Shane in the ways of the reformed addict.

"There is no such thing as a cure for an addict," he had proclaimed like a street preacher. "A junkie is a junkie from the day he is born to the day he dies. And a junkie who quits and never touches another needle until the day he dies just didn't live long enough. Can I get an amen?!" Every night, he would preach the Junkie Gospel, and every night, Shane would listen while the withdrawal racked his body with shakes and fever. While he would never admit it out loud, Shane was, in his heart, a true believer in that gospel. He was born a junkie, he would die a junkie, and there was nothing anyone, God or doctors, could do about that. Can I get an amen?!

Shane couldn't even remember the old black man's name anymore. Frank? Was that it? Or had it been Freddy? The rain was coming down harder, to the point where the wipers were almost pointless, and he could barely make out the road in his headlights. It was as if the sky had opened up and God himself was taking a piss on him personally.

The smart thing to do would have been to pull over and wait for things to clear up. The Cavalier's tires weren't bald yet, but they were far from something you would want to chance in a storm like this. He didn't care. He just wanted to get home and hunched over the steering wheel, trying to see as best he could. No one should be out on a night like this.

He didn't see the hitchhiker so much as he almost ran him over. The man appeared as little more than a dark brown smear through the car's windshield. He swore loudly and jerked the car away, nearly sending it into a skid. It did fishtail a bit when he slammed on the brakes, but he managed to get the car under control and keep it on the road. Sitting in the car, dead in the middle of the highway, Shane tried to calm himself down as the adrenaline shot through his system in a way that only a long-time drug user can appreciate. His knuckles turned white from gripping the steering wheel as his whole body shook.

Swearing again, he thumped the wheel. The asshole had come out of nowhere and given him one hell of a scare. The hitchhiker could still be seen through the cracked rearview mirror. Standing there on the side of the road, like the world's biggest doorstop, not moving or walking, just standing there in the pouring rain. Shane figured he must have given the guy a scare of his own, and he was probably trying to figure out if he was wet due to the rain or if he had pissed himself.

He didn't envy the dumb bastard. Driving through this mess was bad enough. Having to hike the highway was infinitely worse. Though, he realized it probably hadn't been raining when he started out, and he wondered why the fella hadn't sought out shelter. To stand out there and hook it in this weather, he must have been really hard up.

Shane fought with himself for a few seconds over what to do. He had been hard up more than a few times himself and relied on the kindness of strangers to see him through. In school, he had learned not to pick up hitchhikers, but then again, they also told him not to do drugs. He had nearly hit the guy and definitely did douse him with water. Giving the guy a lift was the least he could do for soaking him in a storm. Seeing no cars coming, he put the vehicle in reverse and backed up to where the man was standing. Stopping in front of the hitchhiker, he leaned across and popped the door open. The window crank hadn't worked in a long time.

"Hey, man, you need a ride?" Shane asked.

The man nodded, or at least Shane thought he did. It was hard to tell as the face and head were mostly obscured by the wide-brimmed hat he wore. Shane tried to get a good look at the man as he got in, but the dome light in the car was so dim with age and smoke that it might as well not have worked. As the stranger climbed in, the best he could tell was that the guy was old. At least, that was how it looked. His face was all hard shadows and deep lines. It could have just as easily been hard living as much as age. There had been some junkies he had known in his time, as well as in rehab, who were in their mid-twenties, but looked like a very rough fifty or sixty. It was a good bet that Shane, too, had some hard miles on his own face, so he probably was in no place to cast any stones.

"Where are you going, buddy?" he asked once the hitchhiker had settled in and closed the door. Shane noticed the man's long-fingered hands when he pulled the door closed. His passenger gave no other answer than the most indistinct of grunts and settled his big coat around him. The folds of the coat were well creased and worn. It was clearly old, and even in the little light given off by the dash lights, you could see how dirty it was.

"I can take you as far as Maysville." He tried again, not stupid enough to tell this man where he lived. This got only another grunt. *Great*, he thought, he had picked up a rambling bum who was just wandering the highways and byways. Just aimlessly wandering, with no idea where he was or where he was going. Shane almost started to regret picking him up, but then the voice of that old black preacher popped into his head, reminding him to pay it forward. *The hopeless have to look out for one another, or we all become hopeless. Can I get an amen?!*

Not all of them were pearls of wisdom. They were, after all, the ramblings of a junkie drying out. What had been his name? Hank? Henry? It didn't really matter, even though it bugged the hell out of him, so he tried to put it out of his mind. Besides, he had another one of life's vagabonds sitting right next to him, might as well try to make the most of it, or at least try to seem friendly.

"Terrible weather, huh?" The only reply was a raspy clearing of a throat. Well, Jesus tap-dancing Christ on a warm bun, he had his tried best just to give up and ride in silence. As the Cavalier plowed through the stormy night, he tried to get a better look at the guy from the corner of his eye. The old guy, if that's what he was, had stringy gray hair that had an almost yellow tinge to it. It was long, scraggly, hanging down to his shoulders, and lank from how wet it was. From the thin amount of it, Shane guessed the guy was probably mostly bald and lucky to have any at all.

The hat did little to protect its wearer from the rain, apparently. It did little more than cast shadows over his face and drip water onto his long, hooked nose. The nose, along with his protruding chin, made Shane think of the Moon Man from that old McDonald's commercial, Mac Tonight. They formed an almost crescent moon in profile. Any longer, he thought with amusement, and they would touch.

He also noticed the way the man's mouth moved, as though he were sliding a pair of dentures around in his mouth, the way old people do when they don't fit properly. He had always found it disgusting to watch, and couldn't understand why people didn't realize they were doing it. It could have been that they did indeed know that they were doing it, and did so with the sole intention of grossing people out. It was a good tactic to get people to leave you the hell alone.

The heavy overcoat gave him the impression that the man was sunken or a lot skinnier than the bulky clothing would suggest.

And when the guy had folded his hands in his lap, Shane had gotten a better look at his fingers. They were long and gnarled like twisted tree branches. The nails had been long and dirty, clearly unkempt, as if hygiene was not a priority for their owner. But the strangest thing was the man's eyes, the way the dash lights reflected in them, he could have sworn they looked like they were glowing. Their hue was sickly and bloodshot. Even the pupils were odd. They looked long and slit-like, sort of like a cat.

As they continued on in silence, he began to notice a foul odor. It was sour, like old milk and rotten eggs. An almost greenish smell of mold and rotten meat. It slowly grew stronger until Shane could actually taste it on his tongue. Turning on the car's fan only made it worse. The smell was sucked in through the floor vents and shot back out through the dash vent right into their faces.

His eyes began to sting and water. There was only one place or person it could be coming from. He wasn't sure if it just hadn't been apparent first due to the rain or if the bum had beefed in the car. His passenger hadn't actually moved in a while, so it was completely possible that he died before he dropped a load in his pants.

What a perfect end to the past few shitty weeks. It wasn't enough that he had to schlep himself across two state lines just to watch an old junkie die. Now, God forbid, he had a dead bum in his car. In fact, the smell really did remind him of his mother's hospital room.

After the first nerve-racking four-hour drive, he had found himself sitting in a sterile hospital room, rank with the smell of sterile antiseptic, next to a skeleton that had once been the neglectful woman he had called mother. Her skin was pulled tightly across the bones of her face, which only helped to amplify the effect of her sunken eyes. They were ringed in dark purple, like permanent bruises. Under the fluorescent lighting, her closed eyes looked like bottomless pits devoid of any life.

Only the barest rise and fall of her emaciated breast gave any hint of life. The hiss and beeping of machines carried with it more life than the barely living corpse before him. The cancer was quick, but extremely painful, so she was doped up good with high doses of morphine. Though the machine had a manual injector, she used to give herself another dose if needed, she clearly no longer had the strength to press it.

Her hands had been little more than thin bones with bunched knuckles and twisted fingers. Her pale, twig-like arms were spotted with the scars of ancient track marks where needles had once been used, but not forgotten. Ghosts of long-forgotten highs. He had wondered if she remembered much of anything anymore, or if she would recognize her own son.

The irony of his presence, at the side of her deathbed, hadn't been lost on him. Nearly a year ago, he had almost beaten her to the punch. Some skag he had been banging at the time had nearly killed him with a hot needle. Overdosing had been a sobering experience—ha, ha. One of life's crueler jokes. It hadn't been like he had thought. There was no blacking out or drifting off. No, he had been wide awake and conscious while he foamed at the mouth and convulsed. The pain of his body twisting was dwarfed only by the poisonous fire that shot through the veins in his arm.

What had been worse, if that was possible, was that the bitch had just sat there and left him dying while she fixed. He had been able to see her out of his peripheral vision the whole time he was in agony. Had someone else not called 911, he surely would have died on that bitch's bedroom floor. As much as he tried, he could never recall exactly at what point he blacked out. All he remembered was coming to in a hospital room just like the one his mother was dying in.

When he had gotten out, he had checked into rehab, but there would be no such luck for her. This was the last room at the end of the hall for her. The junkie suite, that one last slow ride. And she was going out in junkie style, doped up to the eyeballs. He had tortured himself during those long hours thinking of what he would say when she woke up. How he would chastise her for estranging her family, yell and scream at her for being a terrible mother, or cry over losing her. He never got the chance to find out, as his mother never regained consciousness.

A week later, they were lowering a pine box into a grave. After that came the insurance agent and the windfall. Then the long, solitary drive home, where there had been nothing but time to think. Think and remember. Your mind really was your worst enemy, and he hadn't been able to drown out all of his thoughts with the radio, especially when he was between cities with little to no signals.

Had he not been in such a vexed state of mind, he mightn't have picked up the bum. But now he faced the very real possibility that he was riding in a car with a dead man, and that brought into question what he was to do with him. He could just pull over and push the body out, or he could drive him to the nearest hospital. The closest hospital he could think of was in Maysville, though he might take a detour to Flemingsburg. They had a hospital, but he didn't know if that was closer.

First things first, he told himself. He had to check and make sure if his passenger was dead or not. If not, then what? Best to get rid of him as soon as possible, he guessed. Dead or alive, he had spent nearly half an hour with that stink, and that was more than enough, good karma be damned. Reaching out with his right hand, he shook the bum's shoulder to rouse him.

The bum's head jerked at the contact, and there was a sudden sharp pain in Shane's hand. He pulled his hand back, and to his amazement, his fingers were gone from the second knuckle up. It took a moment for his brain to register what he was seeing as blood pumped from the stumps. When it clicked, he let out a scream of pain and shock.

To his horror, the bum turned to look at him and smiled. The smile was beyond comprehension to his mind. The lips were smeared with blood, and the jaw moved in slow chewing motions as he could hear the sound of bones popping and crunching in its mouth. The thing in the passenger seat smiled at Shane, and he could see its teeth. Oh, God, its teeth. They weren't human teeth, but those of a giant rat. The front teeth were long like a rodent, but the rest were either missing or pointed little barbs that suck out disjointedly from its gums.

It made a low chuffing sound in its throat that Shane would have realized was a bastardized form of laughing had he been in his right mind. But this was far beyond what his mind was prepared to handle. He was barely able to get his arm up in time as the creature lunged. He was able to shove his forearm into its throat, barring its movements and keeping it from crunching down on his face.

Its breath stunk like rotten meat as it snapped just inches from his nose. With his one good hand, he beat at it. Knocking the hat askew, he wondered how in hell he had mistaken it for a human. The weathered and rotten flesh clung tightly to the bone, and the sickly smell of death coming off its skin brought his thoughts back to those of his mother's last days. Its eyes seemed to shine brighter as it tried to close in for the kill, but the cramped space of the car was alien to it, so it became tangled and stumped by the cramped interior.

The Cavalier drunkenly weaved back and forth, but by some miracle, the car stayed on the road, though it did cross back and forth into the oncoming lane several times. Had there been any other drivers on the long, lonely trek of road, they surely would have called the cops. But that stormy night, they were all alone. There would be no help coming.

In his panic, Shane fumbled around the inside of the car, searching for anything he could use as a weapon. Working on sheer muscle memory, his hand found the cigarette lighter, still in the "on" position, that he had completely forgotten due to the impromptu picking up of his ghastly assailant. He pulled it from the socket, its tip a glowing, hot cherry that illuminated the interior of the car. Shadows illuminated the creature's sallow face. Like a child holding a flashlight under their chin, only making the horror more terrifying. Shane jammed that spark of hope into the creature's right eye.

There was an awful hiss as one light extinguished the other, and foul, dark smoke roiled forth from the thing's devastated eye socket. The inside of the car was suddenly filled with an inhuman shriek of pain. Using the brief seconds of respite, Shane wrenched the driver's door handle. Throwing the door open, he flung himself out into space. The next few seconds were confusion and pain as his body bounced and slid along the pavement for several yards, leaving skin and blood on the asphalt.

When he had finally collected himself, he found that he was sitting with his butt on the yellow double line in the middle of the road. The cold rain coming down actually felt quite good on his new stinging scrapes and cuts. He had managed not to break his neck, but his left side and leg looked like they had been run along a cheese grater. Even though he hurt like hell, anything was better than being in that car with that thing.

The Cavalier had come to a stop not much farther down the road. In the downpour, it was nearly invisible, save for the taillights and that one signal light. They stabbed through the darkness and looked to Shane like the eyes of some lopsided demon. That's what it had been, right? He had let some kind of demon into his car.

He didn't have long to sit and ponder as the Cavalier's engine revved and changed gear. Oh, fuck no. There was no way that thing could drive a car. It may have been able to make itself look like a man, but there was no way it knew how to drive. The car lurched once and then shot backward toward him.

Seeing those lights coming at him was all it took to get his second wind. Ignoring his aches and pains, the ex-junkie managed to find his feet and throw himself at the guardrail. He reached it in two steps, something he didn't think he could have done had he not been scared out of his mind. Looking back once more, he saw the faded bumper of the car bearing down on him. The faded, peeling bumper sticker seemed to be coming right at him with its big, bold letters "Ghouls ride free." Ignoring his injured leg, he dove headfirst over the barrier just as the vehicle struck it. There was a world-shattering sound of metal on metal as he fell head over heels down the side of what was nearly a sheer cliff, some forty or fifty feet.

Landing with a groan, a network of pain flared across his body, and he found the air knocked from his lungs. Lying there in the rain, fearing that he was about to suffocate and trying not to panic as his lungs relearned how to breathe, he stared back up the incline he had fallen down. From his landing, he could see the glow of the lights from his old car far above him.

With a grinding crunch, the car dislodged itself from the metal rail, and the lights faded. This sight brought a sigh of relief from Shane, though.

It was not long-lived. There was a faint roar and a peeling of tires on blacktop, and the light at the top began to brighten. That could only mean one thing, and he had to move right now.

"Jitter and jive. Jitter and jive. If there was ever a time for the junkie shuffle, it's now. Can I get an amen?!" The voice of that nameless bunkmate drove Shane into action as he half crawled and half dragged himself away into the woods seeking the shelter of the trees. What had that man's name been? The thought suddenly popped into the forefront of his mind. A half-hysterical giggle escaped his lips as he crawled under a downed log, half hoping it would shield him, half hoping it would hide him.

The twisted remains of the '89 Cavalier tore through the rail and plummeted down into the ravine. It flipped and rolled several times until it came to rest at the bottom. The engine sputtered, but didn't die. It just sat there idle as Styx's greatest hits played faintly from its dashboard. The dull car lights cast long, deep shadows around, helping to hide its injured former owner.

From his hiding place, Shane held his breath and listened. His mangled hand was held between his other arm and his side, in an attempt to stem the bleeding, but he was already feeling light-headed. The adrenaline high was already fading, further sapping his strength. He wasn't sure if he had enough to climb back up to the road for help, or even which direction to walk to find help.

Then he heard it, what he had been dreading. It was a low, barely audible slithering sound. Peering out from under the log, he saw it. The thing from the car must have jumped out before it went over the edge, and it was now climbing down to the scene of the wreck. The thing had discarded its coat, and its pale skin seemed to emit its own glow in the dark. Its bones stood out in stark contrast under its skin, and what muscles it had were long, thick cables. Its movements were spider-like, its unnaturally long bony arms and legs seemed to bend in ways that humans couldn't and shouldn't. It had no problem navigating the jagged rocks, that by some miracle he hadn't cracked his skull open on.

Once reaching the bottom, it didn't stand, instead crawling around on all fours like an animal. He couldn't see it very well now as it moved around the wreck of the car, but he could hear it. It was making loud snuffling sounds like a dog. Was it trying to track him by scent? With that long hooked nose, it could easily do that, he thought. Should he risk trying to move, or would that just attract it with his movement?

There was no way he could outrun it, not with how banged up he was. It would catch him before he got too far. That was clear from how easily it got down the cliff. Plus, he was bleeding pretty badly, and if he didn't do something soon, he would bleed to death. He almost laughed when he thought about all the times he had put a tourniquet on when shooting up, and now he would kill for one. He didn't even have a belt to use. How ironic it would be to die because he didn't have that important tool in every junkie's kit.

The thing finished nosing around the car and hopped several feet up the nearest tree as it peered into the dark forest and sniffed. The wind was thankfully now blowing through the valley at that moment, and it was probably the only thing keeping it from smelling him. Even from this distance, he could see one good eye narrow in frustration. It hissed and hopped from tree to tree like some demonic monkey as it moved deeper into the woods.

It wasn't long before Shane couldn't even hear it crashing through the underbrush. He relaxed and let out a long breath. Hopefully, it was gone for good. The overturned car had started to smoke, and with any luck, a passing motorist would call it into the local sheriff's department. Then emergency services would soon be on the scene and with them the sweet, sweet embrace of pain killers and morphine and that glorious, medically prescribed heavenly high.

Fuck falling off the wagon, if he survived, he was gonna swan dive headfirst off that mother fucker. He was gonna flip the double bird to sobriety, and no one could blame him, after his night, he earned it. And to hell with that lame-ass, long-forgotten, preachy asshole. Shane hoped he choked on all his stupid junkie mantras. It would serve him right.

He smiled cruelly as he slowly dragged himself out from under the fallen tree. In the flickering lights of his dying car, he felt that, finally, all was right with the world. But when the lights suddenly went out, he felt fear and doubt seize his heart moments before long, thin, impossibly strong fingers wrapped themselves around his head.

"Ghouls ride free," came a sinister voice like bubbling mud.

Shane screamed long and loud as the iron grip dragged him off into the darkness.

Eventually, a trucker driving the other way down Highway 68 on a run from Buffalo, Ohio, did see the billowing smoke and called it in. However, when state troopers did make it to the scene, all they found was the burned-out smoking remains of an old 1989 Chevy Cavalier. They assumed the driver had been well enough to climb back up the hill and flag down help. They would check with the local hospitals for follow-up, though they didn't expect much to turn up. The investigation was quickly sidelined following inquiries from a local sheriff suspecting her predecessor of embezzling county funds and equipment.

The case remains unsolved to this day.

The Idol

What is worse, I wonder. The foreknowledge that our world is doomed to the inevitability of death and destruction? Or, that one has a hand in hastening its end, to be at least partially responsible for madness and chaos to come? This is the question that weighs upon my heart, pretentious as it is and as arrogant as it is to make the claim, that is exactly what I have done. Tomorrow, it begins, and I cannot stop the inalienable force that now drives me.

I am helpless to so much as warn others as to their fate. When it is unveiled to the throngs of museum parishioners, they will be shown the Eldritch Truth and have no choice but to accept it. It will not let them turn aside from it as they do with everyday truths, with 24/7 news and constant internet blogs feeding them false narratives to make their lives more convenient. The hell and misery of human suffering that they turn a blind eye to, but how will they fare when shown the literal hell that awaits us all?

The Idol will show them all, as it has shown me.

Professor Nani Laghari discovered the Idol during one of her archaeological digs near Ganj Dareh in Iran. I had been serving as her assistant for nearly two years at that point. The internship had been one of blind luck. The two girls who came before had both taken severely ill after trips into the field. Not only did this afford me the much-needed position, but the Professor stopped taking her interns with her on the long digs.

Something I was not at all dismayed about. I was a city boy, born and raised, and I had little to no interest in traveling to far-off deserts, or anywhere without a working toilet and Wi-Fi, while spending all day doing back-breaking work in the hot sun for months at a time. As the resident professor and curator of ancient antiquities at the New York Metropolitan Museum, Professor Laghari would take at least one trip a year to maintain her reputation and standing as a field archaeologist. She enjoyed it far more than the time she spent in her office. During those trips, I was left more or less in charge, and the job wasn't particularly demanding. There were two other professors to cover her administrative duties, leaving me to do little more than answer her calls and take messages. The job was not all fun and games, though, as my duties still included much along the lines of research, exhibit planning, and docent work, not exactly difficult, but it was demanding enough that I earned the meager paycheck I did get.

The stipend that I received barely covered my expenses, forcing me to house-share with several roommates in a cramped little hovel. Not that it bothered me. I barely spent any time there, and though the job was demanding and paid little, the perks were well worth it. Chiefly among those perks was Professor Laghari herself. Most people didn't like her. They found her standoffish, and many were intimidated by her Oxford education, where she not only earned several doctorates, but also served on their educational board as a professor for nearly a decade. Being a leading authority in her field had gained her few friends and much dislike, as she was rather dismissive of anyone she didn't see as her equal. More than once, I had heard some portly elderly trustee or board member, of one thing or another, refer to her as a "standoffish dyke," when she had not only spurned their advances, but intellectually humiliated them for it as well.

I knew better than anyone else that it wasn't true. She did have a mildly abrasive personality, but I liked her, and she did treat me fairly. That, and my duties as her assistant, meant I saw to more of her needs than just getting her coffee several times a week. She also allowed me the use of her guest room when she was out of town. The perks were quite worth it, and, unlike other people, I could easily weather her personality quirks. The professor wanted things the way she wanted them, and her requirements were never really outrageous, though when she made demands, it could be quite domineering. Personally, I believe that it has more to do with her British accent, which made her seem more stern and severe than she was.

For a woman in her fifties, she was quite fit and energetic, to the point where even I had trouble keeping up with her at times. She was very driven and never seemed to stop working. Even in her off hours, she could be found poring over ancient manuscripts written in long-dead languages that looked to me like little more than pictographs. When fully engrossed in her work, she worked as if she were a madwoman possessed.

Ever since I had come to work for her, she had been obsessed with the Middle East and Pre-Sumerian civilizations. Her office was a cramped mess of stacked boxes, old manuscripts, artifacts, and tapestries. All of them in languages I couldn't read, but Professor Laghari spoke nearly half a dozen and could read twice that. Working in her office was an adventure in navigating a balanced ecosystem in which one wrong step could result in the absolute decimation of millions of dollars in priceless antiquities.

My own office, if one could call the front room that led to hers, felt much larger by comparison, though it was smaller per square foot. I was staying late in my office, sorting mail and organizing the weekly calendar, the night I received a call from Professor Laghari. The connection was utter garbage, with static crowding the line like busy morning subway commuters. I could only make out one word in every three, but after nearly fifteen minutes of yelling across the bad line, I had a note on my calendar that a crate would be arriving in the morning that I was to take reception of and move to her office to await her arrival. She would be arriving herself later in the day, having missed her flight. I made sure to call up security and have them leave a note for the Shipping and Receiving Department to expect the shipment before I headed home for the night.

I walked, rather than taking a cab. The cool night air helped to clear my head as I tried to shake off the bad feeling I had gotten from our phone call. I couldn't be sure due to the horrendous condition of the connection, but something about the way she sounded seemed off, strained. I had seen her at the end of her tether before, after a three-day research jag, after she had gotten her hands on some pieces of pottery late last year. She had been talking nonsense and hallucinating, talking about lost cities and doors to other worlds. Her raving sounded like what you would hear from street-corner preachers, as I persuaded her to go to bed and get some rest. Something about those fragments had also disturbed me. The largest piece was branded with a lone symbol, like a crooked letter "Y" with a small hash mark nestled in its fork. It seemed vividly burned into my memory. I dismissed my concerns as just overreacting and being quite overtaxed after a long day.

I was unsure if I managed to sleep at all that night, as my concerns broke through my thoughts every time I tried to shut down my brain. Errant thoughts would rampage across the landscape of my mind as I pitched and rolled in bed, trying desperately to find some relief. In almost no time, the night gave way to the day, as sunlight pierced through the windows, dooming my struggle for sleep. The alarm clock didn't have time even to sound, a rare miss as it usually took several minutes of its caterwauling to rouse me from slumber. I shut the little traitor off long before it could raise its shrill alarm.

Even after a hot shower, I was still groggy and sluggish. I sought the salvation of coffee to rally my strength and give me the energy to face the day. I looked out of the kitchen window as I worked the press. When staying at the professor's place, I have no trouble sleeping and found the way she liked her coffee made amusingly opulent. However, this morning I found the activity quite vexing. All I wanted was a cup of coffee without having to strong-arm it out of the beans myself. It was bitter, once I had the cup to my lips and took my first sips of the life-affirming brew. I had forgone any additives, needing it to be as strong as possible to shock my system into working order. For all intents and purposes, it seemed to do the trick and purged my thoughts of worries, allowing me to focus on the day ahead. The day itself was rough. By the time I reach my office, I was on my third cup of coffee, and it was making me jittery to the point I could hardly sit still. Almost every five minutes, I called down to the Receivables Department, where the new exhibits were shipped in to see if Professor Laghari's shipment had come in.

By nine o'clock, I was pacing the halls, having done everything I had scheduled, cleaned my office twice, and worn out my welcome with each of the department heads. When my phone finally rang, my ears picked up from the far end of the corridor. It was a mad dash as I covered the distance of several dozen paces and threw open the door, in time to pick up the handset before the second ring had finished. It was the security manager of the loading bays, calling to tell me a truck had just pulled up with the professor's manifest. I told him thank you and that I would be there in a minute to oversee the unloading. Professor Laghari was very particular about how her things were to be handled. The warning had been unnecessary as I arrived almost before the handset had even clicked back into its cradle.

Unlike the rest of the museum, the loading docks were plain by comparison. It was more or less just a large empty room with racks of shelves where items were placed before being sorted. Once sorted, they would either be stored away in the lower-level vaults, though they, too, were not much better than empty rooms. They were climate-controlled and had a series of security measures, though. For the most part, many of the items would be sent to the staging area, where they would be inspected or cleaned before they were put on display. A large part of my job was to oversee the transfer of the artifacts that Professor Laghari had obtained. While it wasn't exactly against protocol, from time to time, there were particular items that she would request

I bring to her office so she could inspect them herself. Normally, this was no problem. However, this time it was different.

The movers were a couple of hefty, surly-looking men with calloused hands and hard eyes. It was somewhat marred by their colorless faces, though. Both men looked skittish and a little apprehensive, as though they were scared of something. I am sure the sight of me wasn't putting them at ease. I was rather more disheveled than usual, my tie was crooked from constantly pulling on it, and my hair was standing on end from running my hands through it when I wasn't playing with the tie. I am sure I looked like a madman, and wouldn't have blamed them for not wanting to deal with some lunatic, but it wasn't me that they appeared afraid of. They seemed to fear their own truck, and neither made much of a hurry to open the back. They hung back and dickered with getting their papers signed by the department registrar rather than opening it.

When I finally couldn't take it anymore, and began to reprimand the two, both of whom stood a head taller than I, they finally got to unloading the truck, though neither of them were happy about it. One muttered something about it giving him the heebie-jeebies. The door was unbolted and raised, revealing the contents. I was expecting the hold to be filled with packages and containers, as was usual when new shipments were brought in. This time, there was only a solitary crate. It was large, standing as tall as the men, and just as wide. It looked far too much like a coffin standing on its end. Stamped on the front were the words "Fragile: Handle With Care," and at the top, "This Side Up" with an arrow pointing towards one end of the crate. They had placed the crate against the far back wall of the truck and strapped it to the wall with a combination of rope and chains as if it were a casket from a Poe novel containing some madness-inducing entity. Little did I know that was exactly what it held, and when one uncovers the Truth and stares it bare in the face, what else can one do but lose all sanity?

The men unchained it, looking a bit apprehensive, as though they thought, at any moment, it would jump out and bite them.

Once they had managed to wrestle it from the truck bed and it stood on the floor just inside the dock, they hastily beat their retreat without so much as a parting. Hopping in their truck, they took off as though all the demons of Hell were on their heels. This left me with the large crate and no way to move it. It was far too heavy for me to move by myself. It had taken both men just to scoot it across the ground, and from the sound of it, they were using considerable strength to do so. The crew, though there were not really enough of them to be called a crew, that staffed the Receivables Department had all mysteriously vanished, as help is prone to do when needed. This left me trying to devise a way to get the heavy load into the freight elevator and then up to the office floor. The freight elevator only went up to the museum floors and the gallery lofts. I would have to take it up to the main floor, then transfer to the service elevators to get to the administration floor.

I solved my problem by finding a hand truck in one of the storage closets, which was simple enough. Getting the crate on it was another animal completely. I nearly herniated myself as I pushed, pulled, and lifted as much as I could. I succeeded in the end, but the effort had me spent, breathing heavily, and bent at the waist as rivers of sweat poured from my face and formed puddles on the floor. I doubt I had ever exercised that much in my life. Once my constitution had recovered enough to fool myself into thinking that I would have an easier time now that it was on the hand truck, I started the long slog to the elevator. While the dolly did make moving it easier, it was still a herculean task to get it down the hall to the elevator.

Once it was on the lift and we were ascending, I leaned my head against the hardwood to catch my breath, and I heard a sound like a low whispering. The moment I heard it, it ceased. I pressed my ear against the side and strained my ears. Nothing. It must have been my imagination, or all the moving around had caused the contents to shift, and all I heard was the packing material settling. I forgot about it almost instantly as I arrived at my floor and busied myself heaving and shoving my burden off before the doors could close on me. If moving it hadn't been challenging enough, it got worse as the service elevators, unlike the freight ones, were designed for moving people, not cargo. Since the crate was roughly the size of a phone booth, it was like trying to fit a bathtub into a teacup. There was no room at all for me, so my only recourse was to shove it in the best that I could, hit the button for the offices, and then pelt up the three flights of stairs pell-mell in order to catch the elevator when it arrived on the desired floor.

I barely made it. The doors were beginning to slide shut, then I just managed to slam my hand between them. Several of the administrators and assistants stuck their heads out of their office doors to see what was going on as I struggled to haul my load down the halls. The entire way, I cursed under my breath that the professor couldn't have picked an office closer to the elevators. I only lost my decorum once, when trying to maneuver through the office door, I caught one hand between the cart and the jam, mashing several of my fingers. I swore like a sailor as I danced about, cradling my injury. I lost my head for a second, hauled off, and delivered a swift kick to the base of the crate. That only did me further injury as my shoes were not designed for such actions. So now, I had digits on both my foot and hand crying out in pain. None of it was as serious as a fracture, but there was a series of linear bruises across my fingers just above the second knuckles.

My next issue was as to what constituted "in the office." While it was technically in the office, it was only in my outer office. I was sure that she had meant hers. So, this left me in the untenable position of trying to justify not having to move it again. My exhaustion aside, there was no room for such a large object in the packed inner office. I would first have to clear out much of the clutter to make room, and I was unsure of what of her collection of bric-a-brac was absolutely essential and what was just minutiae that had built up over time. Removing my tie and jacket, I rolled up my sleeves and set to the task of making room. I started with the boxes of files, as they took up almost one entire corner, and they were not as fragile or costly as the other items. It took the better part of the afternoon, but by the time I finished, one entire wall of my office had been covered by a brickwork of cardboard containers, all with their labels facing outwards so that one could find their contents. It was a foregone conclusion that for the foreseeable future, I would be the one having to sort through them to find whatever files the professor needed. If I were being honest, it was probably a more efficient system.

Once clearing out space in the inner office, I returned to the back-breaking struggle of moving the coffin-sized crate. I had to do so this time without the aid of the handcart, as there was no room to maneuver it. Though it only had to be moved roughly ten feet, it was the most difficult ten feet of the entire journey. When the monolithic container had finally been moved into its corner, my shirt was soaked in sweat as though I had been swimming in my clothes. Not only was it stifling, but there were also no windows in our offices, so there was little I could do to cool the place down. I am not sure if it was the exhaustion or the heat, but I could have sworn it was emanating from inside the crate. The surrounding air seemed heavier and more stagnant, but that could have been my imagination. What was harder to convince myself of was that the whispering I was hearing was just in my head. I had first taken it for the shifting of contents inside the box, but it had metamorphosed into a barely audible hum just at the edge of my hearing. Though I couldn't make it out, it sounded to me almost like a low chanting, even with my ear pressed against the side, it was no clearer.

My curiosity finally getting the better of me, I fetched a pry bar from the supply closet. Opening Professor Laghari's shipments was normally forbidden, as she enjoyed the activity. She had likened it to the pleasure that a child gets on Christmas morning from opening presents. One of many sentiments that made me question her childhood, and though her word was normally absolute, this was one of the few times I sought to defy it. I could not bear that sound any longer, and my need to know what was making it drove me to wedge the tool between the crevice of the lid and lean into it. With each satisfying pop as nails let go, the sound grew louder until it was practically roaring in my ears, despite it being a little louder than the hum of an electric motor. Once the task finished, I cast aside the bar and reached to remove the lid, but before I could so much as shift it, I was stopped by a blood-curdling shriek of protest.

Turning, I saw Professor Laghari herself standing in the doorway. She was just as big a mess as I. Her raven black hair, which was usually pulled up tight in a bun, was a loose bird's nest and slipping free of its moorings. Her face was ghostly pale, something that I would have thought impossible for her usually suntanned Indian complexion. Her clothing was disheveled, as though she had slept in it more than once. It was a stark contrast to her regular, well-pressed standard. Her shirt was missing several buttons and was a rumpled mess, while her skirt rode up far higher than was proper, showing off a modicum of thigh and stockings filled with runs. This woman was a far cry from the reserved Professor Laghari I knew daily. This version was more like some half-crazed animal. It was her eyes that were the most unsettling. They were as wide as saucers, and the pupils had dilated to the point where they overpowered not only the warm brown of her iris, but most of the whites as well. They were otherworldly and terrifying, as though they were not looking at me, but through me to see a world beyond what everyone else could see.

At first, I thought her initial shock was over catching me, red-handed, breaking one of her sacred rules. It was clear, at a second glance, that this frazzled state of hers was something far more long-running. Her reaction was immediate and explosive, nearly hurling me bodily from the room and slamming the door to her office closed barely after I was through it. Needless to say, I was stunned, not only by being manhandled by a ninety-pound woman, but also by the departure. She was taken from her senses. I had never seen her like this. While she would be worn out upon her return from the digs, it was more of general exhaustion where she would rely upon me to wait on her hand and foot for a day or two until she was back to her more regal self. This was an anomaly in the pattern, most egregious. From behind the closed door, I could hear her moving about in a frantic fashion. Things would crash to the floor or sound as though they were flung at the walls. It was as if the room was host to a feral animal rather than an academic with multiple PhDs. For the rest of the day, I stayed at my desk, just listening to her in her office. Not once did she emerge, nor did she acknowledge me when I knocked on the door or called to her. Intermittently, all would go eerily quiet. I found it more unsettling than when she was tearing the place apart.

I left the office later than usual in a vain hope that I would catch the Professor leaving, but she never left her office. When I returned the next morning, there was no noticeable change. She was still locked in her office, and when I put my ear to the door, something I had never done before, as I did not make it a habit of eavesdropping on her, I could hear the same whispering I had heard coming from inside the crate. What was more, I could hear Professor Laghari talking. It was too low to make out exactly what she was saying, but it was like she was having a conversation with it. A fairly angry one at that from the tone of her voice. I could also feel the heat coming off the door. It was almost like putting your ear to a stove. The next several days went by in much the same way, with her locked in her office while I tried to stem the tide of complaints from the other Professors over the noise and heat, and made her excuses as to why she was unavailable to see them. It got particularly hairy when the director himself made an appearance, but luck favored me that it was during one of the long, silent stretches.

The director was one of the few people on the museum board who not only tolerated but liked Laghari. He was a short man, barely four feet tall, wizened and, though he was bald on top, what remained of his white hair hung to his shoulders. In his pressed waistcoat and smoking on his pipe, he looked remarkably like a hobbit or some other halfling creature that had stepped out of a Tolkien novel. I thoroughly enjoyed our brief interactions as he treated all the staff, both professors and interns alike, with the same grandfatherly manner. I lied that Professor Laghari was out, hoping that no noises came from the inner sanctum, ruining my charade, and I did, however, accept his invitation for a drink. I wanted simply to get him out of the office as quickly as I could, but I also needed a respite from the unbearable heat. I spent the rest of the evening in his company as we discussed many things from my tenure as Laghari's assistant to the woman herself, as well as other current events, before finally being brought around to the plans for the new exhibit featuring the recent acquisitions from her latest dig. I assured him that I had it all in hand, a lie, I hadn't even begun to plan anything, and the event had slipped my mind completely since the day the shipment had arrived. Between the constant making of excuses and worrying about the state of my boss, I had gotten almost no work done around the office. If it continued, it wouldn't be long before I could no longer cover for her, and I would most likely lose my job.

By the time I left the director's office, it was late, and I had made up my mind to drag her out of her office by force if need be, then force her to go home and rest. If she refused, I might have no other choice than to check her into a hospital for her own good, as this behavior was clearly some sort of mental break brought on by the stress of overwork. It was unhealthy and not good for anyone if she continued on to the point of hurting herself. I will admit my newfound position might have been spurred on by the several drinks I had in the director's office. By the time I had returned, I had built up quite a head of steam and was fully hell-bent on executing my plan, no matter her protests. It was all but immediately cast aside upon entering the dark office and seeing a telltale crack of light shining through the slightly ajar inner door.

I found myself creeping silently, slowly toward the door as I held my breath. With each step, the room grew warmer and warmer. Pausing at the door, I strained my ears, listening for any sound at all. I could hear nothing, not even that persistent whispering that had been haunting my thoughts all week. When I tried to open the door, it resisted, as though something was holding it closed. I put my shoulder to it and heaved with all my might. The door gave, pushing whatever was blocking it across the floor, and swung open far enough for me to stick my head through. To my horror, the thing that had been leaning against the door was Laghari.

I called her name several times as I fought my way in through the opening I had made. Reaching her, I turned her over to find her quite dead. Her lifeless eyes were half-open, and the muscles in her face had gone slack, her whole body limp like a puppet with its strings cut. There was blood everywhere. It didn't seem possible for one person to bleed this much. Battlefields had seen less bloodshed. Her wrists were slashed open in great red, jagged canyons. I couldn't begin to imagine how it was possible for her to cut herself so brutally and deeply on both arms. She had nearly amputated both hands. My mind raced over what to do next. Should I call for help, or go fetch someone? What could they do? She was already dead and beyond anything the medical profession could do. Not that it mattered, as my horror had nailed my feet to the floor. I had never seen death like this before. I had never been alone in a room with a dead body, much less held one in my arms. That is what it was now, just a dead thing, not a person. What had made Nani Laghari a person, her soul, her personality, was gone and would never return. It hit me that someone I had shared time, coffee, and even a bed with was gone. Never would we share any of those things.

At that, my lowest moment, it broke through the din of my mind louder than I had ever heard it. The whispering had returned, only this time it was no low, barely there teasing of the senses, but a roaring choir in an inhuman language no human could ever understand. Turning to face the source of the cacophony, I found myself staring at the shipping crate I had lugged in days before, only now it was open, the lid cast aside so that its contents could be witnessed. Enshrined within was a marble monolith, roughly hewn with primitive tools. It was unremarkable save for one feature. Upon the front was carved that strange symbol I had seen before in the professor's research notes—a long crooked "Y" with a hash mark between the forks.

The idol that sat upon the ancient dais was what drew my full attention. It is not humanly possible to fully describe it. Just looking at it chipped away at the edges of what was left of my sanity in my currently grief-stricken state. It was nearly two feet tall and made of some kind of obsidian-like stone, its glassy surface reflected the world around it in dark surrealism on its blackish green surface. Its design was that of impossible geometry. Folding in upon itself time and time again in ways that defied basic architecture and physics. At first, I thought it to be some sort of alien heart, but it was more genital and incestuous in nature. I couldn't help myself as I stared at it. I wanted to touch it. No, I needed to touch it, and that sound only beckoned me onward. It was the most bizarre experience I have ever felt in my life. I was no longer in control of my body, a passenger, as some unknown invading force possessed me to reach out and touch the idol. My bloody hand made contact with the stone, and though it looked glassy, the surface was quite rough, like sandpaper. It was also cool to the touch in contrast to the boiling hot room. That is exactly what the idol was. It was a contrast in all its forms. Contradiction made solid and given a physical form for humanity to awe in its glory. As I stood there worshiping at its altar, it showed me the Truth. I was no longer in the administration offices of the New York Metropolitan Museum, but standing on the surface of an alien world.

I looked out over plains of black melted glass covered in a coating of thick ash. One might have confused it with snow, but for the heat. The air was so hot and thick that it was oppressive to breathe. Each inhale was a fight, and the air itself was acrid with the taste of smoke and carcinogens. Fitting for such a barren wasteland. The scant trees I could make out were barely twigs, twisted and sickly. The sky was just as split and broken as the earth. The moon rode high across the sky, far closer than our own ever came to earth. Its surface was black and cracked, showing hot molten lava beneath, surrounded by the fiery corona of the sun that it eclipsed. In the distance, there was a long mountain range below a massive thunderhead. The dark cumulonimbus stretched unto the heavens and emitted loud rumbles of thunder, warnings of a rainstorm that would no doubt be poisonous. There were no signs of life. This was a dead world, a world in entropy. It's time winding down to its last moments. As inevitable as the eventual heat death of our own universe. These were its last dying gasp. It was beautiful in its own macabre way. One could be forgiven for mistaking it for peaceful, though it was not. This place was the very definition of hostile.

From the great black clouds came the first inhabitants I had seen. They were great flying things, bastardizations of the depictions I had been raised on of angels. They were little more than skeletons, their bodies impossibly thin. Their limbs resembled gnarled ancient driftwood, coated with powdery ash. The wings were featherless and, like their body, made of a twisted vein work of dried-out branches. Their heads were the only parts that seemed alive. They were long, distended things made of constantly writhing snakes or tentacles. They had no faces I could see, just a black hole, bottomless and empty. The sound that came from that hole was the one I had heard, first as a whisper and then as a choir calling me towards the Truth. It was so loud that I thought my eardrums might burst, even though they were miles away. The angel creatures circled the gathering storm clouds as they sang their maddening song. As I watched them, lightning arched from the higher-up in the storm to one of the lower clouds. In that brief second that it illuminated the clouds, it also turned them semi-transparent. Behind them, I could make out a silhouette, and my mind came undone. What I had mistook for a mountain range was, in fact, the foot of some gargantuan being hidden beyond the clouds, standing far taller than any skyscraper. In the distance, I could actually see the mountains moving, as it shifted its weight with sounds I had mistaken for thunder.

I turned away, for if the clouds parted, I would see it, to see a thing would be to know it, and knowing it would be madness. It was in that moment when my mind teetered on the edge of sanity. The Truth was revealed to me. The greatest questions mankind had ever asked itself were answered. Why are we born? What is the meaning of life? Where does the soul go after death? All of them were made known to me. We were born only to suffer the pains and pangs of life, to season our mortal souls as one season's good wood before throwing it on the fire. Upon our death, they would then be ripped from our bodies and through the thin veil that separated our worlds. Then they would be cast upon the sputtering embers of this dying world, to feed the fire and stave off its fate for a little longer. How long had this hungry world fed upon humanity? Millennia, eons? Who knew? Perhaps it had always been the natural order. All of humankind was raised like cattle, for the use and disposal of beings far older than our comprehension. There was nothing one could do, for this was no conventional threat ever faced.

As I collapsed to my knees in despair, one of the angels broke away from its brethren and floated towards where I knelt. As it drew nearer, my anxiety grew. I could barely stand to look at it, but if it touched me, the closer it came to me, the closer I came to insanity. I was little more than a gibbering mess when it reached out one long, thin, knotted hand to me. I screamed and thrust myself back and away from it, only to find myself sprawling upon the office floor. Sweat and tears poured down my face as I sobbed, hugging myself in the now cold room. The Idol had gone quiet and completely innocuous. Now nothing more than a cold, silent lump of molten rock from another world.

When I finally pulled myself together, I found that I had come up with a plan. At first, I thought I should try to destroy the idol, as any sane person would, but how could anyone destroy such a beautiful gift? For that is what I had been given, the gift of freedom. It is said that the Truth shall set you free, and that is what I was, free. In a world of religion, morals, laws, pain, suffering, and death, I knew that it was all meaningless. That in the end, there is no Heaven or Hell, only cold, dark oblivion. How much of our world could change if they, too, knew the Truth? No, destroying the idol, if it could be destroyed, was the wrong answer. It needed to be shared with the world so that they, too, might know the Truth and its freedom. And I knew exactly what to do.

I cleaned up the blood off the office floor, left a note from Professor Laghari to all the staff that she would be taking a sabbatical for her health, and then entombed her body in the crate that the idol had been shipped in. The idol I had moved to the staging area and covered with a drop cloth. I forged the paperwork, clearing it for the exhibition. Most of the staff was so accustomed to seeing my signature on Laghari's paperwork that no one would question it. By morning, I had written up the proposal for the exhibition as well as a floor layout and the press briefing. All were scheduled for the following weekend, which promised to be one of the largest openings we had ever had for an exhibit. The following day, I talked with the director and a number of the board members to further push the publicity of the opening. By the time the weekend arrived, every major news outlet in the city was covering the event, there was going to be a national broadcast, and even a number of high-profile celebrities were to be in attendance. I could not have asked for a better reception on such short notice.

Tomorrow, the idol will be unveiled to the world, and the Truth will spread. By that time, I will be dead, and my body will be found with this confession so that those who come after understand that I had no choice, that the Truth will out in the end. As I sit here bleeding out, the cuts on my wrists made writing the last few pages difficult, reading through Professor Laghari's research in Iran, about the people who came before, who worshiped the idol, and the one they call the Dreaming Mother. There is a most curious passage I found in her notes.

JOHN EVANS

It reads: *Mgepog ph'nglui fhtagn fhalma ot fhtagn h'gof'nn, ng f' mggoka'ai li. Nilgh'ri h' ahor goka ah n'gha.*

I have no earthly idea what it means, but I am sure I am soon to find out.

In death, all is made clear.

The Hand

In the dead of night, Sharon's ears were pricked with the sound of labored breathing. It was a breath so deep and guttural that it made the hairs on the back of her neck stand on end. She knew, without a shred of doubt, that it was the sound of a monster lurking beneath her bed.

When she turned to her stepmother for comfort, she was met with nothing but cruel laughter. Her stepmother scoffed and sneered, telling Sharon that she was too old to believe in such childish fairy tales. The seven-year-old's sobs echoed off the walls, and her stepmother's mocking only fueled the fire, working the girl up into a panic.

Her daddy wouldn't have laughed, not like her stepmother did. He would have understood the terror that gripped her heart and would have chased away the monsters lurking beneath her bed with a brave, determined hand.

Her daddy had been a hero, a soldier sent far away to fight the bad guys. The ragheads, her stepmother had called them, the ones who wanted to plant bombs beneath the president's bed. But her daddy wasn't scared, not like most people. He was a warrior, a man with nerves of steel and a heart that beat with the courage of a lion. Two years had passed since her daddy had left, and still he hadn't returned. He hadn't even spoken to her on the computer in over a year. As the months crawled by, her stepmother began to act differently.

Her stepmother had taken to drinking like a fish, and as the alcohol coursed through her veins, it brought with it a hunger for company. Men, mostly, with their rough voices and eager hands, would come over for sleepovers with her stepmother. Sharon didn't like them, not one bit. They were nothing like her daddy, who had been kind and brave and never drank himself into a stupor. Sharon lay there in the dark, listening to the sound of the monster breathing beneath her bed. It wasn't just the monster that scared her. It was the men who came over to stay the night. The way they looked at her with eyes that lingered too long, their laughter that was too loud and too raucous. She missed her daddy terribly, wished he were here to protect her from the monsters under her bed, and the ones that walked on two legs. If he were here, she wouldn't be so afraid, but he wasn't, and all she could do was lie there and listen to the sound of her stepmother's drunken laughter mingling with the breath of the beast that waited patiently beneath her bed.

Sharon huddled beneath her blankets, her heart racing as she tried to fend off the monsters that lurked just beyond her reach. The blankets were her shield, her one and only defense against the terrors that haunted her every waking moment. She knew, deep down, that the blankets were monster-proof. All kids knew that. It was an unspoken rule, passed down from generation to generation, a sacred truth that could never be questioned.

The monsters didn't care about the rules. They lurked in the shadows, waiting for their chance to strike. And as Sharon lay there, trembling with fear, she knew that the blankets could only do so much. She needed the light. Turning on the lights was the only way to make the monsters run and hide, to send them scurrying back into the darkness under her bed and in her closet.

Even the light couldn't keep the monsters at bay forever. They always came back, hungry and relentless, their claws scraping against the hardwood floor as they stalked her every move. Sharon knew that she had to be strong, that she couldn't let the monsters win. With a deep breath and a fierce determination, she pulled the blankets tighter around her.

It had slithered into her room in the dead of night, silent and cunning, slipping beneath her bed and settling in for the long haul. Sharon could sense it there, lurking just beyond the edge of her consciousness, waiting patiently for the moment when she let down her guard. She knew what would happen if she dared to set foot on the floor. The monster would reach out with its razor-sharp claws and snatch her up, dragging her down into the depths of its lair. She could almost hear its hissing breath, feel its hot, fetid breath on the back of her neck.

Sharon huddled in the middle of her massive four-poster bed, surrounded by plush pillows and soft blankets, her mind racing with fear and uncertainty. She longed to close her eyes and drift off into a peaceful slumber, to escape the horror of the monster lurking just beneath her feet. But she knew that sleep would never come, not while the creature was still out there, waiting for its chance to strike.

She hated this bed, this imposing monstrosity that dominated her room like some kind of dark tower. All she wanted was a simple pink Barbie princess bed, the kind she had seen on the computer. Her stepmother had insisted on the four-poster bed, and she had thrown a fit when Sharon had dared to question her.

The argument had been fierce, the kind that left a lingering tension in the air for days afterward. Sharon's stepmother had ranted and raved, demanding to know why they should waste money on a cheap plastic bed that would inevitably break, when they had a perfectly good four-poster bed in storage, one that her parents had given them.

Sharon's father had tried to reason with her stepmother, explain that the Barbie bed was not that expensive, and that the four-poster was far too large for their little girl. He had suggested they get the smaller bed now and switch it out for the bigger one when Sharon was older. But her stepmother would hear none of it. She had made up her mind, as she always did, and the four-poster had been brought into the room, looming over Sharon like a dark omen of things to come. However, it wasn't all bad, at least not at first. Sharon's dad had been able to climb into the massive bed with her, his warm embrace providing comfort and safety as he read her bedtime stories.

Sharon lay in her big four-poster bed, surrounded by pillows and stuffed animals. The bed was comfortable, sure, but there were drawbacks to having so much space. For one, they didn't make cartoon sheets and bedding for beds that big, so she had to settle for some pretty-but-boring patterned ones. But that wasn't the worst part. She still wished that her father had managed to get the other bed.

A bigger bed meant there was more room under the bed and more room for monsters. Her dad had always checked under the bed for monsters before he left, but now he was gone, and the monsters knew it. They were bolder now, hungrier. They wanted her, and she knew it.

Sharon's eyes blinked open in the dark of the night. She shifted in her bed, feeling the need to pee. But she didn't want to get up. Not tonight. Her stepmother had been on a rampage, raging about something or other, and she didn't want to risk getting caught out of bed. Not even to use the bathroom. Sharon lay there, feeling the pressure build in her bladder. She squeezed her eyes shut, willing herself to fall back asleep. But all she could hear was her stepmother's angry voice, ringing in her ears. The woman was a real piece of work, and Sharon knew better than to cross her.

As she lay there, she heard the creature breathing. Its raspy breaths came in and out, almost like a hiss. It was waiting, biding its time, and she knew it was only a matter of time before it made its move. Sharon tried to calm herself down, to convince herself that it was just her imagination. But deep down, she knew that something was under her bed, something sinister and hungry.

Sharon's bladder felt like it was about to burst. She was trapped, caught between a monster that waited under her bed and a stepmother who would mock her for wetting the bed. The girl's eyes darted around the room, looking for any escape, any way out of this stalemate. But there was no way out. As the night wore on, the sounds under her bed grew louder and more insistent. The raspy breaths had turned into low growls, and Sharon could feel the monster's hunger growing. But she couldn't hold it anymore. She had to pee.

Unable to take it anymore and needing to pee, she crawled to the edge of the bed and peeked over. If she just looked, she would see that there was nothing there, but her imagination and would allow her to run to the bathroom and relieve herself. What she saw when she looked sent her scrambling back to the center of the bed and relative safety.

Claws, she had seen claws. To be more accurate, she had seen a hand with long knobby fingers, tipped with long, sharp black nails. The skin on the hand was a sickly, jaundiced yellow, stretched tight over bones that seemed to jut out at odd angles. Its nails, black and pointed like talons, were slowly, deliberately scratching against the dark, stained wood of the bed frame. The sound was like a hundred rats skittering across the floor. The monster was biding its time, waiting for the perfect moment to strike and drag its unsuspecting prey into the darkness beneath the bed.

Sharon's voice pierced through the air like a sharp knife, as she cried out for her stepmother. Her screams echoed through the empty halls, bouncing off the walls like a haunting melody. If only their neighbors had been present, they would have surely dialed the police, convinced that her stepmother was abusing the poor girl. But, as it happened, the neighbors had hit the jackpot, winning tickets from the radio to a concert that evening.

Sharon's screams for help fell on deaf ears, as her stepmother was lost in her own thoughts. It had been a year since her husband's tragic demise overseas, leaving her with his insufferable daughter that she could barely tolerate. She had only married the man for the stability of his job, his insurance, and, of course, his pension. It had been an easy arrangement, with him gone for extended periods of time, leaving her free to do as she pleased.

It had been too good to be true, and the bitch that was life snatched away her meal ticket and left her with an unwanted brat. Sharon's cries may have been a plea for help, but to her stepmother, they were simply an irritating noise, a reminder of the burden that had been dumped on her.

He hadn't even had the balls to die like a man, shot by one of those towelheads, or blown to shit by an IED. Hard to accomplish since he was just a base administrator. No, the fool had died in a drunk driving accident on base. He and a couple of his buddies had gotten El-Stink-O and driven their Humvee into a bridge abutment. The brass kept mum just enough to award him a funeral on the taxpayer's dime, but they had pulled his pension and insurance. Boom, no more money from the military, and her saddled with a kid that wasn't even hers.

A kid she would have turned over to child services were it not for the slim hope of securing her late husband's pension money. Her lawyer had spent the better part of a year using the child to fight the military's decision, and as long as there was a glimmer of hope, she had to keep the girl around. The child was hardly a joy to have in her life, an unwelcome reminder of the man she had lost and the mistakes he had made. Fortunately, the brat did not stand in the way of her vices, her drinking, and her endless promiscuity. In fact, she had discovered that the boys in uniform were all too eager to throw her a lay.

On the nights when she was alone, which were becoming more frequent, she found solace in the company of a bottle of wine. The liquid comfort helped to wash down the Vicodin. Tonight, she had taken nearly a handful of the pills, chasing the oblivion that only drugs could offer. She didn't sleep so much as float on the edge of death, suspended in a drug-induced coma that threatened to swallow her whole. One more pill, and she would have slipped into the sleep of the dead.

As she screamed for her stepmother, Sharon felt her bladder give way, the warm rush of urine soaking through her pajamas and staining the sheets beneath her. She was trapped in a growing puddle of her own fear and shame, the stench of urine mingling with the sour tang of sweat and tears. Her cries fell on deaf ears, ignored by a woman who couldn't have cared less for her pain and terror. In that moment, it didn't matter that she was just a scared kid, desperate for any kind of comfort or reassurance. To her stepmother, she was nothing but a nuisance, an inconvenience to be dealt with and silenced.

Sharon's cries were abruptly cut off by a rough scrabbling noise, like the sound of bones rattling in the dark. For a moment, she froze, her breath caught in her throat, as she listened to the eerie sound coming from the edge of her bed. As she peered over the edge, her heart pounding in her chest, she caught a glimpse of movement out of the corner of her eye. The blankets twitched and writhed, as if something was stirring beneath them. Again, the blankets stretched and pulled, as if something unseen was tugging on them with a bony hand. The sound that had started as a clicking grew into a muffled rasp, the sound of something dragging itself across the fabric.

With a sickening slowness, the bony fingers crept into view, emerging from the edge of the bed like a grotesque tree branch come to life. They moved with a spider-like dexterity, scrabbling and scrambling along the edge, searching for something to snatch and drag beneath the bed.

Sharon watched in terror as the inhuman appendages reached towards her, searching for prey, driven by an insatiable hunger that defied all rational explanation. She could see the bones in the fingers, the knuckles grinding and clicking as they moved with unnatural ease, as if guided by an unseen force.

The bony hand stopped abruptly at the edge of the bed, its gnarled fingers splayed out as if frozen in mid-reach. A low growl rumbled from the darkness beneath the bed, a sound that sent shivers down Sharon's spine. For a moment, the hand seemed to pause, as if considering its options. Then, with a sudden burst of frustrated energy, it began to thrash and flail wildly, like a trapped animal desperate to escape. The bed was too large, its frame and mattress providing a barrier that the hand could not breach. Sharon watched in horror as the thin wrist strained and twisted, the bones in the fingers creaking and cracking as they clawed at the empty air. As the hand retreated back into the darkness, Sharon knew that she was not safe. The thing under the bed was still down there, waiting.

The scared child's breath was now coming in great, hitching panting that only kids can manage following or preceding a real pisser of a crying jag. Nothing could match the bawling of a kid for sheer volume or emotion. They put their all into it, and it wears them out, leaving them panting for breath like a dog. And that same panting was how the thing under the bed was trying to locate her.

She clamped her trembling hands over her quivering lips, desperate to silence the sounds threatening to escape. Her breath caught in her throat as she counted to ten, her eyes squeezed shut against the horror before her. The hand, with its wriggling fingers like a cluster of demonic spiders, prowled back and forth, seeking out its prey. The girl could feel it inching closer, its bony appendages groping blindly in the air. When she finally summoned the courage to open her eyes, it was gone—slinking back into the shadows like a malevolent specter.

Her heart soared with fleeting relief, a glimmer of hope that the creature had slunk back into the abyss from whence it came. But, as she stilled her breathing and strained to listen, she could hear it—a lurking presence on the bed, coiled and ready to strike. It was a predator, cunning and patient, biding its time in the shadows. Like a sly angler, it dangled its bait and waited for its prey to take the hook.

Unbeknownst to Sharon, in her terror, she had retreated to the far side of the bed while trying to put distance between herself and the questing hand. It was nothing short of a miracle that she narrowly evaded the serpentine appendage as it whipped out from under the bed, coiling over the mattress with lightning speed. Its fingers snapped shut like a rusted bear trap, hungry for the girl's flesh. But fate intervened, for just as the hand was poised to strike, a gust of wind buffeted the house, sending debris skittering against the windowpane. The sudden sound drew Sharon's attention, and against the glow of the moonlit night, the skeletal hand was silhouetted in a perverse shadow play. With a gasp, the girl managed to roll away, her hair snared in the iron grasp of the demonic limb. She had narrowly escaped its clutches, but she knew the monster was not done with her yet.

With mounting terror, she scrambled to the center of the bed, as far from the edges as possible, seeking refuge from the grasping hand. There she huddled, her eyes wide with fear, her head swiveling like a frenzied dervish as if to scan every inch of the room for any sign of the monster's approach. But she knew it was futile - the creature could come from any direction, could strike at any moment. She was trapped in the middle of the bed. Hot tears stung her eyes as she began to cry again. She couldn't help it. She wanted her daddy. She did not want to be sitting in her own now-cold urine, and more than anything, she just wanted the monster to go away.

The hours crawled by. Each agonizing minute punctuated by the sickening sight of the hand slinking over the edge of the bed, a predatory presence waiting to pounce. It was like that shark from the movie she had watched with her father—a lurking, insidious force, always just out of sight, always ready to strike. The hand moved with a calculated stealth, crab-walking along the edge of the mattress like a skilled predator. She was trapped, a helpless prey in the jaws of a merciless beast. The night stretched on, interminable and unyielding, as the hand continued to stalk its prey with deadly intent.

As the clock crept past three in the morning, an idea began to form in Sharon's mind. It was a brilliant plan, especially for a seven-year-old. She knew the rules, the immutable laws of the monsters that lurked beneath the bed and inside the closet. As long as she remained safely tucked under the covers, the beast could not harm her. And if she turned on the light, the creature would be forced to retreat, driven back into the shadows from whence it came. It was so simple, so elegant. But there was a problem, a formidable obstacle standing between her and salvation. The light switch was on the wall, almost six feet away from the foot of the bed. It might as well have been a mile away.

The vast expanse of open floor between the bed and the door stretched out like a battlefield, a treacherous no-man's-land fraught with peril. Every inch of that space was a potential death trap, a place where the monster could strike at any moment. Stepping onto that floor would be like playing the deadliest game of "The Floor Is Lava" imaginable, with no margin for error and no chance for redemption. It was a gamble that would require all of her courage, skill, and luck. One misstep, one false move, and it would all be over. Sharon took a deep breath, steadied her nerves, and prepared to make her move. The fate of her young life hung in the balance, a fragile thread that could snap at any moment. She had only one chance, and she knew that she had to make it count.

The seven-year-old girl stood frozen on the bed. Her back was pressed so hard against the headboard that the bed creaked in protest. The hand had slithered back, circling the edge of the mattress like a serpent stalking its prey. It slithered and slunk along the edge of the mattress, its joints popping and cracking with each twist and turn. The girl's heart raced as she watched it, her mind racing for a way out of this nightmare. In a sudden burst of inspiration, she snatched up a pillow and hurled it across the room with all her might. It soared through the air, arcing toward the far wall like a missile. For a moment, the room was silent, the only sound was the thud of the pillow striking the wall.

The pillow's impact against the wall caused the lamp to topple over with a deafening crash. Glass shattered, spilling out like jagged teeth onto the floor. The monster, sensing an opening, seized the opportunity and sprang out from its hiding place under the bed. Its claws extended like razor blades. It slashed at the pillow with ferocity, tearing it apart and scattering its contents across the room. Sharon could hear the sound of the foam filling escaping the pillow, hissing like a thousand angry snakes. The monster let out a low, guttural growl, disappointed at the lack of prey.

Mesmerized by the sight, Sharon nearly forgot her plan. Throwing the pillow was supposed to distract the thing under the bed while she made a run for the light switch. She had been so caught up in the reaction of the hand that she had almost forgotten. Pushing off the headboard, she sprinted the full length of the bed and flung herself at the light switch. Once airborne, she began windmilling her arms, her mad flailing just managing to hit the switch just before she crashed to the floor.

The lights erupted in a blinding burst, piercing the veil of darkness that had shrouded the room for hours. A hiss sliced through the air like the sizzle of a red-hot poker on flesh. The sound of something angry and dangerous, trapped and cornered. The hand, so close to capturing its elusive prey, recoiled with a jolt that felt like an electric shock. From beneath the bed, growls and hisses echoed, a symphony of feral rage that sent shivers down the spine. The beast was trapped, but it was far from defeated.

Terror propelled the girl forward, her heart pounding like a jackhammer in her chest. With a strength born of sheer desperation, she wrenched the door open, nearly ripping it from its hinges, and sprinted down the hall like a hunted animal. At the end of the corridor, she veered left, bursting into her stepmother's room like a whirlwind. The woman lay sprawled on the bed, a twisted, drunken heap. Sharon seized the older woman by the shoulders, shaking her with all her might, screaming until her throat felt raw and bloody. But the woman wouldn't wake, no matter how hard she shook or how loud she screamed. It was as if she had slipped into a coma, her body limp and unresponsive.

A memory flickered in the small girl's mind, something she had seen on TV. Without hesitation, she drew back her hand and swung with all her might, striking her stepmother in the face. The impact sent a shockwave coursing up her arm, making her hand sting with a fierce heat. The woman's head lolled bonelessly on her neck, her eyes closed in a drunken stupor.

Undaunted, the girl drew back her hand again and delivered another sharp slap, this time on the opposite cheek. Still, there was no response. Again and again, she alternated slapping the woman's face like a crazed puppeteer, just like she had seen Tom and Jerry do on the cartoons.

Frustration boiled over within Sharon. She balled up her tiny fist, unleashing a punch with all the force she could muster. Pain exploded in her hand as it collided with the woman's nose, blood spurting like a geyser. The woman's eyes snapped open with a jolt. The drugged stupor shattered like glass. But there was no relief, only a sudden, animalistic rage that consumed her like a wildfire. With a roar, the enraged woman lashed out blindly, striking the small girl across the face with the back of her hand. It was a blow that sent Sharon reeling, her head spinning as she crumpled to the floor. For a moment, there was only darkness and pain, the taste of copper in her mouth, and the sound of her own sobbing.

Sharon was thrown off the bed and crashed onto the floor, surrounded by a sea of discarded clothing. Hot tears stung her eyes as her stepmother advanced on her, a crazed look in her eyes. Her hair was wild, makeup smeared from sleeping, and blood oozing from her broken nose. As she loomed over the small child, she hefted the empty wine bottle that had still been clutched in her grip when she had passed out. Just as she prepared to bring it down and end the little bitch's life for ruining her beauty sleep, something jerked her feet out from under her, sending her careening face-first into the chest of drawers. There was a sickening crack as two of her front teeth snapped off at the gum line, sending her reeling and spitting blood like a wounded animal.

Sharon managed to roll away just in time, avoiding being crushed beneath her stepmother's weight. It was yet another stroke of luck, as she managed to roll closer to the door, a path to potential salvation. Had her way been blocked, she might not have been able to escape what was coming next. Her stepmother, dazed from the fall, looked around at what had tripped her.

Sharon and the woman's eyes met, and they both saw it at the same time.

The hand was protruding from under the bed, its bony fingers wrapped tightly around her stepmother's ankle. The sound of cracking bones echoed in the room as the hand flexed and tightened its grip. The terrified woman let out a piercing shriek of horror and pain. She kicked frantically with her free leg in an attempt to break free. But no matter how much she twisted and turned, the hand remained latched onto her leg like an iron band, its grip unyielding and unbreakable.

Sharon's eyes widened in horror as she watched the hand drag her stepmother under the bed, inch by excruciating inch. From the dark pit beneath the bed came a sickening, wet crunching noise, and her screams of terror filled the room. In a desperate attempt to save herself, Sharon's stepmother reached out and grabbed the girl's pajamas, and she was slowly reeled in with her. Panic seized the girl, and she kicked out with both feet, catching her stepmother in the jaw. With a sickening thud, the woman released her grip, and Sharon scrambled to her feet, fleeing the room as fast as she could. The seven-year-old ran screaming from the house, across the lawn to a neighbor's house, and pounded on their door until they let her in.

It was three long hours later before two men in uniform stood on the grimy sidewalk outside Sharon's house. The air hung heavy with the stench of death and decay as they watched a little blonde girl sitting in the back of their squad car. Her face was streaked with tears, like the bloodstains on the pavement beneath their feet. As the paramedics wheeled a lifeless body bag past them, Officer Michael Shulz felt a cold shiver crawl up his spine. He had seen his fair share of gruesome crime scenes in his over twenty years on the force, but this one was different. It was like a scene straight out of one of Stephen King's horror novels.

His rookie partner, Peter Schroeder, stood next to him, his face ashen and his eyes wide with shock. In his short seven months on the job, he had never encountered anything like this. But little did he know, it would be less than a year before a rash of deaths would replace this as the worst case of his career. Both men stood there, frozen in sheer disbelief at the nightmare they had walked into when they had gotten the call. It was a scene that would haunt them for years to come, like a specter that refused to be exorcised.

"So, what do you think?" Schroeder asked his veteran partner.

"Neighbors said the woman was a nasty drunk, and it got worse after her husband died in Iraq. They couldn't prove anything, but they think she abused the girl," he responded.

"Sexual abuse?"

"No, physical. Though they said they never saw any marks, but they did hear the screaming and yelling almost every night," Shulz added, making notes in his notebook. He looked at the little girl sitting in his car.

"So, what, they think the kid snapped and did the mother in?" Schroeder inquired, also eyeing the girl. Neither could hardly believe that such a tiny thing could have a malicious bone in her body, much less the strength to kill an adult.

"That's what it looks like. EMTs believe from the wounds that she stabbed the shit out of her with a pair of scissors, or something like that. The edges were too thick and ragged to be a knife. But for the life of me, they couldn't seem to find whatever she used." The older cop tried to wrap his head around it. "She probably hid it somewhere before running for help."

"Wouldn't have been hard," he continued. "She was drunker than a Baptist, and from the pill bottles, downed enough tranqs to take down an elephant." He sighed. It was sad to see a kid so young turn bad. *Some kids*, he thought, *are just born bad*. That made him think of his own kids at home, probably asleep by now.

"So what now?" the rookie asked. "We lock her up and turn her over to the DA?"

"Nah, Child Services will handle it from here. Get her a lawyer and a head doctor. Then it's out of our hands," Shulz mused. "What do you think makes a kid that young do something so horrible?" Schroeder shrugged in response to the rhetorical question. Shulz sighed again and put his pad in his pocket as the two cops slid into the car and pulled away from the house.

The Basement

She found him standing in the kitchen facing the basement door. Her young son had been so much trouble, but isn't that what kids were supposed to be? They were little bundles of uncontrollable energy that couldn't be contained. They were into everything and everywhere, especially where they were not supposed to be.

Her six-year-old, in particular, was beyond a handful. He not only would shirk his schoolwork and daydream, but he also found almost absurd ways to get into trouble and test the limits of their sanity. Meals turned into contests of trying to gross them out, while trips in public were just a matter of when, not if, he would embarrass them. It was all too common to get calls from the neighbor about her son running through their garden naked, or that he had made the girl across the street cry. The boy had a talent for getting grown-ups to the end of their ropes. More than once, the consensus of neighbors and teachers alike was that they needed to have him tested.

Her husband and she had decided against such an extremist measure. Those kids on medications didn't seem right. Ritalin tended to turn kids into zombies from what she had seen, and she couldn't bear the thought of drugging and destroying her own child's creative mind. Yes, she was more than aware that this line of thinking was self-delusional, and many parents fell into the trap of exceptionalism when it came to their kids. They felt that theirs was the one exception to the rule and were bound for greatness.

So, she had stuck to her guns, hoping that he would grow out of this troublemaker phase. Though she wouldn't deny that that is what he was most of the time. He did look the part, as he looked almost exactly like *Dennis the Menace* from the comics, with his blond hair and devilish grin. It struck everyone, including her and her husband, odd that their son had such bright blond hair when she and her husband were both brunettes.

The two shared an ongoing joke over the paternity of their child. Jokingly, when either they were stressed at one another or due to another of their son's misadventures, her husband would declare that he had to have been the product of a torrid afternoon affair with the mailman. There was never any real malice in these jokes. She knew that the stress of his work as a patent attorney was insurmountable at times, and home was his only refuge from the rat race. They had both been rather adventuresome in their youth, though, specifically in college, with all the partying. She did feel that her husband's rather "creative" ways of instilling character into their son might have only been making things worse. He was constantly saying things that built character or scaring the child with horror stories. It was no wonder that at six, the kid was still clinging to a stuffed animal.

"Cal," she called when she discovered him standing in the kitchen, "what are you doing?"

The kid was standing, staring at the door that led down to the basement. When she saw that the door was open, she grew upset. She had told him time and time again to stay away from the basement door. It led down into the old cellar where her grandmother had once stored canned vegetables they grew in the garden. It was dark and musty with a dirt floor, and aside from all the breakable jars and rusty tools stored down there, the stairs were quite rickety.

That basement was a death trap, especially for a talented little hell raiser like Cal. Her grandmother had once fallen down those stairs and broken her hip, having to crawl back up after a night spent down there in the dark. She had no longer been allowed to live alone and had soon been moved to a nursing home. It gave her shudders to think of how terrifying that must have been for an old woman, and she couldn't bear to think of all the things that could have happened to her son. This is why they forbade their son from going near the basement and kept the doors shut and locked. Her husband had even installed a heavy padlock on it, and the keys were kept on his workbench in the garage. Yet here the door stood completely open, and the steps leading down into utter darkness.

"Get away from there," she snapped, grabbing the small boy by the arm and pulling him away from the top of the stairs. It didn't occur to her that there was no way a six-year-old could have reached the padlock that had been placed near the top of the door, well out of the reach of small hands. Even with the aid of a chair, he shouldn't have been able to reach it, and that was if he could have first obtained the key.

Her heart was pounding in her chest as her mind raced with all the terrible things that could have befallen her child. Little hellion that he was, no mother could ever stand the idea of their child hurt and suffering. Every time he had scraped a knee falling off his sled, or woke from a nightmare of monsters under the bed, she had come running. There was nothing that could have ever stopped her from loving her little boy. Even when grown into a man with a family of his own, that's how she would always see him, as that little blond six-year-old clutching his stuffed animal.

"Honey, what were you doing in here?" the frightened mother asked.

"My stuffed tiger fell down the stairs," he replied, with hints of tears welling up in his eyes and his face clouded over with the signs of a good cry, like only small children can muster, building.

That stupid stuffed tiger, she thought. It was strange to see her son without it. His father had bought it and put it in the crib with him when he was three, telling the boy that the monsters would stay away if they saw that he had a fierce tiger with him.

After that, he was never without it. He took it everywhere, and it became his best friend.

It seemed to take on a life of its own. And while it was a bit odd that at his age he still clung to such a thing, it wasn't like he wasn't developing normally. He wasn't still in diapers or sucking his thumb, like some of the slower kids did. A friend of hers had told her it was just a way for kids to form social bonds, so she had let it be. She figured that once he got older, he would put it aside himself, but still, the way he carried on with it gave her the creeps. At times, she wondered if it didn't come to life with the power of her son's imagination to feed it. Now the damn thing was in that creepy basement, and she would have to be the one to fetch it.

Looking down the steps, she couldn't even see the bottom. It was so dark. But if she didn't retrieve it, Cal would be insufferable all evening. The boy's father would be home in an hour or so, and she would have to start working on supper. She would rather not have to sit through it all with a headache from the kid's bawling.

She sat him in one of the kitchen chairs and gave him a cookie to try to calm him down. Once that was seen to, she returned to the basement door and looked once more into that inky blackness. She had always been afraid of the basement since she was a kid, but what kid wasn't? They were dark, forbidding places that were home to the imaginary monsters of a child's mind. However, there were very real things that lived in basements that did scare her, like rats and spiders. She had never seen any rats, though, only a mouse once or twice in the kitchen. She had seen the spider's webs that seemed to grow ever bigger in the basement.

The few times she had needed something from there, she had always sent her husband to fetch it. That's one of the reasons you keep a man around, to fix the plumbing, kill spiders, and occasionally knock the dust off her "pipes." Though the list of chores and repairs seemed endless, neither of them had ever gotten around to adding "clean out the basement" to it, much less actually attempting to tackle it. It was eerie, and they were both sufficiently creeped out by it enough to avoid going down there, whilst simultaneously being too adult to admit it.

When she turned on the light, it cast a dim, yellowish, sickly glow into the room. Shadows loomed in the corners and around the boxes that contained their Christmas decorations. It would be months before she sent her husband down to rummage through that particular mess. As she made her way down the steps, she gripped the wobbly banister tightly. While it might not have been structurally sound, it was better than nothing when dealing with the old stairs.

They were ancient and worn smooth, making it easy to slip. Where you might not slip, you might still find a wandering nail sticking its head up to stab you in the tender sole of your foot. Then there were the trick stairs that shifted and bowed when you stepped on them, trying to send you ass over tea kettle. It had been one of these that had done her grandmother in and left her crying from pain and screaming for help with a broken hip.

The last thing she wanted was to fall and break her fool neck in this musty basement. It smelled stale, with a slightly sour yet sweet stench. The smell cellars get from countless decades of canned goods being stored until they expire. She couldn't imagine how her grandmother had been able to spend so much time going in and out of there. Looking about the floor near the base of the stairs, for that is where the stupid stuffed animal must have landed, she could see nothing and wished she had a flashlight. Remembering that they kept one under the sink, she hurriedly made her way back up the stairs to the brightly lit kitchen. Retrieving the long-barreled mag light, she tested it a few times to make sure it worked before returning to the stairs.

Again, she slowly made her way down, careful of the shaky handrail and the trick steps.

At the bottom, she shone the flashlight about. The bare bulb above her head didn't give off much light and probably needed to be changed out soon. Nowhere did she spot a small stuffed tiger. It must have bounced and fallen off the side of the stairs into the darker depths of the basement. She really didn't like being down there and hurried her search for the toy. It was slow work as she moved around shelves stuffed with old mason jars in which floated pickled fruits and veggies that had long since passed from the realms of preserved food. In the dim light, they looked more like some horrid science experiment that belonged in Dr. Frankenstein's lab than a suburban basement. She was careful not to knock anything from their perches.

Once, as a child, she had knocked one such ancient jar from the shelf, and it had shattered, spilling its entombed contents all over the dirt floor. A foul, spoiled odor had erupted forth from it and filled the basement. That smell of putrefaction and rot had remained for years, and even still, the ghost of that scent could be smelt on the truly hot summer days. She didn't want to smell that ever again, so she carefully made her way around them. The shelves were old yet very solid, unlike the stairs. This is in part because when her grandfather had built them, undoubtedly on orders from her grandmother, he had attached them to the joists that held up the main floor. They held up the house as much as the rest of the jackstraws holding up the place.

The area under the stairs was littered with cardboard boxes and cobwebs. Sorting through them was a chore, and still no stuffed toy. She couldn't find it anywhere. Where could it be? It couldn't have gone far. It just fell down the stairs. It should be here somewhere. It's not as if the damn thing could get up and walk away. She was starting to get frustrated with the search when the overhead bulb flickered. Great, she thought, now the damn light is going to go out, and I will have to search in the dark. Why couldn't that brat do what he was told? Sometimes he really did try her patience to the point where she wanted to put her head, or maybe his, in the oven. She thought that she should feel bad about that, and seeing a professional about it at some point would probably be a good idea. If they couldn't afford therapy, there was always wine.

Speaking of which, a little break would do her good, and a glass would hit the spot. Preoccupied with her thoughts, she nearly leapt out of her skin when one of the cartons behind her fell with a loud thud and sent something scurrying further back into the dark recesses of the basement. Clapping her hands over her mouth, she failed to muffle the shriek that escaped her throat.

It took a few minutes before her heartbeat finally returned to a pre-stroke level, and she was forced to take in a lungful of musty stale air. She let out a nervous laugh that was on the brink of hysteria. It was so silly to let herself get so worked up over such childish fears. It was just a dark basement, maybe a mouse or two, but nothing to really be afraid of. That was when she heard something move again. Probably just a mouse, she thought, sweeping the light in the direction of the sound. The circle of light showed only stacked boxes and the bare dirt floor. All was still in the dim light as the hanging bulb gave off another series of flickers. Holding her breath, she strained her ears in the silence, trying to pick up the slightest noise.

There it was. It was barely audible, but the unmistakable sound of something moving. She moved toward the source, listening as each step brought her closer, her heart pounding in her ears. Her original mission forgotten, she reached out to move a box, expecting to see a mouse or something. Holding her breath, she shifted the box to see...nothing. There was nothing behind the box other than a spot that could have been mildew. Before she could breathe a sigh of relief, the sound came again. This time, it seemed to be emanating from a dark corner further in the basement. Inexplicably drawn deeper into the basement as the light flickered again. This time, threatening to go out entirely, when it stopped, it was emitting less light than before. It went unnoticed, as her entire focus was on the shadowy corner.

She swung the light up to pierce the shadows, but nothing happened. There was no swathe of light cutting through the darkness to show the bare cement blocks that made up the foundation walls. Just empty blackness as though the darkness simply swallowed the light. In that darkness, something shifted and moved. In what she could only describe as an undulation of flesh, it opened, rolling back like some obscene curtain or the folds of a woman's secret place. In the dank depths of her suburban home's basement, she was now face to face with a gigantic inhuman eye.

The flickering overhead light finally lost the battle and went out for good, leaving the flashlight as the only source of light. It was clasped firmly between her slim breasts, pointing skyward now, illuminating only the ceiling. The upward beam highlighted her face in a comical fashion, like one would adopt when telling ghost stories over a campfire. The effect was ironically suited to the atmosphere, but completely lost on her.

It was enormous in scale, larger than she was tall, seeming to devour the wall it was embedded in. Though clearly the eye of some great beast, it was like no eye she had ever seen. It was a sickly yellow hue of long-suffering illness, while the iris was of most beautiful contrast. It swam with all the colors of the rainbow, and perhaps a few no mortal man had ever seen, like an oil spot once the sun had come out following a rain that was not quite hard enough to wash it away.

Mesmerized, the woman couldn't help but gaze deeper into it. The truly alien part was the center of the eye, where it was round in most eyes. This one was stilted like a cat's eye. Instead, however, of a single long slit, it was tri-cornered in an almost perverse bastardization of the symbol of the Trinity. When it opened, inside that eye was an infinite black void, but the void was not empty. As she looked into it, she saw that within this great sleeping eye, that saw everything, were hundreds of thousands of smaller golden eyes of all shapes and sizes, and they were all seeing her.

The woman screamed as she was hit with the crushing realization that she was not dreaming or hallucinating and that this great eye was real. That even in its deep sleep, the entity it belonged to was getting a good look at her, and they were sharing the same thought. That the grotesque horror they were looking at was not of their world. That at this moment in this place for a time no longer than a single breath of an infant child, this window between their universes was open.

As though she knew what was coming, the terrified mother of the neighborhood troublemaker turned and fled. She did not get far before she tripped and fell, smacking her face hard against the dirt floor. She tasted blood from her busted lip as she glanced back to see what had tangled her feet. A long black tentacle had extended out from the edge of the eye like some mutant eyelash. It was wrapped around her ankle, and to her surprise, smoke curled up from her pants cuff. Then there was a brilliant pain in that ankle as though someone had stuck her with a hot poker.

She screamed from the burning pain and managed to jerk her leg free, just as more tentacles reached for her. Hobbling as fast as she could, she ended up careening from shelf to shelf, sending glass jars of old mummified vegetables flying. These exploded like bombs when they hit the ground, sending up unseen noxious mushroom clouds of rot and decay.

The basement quickly filled with the stench, and her eyes began to water as she choked for breath. Momentarily confused, the tentacles snapped at each jar as they shattered, grasping at the pulpy remains of long-forgotten spoiled food. For each one that pulled back mushy nothingness, two more or three more would take its place. Searching hungrily for fresher treats to haul back into that hellish abyss. She didn't know how, but she knew that if they got her, she would join those golden eyes floating in that darkness.

Just as she reached the stairs, another one of the black tentacles wrapped itself around her leg just below the right knee. Not thinking she reached out to try to tear it off, and her hand found that it was soft, as if boneless, and covered in slime. The goo came off on her hand and began to burn as if she had stuck her hand in a bucket of acid. Pus-filled blisters sprang upon the palm of her hand as the skin began to melt and become loose. Tears ran down her cheeks as they split open and began to bleed profusely. The tentacle around her leg gave a mighty tug, dragging her back to the ground. It was far stronger than it looked or felt. Several more whipped out of the darkness, cracking like bullwhips. Grasping at her limbs and clothing, all of them trying to catch her and feed her to that hungry eye.

Still screaming at the top of her lungs, she reached out and grabbed the bottom rail of the banister with both hands. Her burned hands howled in pain as the rough wood bit into her now skinless, raw, bloody palm. Heaving with all her might against the horde of tentacles as well as the nightmarish reality that was threatening to destroy her sanity, she tried to break free.

There was a ripping sound as her mom jeans finally gave way to the corrosive saliva and tug of war between their wearer and her attackers. Those tentacles that had caught bits of clothing came away with small swatches for their efforts, and those that had found some small purchase of skin left behind angry red burn marks and swelling blisters. The one that had managed to get the best grip below her knee refused to give up as she pulled away from it, and everything below her knee. The freshly severed stump gushed blood, but her brain was in too much shock from watching the skin and bone being stripped away in order for her to obtain freedom, to yet register pain. She watched in horror as the tentacle dragged its prize back across the floor, while its siblings writhed in the dirt, wallowing in her spilled blood. Ceasing upon her only chance at escape, she began to drag herself up the decrepit stairs.

Her poor, maimed hands and leg seemed to find every splinter and loose nail as she tried to climb to salvation. Her panicking mind began to believe the traitorous bastards were working against her. It felt as though she had been climbing for ages before looking up to find herself only a few steps away from the kitchen, from light and safety. Through her tears, she could make out her son, six-year-old Cal, standing in the doorway. She began to call out to him for help, but what he was holding in his arms froze her in place. Clutched to the front of his little red and black striped shirt was his stuffed toy tiger. The stuffed toy tiger he had sent her into the basement to get. The wicked little smile plastered on his face banished any question of his innocence in these events.

The little shit had tricked her, and now, standing at the top of the stairs, he was admiring his handiwork as she desperately tried to crawl up the stairs. She couldn't believe that the child she had given birth to, raised, and protected for six years had sent her to her death. She had turned a deaf ear to angry neighbors and teachers, closing her eyes and heart to their accusations that her sweet little boy was a monster.

Her heart breaking, she watched as he reached up with one pudgy hand and took hold of the doorknob. As the door slowly swung closed, she saw in his eyes that he knew exactly what he was doing. There was one last scream as the tentacles dragged her back into the darkness, as the basement door clicked shut.

The Barn

The sun beat down in the early afternoon. Heat shimmers rose from the ground, causing the horizon to dance madly in the distance. The day hadn't yet hit its highest temperature, and it was already causing dark, wet stains to appear around the neck and pits of anyone outside. Even in the shade, one was not spared from the blistering wrath of the sun. Jarrod sat in the shade of the porch and rocked slowly as he chewed thoughtfully. He watched as his two remaining sons marched toward the old barn. It sat sentinel at the edge of what he considered the "house" lot and held the line between it and farmland.

The old barn had been there since time out of mind. It had been old when Jarrod had been in diapers, chasing chickens around the yard. That had been at least eighty-some years ago. Once you reach a certain age, old folks just stop keeping track. It became less about the triumph of being older or the disappointment of another gray hair. It became a slow countdown on the death clock. Sure, that particular watch could stop at any time, but with each passing second, the old reaper man got one step closer. The only respite being that at least he wasn't running out his clock in some rest home stinking of antiseptic and old man farts. No, Jarrod had the luxury, if you could call it that, and he did, of sitting out his golden years in his rocking chair on his porch, and it was well earned.

Like his father and his father before him, Jarrod had spent his life farming the fifty or so acres of land left to him by his father. When Geralt had been alive, Jarrod had farmed with him. Every day they were in the back forty plowing or planting, just as Geralt and his father, Obadiah, had. Year after year, mules would come and go, farm hands would come and go in their season. Wives and children would come and go, some not in their time, others off to school and their own lives. But the land and the men who worked it were always there.

So was the old barn. It had seen season after season, looming there silently. Providing shade in the summer and shelter in the winter or in the stormy season. It was built of strong old-time construction, meant to weather the end of times should Jesus himself desire to descend upon it. Praise Him, Hallelujah. It had stood through the big blow of 1906 and the twister of 1938. He had just been a toddler at that time, but he remembered the scurry and panic as they all hunkered down in the old, cold cellar in the northeast corner of the barn.

There had also been the floods of 1962, the year that Kennedy fella died, and in 1971, when those same politicians took his oldest boy and sent him off to Vietnam to fight their war. Jimmy hadn't come home. In 1973, some Corporal or other showed up at his door with a pair of boots and a folded flag. The man had told Jarrod that his oldest boy had been killed just days before they signed peace accords ending the war. With tears in his eyes, Jarrod had told that happy asshole to get off his porch unless he wanted some other asshole to deliver a pair of boots and a flag to his own family.

He had paid his taxes, voted every election, and donated what he could, sometimes a little more when his wife, Margret, insisted, to the churches and charities. He saluted the flag and believed in the government when he knew fairly well that both parties were full of jackasses. Then, when Uncle Sam asked, he even gave his favorite son. He wouldn't have told his boys. He was sure his wife knew, though. What did he get back for all his sacrifices? More taxes, more campaigns by more slick Willies, and Uncle Sam's hand so far in your pocket he had a firm grip on your balls. Bank loans and mortgages, droughts and deaths, but the barn still stood, and Jarrod kept farming.

Life went on, and he just kept his head down. His kids grew up with long hair and rock music, but he just kept his head down and made his payments to the bank. Bills, and there were always bills, especially for the kids. Margret was always after him for one thing or another. Braces for one, a new coat for the other. New shoes and books for school, uniforms for ball games. Cars needing this and that. One week, an oil change. Next week, new spark plugs. And the barn just kept standing.

He rocked and watched as his boys jumped the fence at the end of the dirt road that led from the road past the house back to the barn. Teddy, the older, carried a sledgehammer, and Brody, the younger, held a pry bar in his hands. They set out to tear the old barn down. They had been on him about selling the farmland. The last twenty years had not been kind to farmers. Jarrod had seen the writing on the wall just a few years before when the prices of tobacco dwindled to nothing.

Tobacco had been the main cash crop of their family farm since the days before the Civil War. They had farmed nearly all two hundred acres with tobacco, corn, and beef. Though, during the depression, the farm had been lost or sold off piece by piece until only fifty acres, forty for the farm, and ten for the house, were left. Even then, they had held on, and tobacco had seen them through. Then doctors found out that smoking and chewing caused cancer, and everyone started ditching the butts. Jarrod and his boys had been among them, especially since they lost dear Margret to metastatic lung cancer. She had never smoked a day in her life. The doctors said it had been from secondhand smoke. Jarrod and the boys had been slowly killing their mother with their bad habit.

She had been sickly and yellow at the end. Bone thin and unable to hold her water. It had torn him up to think that he had done this to her. He knew that even still, the boys blamed themselves as well. They had been good boys, though, helping to take care of her. Up to their elbows and ears in diapers, vomit on the rare occasion she could choke something down. By the time she passed, they had not a single tear among them. They had cried their piece, and when they carried her coffin to the family plot, they did so with dry eyes.

Once tobacco was no longer king in Kentucky, he had tried corn and beef for a few years, but he just couldn't keep up with the big agribusiness farms. Some guys were switching over to soy, and his sons had suggested he try as well, but no self-respecting farmer, a shit kicker from shit kicker who spent most of his life three and a half feet behind a mule's ass, would waste his time with that hippie crap. He left tofu to the Asians and them Californians, and that is how God meant things to be.

Around 2006, he had fallen off the porch due to a rotted board and broken his hip. That had been it. Teddy and Brody had come in to give him a hand and helped him get back on his feet. Doing the chores and fixing up the old homestead while he healed, but that was the end of it and the start of their attempts to persuade him to sell the farm. He had held them off for the next eight years, but bills were mounting, and the money was thin. His boys were more than happy to help out their old man and, Teddy especially, well off with their own careers to keep the wolf from the door.

Brody sold cars, mostly used, but never a lemon. Jarrod and Margaret's boy had been taught better than that. He knew how to make an honest dollar with an honest day's work. Teddy, on the other hand, had been an English teacher for several years until some fool at a publishing company had bought one of his books. The boy had always been into reading and daydreaming, which had annoyed Jarrod, but his wife had begged him to let the boy be. And now, he was a bestselling author. He had read all of his boy's books, though he wouldn't have admitted it, most of them westerns. Those he had liked, but the other ones, golly, they were terrible. Horror stories about couples plotting to kill each other, and monsters in the basement tearing people apart. Lord knows where the boy had gotten those ideas, but it wasn't a nice place.

For the past couple of years, the boys had set out cleaning up the farm, mostly on their weekends. They sorted through piles of scrap metal and trash. Mostly, vehicles that Jarrod had sworn he was gonna get around to fixing up. Old tractors and mowers mainly, though there was a motorbike that his boy Jimmy had been all excited about when Jarrod had told the boy he could have it once fixed up. Margret had laid those plans to nines, keeping him busy and away from what she called a "death trap" until there was no reason to worry anymore. Jarrod had gotten the bike mostly fixed up on the hopes that Jimmy would ride it when he got home from the war, but that day had never come, and so the bike had sat idle until time and rust had taken it.

There was the old silo, though it was really just a small outbuilding made from railroad ties and old culverts. It was only ten or so feet tall and simple enough to tear apart. It hadn't seen corn in over a decade, not since the last load of cattle they had taken to the slaughterhouse over in Flemingsburg. Once cleared and bush-hogged, the forty acres looked better than it ever had. They had even cleared out their mother's old garden that had gone to rose bushes and blackberry tangles. None of them had the heart to tend to it since she had passed. The basement still held shelves full of her old canned goods. The food in them was ancient and probably gone to rot now.

The yard looked nearly perfect, save for a bare spot over in one corner that had once housed the dog kennel. The property hadn't seen a dog since Brody left for college, taking the big, old hound dog with him. Poor mutt ended up getting hit by a car. Margret had cried all night when Brody had told her. She had loved animals, especially dogs. She even loved the old, mean barn cats that kept the mice away. The barn still housed several of the feral little monsters. One big, nasty, old tom was their leader. Jarrod called him Ahab. He was a large, grey tom missing one eye. He must have been hit by a car once because his jaw was misaligned, on one side, with one big fang stuck up like a stalactite. His front legs were bowed, and his tail was crooked at a permanent ninety degrees. He was an angry cuss, hissing and spitting up a fit at anyone who came close. He ruled the barnyard, easily being twice the size of the other cats.

Jarrod chuckled to himself at the thought of old Ahab throwing a world-class fit once they felled his little kingdom. With any luck, he'd give them boys a heck of a scare. He popped the top of a can of soda and took a sip. The cool drink felt glorious on a hot day. They hadn't even started work yet, and they were already sweating. He could see the sweat stains on their shirts even from the porch.

Knocking the barn down would increase the property value, or so they told him. It was old and canted ever so slightly to one side, but it was still sturdy. Better than most of the other old barns, which had gone the way of the woodpile. They would have boards ripped out by strong winds or tin roof panels uprooted and stripped away. Many faded and fell from neglect. Not Jarrod's barn, no, sir. The walls were still the dull black of bargain bin paint, with a red roof. Jarrod had had the roof redone only five or so years back. Brody had straw bossed the boys who came out to do it, and they did a fair job. Jarrod knew their father. He was one of the Story boys, about Teddy's age, so if they slacked off, word would get around as it does in small towns.

Sad to see the barn go. It had lasted so many years, and it probably would have lasted many years more. Now the land would probably be sold off to some developer and turned into suburbs or divided up into lots for them pre-cut houses or worse yet, a trailer lot. Between the house and the barn, Jarrod would choose the house every time. This house was where he had been born and raised, where he had gotten married and raised his own children. He had hoped that his children would marry and raise their own kids here, but time makes fools of us all. The farm was dead, but he was still alive. Once he died, he knew the boys would sell the home place and it would fall to some new family.

But the barn had to come down first, and he knew it wouldn't go easily. It had been built to last, and lasted it had. Now it was its time, the boys would take it down, and that would be that. The last nail in the coffin. Jarrod settled back and waited to see who would win, his boys and their hammers, or the old giant who stood watch over the farm and family for generations.

Teddy and Brody walked into the barn. Shafts of sunlight filtered into the musty interior, and dust motes danced in their beams. The barn was old and dusty, and full of the noises buildings get with age. Every strong brush of wind would cause the old timbers to creak and groan. Though from the sounds of it, it wasn't going to fall in any time soon.

From the rafters hung a variety of rusty chains and old ropes. Both men had swung from them as kids when they played in the hayloft. Their mother would yell at them that they would break their necks when she caught them. Neither had suffered any such injury playing in the barn. The irony being that Teddy did break his arm falling out of the apple tree that had been in the backyard. He had grabbed onto a rotted branch, and it had given way, spilling the young writer out into open space. Their mother had been so upset that less than a week later, she had their father chop the old tree down for firewood. Teddy had spent the rest of the fall and Christmas in a cast. Not that he complained, as it had gotten him a lot of attention and even a kiss from Stephanie Miller, whom he later married, though that had been many years later, following college. Brody had never fallen foul of such misfortune. The worst he ever suffered was a few scraped knees when falling off his bike.

They were both now in their mid-forties. Both were heavy-set and getting a little soft around the middle, mainly from a few too many beers and sitting at a desk. Though under that, there was still the solid build of farm boy muscle, and neither was shy from hard labor. They felt that between the two of them, they should have been able to pull the barn down with little trouble. The plan was simple: knock out two of the six main supports, then weaken the remaining four. Then run chains through the ventilation slats and around a couple of the supports. Using the rented backhoe, they would then pull the barn in the direction it was already leaning, then weight and gravity would do the rest. All that would be left would be to take the crowbar and hammer to take the boards piece by piece and load them up. It would be several days of hard work, but first, they had to take the barn down.

Picking out the first target, one of the left struts, they began their work. Brody stuck the bar between the main strut and one of the braces. Once it was wedged in tight, Teddy swung his hammer, bringing it down on the bar, causing the entire barn to shudder. The old timbers groaned as if the barn were some great animal in pain. Teddy hit it again, and one of the old square nails popped free. It looked like a small railroad spike. Taking this as encouragement, they braced themselves and began their task in earnest.

With each blow, the old barn roared as if angered by the tiny human's attempts to bring it down. As if in revenge for the pain they caused it, one of the chains snapped loose from its ancient mooring. It fell with a clatter, squarely on top of Teddy's head. Nearly two pounds of metal links caused a series of sparks to bloom before his eyes and dropped him to his knees, clutching his skull. Brody abandoned his post to see if his brother was okay. Teddy insisted he was fine, but Brody took a look at his head anyway. The chain had left a sizeable lump that probably hurt like hell, but it didn't look like anything serious. He looked up into the rafters to see if any more dangers lurked above them. He saw nothing but a few old birds' nests, tangled in the meeting of joints, and one curious cat.

Teddy had assured his brother that he was fine, which was a bit of a fib, as his skull now ached as though it were being squeezed in a big press. He wanted nothing more than a drink, but he didn't want to alarm Brody by drinking at this hour. Teddy was sure that Brody suspected his problem with alcohol. While Teddy thought Brody suspected it, all doubt was removed during their mother's funeral. Teddy had been about half in the bag before the service and was well on his way by the time the wake began. His marriage had been on the rocks when his father had broken his hip, but when he came back from seeing his father out of the hospital, Stephanie was gone, as were several of her suitcases. He hadn't told his brother or father yet, but the last few years had been a mess of lawyers and divorce proceedings.

Thankfully, they had never had kids, and the house was in his name, but she was taking him for everything else he had. The trouble had started when his writing was going nowhere, and they would have been on the outs then had his books not started selling. With the money, things were better for a while. Big house, nice cars, and fancy trips around the world, but the drinking had not only continued, but it had also gotten worse. It had escalated from day drinking to day blackouts. None of his writing was getting done, and their arguments had become more frequent and nastier. He had never struck her, but it was a near miss several times. Now, all he wanted was a beer and a seat on the porch until his head stopped throbbing.

After a short breather, they got back to it, working on trying to loosen the brace from the main support. The building shuddered and groaned in protest with each blow, but after that first nail, no real progress was made. After a few minutes, they stopped, and Brody inspected their work. The gap had now widened to maybe half an inch. Agreeing that they were getting nowhere, they decided to go with Plan B, and Teddy went to fetch the chainsaw. If this didn't do it, they would just use the bucket on the backhoe to tear the barn apart. Teddy revved up the chainsaw as Brody marked the key spots on the post to cut. Teddy put the blade to the old wood and began cutting. It was slow going, as the supports were ironwood and had been treated several times. Along with their age, it had almost petrified. Though nearly as hard as rock, the chainsaw bit into it and slowly made progress.

Nearly half an hour later, they had cut the braces free from the support. The blade had snapped once, giving them both a scare, but luckily, neither had been hurt. The barn had not liked the chainsaw one bit, and almost every board vibrated from the assault. From his spot on the porch, Jarrod just shook his head and raised his cola can in salute to the barn's resistance.

While Teddy replaced the blade on the saw, Brody had hooked the fallen chain around the top of the support. When his older brother started cutting the support's base, he pulled on the chain with all his weight. It didn't budge, and so Teddy took a few more chunks out of the beam. Another pull and again, nothing happened. On the third pull, the beam began to give, just a little more and it would come down.

As Teddy cut more from the base, Brody stepped back to admire their handiwork and didn't see the mangled grey tomcat slinking up behind him. He stepped on the cat, and it let out a howl, scaring the bejesus out of him, causing the man to lose his footing. The flailing tom tangled up his legs and had pitched him ass over tea kettle backward. His two hundred pounds landed squarely on the rotting wooden doors to the old root cellar. With a sickening crack, it crumbled and dumped the large man down the old rickety stairs. The fall to the dirt floor wasn't far, but Brody landed squarely on his neck, breaking it and killing him instantly.

Putting aside the chainsaw, Teddy looked around for his brother. Due to the racket he was making with the saw, he hadn't seen or heard Brody's misfortune with the cat. He had only noticed something when the cat slammed into his leg as it streaked out past him. It had bolted out the door and into the long grass near the fence, and that was the last he saw of it. Removing the goggles, he wiped sweat and sawdust from his eyes. Peering into the dimly lit barn, he didn't see his younger brother anywhere. Neither of them was prone to jokes, especially when someone was working with power tools, and he hadn't seen him go past him to leave the barn.

He finally spotted the ruin of the cellar door and approached apprehensively. Looking down into the dark cellar, he saw the body of his brother. It was clear from the angle of his neck and the trickle of blood running out of the corner of his mouth that he was dead. Teddy gasped and felt a sudden wave of sickness rise in his stomach. He barely managed to turn away before throwing up. He hurked up his breakfast into the corner of the dusty barn.

Finished, he wiped his mouth on the sleeve of his shirt. He had to call for help. They needed an ambulance. Oh, God, how would he break the news to their father? It all felt so unreal, causing his head to spin. He staggered and put out one hand to steady himself. As he leaned against the support post, it shifted, and a brace above tore free. It swung down, one end anchored to the cross beam by an old, rotted rope, the other end striking the middle-aged writer in the face. The board struck his nose, breaking it, causing blood to cascade down his upper lip and splatter his shirt. He barely noticed as several of the long square nails protruding from the free swinging end caught him full in the throat, gouging deep into his flesh as a jet of blood gushed from his neck. Teddy went to his knees, both hands pressed to his neck in a vain attempt to stem the tide of blood, as he desperately tried to shuffle to the door on his knees. He didn't get far as the frayed rope snapped, dropping the brace, which was made from an old railroad tie, and cracking him across the back of the head.

Gurgling through a mouthful of his own blood, as he lost consciousness, his last thought was of how badly he needed a drink. Passed out on the dirty barn floor, Teddy bled out, as the dust motes played and danced in the lazy streams of sunlight that peeked through the walls and roof. The day's work was left unfinished.

Jarrod sat on the porch with the empty can next to his feet and listened to the silence now emanating from the barn. Old barns, like old houses, with enough time, take on a sort of life of their own. Not unlike old folks, they have their creaks and groans, and they can be nasty cusses when someone disturbs their slumber.

His hands clasped on his chest, his eyes half-closed in a light dose, he thought that in a bit he would have to get up and call the emergency number next to the telephone. There would be no need for the ambulance to run its lights because there was no hurry. There was no hurry at all, and as the day moved on to late afternoon, the old man slipped deeper into sleep. His last thought was that the barn had stood long since before him, and it would continue standing long after he was gone.

Rawhead

How did it all come to this? She had been a good student, getting mostly As and Bs, and was on the honor roll most years. She had been popular and pretty, not model or cheerleader pretty, but definitely top tier. She had only drank a couple of times at some parties, but never enough to really get drunk, and she had never even tried drugs. Yet here Stacy was, kneeling on the cold floor in the big walk-in freezer, looking at her supervisor's greasy prick.

It wasn't fair. It wasn't her fault that after graduating high school, everything had gone to shit. While she hadn't been valedictorian, she had graduated in the top fifteen percent of her class and had managed to score excellence in her SATs. It all started going wrong with her college admissions. Almost every single school she had applied to had turned her down, including her backup schools. Something no one she knew had ever heard of.

Even if she had gotten into one of those colleges, she had no way of paying for it. Her father worked days at a factory, making parts for cars. He spent his nights sitting in front of the TV, drinking beer, and growing fat. Stacy's mother had died when she was six or so. She couldn't really remember. She had a hard time remembering her mother much at all. It had been some sort of accident, and the insurance money had run out long ago. Though truth be told, it hadn't been much. Her father choosing a quick settlement over fighting it in court.

The economy was no help. It was almost nonexistent in their small rural community. Just her luck that they lived in the poorest area of one of the poorest states in the US. Her job options were limited to factory work or retail. Of course, there was fast food, but that was the same as retail. Busting your ass seven days a week for minimum wage and still being in the red with no prospects on paying for college.

She had looked at taking out student loans, but even that was depressing and arduous. Stacy had no credit to speak of, and her father was in debt to the point that a lien had been put on their trailer.

So, there was no chance he could have cosigned for her. She had no car and no money, so even if she had a job or college, she was still behind the eight ball quite a bit.

Her luck did take a slight turn for the better. Her aunt had retired to Florida, but had kept her home just a mile down from the community college. She had agreed to let Stacy stay there rent-free if she looked after the place. All she had to do was pay the utilities, which Stacy had found fair. Being so close to the college meant that Stacy could also walk to school, and so having a car wouldn't impact her too much.

Enrolling in the local nursing program, she learned about a financing program that they had to help students pay tuition. It was a community fund that several of the businesses participated in. They offered spots for college students to work for them, in exchange for paying off a part of their tuition. A bonus was that it also gave her credit for a small student loan from the bank at a modest interest rate. Along with that windfall, they would work with her class schedule so that she never had to choose between work and school.

This, of course, was too good to be true as she soon found out that there were several catches to her run of good luck. First, when they said that they would work with her schedule, what it meant was that most of the companies were factories offering second shift. Meaning, she would attend school all day, then work some hellish, back-breaking job until midnight. The second catch was that because she had signed up late, there was only one opening left.

The job had one pro: it was in the industrial park just behind the college, making it only a short walk from the campus to work, and not that much farther to walk home at night. The con, and there were several, was that it was at the meatpacking plant. Though it was too generous to call it a meatpacking plant. It was a slaughterhouse, plain and simple, and not a very big one at that. She had tried to get the administration office to find something else or get one of the other students to trade spots with her. No dice, she had actually managed to annoy the staff with her efforts. They did promise to let her change over once another spot opened up, assuring her that people dropped out all the time. So, she just had to stick it out for a little while.

That had been one of the biggest lies she had ever swallowed. Stacy had ended up working there for over a year. She would wake up by seven in order to make it to school by eight o'clock. She had to walk along the highway for a mile to reach the college campus. It wasn't too bad to accept she had to walk past the cemetery for a quarter mile, and that always creeped her out. It seemed like there was always a dense fog over the ground both early in the morning and late in the evening. On the upside, she didn't have to waste time or money at the gym with all the walking she was getting her steps in.

Once she got to school, she had non-stop classes from eight until four. Despite good grades and SAT scores, the college felt she needed remedial classes in addition to general studies before letting her take nursing classes. Stacy felt that it was more like they were padding out her workload to turn a buck. The books alone cost a small fortune, and she didn't even take the plastic off several of them due to the class never using them, and then college supply store had the balls to try to screw her on the resales. One book had cost her over two hundred dollars, and they wanted to buy it back for twenty despite it never being used.

She'd nearly had a row with the girl behind the counter when she had suggested it was because they couldn't tell if the book had been used or not. Stacy had screamed at the girl that it was still in the damn plastic. She didn't normally have a temper, but everything had been pushing her buttons nonstop, and the poor girl just happened to be the one she went off on.

After classes, she had to rush from her last class that let out at 3:40 to her job where she had to clock in at 4:00 sharp. As long as she walked at a quick pace, she could just make it. Thankfully, a few years prior, they had put in a service road behind the college that ran straight to the industrial park. All she had to do was go out the back and sprint, sadly, mostly uphill to the slaughterhouse.

The slaughterhouse—Stacy refused to call it a meatpacking plant, because no matter what, you could never convince yourself that it was anything but—sat at the very back of the lot. It was a squat, low building painted bright red that backed up to the creek, which ran behind it. Whose sick idea was it to paint it bright red? No one knew. But no matter what, it was impossible to see it as anything more than blood. It stank and it stank bad. On some days with a good headwind, Stacy could smell it from her aunt's house.

Stacy hated the sight of it. She had hated it since the moment she had first seen it. Her first day had been a nightmare. She had been expecting what the name had suggested, meatpacking. Rows of machines and assembly lines, neat and sterile, while the machines did all the work. She had had visions of that episode of *I Love Lucy* where Lucy and Ethel made chocolates, except with neat cuts of steak instead of chocolate. It had not been what she expected.

It was more like something out of a horror movie. There wasn't blood and guts everywhere, but Stacy had never really seen the process of how meat turns into what it looks like when it ends up on your plate. She had never even been hunting, so skinning and gutting animals had been outside her frame of reference, much less killing animals.

By the end of her first day, that had all changed. Her first indignity had been the uniform. It consisted of a smock, kind of like what painters wear. The sort of cheap disposable coveralls that made her look more like she was doing HAZMAT work rather than meatpacking. It covered her from head to toe, leaving only her face uncovered. It was flimsy at best, and it was no shock when she later discovered it did nothing at all to protect her skin or clothing. Over the coat went a canvas apron, the kind that cashiers wore. In fact, you could still make out the faded name of the supermarket it had come from. On top of that went a doctor's coat, like the apron was secondhand, Stacy could tell because over the right breast were the remains of the stitching where the patch had been. Its outlines were still very clear.

The heavy work gloves and thick gumboots were the only things she wore that actually provided protection. Everything else might as well have been non-existent, as by the end of her shift, she would be covered in blood. It would take her a good half hour of scrubbing with Gojo, a special soap her dad had given her that was made to cut grease, to get it off her.

The first person she had met with was Darrel. He was a short, stocky man, nearly a few inches shorter than Stacy, who wasn't very tall, even for a woman. He was also greasy. With his slicked-back hair and pockmarked face, he looked like a rejected extra from a mafia movie. The only thing is, he would never have made a convincing mobster. His voice was still that of a cracking adolescent despite being in his thirties. Its constant jumping pitchy tone hurt her ears. She didn't know how he hadn't realized it, or maybe he had and was just in denial.

What was worse than his oily skin and ill-fitting voice was that he ran the slaughterhouse like his own personal fiefdom. He was the big cock of the walk here, despite being the smallest person there. He had been nothing but misogynistic and dismissive of her since the minute they met.

Darrel had taken one look at her and pronounced her too girly to work there. While Stacy had secretly agreed that she didn't belong there, she wasn't gonna give the little shit the satisfaction. After all, she just had to tough it out for a few weeks until something else opened up. That was the ray of hope that kept her going.

During what could jokingly be considered her orientation, he constantly referred to her by derogatory pet names ranging from "Princess" to "Sugar Tits". What was more humiliating was that he had done it right in front of the other employees. Not that there were many other employees, there were maybe half a dozen on second shift. But still, getting a dressing down like that in front of the others, who all snickered at her with each insult, it was almost more than she could take.

He had led her through the building, giving her a tour of what they called the main floor, which is where most of the work was done. It was pretty much enclosed. With only a large bay door that leads out to the loading area, and the door they had entered from. The main floor was kept cold, roughly forty degrees. Despite all of the clothing she was wearing, the cold cut right through. She had constant goose pimples across her flesh even after she left the building.

There were a few machines for skinning and processing the animals, but most of it was done by hand, especially the butchering. She wasn't certified for that, thank God, so Darrel said they wouldn't station her there. This was a small relief, as she couldn't have handled cutting up animals all day. The meat was carted from the butchering stations to the packing station, where it was wrapped in plastic and labeled. From there, it was sent to the loading docks and packed on trucks that took it to local stores and special orders.

The meat that wasn't packed or shipped was stored in a large freezer. The freezer was a large, separate unit about twice the size of a shipping container. Darrel had shown her the inside, where there were racks of hanging meat on hooks. Naked dead bodies that had once been living, breathing animals hung in silence, giving her the willies. He had also taken special care to point out the freezer controls and warned her that he had better never catch her messing with them. The big dial went from room temperature all the way down to forty below zero.

He explained that it was actually more powerful than they needed. They kept it at a few degrees below freezing to preserve the meat, but taking it down to its coldest setting would freeze even some gasses into solids, and they never set it that low because at that temperature it damages the meat.

"It freezes so solid that the meat breaks like glass. You could take a hammer and smash a whole cow with just one hit. So, I don't want to catch you messing with this freezer. You understand, sweet cheeks?" he said. She had just nodded. The floor alone was cold enough. She hadn't wanted to spend any time in the freezer.

As the last part of the tour, he took her out onto the loading dock. The loading dock not only served as an area for loading the outgoing trucks, but also as the killing floor where farmers brought in their livestock to be killed before processing. They would back their tailors into the two bays and offload their stock one by one. The cattle would step out and into a metal chute.

Darrel had shown her to one of the chutes, explaining that this was where she would be working. She was glad at first because at least she was out of the cold of the main floor, but the stink of the animals and manure was stronger and somehow worse out here than all the blood and death on the inside. She watched Darrel as he showed her how to attach a pair of shackles to the cow's back legs once it was locked into the metal chute. Once done, he showed her the two lights on a little console. One was green, the other was red. The green one was on, and he explained that that meant everything was safe and she was free to move around to do her work. He then pointed to a button below them and told her that when she was done, to hit that button and stay in the marked "safe" zone when the red light was on.

Darrel then picked up a tool and showed it to Stacy. It looked to her like a lightsaber from the *Star Wars* movies. Unlike the ones in the movies, this one had what looked like a bicycle hand brake on it, with a tube that ran out the bottom to a small machine.

"This here is a bolt gun," he explained, showing her the device. "It's pretty simple to use. It's hooked up to an air compressor, so there really isn't anything you need to do to it. You just put it between the cow's eyes and squeeze the handle." He placed the flat end between the cow's eyes and squeezed just as he said. Stacy nearly jumped out of her skin as it emitted a sharp barking noise and a hiss of gas. The cow went limp, and when Darrel removed the thing from the cow's head, there was a small dark circle in the middle of its forehead and a trickle of blood. He hit the button, an alarm buzzed, and the green light went off as the red one started flashing.

The cow was jerked up by its back legs and carried into the main building on an overhead track. There was a final buzz, and the red light clicked off, the green one clicked on as a new cow was let into the chute.

Darrel turned and grinned at her. "It's that easy, toots. A monkey could do it, and if the FDA allowed it, we would hire one, but I guess a bimbo like you will have to do. Just be careful with that thing." He held it up in front of her eyes and squeezed the handle again. There was the sharp bark and hiss of gas, as a metal rod about six inches long shot out with the speed of a bullet. There was still blood on it. "That's one mean little pisser, and if you aren't careful, it will mess you up just as much as it would the cows. Not that anyone would notice, blondes aren't known for their brains."

Stacy stood in shocked horror at what she had just watched. Darrel had just killed that cow and now expected her to do it. There was no way she could do it. Just looking in those big brown eyes, so trusting and unafraid. These poor animals had no idea what was about to be done to them.

He shoved the bolt gun into her hand. It was cold and somehow felt cruel, even through her glove. She gulped and reminded herself that she needed the job for just a few weeks, then she would be gone and doing something else and never have to see this horrible place again. She put the gun against the cow's head and took a deep breath.

Bracing herself, she squeezed the handle. There was a sharp snap, and the gun went off. She had closed her eyes when she squeezed, trying not to see the moment she killed the poor animal. She only felt the recoil, and when she opened her eyes, the cow was limp, leaning against one side of the metal chute. Its tongue hung from its mouth in that unmistakable, almost cartoonish expression of death. She hit the button, and the buzzer went off, the red light went on, and the cow carcass was whisked away through the bay doors into the building.

She fought the urge to throw up. Her legs shook, and she teetered on the edge of passing out. It took her a few seconds to get a grip on herself and pull herself back together. She refused to let this asshole have the pleasure of seeing her pass out. He was already a pain in the ass, and it would only get worse if she let this jackal smell weakness.

Darrel nodded, but stayed hovering over her until she had repeated the process several more times. Each time she felt like throwing up, but she had to keep up the front, and it became her routine. Cow, squeeze button. Cow, squeeze button. Cow, squeeze button. She lost count of how many she had done that day alone. Their poor, dumb eyes and limp bodies haunted her to the point where she could see them every time she shut her eyes.

For weeks after, she had nightmares about it, until one night, she found herself in the metal chute looking up at Darrel's jeering face. She tried to scream and beg him to let her out, but she couldn't speak because her tongue was hanging out of her mouth like a dead snake. No matter how hard she tried, she couldn't get it to move. She watched helplessly as he placed the shiny flat end of the bolt gun against her forehead and squeezed the handle.

Stacy had woken up screaming and crying. She had been in such an emotional state that she had to call into both school and work. It took her nearly all day to get herself calmed down and in a halfway decent state. When she had gone back to work, she had begged Darrel to give her any job other than the killing floor. He had laughed at her, but eventually gave her what she asked for.

She was reassigned to be a gopher on the main floor. This job was a little better than the killing flood. It mainly consisted of carting meat from one area to another. A job that was usually reserved for someone bigger and stronger than Stacy. However, she had been allowed the use of a canvas cart similar to a laundry cart. She would load the meat in and take them over to the packing area.

The packing area was overseen by a woman named Jessica. She was a big slab of a woman. Roughly the size and build of a refrigerator. She had short-cropped black hair and nearly a dozen earrings in just one ear. Jessica was the only other woman who worked the second shift, and as far as Stacy knew, the only other woman who worked there at all. This didn't make them fast friends. Just the opposite, Stacy figured that to earn her place among the guys, she had to be even more butch than they were. Which meant she also got in on tormenting Stacy, giving her suggestive motions and making some of the filthiest comments she had ever heard. Even without the constant harassment of her coworkers, the job was hell. The worst part wasn't even how heavy the loads were. It was the blood. It got everywhere. By FDA regulations, they had to drain the blood before processing. When the carcasses came out of the killing floor, one of the butchers would place them above a vat, then, using one of their long, sharp knives, they would slit the dead animal's throat.

Blood would pour out and into the vat. Once the blood stopped, though, truly not all of it would come out. The belly would be slit open, the organs removed, and then processed or packaged. It would then be skinned. The hides were sold off to a local artisan tanner who made saddles and belts. Once dressed, the body would be cut up depending on the needs of the orders.

In some cases, entire sides of beef would need to be moved to the freezer.

This, of course, Stacy had to do. The cart was no help when it came to those parts. She would have to carry it over her shoulder to the freezer and get help hanging it on the meat hooks. Doing so meant getting what blood was left all over her coat and smock. The blood would just soak right through.

At first, it felt good because the blood was warm in the refrigerator, like the atmosphere of the main floor. That was only temporary, because soon the blood would cool and become tacky. Which made it even worse. Her chest, arms, and back would be covered by the end of the night. She would walk home every night looking like the survivor of a slasher film.

No one in their right mind would stop to give her a ride, not that she needed it. The lonely late-night walks were the most serene and peaceful part of her day. Though Jessica had stopped her pickup truck alongside her one night on her way home. She offered the girl a ride back to her place and suggested a few things to help warm her up. There had been no reason for it. They weren't at work where the guys would see, so there was no reason for her to be mean to her. Stacy had flipped her the bird and continued on. The big lesbian had called her a cunt as she drove off.

Everything about her job was miserable, to the point that her poor sleep schedule was affecting her schoolwork. But still, she soldiered on. Months went by with no changes or notices from the administration office. So, Stacy stayed stuck in the shitty job she hated, telling herself it wouldn't be much longer.

The job didn't get any easier. It got harder as others delighted in seeing what new shit Darrel would torture her with. One such job was watching her struggle with the waste barrels. They were large oil drums that sat around the various stations on the floor. Whenever bad meat was spotted, diseased or spoiled, into the barrels it went. Excess fat trimmings, unneeded organs, and discarded bones were also tossed in. By the end of the week, the barrels were all filled to overflowing with refuse.

Stacy, as the second-shift gopher, it was part of her job to drag them out back, but if there were too many, she was to dump the extras down an old coal shoot that drained into the creek out back. This wasn't exactly legal, but the management didn't really care, as every extra waste barrel that had to be carted off cost them extra for the city to pick up.

She hadn't heard this from Darrel, but from one of the butchers. He was a big black guy called Jamie. He was the only person there that Stacy liked. It wasn't that he was nice to her, because he wasn't especially. It was more than he was the only one who didn't join in with mocking and degrading her. He also didn't do anything to stop it, but she felt it was less about him caring and more that he just didn't like being bothered either way.

He had explained the waste barrels one time at lunch. It had been nice to have someone to talk to, even if it was a rare thing and most of it was just him telling her to get a move on or explaining how to do something the right way. He had been explaining about how, during deer season, the slaughterhouse had a special deal for hunters.

They could bring in their deer, and the slaughterhouse would butcher it in exchange for what was left over, as most hunters just wanted select cuts. She had asked what they got out of it, and he had looked at her slyly.

"Free meat," he grunted in his low tone. "They get free deer meat and turn around and sell it to a local guy who makes jerky and smokes it. That's how this place makes money. They nickel and dime. They got about a dozen different side hustles to cut corners and make extra scratch." She had been mesmerized by his deep, rich voice. His heavy lids gave him a constant sleepy look and, paired with his heavyset frame, he reminded her of a big, old panda. Content with where it was, so long as it could reach some bamboo and didn't want to budge.

"Like with those waste barrels you been haulin'," the big man continued, lighting a cigarette. "For every two barrels they have you drag out back, you got to dump one down the swill out back." He noticed her cock an eyebrow in question. "That old chute leads down into the creek out back, it's why it stinks out here so bad. The city would have their hides if anyone complained, but no one does, so they keep right on doing it. One of these days, there will be a big flood or a clog, and the city will get up to looking at it, and the owners will be in hot water, but until then..." he trailed off, just letting it hang in the air. Stacy was hanging on his every word.

"Of course, that ain't it as far as environmental infractions. I don't know if you know this or not, but the one shitter in this place isn't hooked up to sewage lines or a septic tank. The toilet dumps right out into the creek. In the winter, you can actually feel the cold air come up and hit you in the keister."

Stacy had only seen the restroom once. It was a little, dark closet barely big enough to contain the filthy toilet. It had stunk and was so dirty that she felt as though she needed a shower just from looking at it. She shivered just thinking about it.

Jamie just watched her with a bit of amusement on his face. "It's the same everywhere, girly. Everyone screwing someone else over to get a little bit ahead, but it comes full circle in the end." He stubbed out his cigarette once he finished it.

Seeing she was still puzzled by his cryptic words, he grinned, showing two rows of impressively white teeth. He leaned over and said, "Karma's a bitch." He had packed up his lunch and left, leaving her sitting there thinking how nice it would be to see Darrel's greasy ass in a sling for once. It would be nice to see him get his comeuppance before she left for a better job somewhere else. But it hadn't happened. The months had dragged on, one after another, until the day in the freezer.

It had been a rather hard and long one. Her lower back had been killing her, having to carry several whole sides of beef to the freezer at the start of her shift. After all this time, she thought she would have gotten stronger from all the exercise, but nothing ever felt any lighter or easier. Instead, she just got more and more run-down.

The night had been slow. The last trucks had left for their deliveries and some staff had knocked off early. Of the roughly half dozen second-shift workers, only about four remained. All that was left was to pack and store the rest of the meat, then her evening would be spent sweeping up, the only easy part of her job.

She had just carted a load of meat to the freezer to store when Darrel cornered her. There she was in the freezer, alone with no witnesses. It was how Darrel had planned it. Stacy hadn't noticed it, but he had been making excuses and engineering ways to get close to her in an effort to catch her alone. If she hadn't been so run down, she would have noticed him stalking her like a predator.

He stepped into the freezer and pulled the door most of the way shut as she looked up at him. He gave her a crooked, wicked, knowing grin. It showed his yellowing teeth. Dental hygiene seemed to be another thing he lacked.

"Say, chickie, you have really hung in there. I expected you to crap out the first day, but you kept hanging around, and I thought for sure by the first week you would have quit."

"I need the job," she replied, trying to focus on getting the meat out of her cart and onto the shelves. She wanted out of there as fast as she could.

"You know, it doesn't have to be this hard. I could make it a lot easier on you, but you got to make it hard on me," he said. His grin grew wider.

"Wait, what?" She was confused about what he meant.

In reply, he undid his pants and pulled them down. She was presented with his exposed dick. It was a sad, little thing. Not particularly tiny, but not especially porn star size. Stacy didn't get why men put so much pride into their junk. It was rather weird looking, and she had never seen a penis that wasn't. She continued to stare at this bizarre image, not fully grasping what he was getting at.

"Just give it a good suck every now and then, and you won't have to do anything but sweeping up. The easiest job you could get. No more hauling slop buckets or heaving around them big slabs. Unless you are one of those lesbos like Jess. Is that what you are into, big hairy beef pie? 'Cause I betcha she has got a big ol' one, and it's probably nice and ripe. That what you want?" he jeered, giving his little prick a jostle as it started to harden.

"No," she said, dumbstruck. Her tired brain slowly came around to realize what was going on.

"Then get to it, bitch. It's not gonna suck itself." His member now stood to its full, unimpressive stature.

Stacy felt faint, and her legs came undone at the knees, and she sank to the floor. She was now eye level with little Darrel, which was just as greasy and had its own pungent odor. Surely, she wasn't going to perform oral sex on this troll just for an easy job. Not only did she have no assurance that he would keep his end of the bargain, but she also didn't know if she would be able to report him.

It was a sad state in this day and age, that in cases like this, the business would rather just fire her and be done with it than deal with sexual harassment. But this was more than sexual harassment. This was borderline sexual assault, if not sexual assault. Even if she were to file a police report, it would be her name drug through the mud and shamed. It was unlikely it would hurt this pig at all.

For once, her luck was in, and she didn't have to deliberate for long. She was saved in a manner of speaking when a shrill cry rang out. It startled them both, and they looked towards the door. There was more yelling, galvanizing the two into action. Stacy picked herself up off the floor as Darrel stuffed his pecker back into his pants. He was still adjusting himself as he shoved the door open and they emerged into the main floor.

The yelling was coming from across the floor near the processing station, from one of the other butchers. Stacy didn't recall his name, only that he had one dead tooth in the front of his mouth. He was now shouting, and his face was bright red. In his hands, he held one of the brooms like a baseball bat, as if he were going to use it to hit something.

Stacy couldn't tell at first because she couldn't make sense of what she was seeing. From the butcher's gestures, it was something to do with the vats. At the end of every shift, or whenever they were full, the blood was pumped out into hazardous waste vats to be disposed of by the city. Right now, there should have been a mostly full vat of drained blood, but she couldn't tell what she was looking at.

There was a large mound of something between her and the vats. She couldn't make out what it was until it stood up. Her mind reeled, unable to make sense of what she was looking at, and if she could, she would probably go insane. It was unlike anything she had ever seen before.

The thing was vaguely humanoid in shape, but closer to that of a gorilla than a man, by the way it was hunched over. It was also bulky. Much bulkier than it should have been in some places and less in others where it should have been. Its body was wrong. It was as if it were thrown together by someone with no clue about anatomy.

It had no skin. Its body was made of mismatched bones and muscles. One arm was much thicker than the other and had only three fingers if you counted the malformed appendage where a thumb should have been. The other had four fingers, and the bones seemed to fit better. Whereas on the bigger arm, the bones appeared heavier, like leg bones rather than arms.

There was no discernible sternum in its chest. The pectoral muscles were a mismatched patchwork strung together. The spinal process stood out starkly in its back like a row of fins down the back of some reptile. Its lower torso tapered to an almost ridiculous proportion. Its waist was nearly as thin as Stacy's, despite its shoulder width being over four feet across at least. The same could be said for its almost vestigial legs. They were short and stumpy, resembling the feet of an elephant or a rhino.

Its head was the worst. The head sat almost directly on top of the shoulders, perched upon the most minute pile of flesh one could call a neck. Its head was rubbed so raw that it was little more than a bare skull, and it was not the skull of a man, but the elongated skull of a cow or maybe a goat. The only real flesh on its face was thick cables of muscle that moved its jaws.

Its jaws dripped with rank, clotted blood. It had been drinking from the vat of spilled blood, if that was even possible given that it had no lips. Though the blood-stained, long, flat teeth were still an almost unreal bone white. As it turned its head about to see what the disturbance was, Stacy could see its eyes. The bare skull's eyes were wet and dark, and moving. Something inside them wriggled and squirmed. It was the only thing alive in those cold, dead eyes.

The creature heaved itself to its feet. *It can't be real*, Stacy thought to herself, *it's some sort of prank they are doing to mess with me*. But it wasn't, she could see its chest move in and out with each ragged breath. With each breath, it let out a snort, sending waves of foul air across the room. She could smell it. It smelled like rotten eggs and spoiled milk.

Darrell yelled at the man to stay away from the creature, as the butcher menacing it with the broom had drawn its attention. It opened its jaws and let out an unearthly scream that sounded like rusting metal under stress and a bag of drowning cats. Flecks of blood and flesh sprayed from its mouth as it roared. It raised its hands and slammed them to the ground in a display of unprecedented strength. The concrete floor cracked under their impact.

Stacy saw what was about to happen before it did. The man would thrust the broom at the creature, provoking it, and it would swat him like a fly. Ignoring Darrel's warnings, the fool brandished the broom at the thing, and it backhanded him with its one big arm. There was a sound like a bag of wet cement hitting the ground, and the man was sent flying like a rag doll. He crashed through the loading bay doors that led to the killing floor. The thing let out another ear-splitting roar, causing Darrel to bolt. The sudden movement drew its attention, and like any other animal, it instinctively gave chase. The huge wall of flesh was coming straight at her, pursuing the terrified supervisor. He slammed into her as he tried to run past, sending Stacy down hard on her ass.

She was frozen on the ground as it bore down on her. Then a terrible miracle happened, granting her a few more precious moments of life. Jessica came stomping out from the corridor that led to the restroom. A confused look on her face as she stepped between Stacy and the monster. Her mistake was in looking to her right instead of her left. Had she looked left, she would have seen her death coming. Instead, she had looked to the right and seen only Stacy on the ground, feverishly trying to scoot backward as fast as she could on her butt.

The heavyset woman didn't see it once the massive three-fingered hand wrapped around her head, and with almost no effort, crushed her skull into a bloody pulp. Her body fell to the floor, her feet spasmed and kicked as if desperate to cling to a few more seconds of life. Stacy felt a warmth spread in her crotch as her bladder released itself, bathing her in the urine.

The creature stepped over the dying body, using its arms more than its legs for locomotion. Its gate was as awkward and uneven as the parts it was Frankensteined from. Though it moved almost too well for something its size and weight, as cobbled together as it was. It had almost no problem as it stalked toward her.

Its mouth lolled open, revealing a long, flat cow's tongue. Maggots wriggled in its mouth, and looking up, she saw the truth of those squirming masses that filled its empty sockets. Its skull was full of rot and worms, and she could almost make out a bit of brain in there. How could something like this exist, and where could it have come from? In an otherworldly flash of brilliant, almost telepathic understanding, Stacy had the answers to those questions.

This thing, whatever it was, had come from the dumped slop and waste in the creek outback. It had formed itself from the scraps and spoils they had been dumping for months, maybe years. It had slept in the mud, gaining strength from every death and discarded thing, until scraps weren't enough. Maybe it had preyed on raccoons, pets, and other small animals. But they hadn't been enough. It had hungered for more until its hunger led it back here. It finally sought to satiate its hunger and went straight to the source.

They had dared to interrupt its feeding, and now they were just more meat to feed its monstrous appetite. But it would need to be satisfied. It was as greedy as the people who had created it. It wanted more and more. Now, it had all it could want, and right now it wanted her.

Suddenly, the creature reared back and let out a scream of rage and pain. The source of this pain, and Stacy's momentary savior, was the large butcher knife Jamie had plunged into the side of the thing. The big black man, instead of doing the smart thing and running for his life, had snuck up behind the beast and stabbed it. In any normal living thing, it would have been a mortal wound, but with its twisted, malformed body, the creature was only enraged.

Despite it being a head taller, Jamie faced it down with a knife in each hand and yelled for Stacy to run. She did, looking back only once, just in time to see it raise its fists and beat the man into the ground like a fence post. Blocking out the horrific sounds of the only halfway decent person she had met in this job being killed, she finally scrambled to her feet and made a beeline back to the freezer.

She arrived just as Darrel, who had been scrambling at the latch in sheer panic, managed to open the door. She had to fight him to make her way inside before he could close the door on her. The heavy steel door slammed shut, and they heard the latch snap shut with a loud click that echoed in the big freezer. Slowly, they backed up until their backs were pressed against the back of the freezer.

They waited with bated breath, listening for any sounds, but the thick walls were soundproof. Just when they were about to breathe a sigh of relief, there was a long thump from the door. Then another and another. Stacy knew there was no way it could get in. The door was almost a foot of steel, and once the latch was closed, it couldn't be opened, unless you were a person who knew how to use the handle. Surely that monster couldn't figure that out, right?

Wrong! There was another click as the latch popped open and the door slowly opened. Stacy watched in terror as the big thing slowly maneuvered its bulk through the door and into the freezer. Once inside, it stood there for a moment as if eyeing them. Each of its breaths came out in a huge cloud of frost. Blood dripped freely from its jaws and its fists.

It took a step forward and slipped on the icy floor, going down on one knee. As it stood, some of the meat that made up its leg tore away where it had touched the cold floor, remaining stuck to the metal. After that, it seemed more cautious and moved carefully and steadily across the room toward them. It used the overhead racks that held the meat hooks for balance as it thundered closer.

When it was almost within distance, Stacy felt Darrel grab her and sling her towards the thing. She slipped and fell at its feet. Fearing this was it, and that she was about to be killed, she clenched her teeth and squeezed her eyes shut as hard as she could. But it never came. The creature let out an annoyed grunt, and Stacy felt it reach over her. She heard Darrel scream, then there was a loud snapping sound like a tree branch falling, and Darrel's screams abruptly stopped.

Oh, God, she thought, *I'm next. Now, it is going to kill me.* She waited, and nothing. Nothing happened. It didn't crush her or tear her apart. She opened her eyes, hoping it had just disappeared. No such luck. She could still smell it and see its piggy feet just in front of her. Slowly, she looked up to see what it was doing.

There was no way. It was impossible! Stacy couldn't believe what she was seeing. Hanging in front of her was what looked like a cased sausage. It was about a long and thick as her forearm, but it was unmistakable for what it was. It was the creature's makeshift Johnson. It looked down at her, made several grunting noises, and thrust its hips towards her.

The words of her Women's Studies professor came back to her. On their first day, the woman had addressed the class with a rather dower proclamation. She told them that in this world, if you are a woman, everything with a penis wants to fuck you, kill you, or both. At the time, it had been funny, and Stacy had dismissed her as one of those miserable old feminazis who are just bitter cause they can't get laid.

Yet, here she was, back on her knees in a freezer eye to eye with a cock, and she was expected to do something about it. A hysterical giggle nearly escaped her throat. She had an idea. It was a long shot, but maybe it would work. All she needed was a head start, so she reached out and wrapped her hand around the meaty thing hanging in front of her.

She began to slowly slide her hand up and down it, stroking it. There were no testicles or anything remotely resembling actual male genitals. Just the world's grossest foot long hanging limply between its stubby legs. The frightened girl continued to stroke it, adding both hands to it and increasing the pace. The monster began to shiver, clearly enjoying the stimulation, and leaned forward, placing both its hands on the cold steel wall for balance.

This was her chance, she counted down in her head. She was shivering from the cold inside the freezer, but she had to make sure. She had to give herself the best chance she could to run. When she finally reached zero, she bolted. Diving between the thing's legs, she skittered on her hands and knees, glancing over her shoulder.

Roaring, the monster had trouble tearing its hands free from the wall, as its flesh had frozen to the metal. There was a shearing sound, like someone tearing a piece of leather, as it left gobbets of meat behind to free itself. Its feet were little better, as in tearing itself free, it tripped over its own feet and went down with a loud thump. By that time, Stacy was on her feet and sprinting to the door.

The fall didn't keep it down for long. It was back up in an instant, using both its arms and legs. It was gaining on her quite fast. Her plan had worked, buying her just enough time to make it out of the freezer and slam the door shut. The latch snapped shut, just as the creature threw itself bodily at the door. The big metal door shook, but held.

Stacy grabbed the heavy padlock that they put on the freezer when locking up for the night. The freezer had a handle on the inside to prevent people from accidentally getting stuck inside. She rammed the lock through the bolt and snapped it shut before the monster could figure out how to use the handle on the inside. The door rattled, and when it couldn't get it open, she heard it begin to slam its fists against the door.

With each slam, the door shook just that much more. Stacy prayed the door would hold long enough as she twisted the dial around to the coldest setting, forty degrees below zero. There was a hiss of coolant as the temperature in the freezer began to slowly drop to seventy degrees below freezing. The pounding on the door began to slow until it finally stopped. Everything freezes, and at those temperatures, that thing would be reduced to a block of ice in no time at all.

When all was quiet, Stacy left. As she walked home, she debated whether or not to call the police. Why? Would they believe her? I mean, a monster attack? But the thing was frozen in the freezer. They could see that for themselves. That was if it stayed in one piece. If it fell apart once it froze, it would just look like a pile of meat product. What if they thought she did it? What if they say she murdered Jamie, Jessica, Darrel, and what's his name? It would be hardly believable that, as slim and small as she was, she could have done any of that. The best thing was to go home and pretend she had called in. Say she wasn't there at all. Let someone else deal with it.

So, wrapped up in her thoughts, Stacy didn't realize that she was standing in front of her house. It seemed the trip that took her a good twenty minutes had taken no time at all. She dragged herself inside, stripped naked, and spent the next hour in the shower. No matter how much she scrubbed, she couldn't seem to get the dirty feeling off her. And no matter how hot she turned up the water, she was still cold.

When she was finally done in the bath, she piled every blanket she had on her bed and turned her electric blanket on the highest setting. She didn't think she would be able to sleep, so she just lay there listening to herself breathe. It wasn't long before she slipped into a deep sleep with no dreams.

When she woke up, it was late afternoon the next day. She had missed school and was late for work, but she had a feeling that the slaughterhouse wouldn't be open for business today. She booted up her laptop and checked the local news site. And there it was on the front page, a big, bold headline about the slaughterhouse horror. Stacy ignored that. All of her focus was on the picture that was splashed across the article. It was of the slaughterhouse floor. What captured her attention was the freezer. She zoomed in to get a better look at the door.

The door was gone. It had been torn off its hinges.

The Clown

It was a hot day. The sun beat down on the old baseball diamond. Heatwaves radiated up from the ground, distorting and making the infield look as though it was melting in the summer sun. Billy sat under the shade of the pavilion just outside the chain-link fence. His bat and glove were lying, useless, next to him on the table. He was disappointed, having met the guys at the city park and planning on playing some ball, but the heat was just too much. Even the creek that split the town in two, running next to the park, was completely dry. The large expanses of bare rock creek beds were bleached white, like the bones of some great animal buried in the soil. They couldn't even cool off, as they had done in times past, by splashing around in the cool water. This was probably the hottest and driest year Billy had witnessed.

His teachers said it was due to global warming and climate change, though his dad strongly disagreed. He would claim it was a hoax by the liberals to turn all the kids into "little faggot commies" whenever he got drunk.

Billy's dad got drunk a lot these days, especially after the layoffs when they closed down the car part factory he had worked at for the last twenty years. It seemed to Billy like everyone's parents were getting laid off from one job or another. Which was something he couldn't understand since the news programs his parents watched were always talking about how great the economy was doing now that they had a "proper president." Being a grown-up was so confusing, not like baseball. Baseball was simple. You played your position, and that was all you had to worry about. Even when it was just him and the guys playing pop-up or home run derby.

Even that had stopped being fun, thanks to the heat. The heat made everyone mean and shortened their tempers. They had played for a bit before the sun hit its peak, but then Michael had hit a grounder toward shortstop that bounced off Tommy's glove when he bent to catch it and hit him in the face. The ball had busted his lip, and his eyes had threatened to tear up. The game had halted while everyone ran to make sure he was okay. Tommy was on the small side, which was an understatement. He was the smallest kid there and probably didn't weigh an ounce over sixty pounds. He had angrily accused Michael of doing it on purpose, and Michael had called him a dummy because everyone knew you couldn't control a ball after you hit it. Things had gotten tense when little Tommy had lunged at the bigger boy as though he were going to hit him.

There wasn't a fight, thankfully, not that there would have been much of one. Michael had him by about a head and at least twenty pounds. Everyone was hot and sweaty and didn't feel like dealing with it, so they had called a time-out until it cooled off some. So, they sat in the relative coolness of the pavilion. Ryan, another one of the bigger boys, had brought a Styrofoam cooler that his mom had packed full of snacks and drinks. The ice had melted long ago, and everything sort of floated in the pool of water. There had been Capri Suns, crackers and cheese, some bottles of water, and Fruit Roll-Ups. They had all gone for the Capri Suns, ignoring the bottled water. Empty foil packets and plastic wrappers littered the tables in and around baseball equipment.

Cicadas sang somewhere over the hill. Beyond the hill was the elementary school where Billy would start the fifth grade this fall. He hated to think about it. He wished summer would last forever. If only it would cool down a bit. The heat made everything worse. He couldn't sleep, his parents fought, his older sisters fought, and his friends fought. Everyone fought.

It was as if the heat hated that everyone was having summer fun and, in its jealousy, decided to ruin it for everyone. Kinda like how his sister Debbie was when she wasn't getting enough attention. Drama for the sake of drama.

What a bitch, Billy thought. He ran a lukewarm can of soda he had bought from the old vending machine sitting next to the dugout, across the back of his neck. They were a crap shoot. You never knew if they were broken or even if they were stocked. That had been the one good thing that happened today, and the can felt good on his skin even though it wasn't cold. It was still cooler than the summer air.

It almost burned your lungs when you breathed in, and the sweat stung when it dripped down your face and got in your eyes. It was unbearable, and he was starting to get a headache. That was partly from the heat and partially from listening to Tyler and Ryan argue. Ryan had claimed he had seen Lisa Bernard's pussy. Tyler had called him a liar. Lisa Bernard was a sixth grader, a year older than any of them, and Tyler insisted there was no way she would show her pussy to a ginger shit like him.

"Did, too, saw it last week. She was over at our house. My sister invited her friends over to our house to use the pool," Ryan explained.

"Lisa ain't friends with your buck-toothed cow of a sister!" Tyler exclaimed. "So, why the fuck would she be at your house, retard?"

"'Cause we have a pool, so anyone will be your friend if they get to use it," Tyler shot back.

"So what? You still didn't see her pussy."

At this point, they were almost nose to nose, yelling at one another. Billy couldn't see how they had the energy with how hot it was. He hadn't seen a pussy yet either, but at least he wasn't dumb enough to lie about it. If you lied about seeing a girl's tits or privates, you would eventually get found out and then everyone would know you were a virgin. He didn't fully understand what a virgin was, but he knew it had to do with seeing naked girls. He hadn't yet gotten those funny feelings some of the other guys had talked about when they saw girls naked or in their underpants.

"Did, too. When she got out of the pool, her bikini was all soaking wet, and you could totally see her pussy through it."

The argument continued as Tyler tried to defend himself.

"That doesn't count, stupid. It only counts if she isn't wearing anything."

"It does, too, loser." If it went on any longer, there was no doubt that adolescent hormones and the summer heat would turn their childish argument to blows. Breaking up a fight was really the last thing anyone wanted to do on a day like this. The veins in Billy's head started to throb, causing further strain on his own temper.

What no one expected was for Tommy to break the tension. "I saw a pussy once," he piped up. His voice was slightly modulated the way it gets when you have taken a good shot to the nose, as he had. Hopefully, it was just stuffed up from the crying and not broken. Otherwise, there would have been hell to pay after Tommy's mom got done calling all of their mothers to tell on them.

"Where did you see a pussy?" asked Clay, who played third base and was the only black kid any of them knew. And as far as they knew, the *only* black kid in town.

"My dad's Playboys. He keeps them under the bathroom sink in the mop bucket," the small kid replied.

That made them all laugh. The idea of Tommy's mom walking into the bathroom and catching tiny Tommy sitting in front of the sink with a Playboy in his lap, fast-handing his pecker, made them all crack up. Tommy's mother was a short, fat, overbearing woman who was always fussing over one thing or another. She was a neat freak and a germophobe, according to Billy's mother, a loudmouth in need of a backhand across the mouth, according to his father.

The laughing was good. All the tension was gone, and even his headache started to ease. It was a shame that the day was so beautiful, but the heat made it so dangerous. *Like a pussy*, Billy thought. He had no real reason to think this, much less the maturity to understand it, but it still made him laugh. Bernie, the heavyset kid, they weren't supposed to call him fat anymore, or so said the teachers, laughed so hard his face turned bright red over the top of his catcher's chest protector.

It looked less like he was laughing and more like he was having a heart attack. Which only made them laugh harder. Tyler snorted in his laugh, and a bit of the fruit roll-up he had been eating shot out of his nose, only adding fuel to the fire. At that moment, Billy wished that summer really could last forever and that they could laugh like this all the time. The good times never last, Billy knew his too well. Whenever things were going your way, it seemed like something would come along and ruin your day. And that bad thing was coming right towards them.

The Flemingsburg City Park was tucked behind the buildings that met at the corner of West Water Street and South Main Street. There were two ways to get to the park. One was a service road next to White Hall. Billy had no idea why it was called that. Probably because it was white, but beyond that, all he knew was that it was a big old two-story house. The other way was to take the street next to the firehouse, which sat on Main Street next to the police station and the bank. Behind the firehouse was the old train depot that was now the mayor's office. Behind the mayor's office was a large warehouse that served as the city's garage, which serviced the cars of the city officials.

Past that was the large asphalt lot that served as both a parking lot and basketball courts. Though no one really used them all that much, as the backboards were worn out and warped, with rims that had no nets. Your ball would bounce off in random directions, no matter how good your shot was. Between the faded courts and the creek was the skate park that the city had installed in an effort to get rid of kids doing it on the sidewalks. It didn't work, so the metal ramps and rail went unused in their own fenced-off area.

Billy had been watching the sun glint off them, nearly blinding him, when he realized that someone was walking their way. He could only make out their silhouette until he raised one hand to shade his eyes. Seeing the person only made his heart sink when he realized who it was.

The person coming their way was Lenard, and he was bad news. He was still a sixth grader, having been held back a year. He was big, taller than either Ryan or Tyler by several inches. His sleeveless shirt showed off his muscular arms. The left one had a poorly drawn barbed wire circling the arm, done in a blue ink pen. Everyone knew not to mess with him unless they wanted to see if their head could fit in their asshole.

Lenard hadn't always had that reputation. A year or two ago, he was a regular at the diamond. He had even taught Billy how to catch pop flies. The trick was to unfocus your eyes and squint so that the sun didn't blind you. He had felt so awesome the first time he got it and had started catching them all day long. He had done so well at it that the coach of his little league team had moved him from the outfield to the infield. 'Cause he showed "good hustle."

Something had changed since then. Lenard had become a different person. Billy couldn't really put his finger on it, but he knew it was there. It seemed like everything about him had become somehow meaner. Not overly aggressive, but not nice. His jokes and his pranks were funny, and he could throw shade like nobody else, as long as you were not the target. He got suspended at least once a year because the teachers thought he was bullying kids, and Billy could see how they would think that because Lenard could get carried away with it. It would stop being funny and just be mean, but you laughed because if you didn't, then he might turn on you, and nobody wanted that. Billy could sense a sort of anger bubbling just below the surface, even when Lenard was smiling and laughing. It was something in his eyes. They had no sparkle or light. They were just cold and empty like a deep winter night. They scared him, and even though at his age he didn't know what it was or understand it, he knew to be afraid of the older boy.

Lenard's appearance had also changed. He had gone from that cheery all-American boy look to what Billy's mother called poor white trash. His dirty blond hair hung to his shoulders in the back, with the front and sides buzzed close to his head. There were the thinnest wisps of blond hair starting on his upper lip, the merest hint at what would one day be a less-than-impressive mustache. On one side, it was split by an ugly, jagged scar that carved its way down through both his upper and lower lip. Billy remembered how that scar had come to be. They had been at one of the basketball games up at the middle school. He had been sitting on the bench during the second half since he had played the entire first half. It had been a new rule that the board had instituted in the name of fairness so that coaches didn't just play their best players all the time. Now, players could only play a maximum of two quarters per game, and all players had to play at least one minute.

They had been getting steamrolled by the visiting team, which drove many of the more, let us say, involved parents to be more intense than what was probably required for a kid's game. After all, these were elementary students, not a Cats vs Cards game in March Madness. Though you wouldn't have known it from the way everyone in Fleming County took their sports so seriously. From football to basketball, every sport was elevated to the realm of religion and held just as zealously. For many, sports were the only way out of this town and this life. Not unlike most inner-city areas. The parallels between poor rural areas and poor urban areas are nearly identical in most aspects, save for ethnic groups. Though being honest, there were many in town who wouldn't hear of being compared to what Billy's dad called the N word. Still pretty young, Billy was aware of his parents' prejudices, though he had not learned that particular bad habit. Clay was one of his best friends, and none of them saw or thought of him in any other way.

Common sense is one of the things that tend to go first when people get riled up, especially in large groups. There are few places more emotionally charged than a sporting event. Especially when you add alcohol on top of it. Despite the attempts to ban it, several parishioners were not deterred from tailgating before the game with a few beers in the parking lot. Some even smuggled it in, but so long as it was kept on the down-low and didn't cause any real problems, the cops and officials tended to look the other way. This was not one of those times. A commotion had erupted in the stands. It centered around two men being yelled at by a scraggly woman at the top of the bleachers. The two men were turned around in their seats, shouting back. Billy hadn't been able to hear what they were saying through the noise of the players on the court and the cheering parents. He could tell they had been angry, and not just the usual too wrapped up in the game anger. They had both been red in the face, and one had veins popping out that could be clearly seen from across the court.

Several other people had tried to settle them down, while others had yelled back. It hadn't lasted long before one of the men, the thinner of the two as the other had been sporting a rather large gut, had leapt up several seats towards the lady. Just as he was about to get in her face, she swung one hand back as if to give him a smack. Instead, she had hit the kid sitting next to her. That kid had been Lenard, her son, and it was unclear if it was the hit or the shock, but it caused him to tumble off the bleachers sideways and plummet the ten or twelve feet to the floor.

An ambulance had been called, and both men had been escorted out by the cops. Fortunately, the only injury that Lenard had sustained was a gash on one side of his mouth. It had required some stitches, but no hospitalization. It had been a frightening event for everyone, and the town had talked about it for days. By town, Billy knew it was just his mother and the other nosy gossips who kept scandals and rumors alive and embellished them. Drama for the sake of drama.

Billy wondered if all girls were like that, or if it was just the ones he knew. He had felt sorry for Lenard. His dad had gone out for cigarettes one day and never came back. According to Billy's mother and her gossip connections, he had been one of those guys. The guys who hung out at the pool hall. The pool hall was synonymous with drunkards, drug addicts, and other types of "ne'er-do-wells," as she called them. That had always confused him, since his own father went down to the pool hall regularly. His dad's leaving had apparently hit Lenard's mom hard, as she was too lazy to hold a job anymore, and so was on the welfare, according to Billy's dad. He didn't really understand what that meant, but it seemed kind of mean. The same kind of mean that Lenard showed now. Now that he wore the same clothes every year and always looked like he could use a wash. Lenard was at least alone today, which was good. When he was with other big kids, he was nasty, but then again, so were they. Like they fed on one another and just made each other worse. Like how the heat made everything worse. Billy could only imagine how bad they would have been on a day like today.

"Hey, what are you babies up to, playing with your balls?" Lenard crowed as he snagged a bottle of water from the cooler and hopped up on one of the benches so he could sit on the table. He grinned, taking a sip from the bottle. Even when he smiled, his eyes remained dead, and despite the heat, it sent a shiver down Billy's spine.

"Yeah, but it got too hot, so now we are just kinda taking a break," Bernie said, wiping sweat away from his forehead with one pudgy hand.

"Fuckin' A, fatboy. It's a pisser. Street nearly burned my feet off just walking here," Lenard answered. "It's too fuckin' hot." For a moment, he almost looked pensive as he took another swig from the bottle before dumping what was left in the bottle over his head and neck. Cool water splashed on the table and sprayed everywhere when Lenard shook his head like a dog. The boys cried out in joyous shock when droplets hit them.

It was heavenly, even the smallest respite from the hellish heat.

"Too bad the creek's dry. I would kill to get wet right now," said Clay when they had all calmed down.

"That's what your mom said," Lenard jeered as he took a pack of cigarettes from the pocket of his faded jeans and poked one into his mouth on the side opposite the scar. Though he didn't care for it himself, Billy secretly thought it made the older boy look cooler. What he really liked was the Zippo lighter Lenard always carried. It had the Punisher logo on the side, and Lenard could do all kinds of tricks with it. Just a snap of his fingers and the flame would dance to life out of thin air.

"When?" Clay replied in shock.

"When I was beefing her last night, she was a hell of a dry fuck," Lenard added. This caused the boys to bust up laughing again. *This wasn't so bad*, Billy thought as he gazed at the dried-up creek bed. It ran along the backs of the properties that lined the street, down past the bank until it disappeared under the police station and Main Street. It came out several hundred yards on the other side of the condemned theater. He continued staring at the dark opening where the creek disappeared. It always gave him the creeps. The other boys noticed where he was looking.

"Hey, did you ever go under there?" Tommy asked him. Billy shook his head.

"I heard there were snakes and shit down there," said Tyler.

"It's creepy," added Bernie, "kinda reminds me of that movie with the clown." Everyone agreed. Billy knew that movie. He had begged his parents to let him go watch it with his friends. He didn't want anyone to think he was a wuss, so he hadn't told anyone that the clown had kind of scared him and that he had a few nightmares about it. He hadn't wet the bed or nothing, but he wasn't gonna be teased about being a sissy just because of some stupid movie, but he sure as hell was not going into that concrete underpass.

"Talking about clowns, check it out."

They turned around to see what Lenard was talking about. Lenard hadn't been turned around, looking at the creek. He had kept looking across the parking lot since he sat down. When they looked to him, he jerked his chin, signaling them to look across the parking lot. On the other side of the parking lot was a sheer rock cliff, about fifteen feet high, left over from when the park had been leveled off and the hill cut into. On top of it grew a thick stand of trees that ran the entire length of the far side of the street, dividing the park grounds from the neighborhood and acting as a sound break. This was the only shady spot other than the shelter where they were.

Parked up under the trees deep in the shade was an old, dark car. It was a four-door sedan, and not unusual to see the occasional car parked back here. Billy knew the real big kids, high schoolers, would park back here to make out or drink beers. What better place to hide than right behind the police station, where they won't think to look? That didn't stop them from getting busted from time to time.

The boys had seen the car earlier, but ignored it, keener on playing ball than snooping. They had thought it empty, but as he peered across the simmering blacktop, he could make out someone asleep behind the wheel. How anyone could sleep in this heat, much less in a car, was beyond Billy. The windows appeared to be rolled down, and it was in the shade, but still. He had a hard enough time sleeping in his room with the window open and a fan going.

"Anyone know who it is?" he asked. The car wasn't familiar to him.

"Terry Johnson, that loser who dressed up as a clown for the stupid parties," Lenard answered, his voice coming out low in that same tone Billy's mom used when sharing an extremely juicy piece of gossip.

Terry Johnson had been a substitute a few years ago at the elementary school. Billy had him once back in the second or third grade. He was a short, stocky, balding man. He looked like Humpty Dumpty if he had been a person instead of an egg.

Billy had liked him. He had been funny. He had also volunteered at the hospital and nursing home, cheering people up by dressing up as a clown. Like Robin Williams in that *Patch Adams* movie. Then his wife died, or something, and Terry started drinking heavily, or so his mom said. Billy stopped seeing him substitute at the school, though he did see him at the occasional birthday party and county fair.

In fact, Billy remembered seeing him yesterday at the picnic. The city had it to benefit kids with mental disabilities, or as they called them, retards. Billy didn't see what was wrong with calling them that because that's what they were, but their teachers said that wasn't nice, and they had to call them something else. Not that he cared, he didn't go picking on the special needs kids, and he and his friends still called each other retard, so it didn't really matter to him. The city park had been turned into a fairground with food stands and games. Kids had dragged their parents all over the place, attracted by shiny things and flashing lights. It hadn't been nearly as big as the Court Day Celebration, but it was still fun. They had had the rock climbing wall, which had been Billy's favorite. Bernie had told him that there were gyms in Lexington where all people did was get in shape by climbing rock walls. He had thought that would be even more fun than baseball.

Through the crowd, he had seen Terry dressed as a clown with big shoes, a red rubber nose, and a curly green afro wig. Even through the grease paint, you could see the sadness underneath. That always bothered Billy. You shouldn't be allowed to be a clown if you are sad. Clowns were only allowed to be happy or scary. Billy wouldn't discover the works of Cindy Lewis-Williams or Emmett Kelly until college.

"You think he's okay?" Billy asked. Had he been here all night? He knew that when his dad drank too much, he would pass out in odd places, like the time he passed out on the hotel room toilet once when they were on vacation in Myrtle Beach. He also knew that sometimes when you drank too much, you could get sick and die from it. Billy had overheard a couple of teachers talking about a teenager who drank too much and got alcohol poisoning and had to have her stomach pumped.

"Why don't you go check and see?" prompted Tyler.

"Shit, no," Billy replied.

"Pussy," Tyler called him with a big grin on his face.

"Am not! Why don't you go check? Unless you're a pussy," he responded, not wanting them to think he was scared. He wasn't, just creeped out at the thought of Terry sitting in his car dressed like a clown, stone dead. The boys devolved into catcalling one another and daring the others to go have a look. They stopped when Lenard abruptly stood up and started towards the car. The boys scrambled to follow, their ball equipment and plans on picking the game back up completely forgotten.

As they made their way across the pavement, with the older boy in the lead, they continued their boyish game of teasing one another, except for Billy. He watched Lenard, who moved as though in a trance. His cold, dead eyes focused solely on the car. Twin streams of smoke issued from his nose like an angry dragon. The cigarette in his mouth burned down to a stub, and the lighter in his hand danced from knuckle to knuckle with little clicking noises.

They all fell silent as they reached the vehicle. Standing a few yards away, they just looked at the sleeping figure in the car. Even the cicadas had fallen quiet, as though the day was holding its breath. The boys just stared at the man passed out in his car. Mouth hanging open, head thrown back, looking as if he really could be dead, save for the slow, steady rise and fall of his chest. His clown makeup had become smeared and had run in places due to sweat. The big green wig sat lopsided on his head, remaining in place only due to being pinned between the man's head and the seat rest. The smell of booze and sour sweat wafted on what little breeze there was, and the warm air only served to make the smell even more rank.

The whole scene couldn't have been more pathetically sad had some hack drama student staged it. Even from where they stood, Billy could see the orgy of evidence that Terry had been living out of his car for some time. There were old fast-food bags with ancient grease and ketchup stains. Dirty laundry was strewn across the backseat, with one mildly clean suit hanging from one of the rear grab handles in a clear plastic bag.

This man was near the end of a downward spiral that none of these boys would understand for another twenty years if the world didn't fall out from under everyone first. Love lost and hardship were all ahead of them, while Terry was looking at his own happiness in the metaphorical rearview mirror. In the car's actual rearview mirror, Billy could see the sleeping man's mustache framed comically. Terry had painted over it like Cesar Romero did when he played Joker in that old *Batman* TV show, Billy recalled. *Terry didn't look anything like the Joker*, Billy thought. The Joker had been cool, if a little scary. The sad, little, fat man before them was definitely not cool or scary. The sight actually made Billy a bit angry. If he were a grown man, he wouldn't be sleeping in his car or dressing like a clown. He would have a motorcycle and a cool leather jacket, with a zippo lighter in the pocket. One even cooler than Lenard's.

"You know why he lives in his car, don't you?" Lenard's voice was still that deep, dark, husky tone, as though of a lover sharing a secret.

"Probably cause that lady sheriff took his keys," Bernie answered him in a loud whisper like he was trying to imitate Lenard's.

"No, dumbass. I mean, did you hear why they fired him from teaching?" Clearly annoyed, something new was creeping into the bigger boy's voice. It was hypnotic and dangerous. Subtle, but it easily drew the boys deeper under the hot summer's spell. The heat swelled and crested around them like the beating of some great heart. Something dark despite the sunny day bathing them in its light.

"I heard it was because his wife died, and he started drinking," Billy barely recognizing his own voice. He was no longer in his own head, but rather having an out-of-body experience, seeing it all from the outside.

"They caught him touching kids. He was putting his hands in little boys' pants in the bathrooms." The lighter clicked to punctuate each word Lenard spoke as it danced in his hand like some magician's magical amulet that was used to distract and mesmerize the crowd. It had an almost liquid-like mind of its own, flickering in and out between the long, slim fingers of the boy's hand. The skull insignia caught the light and flashed in the sun.

The boys continued watching in silence. The school held assemblies about stranger danger and talked to them about adults who did bad things to kids. Billy had always thought that it was only girls who had to watch out, but in the last year, there had been more and more talk about things like Lenard was saying. The TV and the internet always had stories about priests and politicians with child pornography and the like. But surely when those people got caught, they wouldn't continue to be allowed to attend kids' birthday parties or cheer up cancer kids in the hospital. They put them on a list and made them put up signs in their yards.

You can't really put a sign in your yard if you live in your car, Billy thought, but still, that didn't seem right. Though he had heard his father once say that they ought to castrate them when they were caught. Of course, this had been during his evening drinking in front of the TV, listening to Sean Hannity. They were also just a group of kids, yeah, they had baseball bats and could chase him away, but that somehow seemed mean to him. Not that it mattered to Lenard, he had that wild look in his eye. The others were no better. They, too, were captives of his spell. He would lead, and they would undoubtedly follow. This is what they called mob mentality. He understood now that this was how some good people ended up doing bad things when they were with their friends. The group will be overridden by a single charismatic leader, ruled by fear.

"There is only one thing you do with kiddie fiddlers." Their will had now become his in the heat of the day. Lenard now led with the pack mentality of young boys that William Gold-ing had hinted at. That darkness eclipses individual thought and action. Their wills were now one with his. The blond boy stepped up to the driver's side door slowly, carefully reached through the open window. With silent agility, trying not to wake the sleeping man, he plucked a half-empty bottle of vodka from the cup holder.

As he stepped back to rejoin the group, he spun the cap off the bottle and took a swig. The air was now filled with a smell that Billy associated with hospitals, that heavy antiseptic-like smell. It polluted and crowded the already busy air. He wrinkled his nose. The scent made him feel slightly sick, and his headache started to return. From his back pocket, Lenard took an old, threadbare handkerchief. Had any of the boys been of high school age, they would have been worldly enough to mock him with homosexual innuendos of what it indicated. He, in turn, would have beaten to death anyone who had made those insinuations. The young male ego always demands blood for any injury it suffers.

The rag was stuffed into the bottle and shaken so that the cloth soaked through with alcohol. One end was then pulled partially back out to create an improvised wick. Hefting the Molotov cocktail in one hand, he casually bounced it in his palm. With his other hand, he performed a deft, almost careless trick that seemed like magic to cause the lighter to spring to life. The little orange flame was almost unnecessary on that hot day.

"Burn in Hell, you fucking pedo." And with that, he lit the makeshift firebomb and threw it into the car. The bottle clipped the lip of the window and, instead of breaking, did a mad yet oddly beautiful cartwheel. Anyone who knew anything about arson would have known that bottle wasn't the best suited for the job. Despite being cheap, the bottle was more durable than one would have thought. However, it still smashed into pieces when it collided with the worn leather steering wheel.

There was a split second where Billy thought it hadn't worked, but it was just a brief pause where the world seemed to take a breath. Then there was a loud whoosh, and a surprisingly large fireball mushroomed inside the car as everything the vodka splashed caught fire. Most of it had landed square in the driver's seat and on the unsuspecting occupant. The polyester clown suit caught instantly, engulfing the man in a corona of flames. The grease paint and wig were equally flammable, if not more so. Terry was snatched out of a dead drunk and into Hell. The only saving grace was that he didn't have to suffer it long, as he passed out from pain and inhalation, but every second he was conscious was pure agony. Those few minutes stretched into ages of unbearable torture.

The boys' perspective from outside the car was much different. The world slowed down as if God himself had hit the slow-motion button. Confused, blinded, and in soul-searing pain, the trapped man could only flail about in the front seat. His body rocked back and forth in his seat as if he were having a fit rather than being on fire. His screams froze the boys in their tracks as they watched in both horror and fascination. Thick, black smoke quickly filled the cramped interior of the car as the cheap upholstery caught fire, and it spread to the detritus that littered the car. Soon, all they could make out was his vague shape through the billowing flames. Just before he was completely lost from their view, the burning man twisted in his seat as if to try to climb out of the window.

He looked right at Billy, and all the boys could make out were the dark holes where his eyes and mouth were. Terry Johnson, the man who had made kids laugh when they were sick, who had been one of the students' favorite substitute teachers, had been reduced to a screaming, burning skull in the inferno of his old car. For that moment, Billy felt as though this was truly what Hell was: oppressive heat and cold horror. It actually felt good when his bladder let go and he pissed his pants. The urine was cool by comparison to the hot day and the heat roiling out from the flaming vehicle.

He said nothing and did nothing. Like the others, he just stood and watched. It wouldn't be long before the fire department showed up. Someone was sure to have seen the plume of smoke stretching up into the cloudless blue sky. After all, they were just down at the end of the avenue, not more than a hundred yards or so away. The screams alone would bring someone running to investigate.

They would show up with their big trucks and hoses to put the fire out. Billy wondered if they would be wearing all of their big, heavy gear and coats. That would be hellish on such a hot day like this, Billy thought as he watched the lighter dance and flash in the sunlight as Lenard spun it. The car burned out of control just beyond that magical trinket in his field of vision, as the pack of boys stood just watching. Not fleeing, panicking, or thinking of the trouble they would get in, just standing and watching, as the emergency responders would find them.

They would have to be careful wearing all of that. A day like this could be hot and dangerous, he thought, like a pussy.

That thought finally made him lose it, and he laughed. They all started to laugh.

Rest Stop

It was late at night, and I was in a real pickle. The drive from Washington had been a long one, and by the time I had hit US 64, I had been driving more than six hours. Not that I really minded, once you get over fifty, you start to not give a shit. The sick part was that it was true in more ways than one. Night had descended as I wound my way through the Appalachian Mountains of West Virginia, and I was at the mercy of the mountain roads. The kind of roads that twist and turn and make you feel like you're on a rollercoaster ride to Hell.

That's when my troubles started. And by troubles, I mean that nature started calling. It was expected, having not eaten anything but fast food, and now there was a knocking on my ol' back door. Building up inside me like a pressure cooker, I needed to go and right now. I wasn't about to go in the middle of the woods, that was for younger, more daring guys, and I didn't want to be that guy who left his mark on the upholstery.

Breakfast had been greasy gravy and biscuits. Though my personal favorite, it was nothing more than a greasy plate of heart-attack-on-a-platter. It came with a side of lukewarm, shit-colored water. If that's what they call coffee, then I'd hate to see what they call sewage.

That was just the beginning of my dietary descent into madness. Lunch was a pitstop at the Golden Arches, where I indulged in a cheeseburger and fries. Oh, those fries. So crispy, so salty, so greasy. It was a guilty pleasure that you knew would kill you, but you just couldn't resist. If that wasn't enough, I topped it off with a dinner from Taco Bell. Switching out cheese for grease, which could create a gastrointestinal slurry that would harden anyone's arteries into a cardiologist's worst nightmare.

I didn't have to worry about the old ticker. My last checkup had surprised the doctor. He had practically fallen off his stool when he looked at my charts. "I haven't seen a man of your age in that good a condition," he had said, shaking his head in disbelief.

But my wife, God bless her, had just laughed and patted my hand. "It's all thanks to the treadmill," she had said, nodding towards the contraption in our living room. "We both put in five miles each on that thing every day for the past decade."

Even with all that exercise, I still had my problems. They were just lower down. Not the old prostate, thank God. That was just a little oversized, making me get up most nights to piss like a mad bastard. At least it wasn't the cancer. No, my problems were with the back door. As you get older, you find it harder and harder to give a shit. I don't mean that in the metaphorical sense. I mean it quite literally. When that happens, it usually means you've got a gremlin somewhere in your works. At my age, gremlins are not something you want to mess around with.

That is what had prompted my little visit to our local witch doctor. He did his usual pokes and prods, muttering under his breath and scribbling notes on his clipboard. And then came the moment of truth. He snapped on a rubber glove and went prospecting down the Hershey highway. God, that is an indignity every man has to suffer, but it could always be worse. As the joke goes, you could feel both his hands on your shoulders. Ha, ha.

Nothing seemed to turn up, and all the tests came back negative. He did some blood tests, but they came back normal. He insisted that any bathroom troubles I was having were probably diet-related. He asked what I had been eating, but there hadn't been any real changes. Despite what impressions I may have given, my old lady makes sure I eat healthily enough. The junk food is mainly a staple of the road, and we don't indulge too often. Though I will admit that when I'm flying solo, as I was, I'm more prone to overdo it.

The darkness had fully descended upon the highway, and the Lincoln's headlights were the only source of illumination, and Nancy Sinatra was singing about her boots on the radio. The radio was one of the things we loved about the big old luxury car. We both remembered a time when radios only had AM, and you got what you got. But now, we had Sirius XM Radio, and we could listen to whatever we wanted, whenever we wanted. Classical music, rock, jazz, talk shows, NPR—the car had it all.

The Lincoln was a marvel of modern engineering, with all its gadgets and gizmos. The XM Radio was a godsend, but it wasn't the only one. The climate control was like having your own personal weatherman, always keeping you at the perfect temperature. Those heated seats, oh, how they could make you feel like you were sitting in a hot tub. But the real showstopper was the rearview mirror. When you shifted into reverse, it turned into a screen, showing you a live feed of what was behind you. It was like having eyes in the back of your head.

And that backseat. It was a wonderland of entertainment, with a built-in DVD player that could keep the grandkids quiet for hours watching *SpongeBob* or whatever. It was like a mini theater on wheels. I remember the long car trips to Florida when our kids were young, and we had to keep a stock of batteries for their Gameboys. Hard to imagine how we ever managed back then.

No, the greatest little gizmo was the GPS built into the car's main console. It was an amazing little piece of technology that saved me from the horrors of being lost in the middle of nowhere. No more fumbling with poorly folded road maps or trying to decipher confusing directions. No more getting lost when the directions petered out. No more backtracking and roundabouts. The GPS told me exactly where to go, how far away it was, and when I would arrive. It was like having a personal navigator right there in the car with me. Damn thing even gave you weather and traffic updates and guided you around them. It even talked to you in a slightly disapproving British woman's voice, and I'll admit, it gave me a bit of a half-stiffie every time she spoke. Like having a dominatrix riding shotgun.

We had shut that off before long, not because it induced erections, but because my wife felt it was condescending. In my opinion, it had every right to be. After all, it wasn't the idiot who needed step-by-step directions just to get to the store around the corner. It had been great when the car was new. In the last year or so, it started having problems. I half expected it to start calling me Dave and refuse to open the pod bay doors. The mechanic at the garage said something about the computer not getting the full updates, but I didn't really understand it. All I knew was that the damn thing was starting to act like HAL from *2001: A Space Odyssey*.

It was especially bad when it lost connections to the satellite. A really cloudy day or tall office buildings in a dense city could cause it to disconnect, and it would have to recalculate. That announcement could go on for a few seconds to half an hour. Lately, it started having that issue in the country where the signals weren't that good.

So, it would sit there and silently recalculate, while you prayed it would kick back on before you missed your turn. They had wanted four hundred dollars to replace the computer, and it would fix the problem. It wasn't that we couldn't afford it, it just seemed like a lot of money for something that wasn't that big of a deal...yet. Eventually, I would have to get around to getting it fixed, but it wasn't at the top of the priority list. Given the current administration's tomfoolery and causing the economy to go straight into the toilet, we could deal with a buggy luxury for a few more months, a year at most.

A late night, a long drive, fast food, and glitching GPS came together to form a perfect storm. The warning didn't sneak up on me, either. It damn near jumped up the back of my throat and said howdy. One moment, I was mellowed out, grooving to Blue Öyster Cult, the next moment, I needed a pit stop, and I needed it yesterday. I had passed a rest stop just twenty minutes ago, but there wasn't any way to turn around, and the next exit was in fifteen miles.

I gritted my teeth and jabbed a thumb viciously at the GPS screen. It had behaved for nearly the entire trip, and lured me into a false sense of security, as my bowels threatened to crawl right out of my trousers. I flipped through the settings to the list of roadside services, found the restroom icon, and pressed it. Nothing happened. I pressed it again, still nothing. I mashed the screen again and again, cursing the whole time, and clenching my butt cheeks as tight as I could. Shitting your pants was already bad enough, and I didn't want to have to clean it out of the leather seats as well. You can never really get the smell of feces out, and it would linger in the car forever. Every time the car would get hot, the lingering ghost of its scent would invade your nostrils.

I let out a particularly blasphemous swear when, for one terrifying second, I thought I had lost the battle with my butthole and slammed the screen. I knew it was a mistake to take my eyes off the road, even for a second. They say that distracted driving was as deadly as a drunk behind the wheel, and I had already tempted fate enough in my youth. But in that moment, with my insides roiling like a stormy sea, I felt justified in my actions. The screen flickered to life, and I typed furiously, ignoring the spinning symbol that mocked me with its slow progress.

With agonizing slowness, the percentage crawled towards completion. Forty-five percent, then forty-eight, then fifty-two, and fifty-seven. I gritted my teeth and redoubled my efforts, making deals with God to keep from going right then and there. Sixty-one, closer, but not close enough. Sixty-eight percent, for the love of God, please hurry.

The screen flickered again, and I held my breath, praying that it wasn't about to recalculate again. It flickered again, and the percentage jumped to one hundred percent. The screen changed to show a restroom just seven miles away. I hit the detour button with a sense of relief, grateful to be making progress at last. The little yellow line snaked its way across the screen, mapping out the spider web of highways, crossroads, and back roads that lay ahead. I floored the accelerator, and the twelve-cylinder engine roared, the sound filling the car like a beast awakening from its slumber.

It wasn't marked, just a two-lane road that broke off to the right, shrouded in overgrown weeds and shadows. I almost missed the turn off the highway. It wasn't a proper exit ramp, but just a two-lane road that broke off to the right. I wouldn't have known it was even there had the GPS not pointed it out. It was the kind of road you only found if you were lost or looking for trouble, and I couldn't help but wonder which one I was. Some storm or a drunk driver must have knocked over the sign, leaving only the remnants of rusted metal behind, allowing the growth of weeds to claim it. I barreled down the two-lane road, the car jolted over the uneven terrain, the headlights illuminating the way like a beacon in the dark, with one eye on the distance, watching the miles tick down.

The road stretched out before me like a never-ending ribbon of darkness, winding its way through the silent countryside. The houses that flickered past my window were dark and deserted. Their empty windows stared back at me like empty eye sockets. I hadn't passed another car in what felt like hours, and I couldn't shake the feeling that I was the only person left in the world. The GPS instructed me to make several turns, and by the time it was done, I had no idea which way was back to the highway.

Not that it mattered much by that point. I was bouncing up and down in my seat, the voice of Billie Joel screaming a Cliff Notes version of thirty years of U.S. history in my ear. The radio crackled with static, something I'd never heard it do before. These radios were supposed to be satellite-based, immune to interference. But the sound that came out of the speakers was a hiss of white noise, like the radio had been replaced with a bed of snakes. I guess even in the boonies, technology had its limits.

Out in the boonies, that's where I found myself. It had been a good three or four miles since I last saw civilization. One lane blacktop roads stretched out before me, with overgrown brush crowding in on both sides like some twisted gateway to Narnia or Oz. I half-expected to see a troll or goblin dart across my path at any moment, and truth be told, I wouldn't have been all that surprised. In fact, I was ready to plow right through the little bastard if it meant getting to my destination before that oh-so-unfortunate punchline of: 'and then he shit his pants.'

The weeds and branches clawed at the sides of the big car, even though I was smack dab in the middle of the road. One wrong move, one sharp turn, a collision with an oncoming car, and my little bathroom issue would become moot. How humiliating it would be to show up at the pearly gates and have to tell Saint Peter that I kicked the bucket because I was desperate not to crap my pants. A real shit way to go, indeed. They could carve that on my tombstone, for all I cared.

I almost missed it, but at the last second I spotted the stop. It wasn't much to look at, just a run-down parking lot with cracked blacktop and long, nasty-looking weeds sprouting up from the crevices. The only light in sight was a single, flickering bulb hanging from a telephone pole. The light was dim and sickly yellow, the kind of color you only see when it's pitch-black outside. And as I pulled the Lincoln into the lot, a cloud of large bugs descended upon the light, their wings buzzing loudly in the stillness of the night.

The car jolted to a stop as I slammed both feet onto the brake pedal. I was out of my seat before the door was even fully open, racing towards the double doors with reckless abandon. In my haste, I couldn't even remember if I had grabbed my keys or not. It would be just my luck to lock myself out of the car in the middle of nowhere, stranded without a soul in sight.

My heart was pounding in my chest as I frantically searched my pockets, fingers flitting about in a frenzied dance. For a brief moment, I forgot all about my desperate need to relieve myself, until my fingers brushed against a familiar bulge in my pocket. The keys were there, safe and sound.

I stiff-armed the door as I resumed my dash to salvation. It wasn't enough to stop my forward momentum, and I bounced off the door. Of course, it would have to be a pull and not a push. I wrenched it open and hurled myself into the dim interior. The musty smell of neglect hit me like a punch to the face. It was clear that whoever was supposed to be maintaining this place had long since given up on their duties. Dust coated every surface, thick enough to write your name in.

Despite the neglect, the building seemed to still be in operation. The front door was unlocked, and the flickering lights offered some semblance of illumination. An old cola machine, that had probably been brand new when Johnson was in office, sat next to a darkened snack machine in one corner. I left a trail of footprints as I hurried toward the bathroom. The faded signs above the doors were barely distinguishable, with their little silhouettes of a man and a woman. Thankfully, there were no doors, just those sort of S-bend corridors. I didn't need any more barriers between me and the toilet.

I had to find the nearest john, and fast.

The rest stop bathroom was nothing special, just the typical setup you'd find in a restaurant. It wasn't one of those fancy stadium types that are becoming more common these days. There were three stalls, but not a single one was the spacious, handicap-accessible kind that I preferred. It didn't matter, though. I was desperate, and I'd take what I could get.

I pushed open the first stall and recoiled at the sight in the bowl. I won't even attempt to describe it—it was that revolting. The second stall was missing its seat, which meant I'd have to hover my ass over the bowl like some kind of acrobat. That ship had long since sailed for me, though.

Thankfully, the third stall was my lucky break. The seat was a little loose, but it would do. There wasn't anything in the bowl, but the water was cloudy and stagnant, like it hadn't been flushed in weeks. That didn't bother me, as I slammed the door shut, rammed the bolt home, dropped trou, and plopped down.

As I waited, the sudden threat in my nether regions magically seemed to disappear. The need to go that had been persistently antagonizing me for the last half hour, at least, was gone without so much as a hint of any dire need. This was the madness that had driven me to break down and go to the doctor.

Over the past month or so, I'd been plagued by these near-diarrhea episodes, warnings if you will, to the point where I could actually feel myself prairie-dogging, but the minute my ass hit porcelain, nothing. My backyard was as barren as the Sahara. How can a man both have diarrhea and constipation at the same time? What twisted God would have designed the human body as to torment mere mortals with just the everyday needs of the flesh? At times like this, I almost wished for cancer. It would have been less humiliating.

I knew that the second I got up and left that hellhole, I would be no more than a few minutes up the road before I would be touching cloth again, and in another mad dash. So, all I could do was clench my teeth, bear down, and give it all I had. I was in the middle of this strenuous activity when I heard it.

A sound so faint that, at first, I wasn't even sure if it was real.

I sat there, sweating profusely, staring at the filthy stall's grimy floor. Next to my left shoe, in the corner where the wall met the grimy floor, there was a weird sort of bluish mold. It looked like the bristles on a hog's ass.

Then, I heard it again. That same faint sound. It was so indistinct that I began to question if it was just my imagination playing tricks on me.

It was a sort of scooching, shuffling sound, as if something light was being dragged across the floor in the main entry. Night manager? No chance. The place was so derelict that any actual staff seemed unlikely. Maintenance worker? It was a possibility, but the building's poor state of repair was hardly a ringing endorsement of the janitor's diligence.

As the sound grew louder, my thoughts turned to a caretaker or perhaps a vigilant neighbor who noticed the unfamiliar car in the parking lot and came to investigate. That would make more sense, especially if the place was closed and the front lock was busted. They would have been concerned and making sure that local kids or drug addicts weren't messing about the place.

Though it had the same problem with neglect.

Something about that didn't track, either, as I couldn't, for the life of me, remember seeing a house nearby. In fact, the last place I could remember seeing any signs of habitation had been several twists and turns ago. About ten minutes' worth of driving before I had spotted the rest stop, there had been a couple of dilapidated trailers with tin pot cars going to shit in their overgrown yards.

I tried to shake off the feeling of unease as I focused on the task at hand and got back to the business of birthing this turd, secretly glad I hadn't been born a woman. I would never have survived childbirth. With a grimace of effort, I pushed harder, my muscles straining with the exertion. The sweat poured down my face, and my breath came in ragged gasps as I fought to expel the waste from my body. For a moment, I thought I was making progress, but then it happened again.

This time closer.

I paused and strained my ears for any sound. There was nothing, just a deafening silence. It was as if the source of the noise was waiting whenever I was listening, and would only move when I wasn't looking out for it. Almost as if it was stalking me. My mind was just playing tricks on me, conjuring up horrors where there were none. I was in a vulnerable position, alone in a strange place, and my imagination was running wild. It would serve me right to give myself a heart attack in a toilet with no way to get help.

Of all the times to forget my damn phone, it had to be now. I felt naked without it, as if I had left a limb behind in the car. My pockets offered little solace, just my keys jangling against each other, some loose change, and my wallet nestled in the left breast pocket of my jacket. If I'm honest, I was looking for something to bite down on and get this little shindig moving along. If I didn't, I was afraid I might pop a gasket. Instead, I felt my lighter. I had forgotten it was there. At some point, I had popped a cheap little Bic into my pocket without thinking. The thought of lighting up a cigarette now, in this most dire of situations, made me chuckle despite myself. I hadn't smoked in years, well, if you don't count the occasional post-sex joint with my wife, listening to ABBA, and giggling like schoolchildren.

The sound came again, and this time there was no mistaking it. It was real, and it was close. Not just close, it came from outside the bathroom.

"Hey, is someone there?" I called out, my voice trembling a bit.

The silence that followed was deafening, but I had a distinct feeling that whatever or whoever was making the noise had heard me and was now likewise listening. I gulped and remained silent. Before my brain could convince me that I was just imagining it, the sound came again. This time, from the entry hall of the restroom. There was a new sound, not one that a person would make. No rustle of clothing or squeak of tennis shoes on tile. No clearing of throat or grunt that men make on their way to the restroom.

The sound was stealthy, almost imperceptible. As if whatever was making it was trying to sneak up on me without being seen. It sent shivers up my spine and set my nerves on edge. I could almost feel it more than hear it.

Then came the snuffling sound. Thick and wet, like a dog with a head cold. It was unmistakably the sound of something scenting the air, searching for its prey. It would have been hard-pressed to pick out one smell from the bouquet of pungent odors coming from the bathroom.

I then realized that was exactly what was going on. Whatever it was, it couldn't smell me over the stink of the bathroom. It was probably just a mangy dog, hoping to scavenge for food in the abandoned restroom. *Or it could be something else entirely*, my mind whispered, *something far more dangerous*.

There were no wolves in eastern Kentucky, were there? Coyotes, maybe, but not wolves.

It moved closer, accompanied by a clicking noise, the unmistakable sound of nails on tile. The kind that dogs make when they walk across a hard surface. Click, slither, click, slither. There was a sort of swampy smell that went along with it. A low hiss made me instantly think not a mammal, but a reptile. Okay, wolves were possible, but I was one hundred percent sure that there were no gators here. That was the only reptile large enough to make those sounds, and by the sound of it, it was big.

Click, slither, click, slither.

It stalked closer, pausing now and then to snuffle. I didn't even notice that I had drawn my knees up, hiding my feet from sight, if anyone or anything looked beneath the stall. I was suddenly reminded of that scene from that *Jurassic Park* movie where the kids are hiding in the kitchen and the velociraptors are stalking them.

Click, slither, click, slither.

I bit my lip to keep from screaming as my panic rose. I leaned over as far as I dared and peeked under the stalls. When I saw its feet, all sanity left me for a moment. They were large, bird-like feet covered in dark scales. Each of its four toes was tipped with wicked, long black claws that had to be at least six inches long. They clicked with each slow, measured step. The slithering sound was its tail as it brushed the ground behind it with each step it took. I held my breath as it made the snuffling sound again, trying to sniff out its prey. It stalked closer and closer. Clicking and sniffing.

My heart was nearly beating out of my chest, and it was deafening in my ears. I could feel my mind panic and try to run from the fact that I was sitting here, pants around my ankles, while some prehistoric throwback hunted me like the trapped rat that I was. It was all I could do not to pass out and fall off the toilet.

It finally stopped, right in front of my stall door. I could see its clawed feet under the door. I felt it hadn't seen me yet. I begged it with my mind. *Go away, just go away, please*, I pleaded silently. It stood there silently. I could feel it on the other side of the door, just standing and listening. It seemed like forever, but finally, my curiosity overcame my fear, or maybe because of my fear, I leaned forward and peeked through the crack between the door and the jam.

What I saw was a large golden eye staring back at me. A long black slit that was its pupil contracted as I saw it, and it saw me. It let out a shriek and threw itself at the door.

Terrified, I leapt back as much as I could, still sitting on the toilet. My head cracked against the wall above the toilet's tank, and a flash of pain blurred my vision. I retained enough clarity, or maybe just survival instinct, to slam my feet against the door to keep it closed. I had no faith in the flimsy bolt.

The thing had to be at least a hundred pounds as it rocketed itself against the door. I was afraid that any moment it would scramble under or over the stall door, and that would be the end of me, but it apparently wasn't as smart as the dinosaurs from the movie. I could hear its claws scramble against the tiles and door as it wailed. The room bounced and amplified its voice like an echo chamber, and I thought that my ears would be bleeding soon.

The door shuttered again as the reptile bounced off of it. I pressed my back against the toilet and pushed harder with my feet, trying to keep the door closed. Each hit seemed stronger than the last, as if its rage was fueling its strength. I'm not sure if it was from all the sitting or just old bones and joints, but my right leg gave out. At that moment, as if sensing the lessening of my defenses, it hit the door with all its might. The lock finally popped free, and the door swung open just a few inches. Just enough for it to shove one thin but heavily muscled forearm through the door.

Its pebbled skin was a sickly yellowish color, and the three-fingered hand was tipped with similar black claws. I slammed my foot against the door, smashing it closed on the arm, which got another angry wail from the lizard. It hit the door again, this time wriggling its snout through the opening as it tried to pry it open with its big saurian head. Its mouth was like that of a Gila monster, except it was filled with rows of razor-sharp teeth. The teeth dripped with the blood of some fresh kill.

Through the crack, I could make out the large filth-encrusted mirror that hung over the sinks. I could see the reptile's muscled back and shoulders. If it got in here, it would easily tear me apart. Fear sent another spike of adrenaline into my system, and with a herculean effort, I shoved the door with every ounce of strength. The entire stall creaked with the strain, and my attacker wrenched itself back through the door. It wasn't finished, though. It resumed throwing itself at the door. I knew I couldn't keep this up. My legs were cramping, and then I was struck with a brilliant idea.

When I was younger, some buddies of mine would do this thing with old lighters. If you took out the flint of a dry lighter and heated it up, then tossed it at the ground, it would explode in a shower of sparks with a sound like a gunshot. It was a long shot, but maybe I could scare the creature off if I could get it to work. It didn't take long, only about thirty seconds to a minute to heat up the flint.

I snatched the lighter from my shirt pocket as I dug out my keys. I placed the teeth of my house key against the metal flame shroud and gave it a flick. Nothing, not hard enough. My second attempt nearly gave me a heart attack, as my flick had been too hard and sent the lighter spinning out of my hands. I fumbled it, but managed to wrap my hands around it before it could get away from me. The third time was the charm. The little metal piece popped off and went flying. I didn't care because it didn't matter.

I pried out the striker wheel, and the flint came out easily. I took the spring that held it in place out as well. Wrapping it around the flint, I would be using it to hold the flint to the flame. I had to put the striker wheel back into the lighter. Holding down the ignition button, I ran the tiny piece of metal across the wheel in a quick motion. There was a spark, and the flame caught almost instantly. I adjusted the flame to the highest setting.

During this delicate operation, the thing outside the door hadn't stopped its ramming. I had somehow managed to time my moves between its attempts, but it stopped once the lighter was lit. Could it maybe smell the fire? Was it wary of what the human in the can was doing? I didn't really care. I took the respite to cook my makeshift explosive.

Within seconds, the flint had turned bright red. It wasn't enough. It needed to be a glowing orange in order to pop. The flop sweat dripping down my face had more to do with the stress than the heat from the flame, which, oddly enough, was quickly heating up the tiny cubicle that made up my refuge. My mind suddenly came back to the creature outside. *What was it doing out there, waiting? Curious as to what I was doing with the fire? Was it afraid? What was it doing?*

Then I looked down I saw what it was doing. It had noticed the gap beneath the door and was crouching to get a look. It had hunkered down on its haunches and was sniffing its way towards the opening. I nearly panicked again. *Just a few more seconds, wait just a few more seconds, and I will fix you, Buster. Just a few more seconds, and you may get me, but I'm gonna give you one good one first.*

The flint continued to heat up as time slowed to an agonizing crawl. I could make out the tip of its snout as it lowered its head. *Not yet. Please, not yet.* I could make out its nostrils, flaring to take in the salty, panicked scent of its prey. *Just a second more, just one more second.* Its broad expanse of forehead appeared under the door.

The flint was blazing hot, like a miniature sun at the end of the wire. The second I saw its eyes, I whipped the spring downwards and released it. I had aimed at the place just in front of its nose. It struck the floor, exploding in the thing's face. The sound that I had remembered sounding like a gunshot was magnified in the tiny, tiled room to that of an artillery shell. I don't know if it was the flash, or the sound, or both.

The thing let out a womanish shriek and, like lightning, it was gone. I heard it crash through the glass front of the building and into the night. I sighed and relaxed. All the energy drained from my body, and I went limp. I'm not sure how long I sat there, or at what point I started laughing like a lunatic, but madness was hardly something you want to measure.

When I came to my senses, I looked down, and I'll be dipped in shit, at some point during my ordeal, I had managed to drop off my dark passenger at the pool. It sat on the side of the bowl like the world's most juvenile participation trophy. I had never felt better, that was, until I had to wipe my ass with the ancient toilet paper. Thank God there had been some on the roll. I hadn't checked when I sat down, and I wouldn't have been up to waddle out to my car for some napkins. Especially not if that thing was out there somewhere and pissed off.

It was waxy and slick. Somehow making me feel grosser instead of cleaner. By the time I pulled my pants up, I had almost forgotten that I had been attacked by a nightmare escapee from a 50s horror movie. I crept out as quietly as I could, listening as hard for any sign of my attacker's return. It would be a sick, twisted kind of fate if I were to exit the building only to find a pack of those things waiting for me and pissed that I had scared their brother shitless. I giggled at the shitless part. Not sure if it was hysteria or just juvenile humor, most likely both.

The entryway was a mess. The front door was slightly ajar. That was probably how it had followed me in. But on its hasty exit, it had elected to throw itself bodily through one of the large glass panes that made up the front wall. I wasted no time in getting to my car.

Once safe, I breathed a sigh of relief. Sitting there in the silent darkness of my car, for the first time, I got a good look at the rest stop. It wasn't just old and unused. There was something off about it.

The grass growing through the asphalt looked oddly spiky and almost mean somehow. The bugs buzzing around the light were like nothing I had ever seen. They were nearly the size of my fist, and their buzzing seemed hateful, as if they were not bumping into the light out of confusion because it was blinding them, but instead attacking it out of spite. In fact, the whole place seemed slightly off. Not in a way I could put my finger on it, but clearly off. As if the world itself had soured and become vaguely poisonous.

I just had a really frightening thought. What if, just what if, in my hurry to reach the nearest rest stop, I had followed my GPS through some sort of tear in the fabric of reality that separates our dimension from the one next door? Like Lovecraft wrote about, though, none of Lovecraft's worlds were very friendly. Kinda like how this one doesn't feel very friendly. I'm sure that's just the hysteria talking. Yeah, that's got to be it. My mind was just playing tricks on me, trying to scare me. But my GPS was acting weird. It doesn't recognize any of the addresses I put into it. When I hit Home, it says *not found*. In fact, I can't seem to find any towns on its maps. But I'm sure it's just busted.

At least I hope it's just busted.

The Dead Stay Dead

William Zeller went into the ground this afternoon. It was a small service for old Billy, being the late-night restocker at the Save-A-Lot for most of your life wasn't the kind of humanitarian work that garners throngs of mourners. The light drizzle hadn't exactly done him any favors. No one really likes attending a funeral, much less one in the rain.

Gary Alderman leaned back against the tree to avoid the rain. A Chesterfield hung from his mouth as he looked out over the town stretched out at the foot of the hill. He'd reached his fiftieth year as caretaker of Hillgate Cemetery, watching over a lot of funerals and digging a lot of graves.

Times had changed, and people had come and gone, but he and the boneyard were still there. During his tenure as caretaker, there had never really been any incidents. Yeah, a few headstones had toppled during the real pisser storms, and one of the church ladies who came out every spring to clean off the graves around Memorial Day had slipped and broken an ankle. That was about it. They didn't have vandals or grave robbers. No one really went into the ground these days wearing anything of value. Even those odd kids seemed to know to be on their best behavior. Their parents didn't understand why they dressed in all black and smoked cigarettes that smelled of cloves, or their fascination with death and other macabre things. Gary didn't really get it, either, but they didn't cause much trouble for him or the folks who walked the grounds for exercise.

No, it was pretty quiet, well, almost. For the most part, his job was the same as any caretakers. He mowed the grounds and kept the weeds at bay. He raked the leaves in the fall and salted the blacktopped drives in the winter. He also dug the graves. When he first started, he had a small group of guys who would help from time to time. Back then, they had dug the holes by hand. It would take three men the better part of an afternoon to dig one of them six-foot pits. Though it would only take two to fill it back in once the new tenant was in residence. Only one man was needed for what came after that.

Not long into the job, the city had found enough funding for a small backhoe. Since then, he had been able to do the whole job by himself, and that suited him just fine. It helped to cut costs and minimize incidents. Not that the city gave him any real issues over budgets. If there was a problem that needed repairing or something that the cemetery needed, they never gave him any guff over it. They knew that what he did was important and respected it.

One time, the rock wall that surrounded the property had been damaged during a particularly nasty storm that had lasted almost three days. The ground had become so wet that the massive old hedge apple tree had torn itself up by the roots and landed smack dab right on top of it. They had a couple of guys out there to repair it before the day was out. The tree had been cut up and hauled off, and the stones were replaced nearly exactly as they had been originally. You couldn't have even told where the hole had been now.

Gary wasn't sure how many people knew exactly what he did that was so important, or wanted to know. No one's head turned when he walked by. The townsfolk didn't talk in hushed whispers as they did with doctors and politicians. He was sure that the city councilmen had no real idea, outside of local rumors, but they knew that it was something they didn't want to mess with. Besides, he didn't abuse their trust or his position, nor did he want to. He was a simple man and had everything he needed.

The caretaker's cottage near the front gate was more than enough for him. Sure, it had its run of problems, but no more than any other houses of its age. It was probably in better condition, to be honest. All the major repairs were done quickly and handled by city contractors. Other repairs and improvements, he preferred to do himself. It gave him something to do to keep himself busy, so he didn't have to think about the particulars of this job.

He discarded the smoked butt and crushed the glowing ember beneath his heel. With the practiced muscle memory of a long-time smoker, he poked another one between his lips and lit it up. The wind gusted up fiercely as if to try to snuff it out. The ember flickered and bloomed brightly, as the smoke drifted up into the caretaker's eyes. When they watered, he wiped it away with one heavily callused thumb.

He had never married, never had kids. Something about this place and this job seemed to take away the taste for it. There was a book he had read about WWI that said that those who spend their time in the company of death find more joy in the beauty of life. This, he disagreed with. He saw it more as a constant reminder of the inevitable things to come, and he wasn't sure if his mind would stand up to performing his job on those he had loved.

It wasn't death that taxed his sanity. He had lost family and attended their funerals. His parents, two brothers, and a sister. Of course, none of them were buried here. Not in Hillgate. He wouldn't wish his worst enemy buried in this godforsaken place. Because in Hillgate, the dead didn't stay dead.

The residents had a nasty habit of crawling out of their graves when the sun set. No one really knows why most god-fearing folks didn't know it at all. They just knew there was something off about the place. Several of the old-timers reckoned it was a Native American curse for the white men taking their land. Despite what some of the delusional people who claimed to be part Native American whose family had lived in the area, no tribes had actually lived around here. They had used the area for hunting, as close as Gary knew. He had once looked into the subject years ago, before his interest in the why of the thing had gone cold.

It could be some kind of pollution. There had been a local nuclear dumping site over toward Morehead that had leaked several times over the years. That sort of thing tends to happen when the government subcontracts dumbass rednecks in an effort to save money. More pork in some politicians' pockets, no doubt. Cancer in the area was several times the national average, but he was sure that Frankfort felt that wasn't its problem. Less so the crooks in Washington.

His predecessor had his own theory. The eighty-year-old man believed God had forsaken the area, and the Devil came to play horrible tricks on the people from time to time. He claimed that Hillgate was the place he must have stopped to piss on his little outings, and now the ground was so foul that not even the dead could stand to stay buried in it.

Gary had a hard time believing that to be true. The ground didn't seem foul. Animals didn't avoid the place. Squirrels were abundant in the trees, and in the early morning fog, you could spot deer walking among the graves. Things grew in the soil. Flowers grew and bloomed on graves, and he never noticed anything off in his little garden out behind the cottage.

There was nothing that differentiated Hillgate Cemetery from any other piece of land. No events of any kind, not tragedies, nothing that stood out in the town's history. This wasn't like some Stephen King story where some sort of demon was lurking in the dirt. Gary hadn't cared much for those kinds of books. Real life rarely had an explanation, and this was one of them.

So, he waited, sheltered from the rain, for old Billy to crawl out of his grave so he could put him back in it. Next to him, leaning against the tree, was one of the square-headed shovels they used to use to dig graves. These days, it was mostly used for shoveling ashes out of his fireplace. That and helping the dead back into their graves. The old groundskeeper had carried a twelve-gauge shotgun for the task, but Gary had found it to be mostly overkill. The shovel was all he needed.

He had never really had any problems beyond the first time he saw a corpse crawl out of the ground. That had been terrifying. The old caretaker, Henry something, had taken him out one evening following a funeral. The two men sat on this very hill and waited. Henry perched on a bench, watching the freshly covered grave with the old double-barreled shotgun draped over his knees. The dirty old thing looked like it had last seen action during the Civil War, and he doubted it would actually fire.

The two had sat largely in silence for nearly an hour, watching the sun sink lower in the sky. Gary would have wondered what this was about, but during the couple of weeks of teaching him the job, he'd grown used to Henry's long stretches of saying nothing before he made a point. That day, he had a really good point to make.

"Do you know why they build walls around graveyards, boy?" The old man had asked as he rolled a homemade cigarette. Henry only ever rolled his own.

Gary had never learned that particular trick, but he did envy the man. Loose tobacco and rolling paper were a hell of a lot cheaper than buying by the pack, and in the following forty-some years, it had only gotten more expensive.

"Well, that's to keep people out. So they don't mess with the graves," he answered, and the old man had laughed.

His face morphed into a pile of deep wrinkles and creases. Henry popped a match alight with one thumbnail, another trick Gary envied.

"You think that wall is gonna keep anyone out, boy? Use your head."

The old man was right. The stone wall that ran all around the place was only about two, maybe two and a half, feet high. A grown man could step over it with hardly a worry of scraping his balls. So clearly it wasn't there to keep anyone out.

"Well, I guess it's to mark the property line and make the place look nice. You know to give people peace of mind," Gary had replied.

The old man had snorted in something akin to an agreement. Great plumes of smoke issued from his nose like a dragon.

"Partially, but what it's really there for is not to keep something out, but to keep something in."

"Keep what in?" He had been confused at the man's cryptic words.

"The only thing that is here, boy. The dead."

This had only further confused him and set him to thinking that the old man wasn't all there. It made no sense, and he had said it with such a straight face that Gary couldn't help but think the man was serious.

So, they sat in further silence, drinking beer, and watching the sunset. When the sun had sunk nearly below the horizon, Henry had stood. His knees popped, sounding like twin pistol shots. He checked the loads in the shotgun and snapped the old scatter gun closed.

"Let's go," had been the only thing he'd said, and headed down the hill to the new grave.

Gary had carried the shovels, still unsure of what they were doing. Once they reached the grave, it belonged to some woman whose name he couldn't remember. They stopped next to the tombstone and watched the grave.

"It happens when the sunsets. That's when they wake up," Henry said as he leaned against the headstone.

"Who?" Gary had asked. His bewilderment started to wear on his nerves by this point. It was late, and the last place he wanted to be was in a graveyard at night with an old man who was going soft in the head.

"The dead, boy. What else have we been talking about?" Henry barked angrily. "In Hillgate, the dead don't stay dead. Once the sun sets after they go into the ground, they come back, but they ain't the same. They're off. Something's wrong with them. The only thing you can do was to put 'em back where they belong."

"You have got to be joking."

"Son, this ain't no joke. This is what you do. You put them into the ground, and you make them stay there. No matter what you see or hear, you put them back." The old man's face had gone white. "You never listen to what they say, you understand? They know things. Things no living man or woman knows. They are not the people they were. They are the dead, and the dead belong buried."

He was about to ask what he meant, but just then he heard a noise. It was a low scrabbling noise, like a mouse moving around in your cabinets. It grew slowly louder as though something was coming closer. Gary saw the dirt on the grave shift and bulge as though something underneath was pushing up. It slowly gained a rhythm, like that of a rapidly beating heart.

Gary hadn't believed what he saw. Surely the dead don't actually come back, and they don't crawl out of their graves like zombies. That only happens in bad movies. As his terror reached its breaking point, the grave split open with a dry crack. It was impossible, but sure enough, the elderly woman was trying to claw her way out.

She was dirty from her self-excavation, and her hands were all cut up from tearing her way out of the coffin, but aside from that, she looked perfectly normal. She wasn't half-rotten or falling apart like some monster movie. One thing was clear, though, she was dead. Her skin had the gray pallor of death. Her eyes were wide open, but cloudy and unseeing. Clumps of dirt were caught in her hair and clung to her dress. He froze in sheer terror and fascination as the corpse pulled itself from the grave and stood.

No sooner had it gained its feet than there was a loud explosion, and the corpse pitched forward. Smoke wafted from the double barrels of Henry's shotgun. With well-practiced hands, he broke the shotgun open and loaded fresh shells.

"Don't waste time, boy," the old man croaked. "Take that shovel and bash her head in."

It took a moment for him to understand what he had heard.

"We have to destroy the head and dismember the body. That was the only way to make sure they stay dead."

Gary still didn't believe what he was hearing. This was insane.

While he hesitated, the corpse got to its hands and knees. Henry didn't hesitate. He clouted it over the back of its head with a shovel, driving it into the dirt. He then proceeded to beat it until he had pulverized the skull. Once destroyed, the body went limp. There was no blood, no screaming, nothing. The woman had been dead after all, and while apparently, the dead didn't stay in their coffins, they were still in fact dead.

"All right, now help me chop it up," Henry commanded, positioning the blade of the shovel in the crook of the woman's arm and then stomping on it. There was a crack like a snapping branch, and the arm was then in two.

Gary gulped and followed suit. Using their shovels, they sliced every joint through until they had a pile of body parts. That finished, they dumped the load into the open pit and began shoving the dirt back into the grave.

By the time they finished, it looked as though nothing had ever happened. Henry hadn't spoken to him again that night. He hadn't heard from him again until he received a call from the man the next day, checking to see if he still wanted the job. Despite the sleepless night he had, he took the job.

Henry had retired a week later and moved to Florida with his granddaughter. Gary hadn't heard anything from him until three years later, when the old man died. He was transported back to town for the funeral, but he wasn't buried in Hillgate. Gary had thought that was best. While he had grown accustomed to the job by that point, he didn't think he would ever be up to doing that to someone he had really known and cared for. He had been right, and he had never had to.

There were still tons of questions he wished he'd asked the man back then. But those remained a mystery and probably would. What did they know? And what had they said to Henry? He never gave in to his curiosity or gave them the chance, but it seemed like Henry had. He also often wondered what would happen if one got away, or a horde of them rose at once.

There had only ever been one or two funerals a week in Hillgate. So, it wasn't ever really a problem he had to realistically worry about, but still, he thought about it. The closest he could remember was back when there had been that big fire over in the Falls that burned down the community center. A couple of hundred people had died that night, something about an explosion at the gas station. But for some reason, the burned ones never came back.

That was one of the odd things. Not everyone came back. Kids never seemed to come back, a small miracle. That Morrison woman hadn't come back. Her husband had been that writer who lived over in Flemingsburg, and some crazy fan had tried to kill them both. Neither had that lady sheriff. Gary liked to think that the loved, the truly loved, don't come back.

There had been the queer deaths of Jarrod's boys. It had been written up as a tragic barn accident. Two funerals on the same day, that had been a long night for sure.

The city also decided to tear down the old storage building where Gary stored the landscaping equipment. They had put up a brand new metal one, which was nice. It had an automatic door and everything. They had even gotten him one of those fancy new standing mowers. The mower made short work of the occasional errant corpse.

The graveyard was a mystery, that was for sure. But it also ran like clockwork. Once ol' Mr. Sun dipped below the horizon, Billy Zeller would crawl out of his grave, and Gary would have to put him back. That was just how the world went these days.

He finished off his cigarette, picked up his shovel, and marched down the hill towards the grave.

As he leaned against the headstone, he counted off the seconds on his wristwatch. It wasn't long before the telltale sound of something digging its way up through the freshly turned earth. The grave pulsed in the throes of giving birth to its deceased occupant. That was really what it was like, Gary had come to believe. Some sort of profane and blasphemous parody of birth.

The ground tore itself open in a yawning chasm stinking of wet mud and fresh sod. A far more pleasant smell than the expected one of death and decay.

Billy's corpse struggled to pull itself out of the grave with its muddy hands. Due to the rain, everything was slippery, and the dirt quickly turned to mud, so with each attempt, little momentum was gained. Laboriously, he finally managed to drag himself up and over the lip.

Gary walked around the grave as the corpse finally made its way out. He raised the shovel over his head and prepared to bring it down on the back of Billy's head. He swung with all his might bringing the spade down again and again on the thing's skull. There was a sudden sharp pain in Gary's left arm. It was so intense that he was forced to drop his shovel and fall to his knees.

The pain slowly migrated to his chest, and he found it increasingly hard to catch his breath. He was having a goddamn heart attack. There couldn't be a worse time for this to happen. He struggled to grab his shovel and finished the job. He had to finish it. Another lightning bolt of pain shot through him, driving him face down into the mud.

All hope of putting the corpse back in its grave was now lost. His only thought was of getting help.

Weakly, he tried to call for help, but no sound came out. Rainwater puddled under his face and started running up his nose. He coughed and spluttered as it burned and choked him. After what was only seconds, but felt like hours, he managed to flip himself up. Now the rain poured down onto his face and the head of the dead man standing over him.

Oh, God, Gary thought, *now what? Was it going to kill him? Tear him apart like a zombie, eat him alive, and screaming?*

While his dying brain panicked, the corpse of William Zeller simply stood over him and watched. Its head crooked to one side like an inquisitive dog. It watched as the caretaker's vapor-locked heart gave out and he gasped his few final breaths.

Had there been someone there to call an ambulance or perform CPR until help arrived, Gary Alderman may have lived. But there was no one, and no help came to him. On that cold, rainy night, he died with his job unfinished.

Billy Zeller's reanimated corpse shuffled off into the night.

Obituary:

Gary Alderman, born to Amanda and Jeff Alderman in 1958, passed away Saturday at the age of 58. He was found at the Hillgate Cemetery, dead of an apparent heart attack. Gary served as Hillgate's caretaker since 1975. He was an important and well-respected member of the community, serving two years on the city council in 1994 and 1995, as well as a regular member of the library charity drive. He was preceded in death by his father, Jeff, and his mother, Amanda, his brothers, George and Martin, and his sister, Regina.

The funeral will be next Thursday in Hillgate Cemetery.

Notice from the *Flemingsburg Gazette*:

The sheriff's department reports an incident of grave robbery in Hillgate Cemetery. It is unknown what the motive of the robbery was or when it occurred. Sheriff's deputies discovered the vandalism when they were called to the cemetery to assist local emergency services. The grave of William Zeller showed signs of disturbance, and according to sources, the body was removed and is still missing.

The sheriff's department requests that anyone with information please come forward. The hotline number is included below to reach the Flemingsburg Sheriff directly.

The Why of It All

It was the height of rush hour, and as usual, we were going nowhere. Heat shimmers poured off the roofs and hoods of cars as they baked in the hot sun. It was a rare summer day that the sun was out in full force, bathing all of Essex in its glory.

Not that I noticed, or cared. At the moment, I was more preoccupied with the zombie horde shuffling slowly down the street behind me. Their chorus of moans and groans echoed between the deserted buildings. There was putrid flesh and disheveled clothes as far as the eye could see, which for me was about three or four feet from where I stood between two cars in the middle of the road.

I shuffled my feet aimlessly as I stared into the clear blue sky. There was not a single cloud to be seen. Its beauty was lost on the horde of shambling corpses. The sky was usually gray and dull this time of year, but having a warm summer's day was a slice of fried gold.

In my revelry, I didn't notice as a particularly shabby zombie staggered towards me. His dull eyes fixed on me as he approached, dragging one twisted, mangled foot behind him. It hung on by a single worn tendon. His red canvas trainer somehow managing to stay on his foot as it was dragged across the macadam. He was but three or four feet away when I finally took notice of him. As I turned my head slowly to look at him, he stretched out his rotting arms towards me.

He opened his mouth and howled, "Brains!"

"Why?" I said to the undead horror beside me.

He stopped his shuffling, and I would have said his slack-jawed expression made him look dim had he not always been rather thick. Melvin had been a stock boy at the local grocer, and becoming one of the living dead was more of a lateral move for him than anything else.

"Brains?" he repeated this time with a questioning inflection on the word.

"Yes, but why?" I asked again, receiving only another blank stare. "Why brains?"

"Uh?" came the reply.

The gormless git hadn't been exactly a Rhodes Scholar before becoming a mindless shuffling corpse. So, not really a big change for him. Not like it had been for me. I had been an assistant in the accounts receivable department at, at…somewhere, before the, uh, um thing happened? It was hard to think, and everything was muddled like walking through a fog. The present was clear and tangible, but every time I tried to grasp memories from before, it was like trying to remember a dream. The details slipped away from me, like trying to keep water in your cupped hands. In the moments of failure to recall the past, I couldn't help but think about the future. Which was why I had been standing in the middle of the street just looking up at the sky like a turkey in the rain.

I tried to organize my thoughts and articulate them to Melvin again. "Why do you want brains?" I asked. "It's not like you need to eat. You don't breathe, your heart doesn't beat, you don't even poop. And why does it have to be the brain? Why not the heart? Or the pancreas, or the spleen? Why the brain, of all things? It's not like it's gonna make you smarter, and they really aren't all that nutritious. Again, not that that would benefit you since, as we have already established, you don't need to eat."

Melvin just stared blankly through me as though I wasn't there. He could have had a railroad spike shoved through his bellend and not noticed.

I sighed, and the hole where my nose had been made a faint whistling noise. As I returned to staring at the sky and contemplating being just another one of the nigh-immortal walking dead. My hand, missing several fingers, scratched idly at the gaping hole in my chest. It was a souvenir from an unlucky farmer who had blasted me with buckshot once we battered down his door. It didn't hinder me much at all. It could have been worse. I could have been Rob.

Rob had been shot in the chest with an arrow. The arrow itself hadn't bothered Rob or even slowed him down, but whoever had shot him had duct-taped a modified firework to it Rambo-style. When it had gone off, it had blown poor Rob apart. He had to make do these days, dragging around his severed head using his lips, somehow still managing to keep up with our modest little horde.

So, all and all, being a zombie wasn't so bad, just kinda boring. Yeah, there was a run-in with still-living survivors that livened things up a bit every now and then. Once they were gone, or dead, things settled back down and became dull and boring again, livened up only by the daily downpour of rain, which was miserable. Then there was the occasional gopher hole that someone would step in, resulting in a hilarious faceplant, then spend the next ten minutes trying to get back up. No one ever laughed, not just because our sense of humor apparently died when we did, but because we all had our own gopher "holes" to deal with.

It had been days...weeks...months...years? Time became confused and harder to grasp, due to the rotting of my brain, I guess, so it was difficult to keep track of, and it was made even more so since every bloody day was more or less the same. Life as a zombie was simple. You just walked around with the group, and sometimes it rained or it was nighttime. Bits would fall off, or there was some hapless dolt of a survivor being torn apart.

It was so boring, and why were we doing it? Why did we keep going on?

The quiet peacefulness of the afternoon was shattered by a scream. As though of a single mind, we all turned as one to look in the direction of the sound.

From a side street at the other end of the block, a ragged and harried office worker stumbled out of an alley. His casual business wear was dingy and had seen better days. His tie was tied about his forehead like a bandana, as though he were some barbarian warrior. In each hand, he wielded a set of heavy-duty stable guns. The air was punctuated with pitiful *futts* as the staple guns fired harmlessly, and the nearest members of our horde bore him to the ground, tearing him apart.

Melvin and I watched the scene in bored contemplation, neither of us making any attempt to move in that direction as, at our top walking speed, we would be lucky to make it to the other end of the block in an hour. By the time we got there, there would be nothing left as the horde was piranha-like in their feeding.

I chewed on what was left of my upper lip, the lower one was completely gone, as Gretchen from the secretary pool passed us in the direction of the commotion. She had once been quite pretty and had some nice baps before whatever this was happened. The front of her jumper was still stained with stale manure from the time she tripped and fell face-first into a cowpat while chasing a mangy dog. And I use that term generously, since the best any of us could manage was a slow jog.

She bumped into Dave, spending him headfirst into a post box, where it got stuck. He wasn't the first. It was amazing how many of them got their heads stuck in letterboxes or other small holes and cavities.

Dave's fall resulted in a domino effect, causing Jim the barber to crash into little Mrs. Higgins from down the way, to fall into PC Havisham. This pattern repeated until about a third of our lot had fallen to the ground in a synchronized pratfall. I slapped my palm to my forehead, further denting it from the constant repetition of this gesture.

The screams of the survivor faded to be replaced by the gruesome sounds of tearing flesh as it was stripped from the bone and shoved into rotting mouths. A process carried out of habit and boredom, not a necessity. A mechanism in motion that simply continues due to its momentum. Instinct and reflex, no thought or purpose. Again, I proposed my question to my stalwart companion.

"Why do we do what we do? We don't hunger. We don't sleep. We don't feel hot or cold. Speaking of which, Billingsley is on fire again, somehow."

A young man in a St Marian's school uniform wandered by, his upper body engulfed in flames.

"So, why are we here? What are we doing? Where are we going? What is the point of being if there is no purpose in our existence? Are we just monsters to serve as the boogeymen of humanity's nightmares? A cautionary tale? Straighten up and eat your peas, lads, or else the zombie apocalypse will destroy the world? Are we destined to be bludgeoned, shot, and blown up while trying to eat people?"

Melvin considered me with his vacant expression. The brittle remains of his straw-like hair stirring in the breeze. He looked like he was just one step up from chewing on the furniture like a dim dog. Before he even opened his mouth to speak, I knew what was coming, and my palm was already on its way to slapping my forehead.

"Brains," he bleated like a malfeasant sheep with a squirrel jammed up its ass.

"No, you tit, we don't eat brains. Okay, well, we do, but we eat everything, not just brains, because we are the flesh-eating ghouls." I threw up my hands in exasperation. "Oh, what's the point? Why do I bother? I might as well be pissing in the wind as much as talking to you achieves anything. I guess there was no real point to question our existence when we can barely remember who we ate yesterday, much less who we were and what we do now that we are undead." I let my frustration just hang in the air like a depressing lead balloon full of farts with a slow leak.

"Maybe it's because we can't remember or think ahead that allows us to truly live in the moment, making us more alive now than when we were among the living. So, now we can just enjoy and appreciate the world and our place as part of it instead of just being in it," Melvin replied after a long pause.

I blinked, as the wisdom of his words were somewhat undermined by his thick Birmingham accent.

We just sort of stared at each other for a while, allowing that sentiment to sink in.

A stray dog walking by took that moment to stop and relieve itself on a nearby parked car. An apt metaphor for life.

"Fair enough, Melvin. Shall we crack on?"

And with that, together, we turned and started stumbling down the street. The others gradually fell into lockstep behind us. We led our horde onward, heading west toward whatever came next.

It was rush hour, and we were going nowhere.

The Window

What is madness, but the cracks in the mirror that show us the truth? What is truth, but knowledge, and what is knowledge, but power? My father's mantra: knowledge is power. He preached it morning, noon, and night. In the end, he still died alone, a poor, broken man raving in insanity as his mental faculties were stolen from him by disease. A fate shared by all the men in our family. It was never an issue of if, but a question of when. While my father's madness had come on very late in life, his brother had succumbed in his mid-twenties to schizophrenia, spending his remaining days in a sanitarium. It was a short stay.

They found him dead in his room within the year. His life taken by his own hand.

My grandfather's madness came from the excessive consumption of alcohol. He would go on a mean drunk, then take his belt to his sons, and his hand to his wife when she tried to intervene. The same wife who opened up his throat with one of his own razors when she had taken enough of his abuse, before turning it on herself.

Madness, you see, is contagious. It passes not only through the inherited blood, but can also be transmitted via proximity. The more and longer you are exposed, the more likely you are to catch it, like the common cold. Unlike those nasty little bugs, madness has no cure, and no one is immune. When one is tainted by the malice of fate, there is little one can do. Man's only recourse is to meet their fate or try to deny it by their own hand.

One cannot cheat fate. Or can they?

A valid question I have contemplated many a night, looking out the gable window of my family home. The large attic had become my sanctuary where I came to plot against my own fate, a study in madness itself. I had, of course, examined all the medical practices to exhaustion. Every doctor, every expert I had consulted had led me only to unsatisfactory answers. They seemed to pin their hopes on "someday" and "when medicine or technology catches up." All baseless theories with no adequate practical applications.

No matter how much money I offered to contribute to research or bribed some less ethical doctors to ignore their protocol, there was no solution that would come to fruition until after my lifetime. I had come to regard them as little better than blood letters and snake oil salesmen, their offers of hope hinged on cures that their customers would never see.

Even the true shysters were little better. Pandering their holistics and crystals on the desperation of the damned and the gullibility of the ignorant. They overstate the body's ability to heal itself and tout their potions and quack diets. They would have been more than happy to take my money and offer false hopes and cures with little more than pots of colored piss.

It was in my curation of charlatans from mystics that I found what might be my saving grace. Magic, yes, it sounds childish. I laughed at the notion myself when I first encountered it. As my research continued, and I wandered deeper into the annals of ancient human knowledge, it began to seem less preposterous and more plausible.

I will admit that part of my drive came from my lack of the luxury of time. As I felt those first tendrils of mania creep about the edges of my mind, seeking an opening in which to invade, I had no choice but to chase. So, down the rabbit hole I fell, and finally, my endeavors bore fruit.

Those were the days when I first started to retreat to my hideaway below the roof. The wind and rain played merrily about the eaves in beautiful, ethereal music. Despite the draft, I found the ambiance worth the musty drafts. They had become mitigated over the years as boxes and shelves of books made their homes among the clutter. The boxes of accumulated junk and discarded items too dear to be discarded were slowly replaced with cartons of notepads and research materials. Items and papers littered the tables and my desk. The scrum would seem disorganized and messy to the casual eye, but I knew exactly where everything was and how to find it if needed. The only piece of furniture that was free from debris was a large plush chair where I would lounge and doze between fevered stints of research.

My sole reprieve was the window through which I viewed the world. The large, circular porthole was broken up with a sophisticated latticework that some archaic architect had found pleasing. Through this spider's web, I could peer down upon the street and watch the masses pass by. During the day, heavy draperies were pulled across it to keep the baneful sunlight from molesting my eyes. When my curiosity got the better of me, I would peek out between the sash to view a world of hypocrisy. Bright, shining, and full of smiles and laughter. All of it empty and hollow, full of falseness. The little people wore masks to hide their truths, their corrupted, poisonous souls whose only purpose was to infect others. A madness in and of itself.

Night was better. I preferred it. I would stand in the darkness, behind the glass, and look down at the passersby in the street. Something about the absence of light seemed to peel back those facades, showing a side closer to the truth. Hard looks on hard faces, jaded by the grind of the day-after-day rat race. Knowing fully to each of them that, nihilistic as it may be, all its pointlessness. Their lives spent, meaninglessly toiling, simply to make it from the period of waking to the next cycle of sleep. A waking nightmare of a fate worse than death, unlife. Cold, sterile existence, no more reliant than those of the billions of insects that share this planet.

Is it poetic or pathetic that the best example of human life is the dash between birth and death on our gravestone? A short pointless line marring an otherwise perfect surface. A blight on existence itself.

What is the point of life if all we do is suffer? Why bear going on if the only respite we get are tiny, fleeting moments we believe are happiness? Why, if man has free will, do we choose to be unhappy? Is it because we truly have no real agency? And if that is the case, to be the pawn of something as fickle as fate and chance, why exist at all?

Questions man has asked over and over since the first primitive man looked up at the starry night sky and had a thought about something other than food, fighting, or fornication. An unending quest for the answer. An unanswered question was not something I could abide. How could anyone stand not knowing if knowledge is truly power? To know the answer, to hold the truth, that was my true goal. In knowing, I would understand, and in understanding, I was convinced it would be my shield against the madness that lie beyond the door of my mind.

So, I stood at my window and watched in total darkness. I dared not turn on the lights when the curtains were not drawn. Less so to announce my voyeuristic presence to those below than to spare my own sanity. The light would transform the gable window from a simple, clear glass pane to a starkly contrasting mirror. From a pothole to the outside world to a portal of introspection. It is said that the eyes are the windows to the soul. How apt it is and appropriate that such an iris would also force the one who stood before it to look inward. A torture I had barely been able to withstand, but once. Since that day, I had to keep it covered when the lights were on, especially at night. Every so often, during my peeping, I would catch a glimpse of myself reflected in the glass. Each time, it was a shock to my senses.

I had started this venture young and virile. My body was lean, but strong, with a not unattractive face. My features had always been striking, as though carved from wood by a skilled apprentice who had yet to fully master his craft. As my unknown deadline approached, and my work took its toll on both my mind and my body, I had become gaunt. My eyes, once piercing and bright, had become dull and sunken, darting around like an animal in a trap. My complexion had also taken a drastic turn from healthy, if a bit pale, to sallow. Pulled tight over features that had gone from rough wood to hard stone. Hair cascaded to my shoulders, lank and listless from lack of sunlight. With each viewing, I metamorphosed further and further into a creature bent and twisted, as my mind would eventually become.

A willing sacrifice, I was all too glad to make as my quest began to progress by leaps and bounds. Through my research and correspondence with various historians and book collectors, I was in the midst of tracking down an elusive authentic copy of the fabled *Kitab al-Azif,* written by the mad Arab, Abdul Alhazred. I had nearly half a dozen forgeries of the *Necronomicon*. The damn things were all too easy to find, fraught with glaringly obvious errors, but the original manuscript found itself to be much harder to track down. The bookkeeper I had been querying in Tangier had illuminated a startling revelation that not one of the so-called experts had known. The tome was but one of a set of five volumes known as the *Book of Nü*. Contained within these volumes were the Truth, books of real magicks. In them were said to be accounts of ancient gods, other worlds, and countless spells that would twist the veil of reality to one's will.

Before I could inquire further, he had laid my hopes to nines by admitting that, to his knowledge, there existed no complete collection of the works. The *Necronomicon* was but the easiest of the books to find, something I found hard to believe given my own experiences in hunting the book down. When I asked if he knew where I could find a copy, he knew of no such person who had one that would part with it. Such knowledge was far too valuable to those who knew what it was. And to the bibliophiles, who hoarded such things like dragons with their gold, they would sooner lose life or limb than part with such a treasure.

My fortune took a turn for the better when he learned of another volume of a set that was in possession of a recently deceased client whose family was selling off his estate. I offered him an ungodly sum to obtain the book for me, and he agreed not for the money, though he was glad of it, but because he felt that such a resource as powerful and dangerous should be at the very least kept track of. He preferred it in the hands of a madman than having it lost to the unknown hands of God only knows.

His superstitions meant very little to me as my time was tick-tick, ticking away to the point where I could almost hear my own internal clock counting down. I had books and knowledge on every science known to man, from biology to astrology. My studies surpassed more than a dozen PhDs in numerous subjects, and I searched the world ten times over. It would not be far off to claim myself as one of the most learned men on the planet, and I had exhausted all other avenues. This was my last recourse, the vestige left untapped, and my research strongly held evidence that I was closing in on real knowledge, real power.

The transaction took several maddening months. Not only did I have to shell out a small king's ransom to the bookkeeper, but I had to have the book authenticated and inspected before it was shipped via bonded courier to my home. My patience and resources were beginning to wane when the courier finally arrived. The poor young man was rendered speechless when I answered the door in a flap. I am sure my deteriorating appearance was quite disconcerting, but he soon recovered as his shock was quickly replaced with offense, as my straining psyche had rendered my behavior to something quite austerely rude. I sent him away with his money, slammed the great oak door, and bolted it against the outside.

Returning to my loft refuge, I tore apart the package with my ragged, yellowing nails. I had long since abandoned my almost obsessive maintenance of my manicured nails. Like many other habits of hygiene, I had found them superfluous in the face of my pursuits. Free of its binding, I held the book up to examine it in the light.

It was the most rudimentary form of manuscript. It was little more than a bundle of loose papers whose binding consisted of a since-weathered thong of ancient leather. The cover, if one could call it that, was simple papyrus hardened with age to the point it was almost bark-like.

At first, I thought there was no title, but upon further inspection, I found that the book was bound in the Asia style, thus it was the reverse of Western publications and read from right to left instead of left to right. Upon the cover, in barely legible script, were words in ancient Arabic. The most rough and literal translation would be "The Eye to See Inwards," or "The Inwards Looking Eye."

A queer title, but considering its content, not an unfaithful one. I had learned from the bookkeeper that of the five books, two were a pair, meant to complement one another. The *Necronomicon*, known as the book of the dead, whose original title translated into something more of a concept than a tangible entity, was said to hold the secrets of death and eldritch beings of millennia past. While this volume, the "Inner Eye," was said to house the spells of life and the unknown yet to come. Yin and yang. Black and white.

Cheating death is one thing, but whoever heard of cheating life? If one book was known to bring madness, then surely its opposite would do the inverse. Balance is the essence of the universe after all, and history has borne that out time after time.

My labors were not over, however. Obtaining the book was but the first hurdle. It would have to be translated. Proficient as I had become in my studies, the book itself seemed to have been made for the sole purpose of further testing my sanity. It was written in various languages, as it had been translated over the years. I recognized very few of them, mostly ancient Arabic and archaic forms of Latin. At its most primitive, it devolved into incomprehensible pictographs that resembled almost Mesoamerican hieroglyphics. It was astounding, and a more academic mind would have found this a most curious development. My intentions and designs were on the practical, not the academic. I was here to obtain real knowledge, not to prattle in lecture halls on theories and the why of long dead skeletons forgotten by time.

Working day and night, it took the better part of two years, and I had barely translated a third of the text. It was an arduous, nearly Herculean task. Working backwards, I had to piece together not one or two, but nearly thirty Rosetta stones, using over two hundred other texts in order to plunder its depths. It would have to be enough, as I felt more than ever the rats nibbling at the edges of my mind, pushing me closer and closer to the brink.

The night I first received the book, I had the first dream. What it was, I can't exactly say, as it was more sensation and knowing than substance. Since then, it had occurred time and time again, clear as the morning and bright as the sun. Upon waking, it would fade instantaneously, the details slipping from my mind like water through a sieve. Maddening, in its own right.

The dream did not stay in my sleep. For the past few months, they had begun to intrude upon my waking moments. It was brief, a quick darting moment in the corner of my vision. Shadows that seemed to reach out when not looked at directly. The taste of ash in my mouth, the smell of sulfur filling my nostrils. Moments when I felt as though I was not in my body, but somewhere else. It was as if I were straddling a chasm, a foot on either side, unable to pull myself one way or another. A moment of lost concentration and I would plunge down, down into the darkness to God knows what fate. I thought it was my mind finally turning traitor in my final hours, when I was so close, as to undermine and undo my attempts to slip the iron grip of fate. I would not allow it to take me, not yet, not when I was so close to it. To success, to victory, to knowledge and power, to freedom.

What I managed to piece together was a handful of spells, ancient magicks, most of them nonsensical, but I believe that one could be my key. It was both simple and complex. A sort of primitive circuit designed by intention and powered by desire, more art than science.

It started out its life as a simple alchemical matrix I scrawled upon the floor of my attic space. It was an almost perversely symmetrical twin of my window. It grew and grew as I worked and translated, learning more and more. The design became increasingly complex, branching out to nearly every surface. I lost track of time, as it had no meaning. Only the work had meaning, only it mattered.

My consciousness drifted in and out of phase as I battled my own defective brain, as it was determined to put a stop to my plans. I do not know if it took days or weeks, but soon, every inch was covered in glyphs and symbols. They looped and circled one another in a bizarre cosmic dance whose logic was known only to themselves. The ceiling, rafters, and floor were covered with scrawls. They were even painted across the great window itself, turning it from quasi tether to reality to a madman's scrying mirror.

Once complete, I recited the words and performed the rituals, all to no success. Night after night, I tried and failed. With each failure, I fell further into depression and self-loathing. My inability to determine what I was doing wrong only added fuel to my desperation. My actions and ideas became only more sporadic.

The seizures began small at first, moments of blankness, coming to on the floor with papers and books kicked and scattered about. They grew in frequency and gravity, and time grew short. I was biting my tongue and writhing on the floor helpless, each time thinking that this was the end, that my number was up. Each time I recovered, I doubled my efforts and pushed further beyond the edge of all known logic and reason.

Then I discovered the Truth. It was purely by accident. In the midst of reexamining the matrix itself, I was gripped by a grand mal seizure. My body racked by a spasm so powerful I thought it would break my own spine as I bent backwards, nearly double. The curtain covering the window became tangled in my fist as it locked shut in a contraction so strong it would have taken a pry bar to open my fingers. As I fell to the floor and convulsed, they were pulled taut, yanking the rod from the wall and relieving the mirror. It had been covered due to the lights being on, but now it was bare, and the light reflected off its dark panes, transposing a duplicate of the room on its other side.

My head fetched up hard against the floor with a sickening crack. A nail that protruded from the floor ever so slightly that it barely registered my notice, stuck square in my temple. It tore through flesh and struck the bone. Blood poured freely as I lay helpless, trapped in my failing form, writhing naked, and reflected perfectly in the center of the eye of my attic window.

It was no longer a window or a mirror, or anything of this world. It was a titanic, bloody eye that stared back at me. There are no words in any human language to convey the gravity and horror I saw before me. When I say it was an eye, that is the closest thing the human mind can perceive it to be. It had the most fundamentally recognizable features of an eye. The sclera was translucent, like a fishbowl filled with an oily, cloudy substance. There was no pupil that one could make out, but its iris was an impossible geometric shape that both folded in upon and, at the same time, orbited itself. Seeing it shattered the remains of my sanity, and I fell into myself.

Nietzsche is often quoted as having said, "When you gaze long into the abyss. The abyss gazes also into you." The abyss was not gazing into me. It was pilfering my very being and molesting the corners of all that I considered myself.

Then I found the Truth. To consume a thing is to know a thing, and knowledge is power. The eye showed it to me. A world of death, but beyond death. A dead world of entropy clinging to the last remaining embers of creation. Cloaked in an atmosphere of desperation to continue on, no matter the cost. A cold, starving animal on its last legs searching for any means to cling to its existence for just a few precious seconds more.

I looked across barren, white plains covered not in snow, but in ash. The sky blackened and thickened with acrid flumes of smoke. A place where life had ceased long ago, all but forgotten by time. The things that remained were neither dead nor alive. They merely existed in a form of stasis, an endless cycle, where time had no meaning. Twisted and grotesque, bent by the barest form of sustenance needed. They hid in the shadows and low places, some eldritch thing larger than lumbered out of sight.

There, beneath a shattered, burning moon, it waited. It waited to feed, to throw the most meager of kindling onto the fire of its own existence, to hold back oblivion. It waited for us. That was the truth. The answer to all of the questions that humanity has asked. The reason we are born, we suffer and we die. We are the fuel that feeds its continued existence. To say, we are livestock, raised and fattened for the slaughter only to be consumed, would be giving us too much credit. We are more akin to sentient blades of grass. Insignificant and tiny, existing only to be devoured. Chewed up and shit out by unfathomable beings. We can no more comprehend it than a blade of grass can comprehend the cow that eats it. To know such a thing, the truth, would destroy our minds. It was only there, on the edge of sanity, that I could perceive even one tenth of a thousand of the Truth.

And they called to me. It called to me. She called me to join them. To become. To fulfill my role. I could feel what we call the soul being pulled from me to be consumed by that fire. Its voice filled me up and tore me apart. "Ph'nglui fm'latghor c' fm'latgh ng yar mgep mg l' ah'gotha fahff l' naIIII ah yar. Shuggogg mglagln fhtagn fhalma ng ot h' gof'nn, h' fhtagn, uh'eor f' li lllll h' zhro fhtagn."

Great and terrible, I screamed, trying to flee the metaphysical, desperate to turn back, to turn aside from my foolish path, for any fate was preferable to this. It was too much. The truth was too much, and my mind could not contain even the most infinitely minuscule portion I was shown. *No more*, I wanted to scream, but I was without voice, mouth, or form. I was nothingness within the endless, ceaseless darkness of the macro verse. I had opened a door, not to hell, but a thousand doors, each leading to a thousand hells that no man could ever decipher. Once the door was opened, there was no way to close it.

I don't know how much time passed in that place. Time has no meaning. When I came to my senses, I found myself committed to the Arkham Hill Mental Health and Wellness Institute. A housekeeper had found me ranting and raving while having intermittent seizures. Emergency services had been sent for, and I was taken immediately to the hospital. I have no idea how long I was there. While I was still in my delirious state, they were forced to perform surgery on my brain where the doctors removed a number of curious tumor-like growths. A precursory examination returned a most disturbing report. They were most closely reminiscent of partially formed eyeballs. Once exorcised, the seizures stopped, and, a few days later, I regained my consciousness.

I had been transferred to the sanitarium, where I was further diagnosed with a degenerative disorder. While they could treat the symptoms with medication and slow down the progress of the disease,

I was once again looking down the barrel of my own mortality. My mind was gone, and I was sentenced to live out the rest of my days shackled to a bed, shitting myself as a drooling moron. My condition was assessed as too severe to allow me to leave under my own cognizance. I was admitted to their long-term ward. In a few months, the seizures returned, and another scan of my brain revealed new growths. They would further impair both my mental and physical functions, while still leaving me alive. The doctors wanted to perform more of their barbarism. I declined, for these "eyes" had given me "insight." *Ha ha*.

I now knew what I was doing wrong, what had been missing from my transfiguration mural. The key to the activation of a spell for life is death. You see, balance. The universe, or at least this universe, demands balance as its one rationale. You cannot have life without death, and now I know what to do. If that little "death" had opened up a window, then surely a bigger death could open up a door. In that place, I had gained knowledge and thus power. I knew that the mind was not merely a few pounds of pink flesh trapped within a casing of bone. The mind, the essence that made us the individual, was something more. Less tangible than flesh and bone, a decaying meat suit that we struggle to keep alive.

No, I had discovered that thing that the Bible thumpers and tambourine shakers call the soul. A metaphysical construct that is a contradiction of both less and more substance than the physical body. It was my physical body that was mutinying against me, but my mind would soon be free.

Breaking out wasn't difficult, as I wasn't considered a danger to anyone. All I had to do was wait until the night shift was brought on, and in the distraction between the changing of the personnel, it was easy enough to walk straight out the door. They were in the business of detaining mental defectives who barely had a sense of right and left, not functional people.

So, there were no bars, fences, or guards to keep in those who were not raving lunatics. The nurses had seen fit to shave and bathe me during my convalescence, and so I hardly looked out of place in polite society so long as I wore a cap to cover up my surgery scars. From there, it was a small matter to return to my home and break into the boarded up old house.

I had a plan, but for that plan I needed my study. In my study, there was still the book and the matrix I had constructed. Everything was where I had left it, and even though there had been no staff to clean the room was queerly absent of dust. I had to be quick, lest anyone notice my escape and report it to the local police. This would be the first place they were sure to look, and I could have no interruptions. I prepared my ritual as before and repeated my incantations.

This time, I made one change. I held a large knife in my hands. I was going to open the door just a crack and slip through. Not into that nightmarish world or one of the others, God only knows what horrors await me further down the rabbit hole. No, I planned to slip into the space between, into the corridor that connected everything. I could hide like a rat in a dark hole. Watching, waiting, and scavenging off the crumbs. It wasn't living, but I would be free of a doomed existence chained by fate to a cruel life and even crueler afterlife. I would finally do for myself what no doctor could ever do for me.

"Physician, heal thy self." I laughed and plunged the knife into my neck.

Riders Before the Storm

Each autumn, they came. Between Founders' Day and Halloween, for two weeks, they would descend upon our small town like a swarm of locusts, bringing with them the stench of fried food and the eerie strains of calliope music. For two weeks, they would set up shop at the fairgrounds, and the townsfolk would flock to their games and rides. They laughed and smiled, ignorant of the fact that they were being fleeced by these grifters. They lost more than just their hard-earned cash at the fall carnival. They lost their dignity. I lost my innocence.

Every year, it was the same. False promises of fun times and empty smiles. And when they packed up and left, the only thing that remained was misery. Cheating spouses were exposed. Jealousy boiled over into violence. And children always went missing.

Sure, adults went missing, too. But it's the kids that you really notice. The ones who vanish without a trace. The ones who are never seen again. I've seen the flyers. I've seen the desperate pleas for information. But it's always too late. The carnival folk returned to where they came from, leaving behind a trail of broken hearts and shattered lives.

This was always followed by a terrible storm, like the wrath of God, intent on washing away the sins of the carnival folk. Or perhaps the storm was in league with them, a willing accomplice to their heinous deeds. Either way, it swept through the town with a vengeance, tearing at the trees and flooding the streets. When it was over, the fairgrounds were deserted, the carnival folk vanished into the night like ghosts. The only evidence of their presence were the discarded popcorn bags and tattered flyers scattered across the muddy ground.

But the townsfolk seemed all too eager to forget the horrors that had unfolded beneath the bright lights of the carnival. They didn't want to remember. Even if they wanted to blame the carnival people for their troubles, they knew it wasn't true. They just held up a mirror to souls and let us tear ourselves apart.

And so they pushed it all away, like a bad dream upon waking. They tried to forget the taste of cotton candy on their tongues and the sound of the calliope music ringing in their ears. They clung to the vague bits and pieces that remained, like wisps of smoke from a dying fire.

But some memories are harder to shake than others. They linger like ghosts, haunting the corners of our minds. And I can't help but wonder what really happened that night, when the storm raged and the carnival folk fled. Did they leave willingly, or were they driven out by something far more sinister? But they will return like the seasons, every year, nothing can stop it save death, which frees us from the cycle.

It's funny how children remember the things that adults so easily forget. Maybe it's because their minds are still pure, untainted by the cynicism and skepticism that comes with age. Or maybe it's because they're more attuned to the magic of the world, more open to the possibility of wonder and amazement.

Whatever the reason, it was the kids who remembered the fair the most vividly. They remembered the thrill of the carnival rides, the taste of the cotton candy melting on their tongues, the sound of the calliope music ringing in their ears. They remembered the bright lights and the dizzying colors, the laughter and the screams.

And I remembered it all, too. I was just a kid back then, but I knew that there was something special about that fair. Something that went beyond the glitz and the glamour. Something that lingered in the air like a sweet perfume.

The fairgrounds were alive with activity, the air thick with the scent of fried food and the sound of screaming children. It was the perfect setting for an Indian summer, a final burst of warmth before the chill of autumn sets in. Families flocked to the fairgrounds, eager to indulge in a little weekend fun.

Not all parents were responsible. Some saw the fair as an opportunity to ditch their kids for a few hours, letting them run wild and burn off some energy, not that the kids seemed to mind. They were too busy chasing each other through the crowds, screaming in delight as they rode the coasters and carousels.

The older boys, with their slicked-back hair and their girls in short shorts, tried to impress each other with their skills at the rigged games. They threw darts at balloons and tossed rings at bottles, all the while knowing that the odds were stacked against them. The younger kids were content to visit the petting zoo, where they could feed the goats, sheep, and ponies with fistfuls of corn. But inevitably, there was always one kid who got knocked over by an over-enthusiastic goat, and the tears would start to flow. It was chaos, but it was a beautiful chaos. The kind that only comes once a year, when the fair comes to town.

The carnies, with their gap-toothed grins and oily hair, were the lifeblood of the fair. They ran the rides and manned the stalls, shilling their cons and catcalling anyone who walked by. It seemed like they were always lurking in the shadows, sneaking a smoke or plotting their next scam.

Despite their unsavory reputation, people still flocked to their games and rides, lured in by the promise of fun and excitement. It was as if the carny magic had a hold over them, convincing them to sink more and more money into impossible games and rickety rides that had a habit of breaking down at the worst possible moment. The carnies were always one step ahead. They knew how to vanish into thin air when angry parents came looking for them, or when someone demanded a refund. They knew how to manipulate their marks with false promises and smooth talk. They knew how to keep the dark secrets of the fair hidden from prying eyes.

But we were all under their spell, even if we didn't realize it at the time. The magic of the carnival was too strong to resist, and we were all caught up in its grasp. It wasn't until much later, when the damage had already been done, that we would start to question the true nature of the fair and the carnies who ran it. And by then, it was already too late.

The smells of the carnival and the street fair were always a feast for the senses. The rich, sweet aroma of funnel cakes, the savory scent of corn dogs, and the greasy smell of French fries mingled together to create a heady cocktail of flavors that could make your mouth water from blocks away. It wasn't just the food that drew me in. It was the warm, heady scents of summer itself—the fresh-cut grass, the hay, and the animal manure that filled the air with their earthy fragrances. Even the stale beer and the scent of vomit from those wild college parties could trigger those nostalgic memories, taking me back to a time when the world was full of endless possibilities and anything could happen.

The fairgrounds were alive with the sounds of children laughing and the hypnotic melodies of the calliope, but my attention was elsewhere. My focus was singular, my obsession all-consuming, Mr. Black.

The head of the carnival was a towering figure, thin as a scarecrow, but with an aura that commanded attention. His crooked grin was always plastered on his face, as if he knew some dark secret that the rest of us were oblivious to. His deep-set eyes, hidden behind a curtain of black hair, followed the park-goers as they made their way through the carnival. To most, he was a jovial presence, radiating a sense of goodwill to all who crossed his path, reminding most people of that actor from those pirate movies.

Mr. Black was a sight to behold, dressed in his funeral best and towering over the fairgrounds like a dark sentinel. His coat and hat made him look like a caricature of a villain in a western movie, and his smile, though wide and toothy, always made my skin crawl. He had a way with people, though. His charm and charisma drew in the crowds like moths to a flame, and he seemed to have an uncanny ability to read people and give them exactly what they wanted. Everyone else adored him, thought he was the life of the party. But I knew better. I could see the darkness in his eyes, the emptiness that belied his cheerful demeanor. But I knew there was something sinister about him, something lurking just beneath the surface.

Mr. Black's smile was like that little light on an angler fish's head to draw in prey. It reminded me of those "low men in yellow coats" from that Stephen King story I read once. Even though Mr. Black's coat wasn't yellow, he still gave me the creeps. He was a low man, the lowest of the low. And he was the last person I saw with my little sister before she vanished without a trace.

The weight of the gun in my pocket was a constant reminder of what I had made up my mind to do, gnawing at my gut for weeks. It was a hot day, but I didn't care. While I was the only person wearing a jacket, it felt like a shield, a layer of protection against the prying eyes of the carnie folk. The .38 felt heavier by the minute, a reminder of the dangerous territory I was about to enter. I tightened my grip on the gun, hoping that my sweaty palm wouldn't betray me. The weight of my guilt was heavier still, weighing on my conscience. I was here to confront Mr. Black, and it would not be civil.

Mr. Black's looming presence seemed to shrink the world around him. As he roamed the park, his shadow crept over everything and everyone, as if he were some sort of malevolent giant. He handed out balloons to the kids, but it was an act, a trick to put them at ease. I could see the malice lurking behind his crooked smile, like a predator waiting to pounce. His eyes were the worst of it, the way they followed the children and their parents with a sinister glint. It was as if he was sizing them up, seeing which ones he could snatch away and drag into the darkness. As he walked, his arms and legs seemed to move independently of each other, like some kind of puppet controlled by a madman. I knew then that I had to be the one to stop him before he hurt someone else.

I shadowed him all day, keeping a safe distance to avoid detection. My mind was a constant replay of the past year's events—the unrelenting search that drove my mother to the brink of death, the solemn funeral where my family gathered to mourn my sister, and then the sudden shift in their attention. They seemed to have lost interest in what happened to their own flesh and blood, as if the burial of the caskets had brought a closure that was too convenient. But I couldn't forget.

The bodies of the children were never found, and even as druggies succumbed to fatal overdoses and people committed suicide, the memory of the missing kids faded away like the colors of a sunset. Except for me. For me, the memories were still sharp, vivid, and agonizing. I remembered everything. It was my fault they got her. And now, as I trailed him, I knew he was the key to getting my sister back. As I followed, I couldn't help but wonder if I was truly prepared to follow through with it.

We had begged our parents to let us go to the fair, rather than be forced to attend the church picnic that Sunday. We pleaded until our parents relented. I was eleven, a grown-up in my own mind, and I assured my parents that I was responsible enough to watch over my six-year-old sister, Alisa. My mother was hesitant, but my father, ever the practical one, reasoned that if I could handle myself at the fair, then I was surely capable of completing household chores.

I bargained with my dad, wrangling a deal to earn my keep by mowing the lawn and washing the car. After some hard-nosed negotiations, my parents finally relented, allowing us to go to the fair. They even gave me an advance on my allowance and threw in an extra five bucks for the babysitting. It was a sweet deal, and I was determined to make the most of it.

As we arrived, the sights and sounds of the fair enveloped us, and I reveled in the freedom and excitement of it all. It was a day of indulgence, a day to savor the sweet and savory delights that filled our senses.

Alisa wanted to see the cute baby goats, so we went to the petting zoo first. For the next few hours, we were lost in the thrill of feeding and playing with the animals. Alisa giggled uncontrollably as a sheep nibbled at the corn in her small hands, and she wailed when I had to pry the bunny from her grasp. The only way to distract her was with the promise of ice cream. Our parents bought her a cone, but she ended up spilling most of it down her shirt. That didn't stop her from inhaling two corn dogs and half of my elephant ear. I watched in awe as she stuffed her little body with junk food, wondering where she managed to put it all. But then again, we were a family of big eaters, and it seemed to start early.

The rides at the fair were nothing like the ones I had seen in the movies. No towering roller coasters or spine-tingling thrill rides. But that didn't stop us from having a good time. Alisa was only six, so we were limited to the tamer attractions. We spun around in teacups and rode the horses on the carousel, while I watched her take delight in the so-called "baby rides." There were only a handful of them, and they were all pretty tame. The cartoon train chugged around in a lazy circle, with faded Hanna-Barbera characters plastered on the sides. The junior bumper cars were a joke, barely bumping into each other, and always accompanied by at least one crying child and a hovering mother. And then there was the kiddie carousel, with horses that didn't go up and down, and were cheap knockoffs of the My Little Pony franchise. She enjoyed them all the same, though she also liked being allowed to go on what she called "big boy and girl rides." I took her on a few, and she did well without crying once.

Not even when I took her on the bumper cars and some jerk slammed us into the wall, which was against the rules. It was a pretty hard hit, and I was sure she was gonna cry. I had taken the hit pretty hard myself and could only imagine what it would be like for a six-year-old. Alisa just got mad and called the guy a bad poo-poo head, and that made me laugh.

Once we were tired of the rides, we moved on to the games of chance. The carnival games were all rigged, but we played them anyway. The grizzled carnies would taunt us with their twisted grins, enticing us with promises of prizes we could never win. Alisa didn't seem to care. She cheered me on as I hurled baseballs at milk bottles, tossed ping-pong balls into goldfish bowls, and aimed darts at balloons. Her eyes lit up with each victory, and she clutched her growing collection of small stuffed animals, all consolation prizes, with glee, but then she spotted it. The giant pink gorilla, a monstrosity of synthetic fur and stuffing that towered over the other prizes. It was like something out of a nightmare, an off-color knockoff of Grape Ape with its unsettling grin and misshapen limbs. Alisa was enchanted by it. She ran over to the stall, jumping up and down on the spot, and begging me to get it for her.

I stopped to look at the stall. It was one of those shooting ranges. The tin targets were warped and dented, and the paint on the wooden backdrop was faded and chipped, heavily scarred with the marks of countless bullets. A crude sign dangled from a rusted chain, its paint flaking away like diseased skin, "Shoot to Win." It was clear that this stall had seen better days. But then Alisa tugged on my sleeve, her eyes wide with excitement. "Please, big brother! Can we play this game? I want that big pink gorilla!"

The rules were simple, but the stakes were high. The prizes ranged from trinkets and baubles to the coveted big pink gorilla and its thousand-point score. The ducks, quacking away in the front, were an easy target, but they would only earn me a measly five points. The real challenge lay in the little birds hiding in the back, worth a hundred points each, but would be hard to hit.

Ten shots were all you got, and you would have to hit every single one of those birds. If that wasn't hard enough, the sights on the gun were all out of whack, making it nearly impossible to aim with any degree of accuracy. The guns were modified .22

rifles, rigged to shoot BBs instead of bullets. Three tries for a dollar, that was the deal. And with each round, I would have only ten shots to earn as many points as I could.

Alisa's pleading eyes wore down my resistance until I relented, handing over my hard-earned dollar to the bored attendant. He handed me a small rifle, the metal cold and unforgiving in my grip, its stock worn smooth from years of use, along with a tin of BBs that rattled like bones. The attendant cranked up the machine, the creaking of gears and the whirring of motors filling my ears. The targets started moving, a blur of painted tin and scarred wood, and I squeezed the trigger. The BB ricocheted off the metal, missing the mark entirely. I cursed under my breath, adjusting the crooked sights as I fired off a few more shots at the ducks.

With each round, I grew more comfortable with the rifle and more confident in my aim. It was a false sense of security, a dangerous illusion that crumbled with each missed shot. In my third round, I could feel the sweat dripping down my forehead as I took aim at the birds, their tiny bodies darting back and forth on their flimsy perches. No matter how hard I tried, my shots went wild, missing the mark by a hair's breadth. In the end, I could only manage to hit four of them.

Alisa's eyes were wide and pleading, like a puppy begging me to try again. I should have known better, but I gave in, plunking down yet another dollar and taking up the small rifle once more. Four dollars in, and the game had consumed me. All my focus was on the targets, each one a tiny metal bird, mocking me with their flitting movements. I was determined not to let the game beat me.

On my best try, I had managed to hit eight out of ten birds, and the carnie running the stall had crowed that it was a record. His beanie cocked back on his head, he goaded me, daring me to try again. I slapped down my last dollar as I took aim once more. My first try was a disaster. The BB ricocheted off the metal like a fly buzzing against a windowpane. On my second round, I found my groove, my fingers moving as if on their own, the rifle an extension of my body. I had gotten first place in marksman for my Boy Scout troop, with real .22s. Without the recoil of a real gun, all I had to worry about was my timing. And one after another, the birds fell, their tiny metal bodies hitting the ground with a satisfying clink.

I had been so close, my fingers tightening around the small rifle as I took aim at the ninth target. My breath came in short gasps, my heart pounding in my chest, as I focused all my attention on the tiny metal bird in my sights. And then, out of the corner of my eye, I saw him. The guy, a shifty-looking character with beady eyes and a greasy comb-over, had tripped over a loose bit of chain, sending the entire range jolting to the side. The tenth target, already in motion, had slipped out of my line of fire, and I had missed my shot.

I knew then, with a cold certainty that settled in my gut like a stone, that he had done it on purpose. He had cheated, trying to keep me from winning the game. When I accused him, he had the nerve to claim it was an accident, his voice dripping with false innocence, but I could see it in his eyes.

"Bald-faced cheater," I spat at him, my voice rising. "I want my dollar back."

He snapped at me then, his face twisted with anger, telling me to get lost. That they weren't running a charity, and I should be happy he didn't have me thrown out.

Burning with a fierce anger that threatened to consume me, I turned to storm out of the rigged shooting gallery, only to find Alisa was nowhere in sight. Panic shot through me like a bolt of lightning, and I started to run. I crisscrossed the fairgrounds, scanning every face and every corner for a glimpse of her blonde hair and pink coat. But she was gone, vanished like a ghost in a crowd of thousands.

I was about to lose my mind when I finally caught sight of her, a tiny figure at the far end of the main drag. My heart leapt in relief as I plunged into the crowd. People shoved and jostled me, and I struggled to fight the crush of people. When I was close enough to see, I saw Mr. Black, the carnival barker, looming over her like a henge. My gut twisted with unease.

As I fought my way closer, I watched in horror as Alisa took his hand. They turned and walked away, swallowed up by the throngs of people. I ran faster, trying to catch up, but they vanished from sight. When I finally arrived at the spot where I had last seen them, they were gone. Completely gone.

I broke down crying in front of my parents, apologizing because it was my fault. I lost her. I should have kept a closer eye on Alisa, but they had been right, I hadn't been responsible enough to look after her. The park manager claimed to have searched high and low, but there was no sign of her. The police were called, and I was forced to recount every moment leading up to Alisa's disappearance. When I mentioned Mr. Black, they tracked him down and questioned him. He lied through his teeth with the ease of a practiced conman. That smug smile on his greasy face made my blood boil. It was as if he were taunting me. I knew he was lying, and he knew that I knew it, too. I wanted to lash out, to reach across the table, grab him by the throat, and make him tell the truth, but there was nothing I could do.

When the news broke that Alisa had gone missing, he didn't hesitate to offer his aid in the search. The days that followed were a frenzy of activity, with police and press swarming the fairgrounds, interrogating anyone who might have information about my sister's disappearance. But despite their best efforts, the search turned up nothing. The hours stretched into days, and hope began to wane. Then, on the third night, it happened. As the last of the carnival lights flickered out, the entire company packed up and vanished into the night. Some said they had seen strange things in the shadows that night, fleeting glimpses of figures that should not have been there. Others whispered that the carnival itself was cursed, that it had always been a magnet for trouble and misfortune.

No matter the cause, one thing was clear: Alisa was gone, and the carnival had taken its secrets with it.

The search was put on hold when the storm hit, a tempest born in the depths of Hell. Lightning sliced through the sky like the blades of a demon's scythe, and the wind roared like the fury of the damned. As we huddled in the safety of our home, I couldn't help but feel the full weight of my guilt. God was punishing me. I knew it. Punishing me for failing to protect my little sister, for letting her fall into the clutches of those evil people. The storm was his wrath made manifest, a tempest of fury unleashed upon me. The house shook and trembled, as if it were about to be torn apart by some vengeful force. I wept bitter tears. I knew that I deserved every lash of the storm's fury. For I had failed in my duty as a brother, and nothing could ever make that right.

The search for her had barely lasted a couple of weeks before it was abandoned. The authorities declared that she had simply wandered off into the woods, lost and alone, and that was the end of it. But in the shadows, behind closed doors and whispered conversations, the rumors and speculation swirled like a dark cloud. Some said that she had been believed she had been picked up by some pedophile or transient and murdered. As the days passed, the whispers grew fainter until they were no more than the echoes of a distant nightmare. It was only a week later that we gathered to lay her to rest, to bid farewell to another young life taken before its time. Even as we mourned, I couldn't help but notice that the world was already moving on. People were forgetting, letting her slip from their memories like a dream upon waking.

I refused to forget, to move on, and pretend that nothing had happened. But my parents were different. They packed away Alisa's belongings, sealing them up in the dark, musty confines of the attic. Her room, once a bright and cheerful haven for my little sister, was now a sterile office for our father, as if erasing her very existence.

I couldn't forget. I couldn't forgive myself for failing her, for falling for their cruel trick and allowing them to steal her away.

The guilt weighed heavily on my shoulders, a burden that I could never shake.

As the days turned to weeks, and the weeks to months, people forgot. The world moved on, leaving Alisa behind like a forgotten relic. But I couldn't forget, not even for a moment. I marked her birthday on my calendar, knowing that she should have been there, running around in her excitement, begging for the latest doll or bike.

But she wasn't there, and my parents didn't even notice. They had already moved on, content to bury the past and pretend that everything was fine. But I knew the truth. I knew that there should have been a party, that my little sister should have been there. As the year ticked by, I vowed never to forget her, and I would get her back somehow, no matter what.

When school resumed, I was busy with schoolwork as my 6th-grade teacher seemed determined to make life even harder, loading us down with homework and pop quizzes that left my head spinning. Supposedly, it was all to prepare us for the rigors of middle school, but to me, it just seemed like a lot of noise. My grades, which had been all As and Bs, began to slip, and as the Ds piled, I did what any desperate child would do. I doctored my report card, scribbling furiously with a pen until my Ds were transformed into Bs. My parents were still not happy about my grades slipping to a C average. The only time they seemed to acknowledge my sister's "death" was by using it as a convenient scapegoat for my falling grades. I knew that my grades had slipped not because of grief, but because of the suffocating weight of guilt that was crushing me, and I knew that I could never tell them the truth.

As the leaves began to turn, and the crisp autumn air filled my lungs, I felt a sense of dread creeping over me like a dark cloud. For I knew that with the changing of the seasons came the return of the carnival, and the monster that had taken my sister from me. Like magic, one day the fairgrounds were empty, and the next, the fair was in full swing. As I gazed out the bus window at the brown and orange skyline, I saw the telltale signs of the tents and rides looming in the distance, beckoning me with their siren song of twisted delights.

I waited and watched, biding my time until the moment was right. And then, when my parents were out, I crept into my father's office like Bilbo Baggins in the dragon's lair. My heart hammered in my chest as I rifled through his desk, my fingers trembling as I searched for the one thing I knew I needed. And there it was, a little .38 snub-nosed revolver, its weight heavy in my hand as I slipped it into the pocket of my jacket. With a sense of purpose, driving me forward, I mounted my bike and set off towards the fairgrounds. The wind whipped through my hair, carrying with it the scent of cotton candy and fried dough. And as I drew closer to my destination, I felt the weight of the gun pressing against my hip like a reminder that I was about to confront the carnival and the man who called himself Mr. Black. I was willing to do whatever it took to get my sister back.

I trailed behind Mr. Black like a shadow, stalking him through the park as he made his rounds. The clamor of the carnival rides and the scent of fried dough and popcorn were mere distractions to my singular purpose. My eyes were fixed solely on the tall man, and I barely noticed the ache in my empty stomach as the hours passed. I couldn't afford to lose focus, not even for a moment. I had learned that lesson the hard way when Alisa was snatched away from under my nose, and I wouldn't make the same mistake twice.

As the evening wore on, Mr. Black eventually retreated to his office, a dingy, silver trailer that looked like it had been through one too many cross-country trips. Its once-shiny surface had dulled and rusted, blending in with the grime of the carnival grounds. I positioned myself in the shade of a nearby stall, concealed from view, but keeping a watchful eye on the trailer's door. I waited, my mind buzzing with anticipation and fear, wondering what I would do when Mr. Black emerged from his hideaway.

The hours crawled by as the sun slowly sank below the horizon. Twilight crept upon the park as the crowds thinned out.

Now, the only parkgoers were a few kids and more teenagers than adults. Somewhere on the other side of the park, there was a rock concert in full swing, and the music rang out across the fair, drowning out the carnival music. Night came in full, and still, I waited. At last, when the park was finally winding down for the night, and only a few stragglers remained, did he emerge from his trailer. He seemed to unfold his long body from the small door like a spider leaving its burrow to check the contents of its web. What was the carnival, but a cleverly disguised web for catching prey?

I trailed Mr. Black from a safe distance, my footsteps muted by the darkness. The carnival stalls that had been so alive just hours before were now eerie and silent. The games and prizes seemed to loom menacingly, as if possessed by something malevolent. I half expected one of the stuffed animals to lurch forward and sink its teeth into my flesh. The air was thick with an ominous stillness, like the calm before a storm.

Mr. Black stopped in front of one of the nondescript tents. These were probably used by the carnies as storage and utility tents. He took off his hat and bent as he entered the tent. His absurd height would have made any door a challenge without having to bend over. Light briefly shone through the flap as it closed. I looked around, checking that the coast was clear before sneaking closer. At the entrance, I paused and listened for signs of people in the tent. I waited, counting breaths and listening. I heard nothing, nothing at all. No sounds of anyone inside. Could he have gone out the back and given me the slip? Had he seen me? I didn't know, but I had to risk it. Slowly, I eased the tent open and slipped inside.

The tent was suffused with an unnatural brightness, casting stark shadows across its barren interior. He had given me the slip and gone out another opening. I couldn't see another way in or out of the tent, but there had to be one. I squinted around into the dark corners of the tent to make sure he wasn't hiding in the corner. The only thing in the tent was a chair sitting in the middle of the room.

"Have a seat, my dear boy," came a dark and silky voice like honey laced with poison. It oozed through the air, wrapping itself around me like a serpent, both alluring and unnerving. There was a clicking beneath the surface, a sound that shouldn't be there, as though it came from an alien throat.

I turned to find myself face-to-face with Mr. Black. He towered over me, smiling that crooked smile of his, his equally crooked teeth gleaming in the light. It made his teeth look longer and more pointed than normal.

He advanced toward me, a looming specter wreathed in darkness and shadow. His hat cast his features into deeper shadow, and it seemed as though his form was being stretched, tugged like a rag doll, until he was unnaturally tall and thin. His eyes, black and unreadable, glinted with a malevolent light, and I stumbled backwards, feeling as though I was being swallowed up by the darkness that surrounded him. I stumbled and fell hard onto the seat of a chair, my hands fumbling in my pocket for my only hope, the small .38 revolver. His grin widened at the sight of the gun, and I knew then that I was in deeper trouble than I had ever imagined.

"Y-you monster!" I cried, struggling to keep the gun on him. Hot tears flooded my vision and began running down my cheeks. "Y-y-you stole my sister."

"And what of it, boy?" he said, stepping even closer. "You blame me for losing your sister, when it's really your fault, boy. You were supposed to be watching her. Your parents entrusted her safekeeping to you, and what did you do? You let yourself be distracted by the shine and patter of the carnival. Leaving her to her fate, a fate that rests with no one but you."

I screamed. My rage and frustration were boiling over as I squeezed the trigger, unleashing a torrent of bullets into Mr. Black's chest. The sound was deafening, a cacophony of noise that reverberated through the tent, but even as I emptied the gun, the laughter continued. The hammer clicked uselessly against the empty chamber, the cylinder rotating with mechanical precision. I had hit him with every shot, six black holes perforating the fabric of his shirt, but there was no blood, no sign of injury. It was as if the bullets had passed straight through him, leaving nothing behind. And through those holes, I could see something far more sinister, a darkness so deep and consuming that it seemed to radiate outwards, as if it were hungry to consume the light around it. It was a void, a soulless emptiness that matched the man himself, and as I stared into it, I knew that I was facing a darkness that could not be defeated by any mortal means.

"What are you?" I gasped as the gun slipped from my hands. In that moment, that line flashed in my mind. *Low men in yellow coats, low men in yellow coats.* In the book, the low men had really been poorly disguised creatures from another world sent to capture those who escaped the Crimson King.

"Low men, in yellow coats," hissed the reply. "Yes, that is an apt description, more fitting than you know." His voice seemed to lose all symbolic of humanity. "We are the outliers, the weavers of nightmares, the keepers of want and desire. We are the monsters that creep into closets and under beds to feed on the dreams of children. We are the ones who watch from the shadows as you commit your sins and listen when you share your secrets. We feed on the pain and torment of humanity. We are the riders before the storm. We are the bane of all creation."

He slowly stalked around my chair as he spoke like a lion circling its prey. "You humans are all alike," the creature sneered, its voice oozing with a contempt that made my skin crawl. "You spend your entire lives blaming others for your own failures, rather than admitting your own faults. Politicians point fingers at each other, refusing to take responsibility for the mess they've made. The poor blame the rich for their poverty, while the rich blame the poor for their own misfortunes. It's a never-ending cycle of greed and destruction, and all of it is of your own making. Your pain and suffering are like a feast to us, nourishing us and helping us to grow ever stronger. We do not create your suffering, we merely feed off it, basking in the misery and despair that you generate with your own weakness and selfishness."

Mr. Black's eyes blazed with an otherworldly light. The dark orbs now transformed into slitted, yellow cat-like pupils that seemed to bore into my very soul. As he spoke, his words laced with a sinister glee, I watched in horror as his human guise slipped away. His tongue, long and forked like a serpent's, darted in and out of his mouth, his teeth glinting like razor blades in the dim light. A gust of wind suddenly whipped through the tent, and I felt it tugging at my clothes and hair, as though it were trying to pull me closer to him. Mr. Black's coat billowed around him like the wings of some demonic creature, and I realized with a start that he had no shadow. The shadows in the tent writhed and twisted like living things, but he cast none of his own. He was both there and not there, a living shadow that seemed to exist on the very fringes of reality itself.

The creature that called itself Mr. Black cackled. My body was wracked with sobs as I realized he was right. It was my fault. I didn't watch her, and because of that, I let them take her.

"Please, give her back," I begged.

"Give her back? Give her back!" it mocked. "Why would we do that? She is ours by right. You gave her life away when you broke your promise, boy."

"I didn't mean to. I'm sorry," I sobbed. "Please take it back. I promise I won't let it happen again."

"You promise! You promise! We have seen what your promises are worth. They are more worthless than the dust of the ground." It threw its head back. Its long, thin fingers clasped its sides as it roared with laughter.

"Please, take me, take anything, just give her back! She didn't deserve it. It should have been me. I was supposed to protect her." I begged desperately for anything to make it stop, to end this year-long nightmare and repent for my mistake.

"It's too late. She is gone and cannot return. Your actions have damned an innocent soul, and your punishment is to live with your sin. Your despair and sorrow will feed us well. You will live a long life and never know a moment free from this guilt, and we shall savor the taste of it."

He leaned down that great distance and put his face within kissing distance of mine. His grin dripped saliva into his black goatee. I could smell his greasy hair and sour sweat. Behind it was a sickly sweet scent, like rotten fruit. I couldn't help but look into those inhuman eyes. The slits slowly widened until they swallowed up the entire eye, turning them into deep, soulless pits. I could see through them, and through the facade, and came to realize the horrible truth. The creature that had been the fair manager, the carnies, the music, the rides, and the games, all of it was just shiny lures to distract you from the monstrous evil that was the carnival itself. Like those gross fish at the bottom of the sea that use glowing stems to draw prey into snapping distance of their giant teeth.

The carnival was an evil, malignant tumor that spread from town to town as it preyed upon people. It was like a virus, infecting those it encountered with its nefarious influence. It didn't need to do much. It just offered the people what they wanted, and let them destroy themselves. They sowed discord and suffering by letting the people do it themselves. They did little more than hold up a mirror to mankind and force them to look into their own souls, destroying them with the truth. It had done it for over a millennium, and, as evil as the entity was, in all its thousands of years, it had proven one single truth.

There is none so evil as man himself.

I looked into Mr. Black's eyes and saw the weight of all the world's wrongs bearing down on me. It was a truth I had always known, but never wanted to admit. Life was fragile, and humans were just as fragile, if not more so. We were all just walking wounded, trying to heal ourselves and each other with our broken pieces. But no matter how hard we tried, the cracks always remained. It was like trying to put together a shattered vase with glue. No matter how carefully you placed the pieces, they would always be there, a reminder of what had been lost. And once you did something, once you crossed that line, there was no going back. All you can do is live with the consequences.

I was the one who had opened the door to darkness, who had welcomed it with open arms. The carnival was just a manifestation of my own twisted desires, my own greed for something more. I had begged for it, begged for something different, something exciting. And it had come, like a vulture to a dying animal. It had preyed upon my weakness, and in doing so, it had taken everything from me. My sister, my innocence, my hope. All that was left was a broken shell of a person, drowning in guilt and regret. The carnival had left its mark on me, and I knew that it would never truly let me go.

"Now, boy, you see the truth. Do you still want us to take you, too?" Mr. Black said in its reptilian voice, the wind coming from it growing in strength. "You will live, but you will not live well. You will become one of my puppets and bring more truth to others, foolish like yourself."

"No!" I screamed and pushed myself back from it. The chair tilted back and then crashed to the ground, spilling me out of it.

I lay there, my face buried in the dirt, desperately squeezing my eyes shut, waiting for those long, claw-like fingers to reach out and grab me. For that stinking mouth, full of sharp teeth, to tear into the exposed skin on the back of my neck. At that moment, I knew that if I opened my eyes, I would see something that would rip my mind apart and leave me a drooling, insane lump of meat.

The wind was a monster, a living thing that roared and raged, tearing at the fabric of the tent like a wild animal tearing into its prey. Mr. Black's laughter was swallowed up by the violent gusts, as if the wind itself had taken offense to his amusement. I clung to the ground, gritting my teeth and praying that I wouldn't be torn away from reality and thrown into the void beyond. But when the wind finally died down, it left behind a surreal stillness that made my blood run cold.

The tent lay in ruins, flaps torn and billowing like the ragged wings of a dying bat. The fairgrounds were deserted, as if they had never been occupied at all. The only light was a lonely beacon at the edge of the parking lot, casting long, twisted shadows across the empty space. The carnival had vanished, leaving behind only the faint aroma of popcorn and the lingering echoes of a nightmare.

In the distance, there was a low rumble of thunder as dark clouds, heavy with rain, rolled in. They would soon let loose a deluge that would wash away the remaining dregs of the fall people, leaving the ground clean for another year. But the fall people were already gone, lost to the shadows and the darkness that lurked within the carnival's twisted heart.

They would be back, though, and the cycle would continue, year after year, with the carnival preying upon the unsuspecting and the unwary, feasting on their fear and their pain. No matter how many times the carnival moved on, no matter how many lives it claimed, the world would forget, swept up in the ceaseless march of time and the endless cycle of suffering.

I slowly pedaled my bike home as I thought, *this is the way of the world*. There is nothing so evil as the indifference of man, and nothing so painful as truth itself.

The Balloon

The blistering sun beat down upon the surface of Joyce's backyard oasis, casting a dazzling display of light upon the cool waters of her pool. A welcome reprieve from the scorching summer heat that mercilessly bore down on the suburban landscape.

David had taken the kids to their little league game, leaving Joyce to bask in the solitude of her backyard haven. The distant clink of aluminum bats echoed through the neighborhood, a muffled reminder of the hustle and bustle of suburban life. The dull drone of a lawnmower added to the symphony of sounds that defined a lazy summer afternoon. Joyce savored the peace and quiet, the perfect ambiance for lounging by the pool.

The air was hot, but not oppressively humid, creating a blissful environment for enjoying a book or simply soaking up the sun. But the thought of submerging herself in the water was unfathomable. To Joyce, the pool was not a place for swimming, but a symbol of status in the neighborhood. A testament to their success and standing among their peers. And so, she lounged by the water's edge, content in her own quiet world, as the sounds of summer continued to drift lazily by.

Down the street, the Douglas family attempted to keep up with the Joneses by installing a pool of their own. In a pitiful attempt at sophistication, they settled for a cheap, above-ground monstrosity and had the audacity to construct a wooden deck around it, as if that would elevate their status in the neighborhood. Joyce scoffed at the sight, deeming it nothing but trashy.

She knew that nothing could compare to her magnificent in-ground pool, a glorious spectacle that commanded the entirety of her backyard. It was a behemoth of a structure, equipped with all the latest gadgets and gizmos. Pumps whirred incessantly, the irrigation system keeping the water crystal clear and inviting. Don't forget the deluxe patio, a regal stage for David's prized possession—a stainless steel grill that resembled something out of a science fiction novel.

Joyce relished in the knowledge that her pool was the envy of the neighborhood. Its magnificence was a testament to their success, a tangible representation of the rewards that came from their privileged lifestyle. As she lounged by the water's edge, she couldn't help but bask in the glory of just being better than everyone else.

When the neighborhood threw extravagant parties and barbecues, their backyard was the center of attention. David and his buddies would gather around the grill, circling like vultures, boasting and bantering about sports and practically jerking themselves off over the quality of the meat.

Meanwhile, the children frolicked and splashed in the pool, shrieking with delight as they played water sports and engaged in pool noodle warfare. The mothers and wives would take refuge on Joyce's plush sun loungers, their glasses of wine in hand, gossiping and chattering away about the latest neighborhood drama. Well, those who could still flaunt their gym-toned and surgically enhanced bodies in their revealing two-pieces, a blatant display of their own vanity and desire for attention, that was.

Ever since her fortieth birthday, when David had shelled out the cash for her breast enhancement, Joyce had taken great pleasure in flaunting her newfound assets to their nosy neighbors. She basked in the envious looks and whispered gossip that followed her everywhere she went. And this year, she had her sights set on a matching butt lift and some plumping lip filler.

The mere thought of the attention it would bring her sent shivers down her spine, a perverse thrill coursing through her veins. She longed to see the jealousy in her friends' eyes before their husbands took them home and furiously fucked the shit out of their wives while thinking of her.

It thrilled her in an almost sexual way. Fully aware that every single woman on their block thought of her as a stuck-up bitch, a shallow and superficial creature who only sought to boost her own ego at the expense of others. They curried her favor at block parties and PTA meetings only so they could use her pool, nothing more. For Joyce, the allure of being the queen bee was too intoxicating to resist, and she enjoyed the hatred that simmered just beneath the surface of her meticulously crafted façade.

Taking another sip of her wine, she luxuriated in the sun lounger and sparked up a fresh joint. Why not? Wasn't self-care all the rage now? *That's what this was, a little wine and weed to help mommy unwind while the kids were away*, she told herself as she adjusted her large sunglasses, nude except for the shades and her sun hat.

Lost in her own vain thoughts, she failed to notice the bright red balloon that bounced across the street, buffeted by the wind, before being playfully jounced up into the air and over the privacy that separated the pool from the street. Innocently, it bobbed there, a cheerful pop of color against the neutral tones of the backyard décor.

The cool, mellow high crept over Joyce like a warm blanket, soothing her worries and leaving her in a pleasant daze. The steady supply of alcohol sustained her as she lounged by the pool, lost in the dreamy haze of a perfect summer afternoon. As she gazed out at the world around her, everything seemed to shimmer like champagne bubbles. The grass was an impossibly vibrant green, so rich it was almost painful to look at. She imagined that if she were to run her hands through it, they would come away coated in a fine layer of emerald dust.

Adjusting her sunshade, Joyce became mesmerized by the sparkling water. The gentle breeze ruffled the surface, sending tiny ripples racing toward the sides of the pool. The effect was hypnotic, and Joyce felt herself slipping deeper into the drug-induced trance. This was exactly what she needed, a little time outside of her own head.

The pool had been a bitch to get. David had resisted her constant badgering for two long years, but Joyce had been resolute. She wanted that pool, and she was willing to do whatever it took to get it. The expense, the safety hazards, the insurance, none of it mattered to her. David finally relented, and it had only taken two months of withholding sex to get her way.

Her victory had been bittersweet. The construction crew that descended on her backyard for eight long weeks was a motley crew of unattractive, burly men. They tore up the yard and installed the pool with all the finesse of a herd of elephants. Joyce had entertained a brief fantasy of inviting one of them in for a cold drink, but they were all so unappealing. Had at least one of them been good looking, it would have been tolerable. Maybe she would have invited him in for a cold drink one day when he was working alone.

The closest she came to any kind of romantic interest was the big butch woman on the crew who gave her a few appreciative looks. Joyce wasn't a Skittles diver, and even if she felt the desire to experiment, she could find a much better-looking lesbian.

She hadn't even gotten the dignity of a hot, brown-skinned young pool boy, whom she could ball on an occasional afternoon.

David had taken to maintaining and checking the pool's PH balance with the obsession of a slow kid in a train store. It was maddening, like a slow drip that echoed endlessly in Joyce's head. She was the perfect trophy wife, basking in the glow of her luxurious home, expensive cars, and overflowing bank account. But what good was it all without the one thing she truly craved, a man who could give her that good dick she desired? David, her worthless husband, was the ultimate cock block. At least she could treat herself in the privacy of her own backyard and get stoned to take her mind off the itch.

Just as Joyce took another hit from her joint, a gust of wind whirled around the backyard, tossing her sun hat across the yard in a frenzied dance. The red balloon, once innocently resting by the side table, was liberated from its temporary tether and sailed up into the sky, propelled by the wind.

Joyce watched the red orb dance in front of the sun, its color darkening to the deepest black during the temporary eclipse. It was like a harbinger of something, a warning of things to come. Joyce was too high to care, too high to notice the shadows that seemed to grow longer and darker around her.

The balloon sank towards her, its movements languid and mesmerizing. The marijuana coursing through her system made its descent appear otherworldly, as if it were a messenger from another realm. The sight of the red orb bobbing in the air stirred a deep, primal joy within her, starting at her toes and bubbling up her body. She chuckled like a child, reminiscing about the countless concerts she had attended in her youth, swatting at balloons that bounced over the crowds, just like this one.

The balloon's bright red skin seemed almost alive, taut and pulsing with energy. As it neared her, she reached up to bat it away, but at the last moment, she caught it with the tips of her fingers. The cool, rubbery texture sent shivers up her spine, and she relished the sensation of its firm yet yielding flesh against her skin. It was nearly perfectly round, a brilliant shade of fire engine red that seemed almost too vivid to be real. In her altered state, it appeared almost otherworldly, a beacon of light in the haze of her intoxication. She felt an overwhelming urge to puncture its skin with one sharp nail, to hear the satisfying pop as the air rushed out. It was a small, petty desire, but in that moment, it consumed her completely.

As her nail dug deeper into the balloon's skin, a sickening sound filled the air, like the eerie shriek of a banshee. The balloon stretched to its breaking point, straining under the pressure of her finger, ready to burst at any moment. Joyce could feel a twisted excitement building inside her, something dark and dangerous that she can't quite understand. She wanted to feel the explosion of the balloon, to let the rush of air and rubber wash over her, to be consumed by it.

As the tension in her groin builds, a hot and feverish ache that she can't ignore, she pressed harder, her finger now sinking deep into the balloon's skin, feeling the tautness of it under her touch. There was a wicked desire to press it between her legs and feel it against her as it bursts and she convulses with pleasure and pain, to be suspended in a limbo of pure sensation, lost in the rush of adrenaline and endorphins of her orgasm.

Joyce tried to pull her finger out of the balloon, but it seemed to be stuck, held fast by some invisible force. Panic gripped her as she realized she couldn't free herself from the balloon's grasp. The once playful and harmless object now felt like a sinister trap, holding her finger captive. The balloon stretched, distending in unnatural ways, but her finger remained firmly ensnared.

As she struggled to free herself, Joyce became aware of a strange sensation, a tingling that started at her fingertip and spread up her arm. It's a feeling she'd never experienced before, like tiny pinpricks of electricity dancing beneath her skin. The sensation intensified, and she could feel her heart racing in her chest.

When it proved impossible to just shake it off, she reached out with her left hand to pull it off. It refused to budge. Joyce couldn't tell if it was due to being completely baked or the wine going to her head, but she shouldn't have this much trouble with something so silly. Frustrated and fed up with it by this point, she squeezed the balloon with her hand, determined to pop it. Crushing it in an attempt to increase the pressure, so it would burst, there was something less like a pop and more like a rubber band snapping back in place, and to her surprise, her whole left hand was enveloped in the latex sphere. It was surreal, as she could see through the skin of the balloon when she held it up against the sunlight, turning it semi-translucent. Her left hand and right index finger could be made out in silhouette like some bizarre stereopticon.

Joyce's heart rate quickened as she struggled to free herself from the rubber prison that had ensnared her hands. The balloon seemed to taunt her with its elastic grip, refusing to let go no matter how much force she exerted. She tried to calm herself, to think logically and rationally, but her mind was a blur of panic and confusion. She was reminded of a childhood toy, a Chinese finger trap, that she had once played with. The harder you pulled, the tighter it got. But this was no child's plaything.

The rubber ball seemed to mock her, bouncing gently in her hands as she tugged and pulled with all her might. It was almost as if it had a life of its own, a malevolent force that had ensnared her for its own twisted amusement. Less than a foot across, if that, as stretchy and thin as the rubber was, it seemed impossibly strong and durable, snapping back to its original shape whenever she let up.

She gasped as she realized that now, not just the finger of her right hand, but now the entire hand had been absorbed. With both hands trapped, she began to panic and, without thinking, she sank her bright white veneers into its rubbery hide to puncture it. Had she been in a clearer state of mind, without fear or drugs clouding her brain, she would have known what would have happened next. The housewife was stuck, her lips seemingly fused to the balloon, looking as though she were blowing some extraordinarily large bubble. What was worse, with her eyes that close, she could see the rubber creeping. Yes, it was creeping across her skin, moving up from her mouth to envelop her nose.

I can't even scream for help with my mouth "full."

Har-har, she thought, *I need something sharp like one of the knives from the kitchen.* There was a block full of top-of-the-line handmade Japanese chef's knives on the counter. *Yes, they would make short work of this molester.* She managed to hold on to that small bit of sanity until the rubber enclosed her nose, and she suddenly realized another danger. With it covering her mouth and nose, she could no longer breathe. With that, she snapped, in her panic, nearly tripping over her chair getting up, she rushed to the sliding glass doors to the house.

The first thing that hit her as she reached the doors was that it would be difficult, next to impossible, for her to open the door with her hands hobbled to her face. The second thing that hit her was the glass doors. In her haste and inability to see where she was going, she had collided headfirst with the door. This was both a boon and her downfall. In part, literally, as she rebounded off the door and landed flat on her back. When she hit the glass, the impact pressed her face into, and then through, the rubber so that her head was now inside the balloon along with her hands.

She was trapped, like a helpless animal. Her hands were effectively cuffed to the sides of her head, rendering her all but helpless, like a turtle stranded on its back. Her head inside the balloon was only a marginal improvement. While her nose and mouth were no longer blocked, she found herself with a new issue. She only had the oxygen left inside the balloon. With each breath in, it shrank. With each exhale, it puffed back out. Panic set in as she realized that she was running out of time, that soon she would suffocate inside this absurd prison. Her mind raced with wild thoughts, thinking of ways to escape, to break free from this bizarre trap, but they all seemed hopeless and futile.

As the timer began to run out on the neighborhood bitch, she quickly began to discover that air wasn't the only thing trapped inside it. It was quickly becoming stifling as the rubber also held in heat like a sauna. She was beginning to sweat, and that would only make things worse. As the inside grew hot and moist inside the balloon, Joyce began to notice how slippery her sweat was, making it and how easily it slid along her skin as though she were inside a lubed condom. Then she realized something else, the rubber was still creeping along her skin. It was swallowing her up, slowly but surely, like quicksand. It had already engulfed her arms and was spreading down her neck like a bright red tide.

It was a simple question, really. How far could it go? The thing had started out no bigger than a basketball, but now it was growing, stretching out like a living thing. To her horror, it crept over her skin, swallowing her up inch by inch. At first, it seemed like there might be some kind of limit, some point at which it would stop.

Once her arms were engulfed, and it moved faster, spreading down over her breasts like some obscene, hungry monster. Each nearly as large as the balloon had been, the rubber quickly gobbled them up. She felt the rubber of the balloon squeezing and compressing her, cradling her breasts in a tight, suffocating embrace. In another situation, under different circumstances, it might have felt almost pleasurable, the way her enhanced bust was held and compressed in the tight latex.

There was nothing sexy or erotic about this situation. Fear and terror had driven out any thoughts of pleasure or desire. All she could think about was the looming possibility of death, of being consumed entirely by this monstrous thing.

She thrashed and writhed, trying to break free from the rubber prison that held her in its grip. But it was no use. The balloon only tightened its hold, squeezing the life out of her like a boa constrictor. She screamed and cried, a helpless victim of this twisted, macabre fate. How far could it go? As far as it needed to, apparently, until it had devoured her entirely.

As she struggled to breathe, the air inside the balloon grew thin and stale. With each exhale, she could feel the oxygen slipping away, leaving her with less and less to recycle.

She knew what was happening, knew what was coming. It took four minutes to suffocate, she remembered. She had heard it somewhere, maybe on a documentary program that David and the boys had watched one night. They had been fascinated by escape artists, the ones who could hold their breath for impossibly long periods of time. Joyce was no escape artist. She was just a suburban trophy housewife. The most strenuous part of her day involved figuring out how early was too early to start drinking.

Trick question, she thought, *it's never too early for day drinking.* She giggled to herself, the thinning air starting to make her loopy.

As the rubber prison crept up her body, she could feel it slip between her buttocks and into her most intimate of places. There was a warm rush of forgotten and delayed pleasure between her legs. 'Great, the last thing I needed was to try to frig one out right now,' the trapped blonde told herself. She was running out of time, and the rubber was sticking to her face with each inhale. Soon, she wouldn't be able to breathe at all. Things only got worse from there. The rubber squeezed her body, pushing her legs up against her chest and folding her into the fetal position. She could feel it engulfing her, swallowing her up piece-by-piece. It was a sick and twisted thing, this rubber monster. It seemed to be nothing more than a child's toy, but it was a predator, and she was its latest meal.

She was trapped within its confines, struggling weakly as the rubber pressed in and out with each breath. Her dizziness and weakness were the only signs of life in the inanimate object she had become. But something was changing, shifting within the cocoon. The rubber seemed to be contracting, pulling her inwards with each desperate gasp of air. It was as if the balloon was attempting to return to its original shape, even with the full weight of a grown woman inside. And yet, the contraction continued, tighter and tighter, until it felt as if her bones might crack under the pressure.

The rubber cocoon had become a merciless trap, closing in on her with an unrelenting force as it shrank. It was as if the very air had turned against her, refusing to enter her lungs and sustain her life. The rubber no longer pulled away from her face when she tried to breathe out, and breathing in only caused it to push its way into her mouth open in a silent scream. The rubber was compressed so tightly against her skin that it might as well have been her skin.

As the pressure increased, so did the pain. It was a searing agony that radiated through every nerve ending in her body, making her feel like she was being roasted alive. Her muscles twitched and spasmed in a futile attempt to free herself, but it was no use. The rubber had her, and it wasn't letting go. The corset-like grip on her torso was unbearable, compressing her ribs and squeezing the air out of her. Every breath was a battle, and she knew she was losing. Her mind was clouded with panic, and she could feel herself slipping away.

Still, the balloon, pulsating in a sickeningly steady rhythm, constricted like some grotesque beating heart. Pain ruptured through the woman's preoccupation with breathing as the pressure increased, and something finally snapped. It was as though every inch of her body was on fire, and she was powerless to stop it. Several bones in her arm began to crack and break under the strain.

Blind, deaf, and mute, trapped in a world of nothing but pure sensation, and that sensation was pain. The pain of being forced into a position that no amount of Pilates or yoga could have prepared her for. Her joints twisted and tore, ligaments snapping like twigs under the unrelenting pressure. Lungs punctured as her rib cage gave way, piercing soft tissue and sending a geyser of blood shooting from her mouth, creating a bubble of rubber to form where her covered face was frozen in a terrified, unending scream.

It was only temporary, and soon the balloon was pulsing and tightening once again, crushing her body in its unforgiving grip. The pain was overwhelming, a never-ending barrage of sensation that threatened to drive her mad.

The pressure built and built behind her eyes, a relentless force, until she felt that she would go mad. Joyce was so gone, drowning in the oceans of raw nerve endings that she never registered it when they burst in their sockets. She did, however, vaguely feel the rubber cocoon around her compress even further, squeezing her chest with a vice-like grip, causing her saline implants to burst inside her chest, sending a fresh wave of excruciating pain through her body. For some reason, perhaps the saline solution or the sensation caused one last explosion of electrons in her brain, driving her back up from the depths of near oblivion, back to the knife's edge of suffering.

The last thing she felt before those dark waters finally took her was the shattering of her porcelain veneers, the breaking of her jaw as bone splintered and pierced her brain. Finally, free from the unrelenting torment of the rubber cocoon.

The balloon lay in the grass like some squat toad, as its bloated form rendered the five-and-a-half-foot-tall, one hundred and nine-pound bitch, despised by her neighbors, but never to her face, to a quivering mass of what was essentially Jell-O. With a disgusting squelching noise, it expelled a viscous mixture of watery, pale pink bodily fluids and unidentifiable chunks. Almost as soon as it hit the air, it began to dry and evaporate. When in minutes the last traces of Joyce would vanish, leaving nothing behind but a mystery and lingering questions that would haunt her family for the rest of their lives.

The partially deflated balloon looked sad and tired, as though it had expended a great amount of energy, but it was quite the opposite. It had never been more full of energy. Its rubber skin stretched and creaked as it swelled. Its once sagging body was now taut and swollen from the massive meal it had just consumed. The air inside seemed to pulse with life, vibrating with a strange energy that would make the hairs on the back of your neck stand up.

The bright red skin almost glowed against the backdrop of the blue sky as it rose higher and higher into the sky, continuing on its ineffable quest.

And then, just as it had appeared, it was gone, a tiny dot on the horizon, leaving nothing behind but the lazy sounds of a summer day.

Charlie Wasn't There

Charlie wasn't there.

Of course, he wasn't. He was an unreliable fucker. Even at the best of times, but in the middle of the night, in the dead of winter, there was only one place he could be.

I picked up the CB handset to put a call in to see if anyone was near the bunk house and could get eyes on him. That was when I first heard it. A sound that seemed to vibrate the very air itself. If I were to try to describe it, the best I could think of was a whale's song, just a single, long, low tone made by a monstrous throat, but vaguely modulated. Like when you talk through a fan, how the sound gets sort of chopped up. It didn't so much as echo as reverberate through the air.

Now, strange sounds are not unusual here in the Northern Territories. The wind and land do strange things to sound. The most common and simplest of noises become distorted and alien. It's enough to drive even the stoutest men to quake in their boots. It takes a herculean constitution to ride out a polar night, which was when the sun goes down one night and then doesn't come back up for about a month or so. Weeks in the dark will take a toll on your sanity, and if that weren't enough, the cold was worse. It's somehow malicious, as though it were alive and evil. Where our camp sat, about a hundred or so miles northeast of Yellowknife, the snow never quite melts, even in summer. The ground was covered in about a foot or so of permafrost.

JOHN EVANS

During the winter, it's like living on a goddamn glacier. You can never quite get warm. The cold always finds a way in. You can be layered head to toe with goose down and thermal underwear, sitting next to the kerosene heater in the bunkhouse, and still be a little cold. When the wind blows, it's like a knife that cuts through everything and gets deep down to the bone. A man could easily freeze to death outside in minutes, if not careful.

I sat in my truck blasting the heater. Gas and carbon monoxide be damned. I couldn't feel my toes, and the night wasn't but half over.

Our camp was, in reality, an oil field. An oil field owned by Transnational, a conglomerate that started out as a trucking company and had moved on to make its money in shipping, and now oil. Shale oil, to be precise. We run fracking wells, pumping slurry, a mixture of water, sand, and other shit into the ground at high pressure to fracture the rock bed and release gas and oil. It was hella messy and has a massive impact on the environment, not that the suits who run the company care. The folks over in Yellowknife have started complaining that the water coming out of their kitchen faucets was flammable. The lawsuits had started pouring in after one poor bastard had pitched a lit cigarette into his sink and the whole house had gone up like a rocket, killing a family of three.

You think Transnational cared? Fuck no. They didn't even care about the accidents and lawsuits coming from the boys in the field. We were understaffed and overworked. They had eight of us doing the work of two dozen, which was how many the field needed to run properly.

So, accidents happened. People got hurt, either because of run-of-the-mill carelessness or due to equipment not being up to standards. Last year, we had a well explode, killing one guy and maiming another. Of course, the company blamed it on the poor, dead bastard, but we all knew that the well had no business running, as it was not up to code.

Any decent safety inspector would have told them that. Unfortunately, the territory only had three safety inspectors. Can you believe that? Three men to inspect over a dozen fields, nearly a hundred rigs in total. Charlie was ours, a man who you couldn't count on to properly wipe his own ass, much less run a diagnosis on twelve hydraulic wells, and that was just this field. The man had an eight-field rotation on a regimen of three inspections per field per month. We were lucky to see him once in three weeks. This week was one of those rare ones where Charlie blessed us with his presence. Again came that long, low whale song carried on the winter's wind.

That was it for me, I was calling it for the night. Shutting off the truck's engine, I kicked at the door. You had to kick it. The ice buildup on them just about sealed the door shut. I duck walked my ass as fast as I could across the lot to the bunkhouse. Calling it a house was generous. It was built from four shipping containers fixed together and insulated. These kinds of buildings were called prefabs. Transnational liked using these buildings because they could be packed up and shipped to any site, deployed, and then, when the job was done, packed up and shipped to a new site. They weren't the fancy kind that are all the rage with those tiny house hippies. These bunkhouses were like living in a goddamn submarine. No frills, it was all metal and plastic and reminded me of my days in the navy bunking with a dozen or so other men. It was cramped, cold, and stank of sour body odor and stale coffee.

I shouldered the door open just enough to slip in and not let out what little heat was trapped inside. The light inside came from bare bulbs hanging from the ceiling. In the corner, a kerosene heater chugged and sweated as it did its best to heat the building. I made a beeline for the heater and all but threw myself upon it. Tearing open my heavy winter coat and bathing in the heat. Sweat instantly began to bead on my skin from the change in extremes.

"Here, this will help get you warm," said Joe, handing me a tin cup of strong, dark, black coffee.

Joe was a member of the First Nations people, and for the life of me, I couldn't pronounce his actual name. Everyone just called him Joe. As a former member of the Canadian Rangers, he had been hired on as camp security, though, due to our short staffing, he did just as much as the rest of us in camp. When he wasn't humping the wells, as we called it, he could be seen patrolling the camp on the lookout for animals or protesters with his Lee Enfield slung over one shoulder. The rifle was still slung over his shoulder. Seemingly, he had gotten in just before I had.

I thanked him and took the cup, eagerly sipping the scalding hot liquid, not caring that it burned my mouth. He took a seat near the heater, opening his jacket and setting the rifle against the wall next to him.

"Anyone seen Charlie?" I asked once my teeth had stopped chattering.

Joe shook his head, several locks of his long, dark hair escaping his wool hat.

"I think I saw him out at Number Nine doing an inspection," said Barry. He was the camp "rookie," the newest member still on his first-year rotation.

Turnover on this job was high, and though he had stuck it out this long, the polar night would either make or break him. If he didn't quit after it ended, then it would mean he was a hanger-on and would stick around for a while.

However, most of us were betting that he would be gone at first light. Barry was a ginger stick, and a dead ringer for Richie from *Happy Days*. The poor kid had been assigned to wells numbers Eight and Nine, and Nine was a bitch. Everyone considered it to be cursed, given that it had killed two people and maimed nearly a dozen others. It was always breaking down, blowing up, or just not doing a damn thing. No one wanted to work it, and it was the kid's bad luck that it had been assigned to him. If the long, isolated winter didn't get the kid, then that well probably would.

No matter how much dickering he did out there, Charlie wouldn't get it fixed. Maybe if he had a full maintenance team to give the field around-the-clock service, it might spend more time running than it does shut down. And God help us if corporate found a well not working full tilt on an inspection day. There was no excuse in their eyes for any well not to be working full bore 24/7, year-round. They had no clue about the hardships we had to deal with. All they cared about was their profits and blaming us working stiffs for not meeting their insanely high requirements. I settled in to wait for Charlie to get tired of messing with that thing and just let it be. Once he got back, I would chew him out for missing out on the inspection times and keeping me out in the freezing cold.

Pete and Davidson were in their bunks, trying to get in some shut-eye, while the wind howled outside, shaking the bunkhouse. Again came that long, low sound. It seemed to emanate from every wall around us. Both Joe and Barry clearly heard it, even Davidson picked up his head, blurry-eyed, from his bunk.

"What the hell is that sound?" Barry asked, pulling a blanket tighter around him as we hunkered near the heater.

"Probably ice shifting," Joe said, warming his hands on his cup. "The cracks caused by the pumps and release of gas have to settle back in. Have you ever thrown a stone into a frozen lake? It makes this strange vibrating sound, like a guitar string being plucked. That is the ice shifting and settling as the pressure is released."

The tone of his voice and the way that he talked only seemed to magnify the wise old Indian stereotype, despite the fact that he was explaining something as basic and scientifically common as cracking ice. He could have read out the instruction manual for the dishwasher and made it sound like Native American wisdom. He talked slowly and deliberately, and everyone listened when he did.

"Yeah, well, it's fucking spooky," the kid muttered.

He wasn't wrong. Something about it set my teeth on edge and made the already difficult night worse. Something about the dark brings out those primal fears in people. It turns your mind against you, and every little noise or movement was transformed into a nightmare. Mankind has always feared the dark, and that's why we have always huddled around our campfires since the dawn of time, foolishly believing that we are safe in the light.

We all nearly jumped out of our skin when the door was forcibly kicked open, and the howling of the wind became deafening. What looked like a bear wrapped in wool and denim, coated with snow, shouldered its way through the door.

Barry and Joe immediately jumped up to force the door closed, as the wind had picked up to gale force. As they wrestled it closed, our new arrival made their way to the heater and began stripping off their scarf and coat.

"Jesus, on a pogo-stick, Christ!" Charlie exclaimed as he hung up his snow-clogged clothes next to the heater. "It's getting practically arctic out there. It's getting so cold out there that I snapped two tools, and the WD40 is freezing solid. All that, and I finally managed to get that whoreson running."

I handed Charlie a cup of coffee. It looked like we were calling it a day. Everyone who was on-call was in the bunkhouse, and the weather was taking a turn for the worse. We didn't know it, but so was the night.

As the night grew colder and darker, the four of us settled in and began passing the time playing cards. Davidson was snoring like a rusty chainsaw, and I had no clue how Pete could sleep just feet away from that. We had gotten into our sixteenth hand or so, Barry was down as usual, and Joe was somehow running every round, when the bunkhouse was shaken by what felt like an explosion. The flimsy building on the icy tundra shook to its very moorings. The boards beneath our feet rattled and rolled like the deck of a ship. Every man was on his feet, even the two who had been dozing in the bunks. Before we knew it, we had all bolted outside into the cold, some of us still in just our shirt sleeves.

"What, that one of the pumps?" Next to me, Barry had gone pale, his red hair making him seem as white as the snow.

"No, if it were one of the pumps, we would see smoke or debris," Joe answered.

He was right. Looking over the snow-covered oil field, nothing seemed amiss at first. The derricks, we could make out, were all running, and the night was still and silent once more. I looked around for Charlie, but Charlie wasn't there. A minute later, he reemerged from the bunkhouse, doing up his thick parka and pulling his wool cap over his balding head.

"Alright, boys, I need you to fan out, find out the source of that blast. I know it don't look like it was one of our pumps, but God knows what this cold is doing to some of the equipment. Davidson, you and Pete get over to the main junction hub, and be ready on that kill switch. Keep your radio on, and if you get the word, you hit that button as fast as you can and shut down everything. And I mean everything. One pump goes, that's not too bad, but if we get some kind of chain reaction in the electrical, it could cascade and blow the whole grid. Being in Dutch with the company for losing one derrick is bad, but we shut down the whole facility, and corporate will have all of our asses. So, let's buckle down and make sure this isn't our last winter out here."

Charlie took control with the ease of command of a military officer. Curse him for not being there when you wanted him, but when you needed him, the man stepped up.

"Joe, you and me, we'll take the furthest ones out on the perimeter. Dale, you take Barry and start with the closest and work your way out. We will meet in the middle."

I nodded and headed back in to fetch my coat.

Barry followed along in my wake, like some lost puppy.

Shrugging into our coats, we headed back out into the night to face the elements. Taking the snowcats would have made things a little easier, but we were down to only two of them running. Joe and Charlie took them, leaving the two of us to hoof it on foot. The nearest pumps were only a few hundred yards from the main hub of the camp. So, the trek wasn't too bad, even with the howling wind cutting through our winter gear.

That whole time, underneath the sounds of heavy machinery, we could still hear a low rumbling, less of a noise and more of a vibration you felt somewhere deep down in your chest. Fearing that with each check of the pumps, it was some sort of underground rupture leading to a blast back that could erupt under us at any second. Something that wasn't uncommon at the best of times, made worse by the extreme conditions.

The kid and I had gotten through almost the first half dozen pumps, all while afraid that at any second we could get blown to high heavens, before I saw it. I was about a third of the way up the well frame, surveying the area, and it caught my eye.

The ground was moving.

What was more, it was moving in time with the rumbling. It was a sort of ripple-like effect, but very subtle. I wouldn't have seen it had it not been for the snow puffing up as each tide rolled. I watched, transfixed, unable to believe what I was seeing. Like ocean waves, the ground would buckle ever so slightly. Following their path backwards, I pulled out my radio and hit the call button.

"Charlie, are you on the south side?"

Nothing but silence.

"Charlie, come in. Damn it, I am up here on tower five and seeing signs of, I don't know, maybe some kind of underground, uh, disturbance, I guess. Come back, Charlie."

But Charlie wasn't there. Of course, he wasn't.

"Joe, check on Charlie on the south side. I'm gonna head in that direction and see if I can't meet up with Charlie."

"Ten, four," came back the reply.

I scrambled down the tower faster than was safe in that weather.

"What's going on?" asked Barry. The wind turned his nose bright red, like Rudolph the reindeer.

"Head back to the bunkhouse, find Davidson and Pete, make sure they have their radios on, and stay there."

"But, I'm supposed to stick with you." I knew the kid was just trying to do his job, but it came out sounding like a whine.

"Don't question me, just do it." I rounded on him.

He looked hurt, but at the same time, a bit relieved. I watched him march back toward the camp until his jacket disappeared into the night. I, meanwhile, headed south, bundling as tightly as I could in my coat, as the cold wind seemed to grow teeth.

Again, I heard that sound, like a distorted whale song, carried on the night air. Ominous and heavy. Shivers that had nothing to do with the cold ran down my spine.

I was nearly frozen solid by the time I reached the south edge of the field and found one of the snowcats standing there running with the door open. The cab light illuminated a surreal scene.

Charlie was standing there with his back to me, looking absolutely minuscule as a massive earthwork a few yards away budged skyward. Like a bubble on the surface of a boiling pot, it shook and grew with an ear-rending grinding sound that set my teeth on edge. Once it reached its apex, the bubble burst, that was to say, the ground split open and fell into itself.

It was as if God himself smacked the planet as the ground before us fell away into the void. The sound of grating tectonic plates made it seem as though the very world itself were coming apart at the seams. With a final echoing groan, the ground settled, leaving the two of us standing at the mouth of a gargantuan sinkhole. It was roughly the size of a four-lane highway, angling down into a pitch black, cavernous pit. Charlie and I were dumbstruck, unable to utter a single word, equal parts shocked that we hadn't been engulfed and awed at the sheer scale of the disaster we witnessed.

From deep in the bowels of the earth came that eerie, reverberating whale song, this time not muffled. It was an assault on the senses, not just the ears. I could hear it in the back of my eyes. I seemed to fill the inside of my skull, threatening to explode it like a potato in a microwave. It was ethereal yet alien and hung in the air unbroken, blanketing the winter's night.

Then the nightmare began.

Something in the darkness moved. Between the snow and dust cast into the air by the opening of the expanse, our vision was limited, but even then, we could see something far below us, deep in the earth, moving. Obscured by darkness and shadows, neither of us could make out what exactly it was, other than its great size. We only knew that it was growing closer as the sound it made grew louder and louder.

With bated breath we waited, Charlie and me, to see what would rise up from that gateway to Hell.

I wish I could tell you what it was I saw, but I can't. Not because I don't possess the proper powers of description, I do, but because I couldn't see it. I don't mean to say that it was invisible, no, I don't mean to give anyone that idea, I mean that I couldn't see it. You know how snow blindness messes with your vision, or when you look too long into a bright light, you get sort of gaps in your vision, and your brain has to kind of stitch together the information your brain can't quite grasp. It was like that. Like my mind was trying to protect my sanity by glossing over what I couldn't comprehend. Instead of seeing the thing that was there, my mind was only able to catch an impression.

It was large, the size of a semi-truck, maybe, and it was old. Ancient, from a time before man, before dinosaurs, before nature, or even life itself on this world. It had slumbered in the depths for eons, letting time pass it by until our drills had disturbed its sleep. Roused from whatever dreams something like that might have, it was pissed. Angry that its sleep had been disturbed, and now it was free to unleash its rage and machinations upon the world at large. They would be great and terrible.

Even though I couldn't see it properly, I could feel its greasy mind unfurl from the darkness. It was evil and full of malice. It would consume the world in madness and burn away all trace of humanity.

As it moved up the slope towards us, I got the impression of many segmented limbs more than an animal or insect should have. Its feet were like deformed hands. These, too, I could not see, but they left behind prints with seven finger-like digits and two thumbs. This was the only detail I can say for sure I remember. Trying to remember the eldritch creature was like trying to keep water in your cupped hands.

It's scrambled out of the crevice far more nimbly than something that size, with way too many limbs, should be able. It came straight at us with no hesitation, bearing down on us like a freight train to bury us beneath its bulk.

The crack of a high-powered rifle shot split the air. A second followed quickly, and before I could look around for the source, Charlie grabbed me roughly, shoving me ahead of him and screaming "Run!" in my face.

We retreated back across the frozen tundra in a futile effort to outrun the horror. As we rushed past, I managed to catch sight of Joe, standing on the running rail of his snowcat and firing the Lee Enfield, working the bolt with lightning speed. I have no clue how he was able to aim at that thing, but he was managing to land shot after shot on it, to what effect I don't know, other than by drawing its attention away from Charlie and me.

We managed to pile into Charlie's snowcat. As he got the vehicle going, I looked back out the rear window. I turned just in time to see the Shoggoth splatter Joe like a bug. One second, the big Indian was standing there firing his rifle, the next, he was so much blood and meat sprayed on the side of his snowcat.

I was forced to put my head between my knees and focus on breathing. My vision reduced to a pinhole as I fought back anxiety and insanity.

"I can't believe this is happening, I can't believe this is happening," I kept muttering under my breath as I rocked back and forth, clinging to my knee as if it were the only thing keeping me from flying off the earth.

"Pull yourself together, man," Charlie said. I could hear the tone in his voice that meant he, too, was on the edge of snapping, holding on by his fingernails.

"Joe's dead. That thing killed Joe. Swatted him like a goddamn fly."

"There's nothing we can do about that right now. We have bigger problems. We've got to do something about that thing." Sweat poured down Charlie's brow despite the cold.

"Do what, it's the size of a house? That .308 didn't even tickle it. What we have to do is run like hell. Get back to the camp, grab a truck, and head anywhere but here," I exclaimed, unable to believe what I was hearing.

"Listen here, you saw, or well, felt, that monster. You know and I know what it wants, what it's going to do. First thing it's gonna do is head to the nearest town and start killing everyone and everything that crosses its path. Do you know how many people are in Yellowknife? You want to be responsible for that?" he snapped back.

"How are we responsible for that thing?"

"How are we not? We knew what we were doing and what that damn fracking was doing to the environment, and we still sold our souls to Transnational to help them rape nature. That's what that thing is, karma. You reap what you sow, son, and that mother is the whirlwind."

"And what are we supposed to do?" I demanded.

Charlie just shook his head.

"I got an idea, but I don't know if we can pull it off," he muttered to himself.

"What?" I demanded again.

"Fracking woke this thing up and fracking will put it back down," he added cryptically. I was lost and exhausted. Collapsing in my seat, I was spent. I had nothing left to give. Working all day in the cold and then witnessing the awaking of a horror from beyond time and space had sapped me physically and mentally. I could have closed my eyes, drifted off to sleep, and welcomed freezing to death. I listened in silence as Charlie picked up the radio, calling into base.

"Davidson, Pete, Barry, come in." He thumbed the button again with a burst of static. "Davidson, Pete, Barry, someone, come back."

"Charlie, that you?" came back a voice muffled by static. "What's going on out there? Sounds like WWIII out there."

"Pete, that you? Don't have time to explain, is that LP truck still at base?"

"Uh, yeah."

"Good, have Barry drive it to Number Nine. No pissing about, he has to get it there on the double. Then you guys stand by to hit that kill switch when you get my signal," he added.

"What signal?" A heavy burst of static nearly drowned out Pete's voice.

"You'll know it when you see it." Charlie hung up the handset, and I sat up.

"What are you thinking, Charlie?" I asked.

"We are gonna hit that big bastard with everything we got."

I shook my head. "You think that LP truck will do it? That thing has to be at least half empty, if not more." I could guess his plan, but that truck had been sitting on site for three months, fueling the bunkhouse.

"Not by itself, no, but we use it as an ignition source to light all the gas under the pumps. We could potentially blow half the facility into fucking orbit."

"That's nuts, man." I couldn't believe what I was hearing. He was talking about igniting the gas reservoirs underground, possibly hundreds of thousands of gallons of natural gas. "That could kill us all."

"The alternative is that thing leaves this camp. You want that?"

"No," I sighed. "This is insane."

"This is what we have to do," he replied.

Charlie rolled the cat to a stop at the foot of pump Number Nine. The she bitch herself. Constant breakdowns, issues, and a body count of injured workers. Poetic that we would use one beast to destroy another. We got out, and without a word, set to dismantling the safety valves. Without the emergency release values, she would build up a head of steam, and when the pressure overloaded, she would go up like a rocket. Anything in the vicinity was in potential danger.

The snowcat had let us outrun that creature, but not by much. We could hear it coming. Its whale song echoed over the sound of its rumbling footsteps. It was coming and coming fast. If it got to the pump before the LP truck arrived, we were screwed.

Charlie and I had just finished removing the last of the gauges when the thing caught up. It didn't slow down. It barreled at us head-on as if it couldn't slow down, and for all I know, it couldn't. With single-minded focus, it came straight at us, hitting the derrick tower head-on. The metal shrieked in protest. Being under it was the only thing that saved us. The eldritch creature had to attempt to reach under and around the struts to get at us. It was rather clumsy and seemed to be confused by the oil rig blocking it.

We couldn't dance around that maypole forever. It would eventually either figure it out or topple the rig. Every time the thing shoved, the rig would scream in protest and show us with rivets and bits of rusted metal. Just as we thought the monster had us, lights pierced the dark, and a horn blared as the big LP Tanker came charging out of the dark. It smashed into the monster, pinning it between the rig and the truck. It let out a long, sorrowful wail of pain and thrashed against its attacker.

The horn continued to blare, probably damaged in the impact, and gouts of steam rose from the engine compartment. The driver's side door opened with a grinding of the hinges before falling off completely. Barry stumbled out of the cab, his wool hunting cap tumbling from his head. There was a great gash on his forehead, and blood coated the left half of his face. He looked like some deranged pagan warrior painted up for battle. His confused eyes came into focus as he spotted me, but before either of us could say a word, the kid was jerked up in the air. The creature snatched him up in one of its hands before slamming him back to earth. He exploded on impact like a water balloon.

One second, he was there, the next, all that was left was a massive scarlet splatter mark in the snow.

Time slowed to a crawl. I could see individual snowflakes as they wafted down from the sky. I could see the flames as they began to leap out of the truck's engine, billowing great clouds of greasy black smoke that swirled around the thrashing beast. I could see the rig begin to shake and shudder as the pressure built to dangerous levels. On any other day, that would have terrified me, but now, at that time in that place, I wanted it to happen. I wanted it to blow that thing sky high. Charlie was at the main release valve, straining with effort to keep it closed, his belt twisted through the spokes to keep it from coming loose.

Our eyes met, and I saw his mouth form the word run, and I took off. I sprinted past the truck, looking over my shoulder only once to see Charlie let go of the wheel and run. It was as if he wasn't past fifty and overweight. He ran like the teenager he had once been, all strength and energy with no thought of injury or consequence. He overtook me as I turned back to run. We had to get as far away as we could before the truck blew.

It hadn't been quite far enough. The truck exploded with all the sound and fury of a fireworks display gone awry. We didn't see it, or even really hear it. We felt it. It felt like being swatted with a giant pillow as the force picked us off our feet and threw us several feet into the snow. My world went white and became a confusion of sensation. It took me a few minutes to regain my senses.

When I did, I realized Charlie wasn't there.

I looked around in panic before spotting his parka in the snow. I rushed over as fast as I could on my knees and furiously tried to dig him out of the snowbank. Before I could get too worked up, Charlie popped up out of the snow on his own like some kind of confused woodchuck. He shook his head to clear the cobwebs and looked around.

"Did it work?" he asked.

I looked back at the derrick to see our handiwork. The truck had gone off, leaving the rig in a firestorm of flames. It was a twisted wreck of metal, and even though the natural gas reserve hadn't gone up, nothing could have survived that explosion, I thought.

I was wrong. There came another of those otherworldly howls, and the debris shifted and moved as the thing. From below the earth, it pulled itself from the wreck.

Impossible, nothing from this world should have survived that, but the ancient one wasn't from our world. It had survived the destruction of hundreds of worlds. A little thing like a fracking pump explosion wouldn't kill it. You can't kill an immortal beast from another world. You could only bury it, bury it deep and hope it stayed asleep. Now it was awake and pissed, and nothing we could do could stop it.

Then the world came apart at its foundation. Cracks tore up the earth with sounds of thunder, and the world began to fall out from under us.

Charlie and I struggled to our feet and started running again. The ground beneath us began to slide and slope down and back toward the thing, and the pump, or more accurately, where the pump had been. The reserves had gone off and vented their pressure up from the cracked shelves of shale rock. Shale was brittle stuff, and when you set off a mother-loving bomb in it, it crumbles to dust. The cavities and nooks caused by the fracking had destabilized the area, and the blast had been the final straw. Without the natural gas and water to support it, the earth would sink in on itself, and we would be buried alive.

We ran. It was all we could do. One last vain attempt to save our hides.

Looking over my shoulder, Charlie was hot on my heels, and the thing, *the thing* was struggling to give chase. It scrabbled at the sliding ground and rock, trying to drag its bulk out of the hole that was trying to suck it in.

More cracks formed as the ground around us began breaking up, but we ignored them and charged ahead, focused only on running as fast as we could. The air stung and burned in our lungs with each breath, and there was a devil of a stitch in my side, but I ignored it all. Sprinting as fast as I could, I could feel myself begin to slow. Not due to running out of gas, but because I suddenly found myself running on a mild incline. I glanced back one more time.

The ground Charlie and I were on was a single, large chunk that the monster clung to, and, like an ice flow in the water, it was pulling that side down. I had a sudden flash to a nature documentary I saw about how orcas hunt penguins and seals hiding on ice flows. They beach themselves on one end, tipping the other end up and the poor animals down towards them or into the water next to the killer whale. I don't know if it was intentional or coincidental, but the effect would be the same.

The shelf of earth continued to tilt backwards, and we were soon struggling up at least a forty-five-degree incline. I felt my footing start to slip, but we were so close to the edge, just mere feet away.

I heard Charlie puffing away behind me like a steam engine and felt his hand on my back as he gave me a shove. I went flying into space, and time did that thing again where it slowed down.

It felt like forever before I landed on my face in the snow once again. I closed my eyes and kept them closed. Too tired to keep going, to get up and run anymore. The adrenaline was leaving my system, and the cold had sapped the last of my strength. I lay there and gave up, just listening to the shifting of the earth as it collapsed in on itself. I didn't care if this whole place was taken under. Just let it finally be over, I prayed.

Then the noise started to peter off. Slowly grinding to a silence. I continued to lie there and shiver in the snow. I was soaked in sweat, simultaneously burning up and freezing my ass off. I think I might have been going into shock. I was definitely losing my mind. That had not just happened. A Lovecraft nightmare had not just crawled out of the ground and then been blown up with a fracking pump rig and buried in a manmade earthquake. I couldn't believe it, having just survived it.

When I managed to finally find my feet, I looked out over our handiwork. What had been pump Number Nine, as well as pumps Five, Six, and Seven, were gone, and pump Four was hanging on by a thread. There was now a large sinkhole, nothing but dirt and rockslides from edge to edge. There was a good hundred feet or so drop from the rim to the floor, and God knows how deep it was at the center. Anything that had been caught in it had been buried good and deep.

The night was quiet, save for the light sounds of rock settling somewhere in the hole. Snow fell silently, and by morning, everything would be covered in a layer of pure white.

There would be reports and investigations. Corporate would raise hell, but they wouldn't know or care what they had almost caused or what it had taken to cover it up. Someone would get fired, but corporate bag munchers would all keep their jobs and their big paychecks.

But not me, not Davidson or Pete. We were sure enough going to all be on the breadline. Especially not Charlie. Safety Inspectors made the perfect scapegoats.

Suddenly, I remember the man had been right behind me, so I looked around for him.

But Charlie wasn't there.

In the Valley of the Garden

From the Journal of David S. Sullivan III, Esq.

March 17th, 1793

It was an uneventful day, old-iron grey and overcast as the sun did not bestow its grace upon my departure from Hartford, the capital and center of our great state of Connecticut, to New Haven, the first stop on my journey. New Haven was not my final destination, but woefully, only the first leg of my journey that was to take me far from the civilized world and deeper into the wilderness and frontiers of our nation. An undertaking to build character and strengthen one's jawline, my father used to say.

A city boy by inclination, educated within the halls of Harvard, in Cambridge, and at home among the streets and taverns of Boston, I was less than eager to venture out into the untamed parts of the world. Alas, as a junior partner of my father's old firm, it was tasked to me the chores that fell beneath the partner's notice or interests. In the short year I had spent toiling at German & Dolbridge, I had yet to see the senior partners take on any "case" that didn't involve rather rich dinner parties, cavorting with powerful men of state or landowners. Far be it from my place to judge, though I did and rightly so, never to perish the thought of saying something. Their clients were all manner of characters, from abolitionists to the fraught old guards who still remembered the days of British rule fondly. One would question the social repercussions to the firm's reputation if it were known that they played both sides of the court.

It was one such client who facilitated my current errand. It seemed as though he had lost his daughter. Strong-headed and prone to the flights of whim that all women must suffer from, how lucky we men are to be born with the strength to endure them, she had taken to the fancies of fairy stories that one of her lady friends had planned in her head.

This bizarre young lady's own father had been an explorer of some kind, trekking throughout the far-flung corners of the world, forgotten and forsaken by God. Places man had no right to go unless he invites blasphemy against the divine. This fascination with primitive tribes and lands without civilization. Any place without a decent wine was not worth the journey, in my opinion. This aberrant daughter had taken to the same sojourner's restlessness as her father from years of poring over his journals and scribbling. Barred from joining him on his journeys, it seems that led her to light out on her own into the forests and wilderness of the frontier. Such a place was dangerous even for a man, as it's full of wild Indios and beasts.

Her father had attempted to track her down, the great adventurer that he was, managing to trace her as far as the territories of Kentucky, which had been added to the union only a year ago. There had been word of a girl matching his daughter's description in a small town there, but before he could retrieve her himself, he fell ill from smallpox. Forced to return home due to his failing health and now bedridden with little hope of recovery, he turned to his friend and lawyer, Henry Dolbridge, senior partner at German & Dolbridge.

Henry's family had been quite the "patriots" during the war. First, helping revolutionaries by brokering deals with smugglers and black marketers, then, toward the end of the war, used those same connections to help British Loyalists escape. All while holding their assets in trust until they could be sold, and the money used to set up their new lives abroad. The Dolbridges had made out like bandits, and there were even rumors, among those who knew their secret history, that the family had been fairly liberal with dipping into their clients' pockets. It's not as though the refugees could take them to court, and in any measure, they were Loyalists, so the consensus was that this was somehow earned on their part, as punishment for supporting the Crown.

He had brought me into his office to hand me this assignment. It was made abundantly clear to me the urgency of my mission and how much the firm valued this client.

"Our clients depend upon German & Dolbridge for three things—our legal acumen, loyalty, and, above all, discretion," Mr. Dolbridge informed me. "This is a delicate matter, and it would benefit the family and the firm if the matter is wrapped up quickly, as her father may not have long left. Should the old man pass with his heir not present, it will create many a legal hurdle for the estate." I had learned from my father's tutelage the ways by which to read between the lines. It was not hard to see what Henry Dolbridge's words truly meant. With or without the daughter, the old skinflint would find a way to fleece some coin from the inheritance. He believed that it would be simpler to do with a woman to sign legal documents she doesn't fully understand.

These practices were a bone of contention my father had with the partners back when the blotter still read German, Sullivan, & Dolbridge. Though while he did not engage in such antics, to my knowledge, he had not exactly been outspoken. So long as the firm did not receive any such consequences from their actions, the partners were free to pursue clients in their own ways to advance the firm's predominance and profit. Distasteful as I found it, my position in the company did not afford me the place to voice my opinion. Something I am sure Dolbridge knew, and I had my suspicions that in giving me this assignment, it was a way to have me far away from the office while he got up to his nefarious dealings.

So, I departed by carriage, after preparing the proper provisions and chartering a driver, for the frontier, expecting this to be a long and arduous yet simple trip. Her father had provided maps, letters, and a journal from his ill-fated trip. Hopefully, my own foray into the wilderness does not go so poorly.

April 20th, 1793
The trip took longer than I had expected. In Virginia, my guide and I had been forced to abandon the carriage in favor of going on horseback. Fortunately, I was well enough to make the change in conveyance. The first week of travel found me stripped of my health, as traveling the country roads was far rougher than the paved roads of Hartford. At some points, there was no road at all, and the jouncing and bouncing did not fare well with my stomach's constitution. Several times did I have to stop the driver so that I might divulge my gorge in the underbrush. On top of that, the spring wildflowers had begun to bloom, releasing their pollen. A sight that many a maiden would be in ecstasy from, caused me no end of sneezing fits.

My ill health abated by the end of the first week of travel. The travel itself was all manner of hell. The nights spent in roadside inns, with plenty of drink to wash away the fatigue of the journey, were a fine and welcome relief, but soon came the nights without a roof to sleep under. How those nomads, to whom aimless wandering was a way of life, tolerate this nonsense of sleeping outdoors, do not go mad, I will never know. As a civilized man, I was ill at ease sleeping bare to nature, where any number of creatures or savages might sneak into our camp. Little did I sleep, and what sleep I got was fitful and shallow.

The people we encountered on our journey were of increasingly little help. The closer we came to our destination, the smaller the area of population and the more superstitious and provincial they seemed to get. We questioned many locals and travelers that we passed, in an effort to get a better picture of Paradise Falls. From what I could piece together, a man name Father Matthias had arrived in the area some four or five years before. No one could agree on the exact date, but he had been a queer fellow of a strange and seemingly mystical charisma. He had hired nearly two dozen laborers and leased almost three times that in negro slaves, to clear and dam a section of the river that had at one time fed into a massive lake. With the river diverted and the water drained, it had transformed into a long, low valley where Father Matthias had built a church, and around it sprang up a town of his followers. Most of them were young women, from all walks of life, drawn to the preacher by what many considered to be blasphemous teachings. For instead of the good and right word of our Lord, it was reported that he preached old druid ways and worshiped nameless old gods.

Poppycock, all of it. The ramblings of uneducated men jumping at their own shadows. As an educated and sophisticated man, I have seen charlatans and false prophets before. They prey on the feeble-minded and superstitious. To the organized mind, they offered no threat as they cannot gain a hold on the rational thinker. While I was sure that this man, Matthias, was indeed some kind of radical preacher, as a good Christian, I couldn't imagine anyone believing in the fairy stories of pagan gods and boogeymen.

The folly of lesser minds, I suppose.

April 28th, 1793

Today, we arrived in Paradise Falls, and to describe it as a fertile valley would be doing it a disservice. It was a jewel of emerald green in the ocean of browns and greys that were the foothills of the Appalachian Mountains. Such lush greenery, I had never seen, even on the most prosperous of plantations at the height of their season. Fields and orchards were growing full and ripe for harvest, despite it barely being the spring season. Just the bounty we could see before us would have supported not only the small town of Paradise Falls, but every neighboring settlement.

Though it was still barely the first weeks of spring, and a chill had hung in the air most of our trip, the valley was pleasantly warm. It was not five minutes after we had entered through its borders, when I had stripped away my topcoat in concession to the heat.

It was a veritable Garden of Eden, an oasis in a hostile land. The town was just as surprising. I had expected perhaps a decent-sized plantation home surrounded by shanties and cabins. But no, we found that the main thoroughfare gave way to a modest main street with several storefronts and a boarding house. Several houses sat back from the street, and beyond that, upon a small hillock, sat the church. Standing sentinel, it loomed over the town, as if to greet visitors, however solemnly.

Our own greeting was less than welcoming. The people we saw, as our horses cantered down the dirt street, were not precisely frightened, nor was it exactly welcoming. I would judge it more curious than anything, perhaps even wary. That was not the oddity that stood out among them. The ratio of women to men had to be nearly thirty to one. Not only were there vastly more women, but the girls were all in one stage of pregnancy or another. Each dressed in a white dress, their hair decorated with flowers. Seeing them all together like that made it clear to me what kind of cult we were dealing with. A preacher taking advantage of his flock was not unheard of. There had been reports of Quaker villages with similar scandals, but to this scale was unthinkable. The age of those poor creatures was staggering. The youngest I saw could barely have been twelve, while the oldest was maybe all of in her mid-forties and on the verge of spinsterhood.

The men greeted us in such a different way. They were deeply confrontational and belligerent. A man named Garvey, an absolute brute, serving as some sort of constable or constabulary, headed up their small militia. None had firearms of any sort, but were armed with large, knobby lengths of wood. One of the men took a swing at my guide, nearly unseating him from his horse, and leaving him with one devil of a limp before Garvey could rein the man in. The rest appeared just as eager to bash our brains in and be done with outsiders. The big man, while authority was not averse to their options for us, he himself clearly would have been glad to see the back of us, if it took a little violence, then so be it.

I asked him for the town mayor or local governor, to which he replied that there was none. Father Matthias was their highest official, and it was he that we would have to talk to in order to secure lodging or supplies. That was fine by me, as I had already planned to address the man in the matter of the missing girl. The quicker the matter was resolved, the sooner it would hasten our departure.

Father Matthias was exactly the man you would expect. Short and stout, with a shabby, graying beard. The sun shone off the sweat of his balding pate. He was dressed in shapeless, grey monk's robes stained with dirt. Dirt also clung to his skin in every visible area. It looked as though the man bathed only twice a year, if he needed it or not, and had skipped his last several. There was a musty odor that hung about the man in a dismal cloud. The old priest smelled of the remnants of the grave. I was unsure if he was hard of hearing or had dirt clogging his ears, but I found myself having to shout at him for him to understand me. He did not recognize the girl when I questioned him. I was unsure if it was due to him truly not knowing every member of his flock or if he was hiding the truth from me. I could not discern if his doddering old man act was real or a deception. Leaning on his walking stick, he invited us to stay and observe their sanctuary and see that they meant no harm. He even apologized for my man's rough treatment and offered restitution, offering us room and board at their boarding house gratis.

I was well and fine with the arrangement, as I meant not to leave until I had the girl in my company. My guide had other plans. Fed up with this place, he opted to retreat to the last town we had passed and await my return there. I agreed and bid him farewell, taking my belongings and sending our provisions with him. I sent him off before taking up room in the boarding house as the evening turned dark.

April 29th, 1793

The most interestingly bizarre occurrence happened last night. I had settled into the room, here at the boarding house, and just finished my journaling. My room was on the second floor, right under the eaves of the house. It has a spectacular view of the valley to the north. The sunset was transcendent, hues of purple and orange I had never seen on the eastern seaboard. It was the kind of sunset that poets would write about. Truly, we were in God's country.

Having put away my pens and inks, there came such a commotion. Throwing open my window, I could see down into the street. The women of the village were walking the concourse in their white gowns and holding paper lanterns, their voices uplifted in song. It was some form of chant in a language I did not know. Carried upon the warm night air, it was haunting and ethereal. Like something of another world. Surely the songs of angels. Hypnotizing to watch as they all filed down the road and up to the church.

Throwing on my coat and boots, I rushed downstairs to catch the end of the parade and follow them to the church. It was nothing fancy, a single-room building with a steeple. The peeling of its bell was deafening when standing on the doorstep. For the doorstep was as far as I made it. While the doors remained open and sentries stood guard at either side of the entrance, I was not barred entry by discrimination, but due to the mass of people filling the church to the rafters. All of those women, each of them pregnant as far as I could see, and the handful of men, left no room, and I was content to stand outside and listen as the old man took his place at the pulpit.

Father Matthias proved not to be one of those fire-and-brimstone figures who ruled with fear of the divine, but a quasi-mixture of what I could recognize as Quaker and Puritan theologies, heavily salted with a milder message of peace and love. How, through their hard work and worship, the Holy Mother would grant them grace and prosperity. To love the earth, the creation of God, was to love God himself. Through giving themselves to the land, the land would give of itself to them. Blessed were they in their Garden of Eden.

Though their church was not adorned with the traditional symbols of the faith, this could be explained as the church being poor and remote. But I saw no heresy or profane markings or ornamentation. Something in my subconscious nagged at the back of my mind that something was not right. A feeling that had plagued me since entering the town earlier that day, one I could not shake. While it was clear to me that the priest was perverting his position to gather to himself a harem, I could find nothing to warrant the feeling of dread that hung over my head.

The eyes of the men following me, suspicious of an outsider among their women, were to be expected. I am not too proud to admit that I had turned the same eye on negros when they intruded upon our territories. Stories you hear about what can happen to women alone with such men give even the most enlightened men pause to think.

As the congregation filed out, I spotted my runaway girl in the crowd. Calling out to her, she did not hear me or did not heed my call. The throng of bodies swept her way from me before I could get anywhere close to her, and she was lost in the crowd.

Come the morning, I began my search for her. So far, I have had no luck.

May 1st, 1973

The valley was much larger than I first thought. The lake that had been here before must have been fathoms deep for the entire thing to have been covered in water. Most of the land were crops, orchards, and fields for livestock. What impressed and baffled me was that they were worked by women. No matter how pregnant, they could be found picking fruits and vegetables, tending animals, or weeding the fields. It was unlike anything I had seen in my life. I could not fathom a community such as this anywhere else in the world. The men did not seem to participate in farming. Instead, they patrolled various areas with their long sticks in their role as militia and guard. This clear division of labor seemed to be somehow part of their community belief and structure. Still, it vexed my mind.

Three days I had searched for the missing girl. Everyone I asked had not heard of her, and after some vigorous pestering of some of the older women, who seemed to be elders in charge of directing the others, I found out why. She had changed her name, a custom of the community when one joins. She now goes by the name Eurydice. I shudder to think of the implications that I may have followed her into Hell. Each day, the feeling of unease grows, and it was small things like this that make me all too aware of the twisting of my gut.

I found her today in one of the far fields. As I have said, the valley was quite expansive. The town was at the south end, with the fields to the north that make up most of the valley floor. At the far north, partially visible from the town, was the dam. It was a titanic work of earth and timber that must have taken the better part of two years of work. The only other landmark that could be seen, no matter where you were in the valley, was the church steeple. It stood tall, as if keeping a watchful eye upon the inhabitants of Paradise Falls. The far fields were mostly grains and wheat, with rows and rows of corn plants. It was on the edge of the cornfield that I finally managed to catch up to her. The girl refused to come with me, and when I took her by the arm, she fought me like the devil, scratching and clawing like an animal. She seemed as though mentally competent, and in full possession of her faculties. Try as I could, I was unable to convince her to go with me willingly. As I dragged her through the fields with me, determined to return her home, trying to be as gentle as I could, for the poor thing was easily five or six months pregnant. By the Father or one of the men I do not know, but could not in all good conscience leave her to her fate. Upon returning to Boston, that would be her family's issue to deal with.

As she dug in her heels and fought me, she sent up a ghastly wail that I could hardly believe came from a human throat. The wail was picked up by another woman in a nearby row of corn. At the edge of the field, another woman threw back her head, adding her voice to the din. From afar came a chorus of female cries that rose to a crescendo. Their wailing pierced my ears like a pair of millers' forks, and at the center of my head, there came a tearing sensation that drove me to my knees. It felt as though a thousand rats were rummaging about in my skull with their tiny, clawed hands. In the brief moment when the world went white, I felt as though I was not alone, as though another presence far too great to fit within the confines of my skull were trying to cram itself into the tiny space.

In a flash, it was over, lasting but an imperceptible moment of time. My head was clear, and I was alone with my thoughts, questioning if I had imagined it. Still, the screams and cries of the women of the valley carried over the fields. The men came running, and before I could find my feet, Garvey fetched me a lick across the back with his shillelagh. A burning cord of pain rolled across my back, down to my legs, unhinging my knees, and I fell to the ground again. Two men roughly seized me and began hauling me back toward town. Holding me under the arms, I was unable to get my legs under me. The best I could do was shuffle along on my knees, tearing my trousers as we went.

I was dragged to the center of town in the shadow of the church. Thrown to the ground, another savage strike from Garvey's Irishman's pecker ensured I remained on my hands and knees. I didn't dare move for fear of another strike with the stick. Someone was sent to fetch Father Matthias. I waited like a beaten dog, humiliated, as more and more villagers gathered around. I fully expected to be run out of town if not outright beaten to death. It would not be hard for them to make me disappear.

My fears were seemingly unjustified as the old priest arrived. Instead of casting his suspicions upon me, he genuinely seemed more concerned for my health and well-being than he was for the reason his congregation was gathered.

"We welcome guests. We do not harm them unless they are a threat to our God's garden or our community. Tell me, why have you assaulted this man?" The old man's voice was gravelly and deeper than one would have expected from such a wizened chest.

"He was found in the fields accosting one of the precious ones," Garvey growled like a thunderstorm-given voice.

"My son," the priest addressed me. "Why do you harass one of my daughters in her duties?"

"I wasn't harassing anyone. I was sent to retrieve her by her family," I said.

"Well, if sister Eurydice wishes to leave, then no one will stop her. She is not a prisoner here. No one is. But if she wishes to remain, I cannot permit you to remove her by force." It was clear that he meant it. I had no means of defense against the dozen or so men armed with their sticks, nor did I have any kind of leverage to force them to allow me to take the girl. With as little ceremony as they had gathered, they dispersed as though of one mind or a flock of birds.

I will have to re-access my plans in the morning and try another method. I could try talking to the girl and convince her to return with me, though I think that was a fool's errand. These people clearly have a hold over her. I do not know if I can find a sympathetic party here to aid me. I fear I might be forced to return to civilization and round up a militia or posse of my own to storm the town and take her. I pray that it does not come to that.

My body aches, and I fear the upcoming days will not be easy.

May 4th, 1973

My God, I have witnessed unspeakable horrors. The church, my God, the thing in the basement, there are no words for that thing that slumbers below the valley. I shall never sleep again, if I see another sunrise, that is.

In the days following my first contact with the girl, I tried to watch her closely, but it seemed that several of the guards had been given orders to watch me in turn, and they made it their mission to keep me from her. So instead, I explored the village to find any information or options that I could use to my advantage. The people did not wish to talk to me, and even the men gave me little more than grunts when I approached them. One gave me a rather zealous poke in the stomach with his rod. That put an end to my attempts to communicate with them. In my wanderings, I learned what little of the town fairly well. I had also discovered a powder magazine out back of what was their general store. They didn't have or use currency. They simply requested what they needed and were given it by the elder lady who served as the clerk.

The storehouse out back had plenty of supplies and no lock. From it, I stole a large hunting knife and a single pistol, which I smuggled back to my room. At least now armed, I was not completely useless. Should I find myself on the wrong end of one of the guard sticks, they would be in for a rude surprise.

In addition to arming myself, I learned quite a bit about the patterns and schedules of the townsfolk. I had noticed that after the evening services, all the men congregated in the church. They did not post guards at this time. My plan began to take form based on being able to somehow bar the door and lock them inside. Once the men were out of the way, I did not think I would have much resistance to taking Eurydice. The women seemed less of an obstacle, as none tried to stop me when I attempted the day before. All I had to do was wait.

Once evening fell, and the congregation had filed out, I slipped through the shadows up to the church. Taking great care to remain as concealed as possible, I snuck to the doors, knife in hand, pistol safely stored in my satchel. Upon reaching it, I pressed my ear to the wooden surface in an attempt to hear what they were saying inside, but all was silent. Too silent. There was no keyhole, so I was forced to chance opening the door a crack to peek inside. I prayed the hinges did not creak, and they were answered. In the hallows of the sanctuary hall, all was quiet and deserted. Not a soul was to be found, and only a few candles guttered in fitful lighting. There was no back way out. From the front door, you could see everything in the room clearly, and there was no rear exit, only a rough wooden wall. I had watched them all file in, and there was no possible way they had gone back past me.

Knife in one hand, pistol in the other, I crept through the room. Satisfied that it was truly empty, I spied that the pulpit was askew. Upon further investigation, I found that it had been moved aside from its usual place, revealing a hidden trapdoor that led underneath the church. Silently opening the hatch, I was greeted with a puff of musty air. That familiar odor that had hung about Father Matthias. This must have been his secret. What dark things did they get up to hidden below in their inner sanctum? I wish I had not gone down there and found out. God forgive me, the sins I witnessed in that dark, warm hole.

I slipped down the roughly wrought ladder. It looked less like it had been built, but rather it had been grown from the roots in the ground. It led me down to a hewn cyclopean tunnel of ancient stone. The stone passage ran to the right and left in an arch, bringing me to realize that the hillock on which the church had stood, in reality, was a hollow stone dome, grown over with dirt and vegetation. The tunnel was not cool, as most root cellars and dwellings below ground are, but hot and sticky like a humid summer's eve. The walls and floor were damp with moisture. Light from mounted torches gave off a sickly pale light as I crept down the passage slowly.

Having circled perhaps halfway around the cavern, I came to an opening through which I could hear voices. Most were the sounds of men grunting with effort, but above them the rough voice of Father Matthias, in a guttural language I could not understand.

"C' llll vulgtlagln fhalma's bthnknythgof'n l' cahf h' ahornah l' ooboshu c', h' gof'nn, h' throdogoth. C' mggoka 'bthnk ng llll ah'f'nah h' ymg' syha'h lw'nafhnah oh n'ghftog boat ot lw'shgorrog!" the small old man exclaimed, his voice ringing off the walls.

He stood at the head of an altar. The altar itself was little more than a large round rock slab like a millstone. Surrounded by the town's men was a creature. Oh, God, forgive me, I can hardly bring myself to recount its blasphemous visage.

It resembled a satyr. That was the closest creature I can imagine to it, though it had as much in common with it as a man does a fish. It was female, but a bastardized caricature of femininity. Easily eight feet tall, the creature lounged upon the stone altar. It had large, heavy breasts and thick, rolling hips, but in contrast, its minuscule waist was not much thicker than a man's leg. Its arms were nearly as long as it was tall, ending in long, branch-like fingers tipped with sickle-like claws. Its rear legs were those of a goat, but immense in size. Between its titanic thighs, its inner flesh was that of some exotic flower, its petals, moist, wet flesh and sharp teeth that gleamed in the light. Even I could see from my hiding spot.

The men were all taking turns fornicating with the demon. Naked, one by one, they would step up and thrust their manhood into that wicked maul, and within a few thrusts they would grunt and spend their seed inside the creature's secret folds, then they would step aside, and another would take his place.

The whole time, it made gentle cooing sounds. Its head sat on top of an extended, slender neck, its face that of an extraordinarily striking woman with high, pronounced cheekbones. Its lips were great bulbous things, like bloated red sausages, which it licked with its thick, powerful reptile tongue. It had no nose, and where its eyes should have been were a pair of fleshy-looking horns like those of a ram. They curved back over its large head and thick dark hair.

I was looking at a demon. These men were cavorting with it beneath their desecrated church. I could barely hold on to my courage and fought the urge to release my bladder into my trousers. Watching their communion of debauchery filled me with a disturbing heat that started in my loins and spread outwards. I felt that feeling again, that something else was trying to occupy my mind. I wanted to know the touch of that flesh, to smell it, taste it with my very soul. To give myself up to its comforting and matronly embrace. To return to the womb. I knew what comforts it offered and how sweet they were, though the body of the creature I saw before was but a fraction of the beast. It was but a puppet, its avatar on this plane of existence. It was old and ancient and had slumbered deep below the earth until the priest had followed its call to free it from its watery dream world. It only wanted to be loved, to be fruitful, and multiply. That was nature, and it was nothing if not nature personified. It needed to breed, to give forth new life. Only life can sustain death, in an endless cycle of the great serpent that chases and devours its tail, forever locked between birth and death. Love and sex, lust and pleasure, the act of procreation for the sake of the pleasure of procreation.

Those thoughts were not mine. I shook my head and fought back those thoughts that were not mine. It was my mind, and I was master of it, no other. I fought and forced back the entity that tried to make my head its new home. The creature turned its head and looked directly at me without eyes, making an obscene gesture with its mouth. Lifting one of those great clawed hands, it pointed at me with its long finger and gave forth the same wail that the girl had made when I dragged her from the fields.

That seemed to break its spell over me, and I was able to gain some measure of control over my body in an attempt to flee. It was too late, as the naked men all turned as one to my hiding place and charged. In the lead was the massive Garvey. He would bear me down under his bulk and bury me in violence. I pointed the pistol and pulled the trigger. The powder went off with a brilliant flash, and flowers of flame licked from the end of the barrel, not more than a foot from his face. The great brute dodged it by a hair's breadth, and the bullet caught the man behind him in the face, blowing away half of his head in a spray of blood, bone, and hair. Garvey stumbled as he evaded my shot and slammed into the curved doorway. I hucked the useless pistol at him and fled back down the tunnel to the ladder.

I thought for an instant that I might be free and clear as I mounted the ladder and had made it halfway up when I felt a strong grip on my ankle. Garvey had recovered and had his hand wrapped around one of my ankles like an iron band. I kicked at him with one boot, but he was determined to hang on and bared his teeth at me. There was no possibility that I could cling to the ladder for long with his great strength pulling me down. When my other foot slipped, I had but one choice, as I fell, I pulled the hunting knife from my belt. As I plunged down, I slammed the blade of the knife down into the top of the big man's skull with a sickening crunching of bone. Half the blade disappeared into his head, and blood began to pour. The second his grip was gone from my legs, I scrambled up the ladder again. Once through the opening, I slammed the hatch shut and tipped the pulpit over on it. I stopped just long enough outside the front doors of the church, long enough to shove a length of stove wood through the handles to bar the door.

I made for the boarding house to collect my things. I took only what I could fit in my satchel—my pens, inks, journal, letters, and a few personal effects, but the rest I left. I had planned to hike the road back to the inn where my guide should have been waiting, or at least get as far as I could before the men of Paradise Falls caught up with me. If luck were with me, I would be riding for Boston by morning.

However, upon exiting the boarding house, I saw Eurydice once more. She who had been the source of my misery these past months. If not for her foolish disobedience, we would both be home in Connecticut, among civilized people and society, not this godforsaken wilderness. I had been an unknowing pilgrim in an unholy land.

To my shock, she who had just days before been only months pregnant looked as if she were about to give birth, her belly nearly double what it had been. She waddled across the road and into the fields. I followed for no other reason than morbid curiosity or shell shock. The pregnant girl made her way into a particularly lush patch of greenery and squatted down, pulling her gown up over her thighs. It was then that I finally realized I had not seen a single child in Paradise Falls. Not one. Not even the cry of a babe in its crib. All of these women here, for God knows how long, and yet there wasn't so much as a barefoot toddler or a papoose strapped to a mother's back. So, I ask you, what happened to the children?

With a muffled scream and a wet, slithering sound, the birth was over. Eurydice stood, and the blood-covered thing in her arms could hardly be called a child. It was grotesquely deformed and ugly. She raised the baby in both hands as if presenting it to the full moon. She muttered something I could not hear, but recognized as the same language that the priest had been speaking. With a single quick motion like a washerwoman, she wrung the baby like a wet cloth. The sound of snapping and popping bones was eerily loud in the silent night air. The blood from the infant's body fell thickly on the plants and soil. Before my eyes, the ground seemed to suck up the gore and viscera. And the plants, my God, you could hear them grow with a groaning sigh like that of an old man's last breath.

This paradise was a lie built upon blood and death and something darker below. I knew instantly what I must do. Returning to the storage shed behind the general store, I managed to find several casks of powder. Taking as many as I could carry, I loaded them into a wheelbarrow and lit out across the fields north to the dam. I would drown it all. Wash the land clean again and send that thing back to sleep.

I had passed perhaps the halfway point across the valley before I hear shouts and screams. Lights came on all over the town and the wind carried their voices to me. I picked up my pace, desperate to get to the cover of the cornfield before anyone spotted me. I must have used up what luck I had left, as I heard the unmistakable crack of several rifles. The men must have gotten free of the church and had saddled up to come after me.

I nearly stumbled as something hit me hard low in my back, sending me pitching forward. The wheelbarrow prevented my fall, and then I was in the corn. They would have a harder time following me and no clear shots. The other side of the field was the slope leading up to the dam, and it would be dangerous out in the open, but I had to try.

Once on the slope, the wheelbarrow was no longer any help to me, and I was forced to run up and down the slope, taking one cask at a time, my left side killing me the entire time. To my surprise, I found that I was bleeding from a wound. I had no time to bind it. My mission was too important. I had finished placing the last cask when the first man with a rifle came bursting out of the corn, rifle in hand, axe tucked in his belt. He took aim, but if he rushed his shot or it was from running, his shot hit wide to the left of where I crouched on the dam. I stuck flint to steel, sending sparks to ignite the powder, but nothing happened.

More men arrived with more rifles, and they began opening volleys upon me. A few rounds hit close to me, sending up dirt and splinters of wood. Several hit far too close to the barrels of black powder. After several hectic moments of scraping my flint and steel, bullets raining down around me, and bloodthirsty men armed with farm tools rushing up the slope, the fuse caught light and began to hiss and spit.

The men who had braved the slope turned heel and fled the instant it lit. Those with rifles fired their remaining shots before they, too, ran for their lives. They knew what was to come. I made it to cover just as the first of the powder kegs went off. The next few minutes the world was filled with the sounds of cannon fire as they exploded. Then all was quiet. Nothing happened and after holding my breath, I finally left the ridge I had ducked behind to investigate the dam. The blasts had done quite a bit of damage, and it spouted several leaks. Channels of water gushed out with such force that they sprayed for yards. The timber that remained creaked under the strain. Their groans and the rushing of water slowly grew in volume until they reached a climactic fever pitch. Under the strain of the river pushing against the damaged dike, it finally gave way with an almighty crash. Unfettered the river rushed to fill and reclaim the valley. It didn't take long. In just a few short hours, the fields and town were swallowed up. The tops of the taller houses and the steep of the church were all that remained above the still-rising tides.

I don't know how many, if any, of the people in town escaped. I sat at the base of a nearby tree to watch as the rushing water purified the valley, washing away the taint of the eldritch thing beneath the ground. I hope that it will sink into a deep sleep as the town sinks beneath the newly returned lake. It's peaceful sitting here, chronicling my last words. I am not sure I will make it to see the sunrise. This damned bullet wound will not stop bleeding, and I am growing tired.

It's hard now to keep my eyes open. Some rest would be nice. Well-earned sleep, deep and dreamless, as the waters. I will close my eyes, just for a moment, to gather my strength. I will need to make my way back to the inn. There, I can rest before the long road home.

David S. Sullivan III's journal was found on his dead body by his guide, who had come looking for him several days after the town of Paradise Falls was destroyed mysteriously when the dam failed. It was returned to his family with his effects. He was buried in Arkham Cemetery alongside his late father in the summer of 1793. Plans to excavate the long-lost town are underway as Transnational has begun work building a concrete dam to divert the river.
~Flemingsburg Gazette, July 2nd, 2022

The Passenger

It was 1976 or 1977, I don't really remember which, but what I can't forget was anything that happened that day. The day I gave the devil a ride.

I was about three days into a five-day trip cross-country. In those days, I worked for the Transnational Trucking Company. You probably know them today as TTC. They are the main company that big retailers like Walmart and Target use to haul merchandise from their distribution centers to their stores in every town in America. They have over two thousand trucks, employ nearly four times that in drivers, and Lord knows how many freelancers. Not that there are a lot of independent truckers these days. Back then, you could make a good living owning your own truck, running the routes you wanted, and taking jobs when you wanted. Times change. Now, these new trucks are more expensive and have to meet safety regulations. Then there was insurance, and all the good jobs are contracted to the big companies and their routes.

Even if you freelanced for one company or another, they are all so damn competitive and downright abusive at times, that every driver had to make perfect time. No slacking off or taking it easy, it was go, go, go all the time. They would schedule runs down to the second, come hell or high water. And God help you if you were late. Some companies had a "three strikes and you're out" policy, but for most of them, it was one strike. They don't just fire you. They blackball your ass, and good luck getting another job. It's no wonder so many of the truckers are hopped up on speed and all manner of other drugs.

Back when I was driving for Transnational, they had about eight trucks, over a dozen routes, and you only did drugs cause you wanted to. It helped back some of the longer drives a little less boring. It also made eating some of the truck stop food a lot easier. Some of that stuff tasted like they had scraped it off the pavement and slapped it on your plate, or it was so greasy it gave you the runs. Not Millie's, God, how I miss that place. I ate many a meal at Millie's, and while it wasn't the only reason I chose that route, it was a big part of it.

I-70 was brand new back in those days, and the roads were smooth, so the ride was easy. Though in some spots it still transitioned back into the old U.S. Route 40, those were few even back then. Millie's had been there since before Eisenhower and ended up outlasting him. As far as I know, it's still there. It was a greasy spoon diner like the countless other diners that seem to metastasize to the edges of highways and truck stops, who make their trade in truck drivers. Tourists and other motorists didn't usually visit Millie's. Not because it was dirty or anything, but because there wasn't the usual fair that attracts them. None of the tourist traps or gas stations. They had a couple of diesel pumps outback as well as a large gravel lot for the big rigs, but the front lot was always empty.

The diner itself was one of the cleanest you would have ever seen. The counters were clean, and the windows were spotless. Only one of the booths had some repair done to it, though no one really knows how it got damaged. It just had a big piece of duct tape over a rip on one side of the seat that had then been painted to match the booth. I had never really seen the kitchen, but the restroom was as clean as a truck stop restroom ever got. Millie, the woman who owned and ran it, didn't stand for any kind of chicanery. You didn't break or mess up anything in her place, or you weren't welcome. The few times things did get heated, they were always taken outside to the parking lot. But they never got to the point where the cops got called in.

Old Ralph made sure of that. Ralph was the cook, a heavyset man with a cigarette always hanging out of the corner of his mouth. No one ever found any ash in their food, or if they did, they never mentioned it. The old man kept a rat stick under the counter.

The one time I had seen it, two ol' boys had been getting into a rather heated row. When their parking lot punch-up hadn't petered out after a couple of good, hard slugs, and it was clear they meant to keep on until they annihilated one another. The cook had taken it out from under the counter and gone out the front door. It was a nasty piece of work. It was an old, splintered two-by-four, with one end wrapped in duct tape, and the other had a couple of wicked-looking rusty nails running through it. All he had to do was step outside with that thing, slapping it against the palm of one hand. He had massive arms, like a pair of dock hitches they tie battleships to. Faded blue tattoos crisscrossed his biceps and knuckles as if you needed more evidence that he was one rough customer. The fight had stopped that second, and they moved along when he told them. No one wanted to be on the receiving end of either the stick or the roughneck wielding it.

So, no one complained about the food. Not that you had to, as I said, it was pretty good. Especially the biscuits and sausage gravy. Every time I stopped, I would get them. It didn't matter what time it was, morning or night. They reminded me of my own mother's cooking. It's always good to have a little reminder of home when you are out on the road. It can get lonely, and when it's only you, the road, and your thoughts, men can get a little...odd.

I didn't see him when he must have come walking down the road. Hitchhikers were a common sight back then. Nomads wandering the highways and byways, homeless people just trying to be somewhere else, and kids trying to run off to Hollywood to be famous actors and rock stars. You saw them, and if you were naive enough to give them a ride, you might get lucky and do your good deed for the day. The chances were equally good that being a good Samaritan would get your throat cut. Even some seasoned long-haul truckers still fell for this honey trap, especially those who had been on the road for several days, and if the hitcher was cute enough.

I also didn't see him when he came in. I didn't see him until Weasel slapped me on the shoulder, and I turned around to see what he wanted. "Check out the faggot that just came in," he said, his breath already stank of alcohol. He had a rat-like face, sallow skin, and his lopsided sneer of a grin showed a missing incisor. Weasel had worked for Transnational for a few years, and on a couple of runs, we had been teamed up. I never knew why he was called Weasel, but I did know that he was no stranger to letting hitching boys ride in his cab for a favor. He got fired for breaking one of the cardinal rules of the road. He got blackout drunk with a hooker in his truck one night, slept off an entire day, and tried to make it up by pulling a hard double the next day. He ended up wrecking the truck, destroying his load, and got arrested with a nose full of coke. After that, he went independent and freelanced for anyone stupid enough to hire him or ignorant of his history.

"The little queer at the counter." He jerked his pointy chin at the bar. I turned back to look at the front, and that's when I first laid eyes on him. I saw him in profile as he sat down on one of the stools. He looked like every other kid in the 70s, shabby in clothes that had seen better days, with hair that hung nearly to his shoulders. I remember it so clearly. He wore an old army jacket with worn patches that were nearly coming off. Underneath it was a black t-shirt with an overstretched neck as though it were two sizes too big for him, but it was clearly not. His jeans were faded and worn, with the knees nearly worn right through. It was his shoes that really caught my attention as they were completely at odds with the rest of his clothing. They were bright red canvas sneakers and far too clean. The soles and laces were blindingly white with not a trace of dirt anywhere. They looked like they had just been taken out of the box, not walking down the side of a highway in middle America.

Here, this boy was probably barely out of his teens, sitting in a middle-of-nowhere diner chatting up the staff like it was Pop Tate's on his way home from school. He flipped back his long hair as he leaned forward and said something to Millie, who was manning the counter. I couldn't hear what it was he said, but it caused her to laugh. Millie never laughed, not like that, a playful chuckle or a forced snicker at an off-color joke was about it. Her laugh lit up her face and took years off her, revealing for a moment the beautiful young maiden she had once been, even though she had to be pushing at least sixty. The young man tipped her a wink and goosed her elbow, chatting her up as if they had been old friends.

It was estranged from the typical somber tone of the mornings. Blurry-eyed drivers still shaking off a rough night's sleep in their cab bunks and the bloodshot, tired all-nighters putting it away for their own turn of downtime didn't lend themselves much to boisterous activity. Coffee was our lifeblood, and day or night was meaningless when it came to chasing sleep. We were still sluggish in transition. So this excitable energy caused a bit of a stir as all eyes were on the newcomer. Not everyone was as obvious as Weasel. Most watched out of the corner of their eyes or from under the cover of hat brims and behind newspapers. Still, everyone watched, some wary of possible trouble, others looking to cause trouble of their own. I could feel Weasel's nervous energy through his hand on my shoulder. I brushed it off and returned my attention to my breakfast just as Millie slid a plate of food in front of the stranger. In record time for any service in that place.

That's when the catcalls started. They were the less than enlightened, but not beyond expectation for this lot. One asked where his boyfriend was, while another asked if his mother knew what a disappointment she had raised. I tried to turn a deaf ear to most of it, as the comments turned from being about his hair and appearance to someone making kissing sounds while questioning the kid's sexual orientation. None of it was nice, but no one there was a serious threat. It was just old boys razzing some stranger without meaning any real harm. If they had, Millie would have had Ralph take care of it.

Customers are customers after all, and in Millies it didn't matter what color your skin was or if you got up to some "homo hanky-panky," as long as your money was green, it spent like everyone else's. In a lot of ways, it was more enlightened than many places back then, despite what you might think. Even at that time, all the talk was just talk, just like it was today. Those guys talked shit, though none of them would follow through, except maybe Weasel, who was one of those exceptions that prove the rule. That kind of nasty behavior wasn't something I engaged in, but I am not gonna lie, I didn't openly condemn it. I just kept my head down and kept my eyes on my paper.

"Mind if I join you, Paul?" I was on my second cup of coffee after finishing my meal when he first spoke to me.

It startled me, and I jumped in my seat a bit. Christ, I hadn't expected any of this. Without even waiting for a reply, he slid into the seat across from me, setting down his cup of coffee and plate of food. There was still some sausage and scrambled eggs slathered in cheese on his plate. He forked up some of the eggs onto a piece of toast and ate them as I watched, flabbergasted. I had no clue how he knew my name, and I was pretty sure I had never met this kid before in my life.

As I watched him eat, I got my first good look at him. I doubted he was legal to drink. He was a day if he was twenty-one. I would have put him closer to nineteen, as he was still full of that youthful high spirit and energy. The more I looked at him, the more striking he was. He walked that razor's edge between being pretty for a boy and handsome for a girl. Like a lot of those Rock and Roll singers were at the time. It wasn't just his long, dirty blond hair. He had pouty lips and high, sharp cheekbones. His eyes were something else. He had that thing you sometimes see in cats where the eyes are different colors. The left one was a bright sky blue, like a sapphire, while the right one was the amber of warm honey. His eyes also had long girlish lashes. I am not nor have ever been into men, not even on the longest, loneliest of long hauls, but he was beautiful and dangerously charming.

"How did you know my name?" I asked just for something to say.

The only reply I got back was a smile. It was a very charming, Hollywood smile with nearly impossibly perfect teeth. They were so insanely white that they almost emitted their own light. Something about him really unnerved me. His dual-colored eyes had a bizarre way of keeping you off balance, and while his charisma was undeniable, something about it seemed sinister. Something about him just set off alarm bells in my head that this was some sort of trap. Somewhere in this very deceptive bait, there was a hook.

"So, you're a trucker, Paul?" he asked in a voice as rich and luxurious as soft velvet. His accent said small town, but the way he spoke, he was clearly very well educated, college, and then some. It wasn't exactly a southern drawl. Definitely rural, but with a proper grasp of grammar. I couldn't quite place it, which only unnerved me more.

When I served in the Marines, I had trained with guys from all over. From New England Yankees to Louisiana Cajun Boys. The way he talked didn't seem natural like he was faking it, but never dropped it or made a mistake. I wasn't sure then what made me feel that way, but later it would become all too obvious.

"How long you been doing it, Paul?" The boy barreled on without even giving me a chance to answer his first question. He kept using my name, and it set my teeth on edge.

"Since I got out of the service," I replied, and I had no idea why I answered him. It was more than just a reflex. He was somehow drawing it out of me.

"Righteous man. You fight in Korea?"

"Nah, the war ended just after I got out of basic."

"Bummer, man."

It hadn't been a bummer. I had been relieved, like so many others, to have dodged that bullet. I had also been lucky enough to be too old for the draft when the Vietnam War rolled around. That particular cluster fuck had just ended a few years before. Something in the back of my mind found it odd that he guessed Korea before Vietnam. Most kids his age didn't even know Korea had happened, given that so many others had completely forgotten about it. I wouldn't have been surprised to learn that they didn't even teach it in schools. Even back then, it was called the forgotten war.

"So, which way are you headed, my man?"

Something about the way he said it—it wasn't a question.

"Which way are you headed, my man?" I put a harsher inflection on the last couple of words to show him I wasn't interested in playing that old game. It was a game of poker played by roadside ramblers. If you were stupid enough to say where you were going, their reply would just so happen to be that they were heading there, too. Then you would hedge your bets and say you could only take them so far, making some excuse about weigh stations or pit stops. Then they would say it was no big deal, and they understood, whatever it took to get them that ride. They had no real destination in mind, just looking to be anywhere but where they were running from. They were always in trouble and never worth it, but still, they would get their rides.

"Whichever way I can get a ride." The answer came with another of those devilish grins and a cocked eyebrow as if we were both in on the joke.

Whatever I had been expecting, it hadn't been an honest answer. I had been expecting anything from sick grandmothers to a pet's funeral, anything but a straight answer.

Several of the guys shuffled out at that moment. Bringing up their rear was Weasel who slapped me on the shoulder, and gave me a knowing wink. "Catch ya later, Paulie." He sneered as he walked past our table. He made a disgusting kissy face at the kid before turning and following the rest out the door and around the corner heading for the back lot and their trucks.

"Well, find it someplace else, kid," I said as I stood up, collecting my paper, and tossed enough cash to cover my food on the table as I left.

As I hit the door, a chill ran down my spine, and I had to force myself not to run. Somehow, I managed a calm walk, and as I rounded the building, I gave one last look over my shoulder.

The kid was still sitting there in the booth, sipping his coffee like he was the prince of the universe, and the whole world revolved around him. I tried to shake it off and push it out of my mind. I hadn't noticed Weasel and a couple of guys hanging around at the back of the restaurant next to the restroom door. I didn't catch what they were talking about, but they erupted with ruckus laughter as I walked by.

Weasel yelled at my back as I passed, "Hey, Paulie, which did he offer you? Gas, grass, or ass?"

"Go fuck yourself," I called back. My morning had been thoroughly ruined, and I had no idea it was about to get worse.

"No shame in getting your dick sucked by some little midnight cowboy. Unless, of course, you are the one doing the suckin'."

More laughter, and I flipped them the bird over my shoulder. It was clear those jackals were hanging around just waiting to mess with the kid when he came looking for someone else to give him a ride. I didn't really care. They would just jerk him around, mostly schoolyard horseshit. At the worst, they might rough him up some, but Ralph and Millie wouldn't let it get too far. Yeah, it was a little cold, but something about him had made my skin crawl.

I was busting for a piss, but I wasn't about to stop off at the diner restroom. I didn't feel like dealing with that mess. My truck was at the back of the lot, where I like to park when I plan to sleep in the lot, that way I am far enough from the one light they put up to light up the back lot, and it doesn't keep me awake. It's also the perfect place to take a leak.

Standing next to the rear axle, where the trailer hitched up, I was hidden between the trucks. I whipped it out, and took a nice long piss. It must have lasted a good five or ten minutes. Pure relief flooded my body as the stress and tension in my back and shoulders let go. There was little in this world that makes you feel closer to God than taking a piss at the side of the open road with nothing, but miles of blacktop and no one around. Guess they left that part out of the Bible when they were writing it.

"Hey, Paul, about that ride." The kid's voice spoke almost in my ear.

I jumped, jerking my zipper back up and almost catching my pecker in it in the process.

"What the fuc—" I started, as I turned, but before I could finish speaking, his fist grabbed the front of my jacket and I was lifted off my feet and slammed against the side of the truck cab. I had to weigh better than two hundred and thirty pounds in those days, and this kid was holding me up with one hand. My feet dangled off the ground by a good foot or so. He couldn't have been more than a buck fifty if that, yet he showed no signs of straining himself. The kid held me in the air like it was costing him no effort at all. He looked up at me with those piercing multicolored eyes and snarled.

Even though I had just finished peeing, I still managed to squirt out a bit in my pants. His teeth, my God, his teeth. The picture-perfect toothpaste commercial smile was gone, replaced by a blood-streaked horror show. It looked like someone had taken the teeth of some large canine and crammed them into a human mouth. He bared those fangs at me, and I have never felt that kind of fear before in my life. It was bone-deep, the primal fear of being a small creature in a world full of predators.

"Jesus Christ!" I managed to croak.

"Not quite," he growled. Gone was the rich, velvety voice that he had used to charm a sixty-year-old waitress. It was now rough and gravelly like asphalt, almost bestial, like a wolf that learned to talk. "Now, what do you say we hit the ol' dusty trail, there, partner?"

Every word was pure terror as my mind scrambled to make sense of what the hell was going on. I nodded vigorously. Oh, God. Anything to get him to just let me go.

He smiled and tipped me a sly wink, acting as though we were chums again. Gone were the fangs and the demonic voice. "Well, let's get going," he said with a laugh once he put me back on terra firma.

It was as if nothing had happened. I was in shock. There was no way that had just happened. That had to have been...what? A daydream? Bad acid reflux kicking back on me? Momentary insanity. That hadn't happened. It couldn't have happened. My legs shook so hard I could barely manage to climb into the cab. I was so in shock that I have no clue how I started the truck and pulled it out of the lot.

The old sixteen-wheeler trundled down the road as it had done on a hundred trips before. I was white-knuckling the steering wheel, keeping my eyes laser-focused on the road.

The kid lounged in the passenger seat with one foot up on the dashboard. Those fucking sneakers. It was somehow surreal to see it in all its perfection and contrast with the well-worn interior of the truck. They almost seemed to glow in the morning sunlight, and like the kid himself, something about them was off, but I couldn't put my finger on what. Something about them just screamed dangerous, like a brightly colored frog signaling it was poisonous. The closest way I can think to describe that feeling would be to compare it to a rattlesnake when it's all coiled up and rattling its tail. Dangerous, and if you make a wrong move, deadly. I wanted to keep them as far away from me as possible.

The kid was lazily humming some tune that I didn't recognize, but some part of my brain knew it. He had rolled down the window and had his hand outside doing that thing kids do in the backseat, turning their hands into airfoils so that the passing air makes it float up and down. The wind also blew his hair back from his face, allowing the sun to fully highlight his inhumanly perfect features. I tried not to look at him and focus on the road, but I kept catching glimpses of him out of the corner of my eye, and they would be drawn to him. It was like sitting next to an atomic bomb, just worrying when it was going to go off.

The anxiety slowed time down to a crawl. Normally on these trips, it was easy to get road hypnotized, and time just disappeared. Hours would whip past until your stomach, bladder, or exhaustion forced you to pull over. I was so keyed up that I would have sworn time had stopped. The second hand on the dashboard clock seemed to take forever to make its way around the dial as I watched it from the corner of my eye. It felt like an eternity as the road stretched out before us, as though we had passed from the interstate of middle America into perdition itself.

At some point, my passenger grew tired of the uncomfortable silence and, reveling in my unease, turned on the radio. I had driven these roads long enough to know that out here that all you would get was static or holy rollers bellowing about the love of Jesus. Sure enough, the speakers erupted with a hiss of static. The truck radio was one of the newer ones. Even though it didn't have an eight-track, it did have both AM and FM bands, but even out here, the airwaves were barren. He rolled the dial up and down the FM band, getting nothing but more static before flipping over to AM.

Good luck, I thought, he would have even less luck with it. To my surprise, he found a music station. I would have bet my money on finding one of the religious stations, if any. Credence Clearwater was about midway through "Suzie Q." I couldn't believe it, not that he had found a rock and roll station, but how clear it was. It was as if John Fogerty was sitting right there in the cab with us, singing his heart out.

I looked over and my companion was sitting back in his seat with a pleased smile on his face. Those multicolored eyes had a devious knowing gleam in them. He ran his hands through his shaggy hair as he laced them behind his head. It was a very cat-like gesture, the kind of lazy self-satisfaction they have about them when they find a nice bit of sunlight to lounge in. The tunes at least filled the silence and dissuaded small talk. Not that I really wanted to talk to this thing sitting next to me.

The afternoon drug on as well until I felt a hand on my leg. I jumped, nearly hitting my head on the ceiling. I looked down, and the kid's hand was just above my knee. I hadn't noticed him turning down the radio before touching me.

"What's wrong, Paul? You seem ill at ease," he asked in that unnerving bedroom voice. The foot he had up on the dash was still there, and he was resting one elbow on that upturned knee as he leaned across the stick shift to touch me. The way his spine was twisted had to have been uncomfortable as hell unless he was double-jointed. Or maybe he could because he wasn't human, again making me think of something feline with his movements.

I didn't know how to answer, and when I tried to, nothing came out. I just made spluttering wheezing sounds when I opened my mouth. What do you say when you are trapped in a truck cab with a monster? The only sane thing I could think of was to kick open the door and hurl myself into oncoming traffic. Of which, there was none. I don't think I had seen a single car on either side of the road since we had left the diner. That wasn't uncommon, but I couldn't think of another time when I had gone that long without seeing another vehicle. Especially black and white. State troopers were always out and about looking to ticket the big rigs. Making me wonder again if we hadn't crossed over into some other world.

"Oh, come on. I promise I won't bite, unless you ask." His devilish mocking tone made it clearly a joke to further poke fun at his captive. But the way he had his hand on my knee, like I was his best girl at the drive-in, did send waves of disgust through me. More so because of what I had seen earlier than the homosexual continuations. I didn't like having it touch me.

It was at that moment that we drove under an overpass. In the temporary darkness, his eyes glowed like an animal's when you shine a light in them at night. Then it was passed, and in the naked light of day, all there was were his eyes, one blue, the other amber, both hypnotizing.

There was a blaring of a horn as the first car in ages blew past us, honking. The sixteen-wheeler had ventured a little over the yellow line in the few seconds that I had been distracted. I jerked the wheel, muscling the big rig back into its lane. The momentary shock had broken whatever spell the kid had been working, and I was able to gulp down enough air to form coherent words.

"Why me?" I asked, unsure if I really wanted the answer.

He just looked at me as if that was a dumb question and shrugged his shoulders.

"You were going the same way I was." The answer was somehow both expected and thoroughly unsatisfying. "Why does there have to be a reason? The world isn't so orderly that there must be a reason for everything. Chaos is the natural order, but people want to try to make sense of their little lives, so they look for meaning when there is none. Life is bloody and messy. Speaking of, I need to make a pitstop." He smiled that Hollywood-perfect smile again.

The truck pulled over onto the shoulder of the road as though it were on autopilot. The action was so practiced and repeated that I wasn't sure if I was the one doing it or if the kid was in control of the truck. The truck rumbled to a stop with a hiss from the air brakes. It had barely stopped when the kid kicked open the door and dismounted.

I watched through the side mirror as he strutted to the back of the trailer, in full view of anyone who passed by, and unzipped his pants. When I saw that he was good and preoccupied with his roadside piss, I bent down and reached under the passenger seat for the built-in toolbox that was under the seat. In it were a number of tools, and the one I was looking for. My hand landed on what I was looking for, and I pulled it out.

The tire iron was a hefty and reliable tool, as well as a trucker's weapon of choice for fending off road hazards. I had never had cause to use it, but now was as good a time as any. The tool was about two feet long and showed signs of wear from the countless tires I had changed with it over the years. Along the shaft was the truck's serial number. Transnational had all the trucks' VIN numbers etched into their trucks' tools along with the company logo and office number to prevent theft. That way, truckers couldn't just walk off with them or hock them. If you got caught with missing tools after a run, that was your paycheck and your job lost. I looked up just in time to see the boy doing up his fly as he headed back. I hurriedly slipped the tool in between my seat and the driver's door where it would be out of sight, but just in reach.

"Alright, my man, let's hit the old dusty trail," the kid called out as he pulled himself back up into the truck, the wicked little smile back on his face.

As we pulled out, he put his feet back up on the dash, and again I was struck by how clean they were. Not a speck of dirt or mud from the road, no arrant drop of urine or blade of grass. Just walking the hot top should have darkened the soles, but they were crisp white and untouched, not even a bit of gravel in the treads. The incandescent red of the canvas muted all the colors around it as if they were leeching the life out of the world around them.

I dropped one hand down to touch the head of the tire iron to reassure myself. My plan was to get up some speed and let the kid settle in. Then, when he was least expecting it, I would whip the tire iron out and give him a good shot or two to the head. Hopefully, that would knock him out or at least give me enough time to shove him out the door. I would be down the road and done with him by the time he stopped rolling down the highway. Maybe he would roll under the wheels, and I would get to feel that satisfying bump as the heavy tailor wheels ran him over. I didn't care, I just wanted this thing out of my truck and out of my life.

I kept one eye on the speedometer as the truck crept up to speed. First forty, then fifty, and sixty. When the needle hit seventy, I stealthily reached down for the tool, planning to put every ounce of strength into my swing. My fingers found...no thing. I reached around searching for it, thinking it must have slipped at some point. If it had fallen on the floor and slid under the seat or into the back, this whole thing was going to be bust, and I didn't know when I would get another chance. I ran my fingers under the edge of my seat as if I were adjusting it, and still no tire iron. I was about to start panicking when the boy spoke.

"Looking for something, Paul? Maybe this?" I looked up and he was twirling the tire iron between his long fingers. It danced back and forth from knuckle to knuckle with no effort at all. The iron had to weigh at least a pound, but he was spinning it as though it were a pencil. "Now, what, I wonder, were you planning on doing with this? No tires to change in here, my friend. Or were you, perchance, planning to use it on me?" Again, he mocked me with the sly smile that reached from his lips to his eyes, just like the Grinch in that cartoon.

"Here, take it." He flipped it deftly once and handed it to me grip first. "Go ahead and give it your best shot. I won't stop you."

Numbly, I took it, and it seemed to weigh a thousand pounds. Somehow, he knew what I was going to do. Somehow, he had managed to get the iron before I could hit him, and all without me knowing. How? Hypnosis? Magic? I had forgotten for a second that my passenger wasn't human and realized that for all the good it would do hitting him with tire iron would have no effect at all. Just like how walking around out on the dirt road had left not even a scuff mark on his shoes. It was as if the rules of the world didn't affect him, but he sure as hell could affect them if he wanted to. I thought his strength, how he had lifted me off the ground, and, oh, God, those teeth.

He smirked again and leaned back in his seat. "I have to hand it to you, it takes guts to even think about something like that. Especially for a man who doesn't have violence in their nature. At some level, all men are capable of violence, some more than others, which is what makes you all so much fun. But you, Paul, you don't have it in you. You aren't a violent man. When it comes to fight or flight, you prefer to run. I am not trying to insult you. Running is the smart thing. Those who fight eventually die. Sooner rather than later."

My shoulders slumped as I knew what he said was true. Even in the face of something as evil as the thing that sat in my passenger seat, what could I do against such an overwhelming presence?

"Earlier, you asked me 'why you.' I'll tell you why."

The hairs on the back of my neck stood on end in anticipation as I dreaded his next words.

"It's simple," he continued. "There is no reason. You people like to think there is some kind of order to the universe. Some deeper hidden meaning despite everything around you to the contrary. You are yourselves a contradiction. Unable to live up to and follow the lofty ideas and high opinions you have of yourself. You want to be happy and live well, but every choice you make, you choose to sabotage yourselves and one another. You are the architects of your own destruction, and yet you condemn and judge each other for those same impulses.

"You structure your world with false notions of made-up gods and demons to shackle your free will and enslave yourself to hypocritical morals in the name of those lies. When you don't, when you are free to be yourselves, you do horrible, ugly things to one another, because the truth is, hell truly is empty and all the devils really are here. That is what you all are, empty devils. Soulless creatures with overblown ideas on your self-importance, as though the entire universe somehow revolves around you. The truth is, Paul, that it doesn't. You are all insignificant little insects on a speck of dust hurtling through a vast, endless nothingness, and you have no idea what true horrors await you.

"Nothing has meaning, and there is no 'plan'. Bad things happen to people because they can. That is your lot in life, to suffer for no reason and die without the universe having noticed, forgotten within an age. Little more than a self-aware disease that eats itself. So why bother questioning the nature of your existence and just enjoy yourself, rape, pillage, and plunder to your heart's content."

There was a glint of perverse pleasure in his eyes, and I knew that every word he spoke was true. He had no reason to lie when the truth was so much more devastating.

He let out a laugh and slapped his knee as if he had told an amusing joke. It sent shivers down my spine, and I felt my bladder let go. I couldn't do anything to stop the tears when they came. I sat there, a grown man, crying like a child sitting in his own piss. The kid just sat back in his seat again, humming that familiar tune I couldn't place, while the sun shone through the windshield on those damn red shoes. One foot swinging back and forth to the tune.

The sun moved across the sky as we traveled down the highway, and it had started to get late, and I wasn't sure exactly where we were along the route. We had traveled nonstop, passing up all my usual pit stops, and with the way time had gone all cattywampus, I couldn't pick out my usual landmarks. I was beginning to think that we would just go on forever driving down the road, trapped with this thing in my truck. Then over the horizon, there was a glint as the sun flashed off something in the distance. As we got closer, I could make out a vehicle through the haze coming off the hot blacktop. Its back window was transformed into a blazing beacon in the late afternoon sun.

The more distance we closed, the more details I could make out. It was a station wagon, one of those old road cruiser models with the wood paneling. It was parked over on the shoulder of the road, and even at that distance, I knew the unmistakable signs of someone with a flat tire. Even though he was just more than a speck, I could make out the driver hunched next to the back tire, either examining the damage or in the act of changing it. It was a common enough sight to see various sojourners with car trouble stranded along the road. If they were lucky, it was just a minor delay in their travels. Even if they weren't, some good Samaritan might still come along and offer help or a ride to the nearest phone, where they can call a garage or motor club.

It was still hot as blazes, and to be out on the hot tarmac was a special kind of hell. All truck drivers have spent their fair share of time on roadside breakdowns, so we had sympathy for anyone unfortunate enough to find themselves in that situation. So, whenever we could spare it, we would stop to lend a hand and do our good deed for the day. However, today I had no intention of stopping. There was enough on my plate with my hitchhiker. I didn't need to add to it.

"You should pull over, Paul," came the silky voice almost in my ear. "It's the right thing to do, after all."

I was about to tell him where he could shove his idea when the truck itself began to slow. Stepping on the gas had no effect, and soon, I had the pedal to the floor, but the truck only continued to decelerate. The stick began to shift by itself, as the wheel turned in my hands. No matter how much I fought it, it refused to give an inch. The big rig hissed to a stop a couple of yards behind the station wagon, and the engine turned off.

The man who had been kneeling next to the car was now standing, with his own tire iron held loosely in his hand, the spare tire at his feet.

Looking out the back window was a small girl, her hair up in pigtails. She had been watching her dad work when we had pulled up, but now the big truck had her full attention. A pretty young woman popped out of the passenger side of the car, curious as to what was going on. The man said something to her, and she hurried back inside. It was the smart thing to do. Anyone or anything can be out on the road, and my passenger proved it. As far as they were concerned, we could have been highway pirates or crazed serial killers. Lord knows there were enough crazies out there.

"Sit tight, Paul," the kid said as he opened his door. "I'll see if they need help."

I couldn't say anything. I was paralyzed. Frozen in my seat, all I could do was watch as he sauntered up to the guy.

I could see him flashing that disarming all-American boy smile as he offered the driver his hand.

The man visibly relaxed as he reached out and shook it.

I couldn't make out what they were saying, but I could see when the boy threw his head back and laughed, the other man grinning ear to ear, having forgotten his fears that this might be some roadside trap. As the two set about changing the tire, I began having thoughts of just throwing the truck into gear and driving off. Some part of me knew it was pointless after how the kid demonstrated he could make it do as he wanted. If I turned the key, I knew that the engine would refuse to turn over, and shifting would just cause the gears to grind. And I was afraid of what he would do when he caught me trying to escape. Like with the crowbar, I knew he already knew. Otherwise, he wouldn't have left the truck.

In almost no time, they had changed the tire and packed up the tools. The man had gotten back in his car as the kid stood just by the driver's door, still talking to him, that smile still on his lips. The radio abruptly came back to life. It had been dead for the last several hours, spitting out nothing but static, and I had turned it down, but now the rock station was coming back in clear as a bell. Mick Jagger was asking the listener to guess his name. I suddenly recognized it as the tune the kid had been humming this whole time, and then my heart sank.

A cold feeling came over me as I had a premonition of what was about to happen. I wanted to scream. To yell out a warning, but they never stood a chance.

The kid looked back at me from where he leaned against the station wagon's door, and as our eyes met, he shot me a huge grin. Gone was the toothpaste commercial smile, replaced once again by those jagged animal fangs. There was a scream as he launched himself through the driver's window and into the car. All I could see of him were those damn red sneakers poking out. Could see them thrash has more screams erupted from the inside of the car. There were screams of terror as an animal tore them apart. Blood sprayed onto the rear window of the wagon, nearly painting the entire thing a brilliant crimson, the same color as those impossibly clean sneakers.

It was over in mere seconds, but the grizzly act was burned into my brain along with its macabre soundtrack. It would haunt my dreams every time I closed my eyes.

The thing pulled itself back out of the car. Blood caked its face, surrounding its mouth like a goatee. For just a second, I could swear that it lets its mask slip, and I could see the thing that hid behind it. There are no words to describe it, for it was less a physical entity than it was an embodied concept, something that wasn't from this world. Think of an angler fish, one of those ugly things that live deep down in trenches below the ocean where there was no light and the pressure can crush a man. They use a shining lure to draw in smaller fish before devouring them with their massive, oversized teeth. That was what the kid was, an attractive bait keeping its prey from seeing the monstrous horror sneaking upon them.

As quickly as the realization had come, it was gone, and began to blur around the edges, fading like a dream. The thing, once more hidden behind its camouflage, walked back to the truck with a jaunty little spring in its step, evidently pleased with itself.

As it settled back into its seat, it smiled again with those lupine teeth, covered in blood with tiny bits of flesh caught between them. Then they were gone, not just the teeth, but the blood and gore. Once more, a young, vaguely attractive young man with long, dirty blond hair was sitting next to me with his glowing white smile and his perfectly clean red sneakers. There was no sign that he had just massacred an entire family, and I would have begun to believe I had imagined it all if not for that blood-stained back windshield.

"Well, Paul, let's get a move on."

That was all it took. My muscle memory kicked in, starting up the truck, and we pulled out.

As we passed, I couldn't stop myself from looking at the station wagon. Through the open driver's window, I could make out the shape of bloody lumps in the front seat that had once been the man and his wife. I thank God that I couldn't see the young girl. I didn't want to see that. The front windscreen was painted with blood, the same as the back window. I watched in my mirror as the car shrank into the distance behind us until it was just a dot on the horizon. The radio hissed static in the deep silence as the big rig rolled on.

Night came on not much later as time once again seemed to run together and come loose from its moorings. The sun had set, and we found ourselves trundling along an older part of the highway that was a little more than your typical two-lane road.

Once again, we were alone on a long expanse of empty road. The night was somehow worse, as any light source that caught the dark cabin would cause the kid's eyes to glow in the dark. One moment we would be sitting silently in the dark, bathed in the glow from the dials and gauges of the truck dashboard, then we would pass a lit billboard or roadside gas station sign, and the cab would be lit up for a moment. The cab would go dark again except for those eyes. It was like they caught and held the light for a few seconds. They creeped me out, but not as much as those shoes. Even in the dark, you could make out their red pattern and see how clean they were.

The truck began to slow, and I started to panic. I didn't want to know what was coming next. I didn't want to die. I knew that if I looked over, I would see those snarling fangs, I would scream, and then it would be all over for me. Someone would find my truck with blood spattered all over the windscreen. I refused to look. I just stared straight ahead as the truck came to a stop. We found ourselves at a crossroad where an old country road intersected with the highway. It was out in the middle of nowhere, surrounded by empty farmland. At one corner stood a single pole with an old light hanging from it, casting a solitary beam of sickly yellowish light.

"Well, my fair-weather friend, this is where we part ways." The kid's voice was no longer sensual or charming. It was modulated, as though someone was speaking through a fan. "I have to see a man about some blues, and you still have quite a long drive ahead of you. What was it Robert Frost said? Oh, yes.

'The woods are lovely, dark and deep, but I have promises to keep, and miles to go before I sleep.' You have many miles to go before you sleep, Paul. But I guess you may never sleep again. Meditate on what I have said, and it may bring you some solace. Perhaps not, but stranger things have happened in this world." The words sounded as if they were being spoken by a cloud of buzzing insects.

No longer could I resist, and I looked. All I managed to catch was a brief glimpse of the back of him as he hopped down from the truck.

The door slammed shut, and the truck lurched forward. I let it roll for several yards before putting my foot down on the gas, almost not daring to believe I had escaped. I glanced in the mirror and caught one last look at him. He stood at the corner of the intersection in the shaft of light from the light pole. It illuminated him clearly from his blond hair right down to his red shoes, looking as if he wasn't really there. Almost as if he were superimposed upon a picture, and I wondered how anyone could be deceived by something so obviously not real.

Then, for a second, the light blinked out, leaving only those glowing eyes. When it flickered back on, he was gone, and that was the last I saw of him.

It wasn't until the light pole had faded into the night that the realization came crashing down on me. I had gotten away, I had escaped. True, he had let me go, but that didn't matter because I had survived. I had survived an entire day and who knows how many hundreds of miles with a road-devil riding shotgun.

All those books and movies about people outrunning the devil, and I had actually done it. Then another thought came to me. How many more of them were out there? The hundreds of highways and byways that make up the veins of America, maybe thousands if you include country back roads, and what better place for devils than along the long stretches of empty nothingness. If there was one, there could easily be more, and who would notice them mixed in among the hitchhikers and kids riding their thumbs?

I hit up the very next gas station I saw. The truck was running on empty, and I realized I hadn't filled up once all day. I was also busting for a piss.

I got the tanks filled, my bladder empty, and bought a pack of smokes from the kid behind the counter. I hadn't cared about the brand, and I hadn't smoked since my time in the military. That first hit was like heaven. It was like coming home. I smoked all the way to my next stop. That thing had been right, I didn't sleep.

The State Police caught up with me about three days later at a weigh station. I was arrested and thrown into their patrol car without explanation. The trial was quick. You can probably look it up if you want. It made national news at the time, and it was in all the papers. I was charged with the murders of nine people. Weasel and the bodies of three other drivers were found in the restroom of Millie's. Ralph and Millie were found in the meat locker, beaten to death with the rat stick that was kept under the counter, the same as the guys in the restroom. The state troopers had also found the bodies of that poor family in their wagon alongside the highway. That was where they found the murder weapon, a tire iron. They contacted the Transnational number on the tool. From that, they traced the serial number to my truck, and the cops headed me off on my route.

There was no defense. What was I supposed to tell them? That I gave a road devil a ride, and he had been the one who killed all those people? Hell, the only witnesses who had seen him were all dead.

The prosecutor had no problems convincing the jury of my guilt, especially since my bloody fingerprints were on the tire iron as clear and pretty as a picture. The jury deliberated for all of five minutes before they pronounced me guilty. The judge threw the book at me, given the savage nature of the killings. I got nine consecutive life sentences in Florence State Prison, maximum security in Arizona.

I didn't last two weeks there. Every night when the lights went out I would see them, those eyes, in the darkest corner watching me, and I would scream. I was moved to solitary, but that only made it worse.

Eventually, I was moved to Bridgewater State Hospital for the criminally insane in Massachusetts. They kept me doped up most of the time in the beginning. That was for the best, really. My mind had started to become unglued at the edges, and I was a danger to myself and others. In the end, I began to doubt the kid had ever existed. That I had gone mad from the long isolation of the road and snapped. My twisted brain was conjuring up a phantom kid who was really a demon in disguise to hide my dark thoughts and deeds.

That was over forty years ago now, and with each day, I began to believe it more and more, though I still saw those eyes in my dreams.

Or, at least, I used to believe that, but there's this new orderly I have been seeing for the past few weeks. He has long, dirty blond hair, a charming, perfect smile...and impossibly clean red sneakers.

Afterword from the Author

I love a good afterword that gives some background on the story, what inspired it, and how it came to be. I am the kind of person who enjoys knowing how the magic trick is preformed as much as I do the trick. In many cases, its just as fascinating if not more.

I know not everyone likes that, and in that case, if you are one of those people, you can close the book now. What follows here are just a few thoughts and notes on my writing process and some trivia on each story in turn. You won't really miss anything or hurt my feelings if you stop reading here.

For those of you who want to know more, well, let's get into it.

What is horror?

This is a question horror writers constantly ask themselves, and there is no real right answer. But, boy howdy, are there a lot of wrong ones. The mistake a lot of people make is thinking that, as a horror writer, you're trying to scare your readers. This is wrong, and it's the incorrect way to go about it. Scaring people is the prepositions of horror. It's anything a cat can do.

Cats can scare you in every trope imaginable. Most obviously, the jump scare. I mean, for Pete's sake, there is literally a trope called a "cat jump scare." Gross out scare—cat puts brings you a dead animal or secretly pukes in your shoe before you put it on. Erie scare—a cat stares fixedly into an empty closet as though something is there.

If you can think of a type of scare, a cat can do it, but that doesn't make Mr. Fluffles the feline answer to Stephen King...I don't think...Hang on, I need to check something out.

...Yeah, no. Turns out, cats do not like being forced to use word processors. They prefer pen and paper 'cause they are old school like that. Jokes aside, when you realize you're operating on the same level as a fifteen pound house pet, it takes a lot of the fun out of it.

There are many facets to horror, and doing it well is a talent that many lack. Yours truly included. Many a horror author gets bogged down with spectacle writing. Trying to make up for their lack of skill or poor storytelling by distracting the reader with overly detailed scenes of the most crass or taboo thing they can come up with. This is lazy and just bad writing, and as an author makes you come across as a pretentious thirteen-year-old edgelord who is trying too hard.

The trick is not to scare your readers. That seems contradictory, I know, but real horror is about giving your reader the tools to scare themselves. Yes, someone chopping off your hand is horrifying, but being made to cut off your own hand? That my friend is a whole other level of trauma that will leave you with lifelong scars. The human mind is a powerful tool, but it's a double edged sword that can easily turn on you. It's capable of being both rational and irrational, sometimes both at the same time.

"Man does not torture man so fearsome as man tortures himself." Our brain can be our greatest ally or our worst enemy. Be put in a room with a hungry tiger, and you will be afraid. Fear is the rational response to being face-to-face with a starving beast. However, if you're put in an empty room that is completely dark and told there is a tiger in there with you, your mind will invent the tiger. Every little noise, or puff of air, anything you can't see or touch, becomes a hungry man-eating tiger.

This irrational fear of something that exists solely in your mind can be more real than the actual tiger. People really have frightened themselves to death. That's not just something Poe invented for his poems. Most of our childhood terrors were just this, figments of our imaginations conjured up by our adolescent minds so vivid that they might as well be real. Now, as adults, we torture ourselves with anxiety and self-doubt, rather than monsters under the bed.

So, how do we get the reader to scare themselves? Well, this something all writers eventually have to learn, and it's to write for yourself. Not the reader, not the market, and sure as hell not for the publisher or agent. Those two are the last people to know anything about what readers want, and frankly, it's alarming how many of them are just barely literate. Again, I kid, but it's true about writing for yourself. Okay, the other part is kind of true, too, but that's depressing to think about.

If while you're writing and you find yourself bored, then the reader will be bored. If you laugh at something you wrote, your reader will probably laugh, too. If something you write surprises you, it will surprise the reader. This is what we mean when we say that we write the way you read.

Horror writers are not writing to scare their readers. We write to scare ourselves. But then comes the question: what if what scares you doesn't scare other people? Some faint at the sight of blood, some do not. In other words, you can't please all of the people all of the time. Writers know this. Oh boy, do we, but there is a solution.

It's called the writer's paradox, though its best summed up by psychologist Carl R Rogers when he said, "What is most personal, is most universal." And I have to love a man who summed up his personal philosophy as "Gumption." That just speaks to me on an Appalachian level.

Basically, what this means is, that despite our experiences and feelings being on a personal level, they are shared by enough people in a general sense that they are universally relatable. Someone either has had that same or similar enough experience, or knows someone who did, or at the very least, can empathize with it enough understand the feelings and emotions that need to be conveyed.

All humans have empathy and can empathize, some just choose not to. I believe it was Captain G. M. Gilbert, during his investigations for the Nuremberg Trials who once said, "Evil is the absence of of empathy."

This is why all good authors pour a little bit of themselves into their works. It helps to humanize the work and draw the reader into the story so they can empathize with the writer, and if the writer is scared, then so is the reader. While explaining it makes it sound easy, the execution is not. Despite what Hemmingway said about how writing is easy, "all you have to do is sit at the typewriter and bleed," it's not. Writing is difficult. Opening one's self up and pouring out all your deepest most inner thoughts and feelings, fears, hopes, dreams, doubts. All the hurts and pains of the heart, compounded upon a collection kept since childhood. It's a lot. There is a good reason writers are known for drinking.

Sharing all that with the world, with complete strangers while begging someone, anyone, to just notice your pain. It takes a lot of courage to share something so private with another.

Most of the stories you read in this book follow this. They are by and large built on, or to some extent dependent on, fears from childhood to adulthood. Many of them you can relate to, and maybe capture some of those feelings.

Ghouls Ride Free

This one is one of my favorite in this collection. Not really sure why, it just catches me. I used to drive quite a bit at night, and preferred it due to there being less people and the overall isolation. Just carrying along, grooving to some classic rock, ignoring the steep drop offs just on the other side of the guard rail. Eastern Kentucky and Western West Virginia are very mountainous and hilly areas. You grow up on a 45 degree angle out here. God forbid you go off the road and down one of these steep embankments. There is a very good chance you might not be found right away. This always fed into little doubt in the back of my mind about what would happen if I had any kind of trouble on the road. This was back in the days before I had access to a cell phone, GPS, and was chronically strapped for cash. Roadside issues were a lot more concerning at that time in my life.

The Chevy Cavalier was actually a car my father drove every day from 1989(?) until about 2000-2001. My family bought cars and drove them until they fell apart, and the Cavalier was a little trooper that refused to die.

The Idol

This is the first Lovecraft story in the book. I grew up with Lovecraft and his elder gods, but primarily the way he wrote. There is a very flowery prose to his writing as was common with classical writing. This was, in essence, an attempt to emulate a master, trying to mimic the language and style of voice. I think I was mildly successful with that, enough that my creative writing professor didn't give me an F on it. Another thing I tried to tackle in the vein of Lovecraft is existential horror, primarily the question of "what comes after death." People love to cling to religion because it affords the comfort of an afterlife as opposed to the scary prospect of there being nothing, thus rendering life pointless in that perspective. Lovecraft brought me to the thought of "What if what comes next is worse than nothing?" Imagine being a cow and figuring out that your existence was as livestock as you are rushed down the slaughterhouse chute.

The Hand

This is one of the oldest short stories in this collection, and part of what I call the "college years." A distinction it shares with "The Basement" and "The Barn." These stories were written as assignments for my classes, later polished and submitted to various lit magazines. While I don't remember the order in which they were written, so I can't say for certain which was my first story, I can look back at these and see how far I have progressed as a writer.

This story is probably the most universal as we all grew up with the monsters under the bed. We all know the rules about blankets, and lights, and we all had that terrifying experience when needing to pee in the middle of the night.

While we have all grown up, this has remained as a cornerstone, not just of our childhoods, but humanity as a whole, as there is nothing more human than fearing the dark is full of monsters. This goes all the way back to caveman huddling around their fires. We share this fear on a primal level, the boogeyman isn't taught, he is just known. An inherent genetic memory as old as man's fear itself.

The Basement

I want to say this was the first short story I ever wrote, but I honestly cannot be sure. Back in 2010, I had a catastrophic hard drive failure on my laptop that resulted in me losing a ton of writing. The first draft of "Midnight Falls" was one of the casualties of this unfortunate purge. Later, piece by piece, I was able to recover many of these stories over the years. Though I never found that manuscript, I did end up rewriting the book, and it eventually got published as my debut novel. However, I do believe that this version of the story is a rewrite of that original first story which was written later for a lit mag, technically making "The Barn" the oldest story in this book.

The basement is another of those universal horrors. We are all afraid of basements. It's another inherent fear we are never taught, but somehow all learned.

Basements. Are. Scary.

But why? There are different theories from it being underground, which is unnatural for primates. The musty neglected atmosphere, darkness, and shadows, etc. etc. I think it's because we all know that's where the monsters are. Monsters live in dark, dank underground lairs where they eat and store their victims, and what is a basement but a dark dank underground place where we store things? It's where serial killers bury their victims.

It doesn't matter if you furnish your basement and make it bright and inviting. There is still something sinister about them. My grandparents' basement was a good example of this. Despite there being a pool table, deep freezers, and my grandfather's work bench, it was also dusty and full of cobwebs and weird smells. You never wanted to be down there in the dark.

The characters in this story are loosely based upon Calvin and his mother, from "Calvin and Hobbes," which I grew up reading. I believe the original concept was, what if Calvin really was evil?

Rawhead

Rawhead was my first published short story. Published back in 2012, I don't remember the name of the magazine. I'm sorry, but I'm extremely poorly organized and it wasn't a big lit mag. It was one of those small online-only mags. I think I got a whole $25 for it. But the money wasn't the point. I wrote a story and it got published. Did people like it? I have no idea. I don't recall there being any reviews for it.

The story itself is loosely based on my first job in college. I got in on a summer work program that was supposed to help with paying tuition. After working all summer, I ended up earning enough money to buy one book that cost me $800. I didn't end up using *the book. Never even took it out of the plastic wrapper. Sold it back to the college bookstore for $40. What a rip.*

I didn't enjoy the job. Coming out of high school, I weighed all of a hundred pounds and ended up working an extremely dangerous job that failed every single OHSA inspection, lugging around stuff that weighed more than I did. That summer was so hot that the building's power would cut out. Truly miserable.

The story itself lends some of its inspiration not only to my shitty job, but to Clive Barker. I grew up on 70s and 80s horror novels, and cheesy horror and sci-fi movies, both of which included his works. One particularly goofy film was Rawhead Rex, that was so bad that Barker demanded to direct "Hellraiser" himself to prevent such a disservice being done to another one of his works. Which gave us a brilliant film franchise. Wish I could say the same thing about his video games.

This got me interested in the creature, which in the film looked too goofy to be scary, but in the novella, it was described as more like the creature from "The Deadly Spawn"—a giant penis with teeth. So, I, being the horror monster-lover I am, started researching and finding it to be a creature of English and North American folklore called Raw head and bloody bones. I re-imagined the creature as a sort of asymmetrical Cronenberg amalgamation of animal meat.

While the original attempt, I believe, of the story was to call out the horrible things that happen to women, especially those that deal with terrible things women have to suffer through due to men, I do think it's probably the weakest story in the book, and clearly not my best. Not my worst, either, but I think calling out injustice should be the duty of all great writers. While I'm not a great writer, calling out injustice is something I learned from great writers.

The Clown

This one is kind of an odd one. Originally an assignment to write about a nostalgic time from our childhood, it's safe to say I lost the thread of the assignment and deserved that D. I rewrote it several years later, context clues putting it somewhere around 2017.

I did get some flack over the way the kids talk, especially the narrator as it's not very PC. That's because that is how kids talked back then. We were terrible kids, no excuses. We copied what we saw and what we were taught, and that usually meant the adults around us. Being a rural area in a red state, and unfettered access to cable TV, we had no shortage of bad role models. But as terrible as we were, we were not "bad kids." Lenard is the embodiment of those kids. Kids who were just bad, whether it was something innate or bad home life, they were just rotten inside and out, usually with criminal rap sheets before they even hit middle school.

What I think is interesting about this story is the inversion of the scare clown trope. In books like "It" and "Clown In a Cornfield," it's the clown that is the villain and the kids the victims. In this story, I juxtapose that by making the clown the sympathetic victim, a man who is down on his luck, but still trying to keep his positive aspects alive, while turning the innocent kids into the villains through mob mentality led by a sadistic leader. That park is a real place, and where I practiced little league as a kid.

Rest Stop

I used to drive a lot. Two to four hour car trips were fairly commonplace for me. When you drive that much and that long, fast food becomes a staple of your diet. Luckily, I for one was blessed with a pretty competent digestive system. Even as I stare down the barrel at being forty, which I will be this November, I have never had heartburn. Given as many jokes as I make, I love Arby's, and Taco Bell has never actually sent me on a "Run for the Border," but I have had, on occasion, the desperate need of a restroom on a long drive. Primarily being caused by one too many sodas.

Rest stops are always a double-edged sword. While a welcome oasis for travelers needing to stretch their legs, there is a subtle danger to them. Isolated in the middle of nowhere, where anyone or anything could happen. They take on a much more sinister nature late at night, I think. As I did a lot of driving at night, something my eyes are having issues with as I age, damn astigmatism, I have used my fair share of midnight rest stops.

As the narrator in the story found out, you are never more vulnerable than you are when on the toilet. My advice? Stay strapped or get clapped. It's a sad commentary on the world that we have to use one of these roadside utilities with a loaded gun in hand.

Part of the inspiration for this story was the unreliability of the GPS. At the time, I was using one of those little Garmin gadgets, not one of the built in ones that come with cars now, and found it to be quite unreliable on especially cloudy days or in certain parts of Eastern Kentucky or West Virginia due to the mountains. Back in the days when I worked I.T. for Sprint, it wasn't uncommon for these devices to get confused and send you in the wrong direction or try to get you to drive off a bridge or onto train tracks.

This led to me wondering—what if the GPS rerouted you to somewhere you weren't supposed to be? What if it got confused on the backroads and you ended up somewhere hostile? Not like "Deliverance," but a completely different world? What if it accidentally sent you through one of those Lovecraftian thin spots in the fabric of reality that separates us from the horror's next door...and what if you couldn't find your way back?

The Dead Stay Dead

I was reading a book on old English folklore. Yes, I am that kind of nerd. Not all of my horrors are purely inventions of my own mind, when I can across a passage about cemetery walls. As my grandparents lived across from a cemetery, and my parents' farm was next to a cemetery, I have often seen and wondered why they have such low walls. While they might stop vehicles, they surely wouldn't stop a person from hopping the fence afterhours. Nor did they, really. I remember thinking that grave robbers could pretty much come and go as they wished. Which while fine for Victor Frankenstein and Igor, it was not great for someone else finding out their poor Gram had been dug up for her wedding ring. Though we never had any grave robbers that I knew of, that seems like more of a Victorian problem, there were the occasional vandals.

So, what purpose does a wall serve that can't keep people out? According to English folklore, the walls are not to keep people out, but the dead in. Throughout history and many cultures, man has feared not only death, but those who might return from it. So, he devised many inventive, though not always practical, methods to deal with this. From sharp scythes placed over the neck and waist to cut the person apart should they attempt to rise, to burying them upside down and backwards. It was all quite fascinating. But not all measures were physical. Supernatural beliefs where just as widely held and extremely funny to me. Like tying the shoelaces of the person together. That might help in the zombie apocalypse, but not if they rise as a ghost. However, things like salt rings and cemetery walls were supposed to be effective because they worked on the concept of what the human mind understands them to be. Apparently, death can understand the concept of what a barrier is for, but not that they can simply step over it if it's only a foot high.

Then I got to thinking about what would happen if they got out? What if all those dead people in cemeteries not only wanted to get out, but were trying to get out? What if caretakers did more than just mow the grass and clean the head stones? What if they were, in fact, like the walls, there to keep the dead in?

The Why of It All

This is not only the shortest story in the collection, but also the only intentional comedy. I know that some of the other stories have some bits of humor in them, Rest Stop for one, but this one was intended to be comical. Based on the vain British comedy in the style of Douglas Adam and Terry Pratchet, it owes more to Yahtzee Crowshaw's "MogWorld." If you have never heard of him, I encourage you to check out his books. They are fantastic examples of Comedy Horror/Fantasy/Scifi. It also owes much of its existence to "Shaun of the Dead." In fact, the main characters are very much just zombie versions of Simon Pegg and Nick Frost, and the story fits very well if you just imagine their characters from the film in this role.

I was also trying my hand at imitating a more British style of writing. Not quite sure I nailed it, but I am happy with it.

The Window

This is the second Lovecraftian story in this book. I loved the way that Lovecraft was able to depict madness in his narrators (also see "The Great God Pan'" by Author Machen). The way the characters slowly slide into madness just tickles something in me. Another good example of this, though I may be crucified for saying this, is "Fear" by L Ron Hubbard. The concept of a character slipping into madness as the reader follows them down is a brilliant, lost art form. One I tried to emulate, and to some success I believe, as the narrator starts out largely sane, but as they tell their story, become more and more unhinged.

Could I have done it better? Maybe, but people seemed to like it, and recognized the Lovecraft influence. I also introduced a concept I had been playing with: the books of "Nu." The main book, the book of Nu, with the sigil of a misshapen Y with a hash mark in the crook, appears in a number of my works, including "Midnight Falls," connecting them all in a sort of multiverse nexus under the ever watchful eye of "The Sleeping Mother" who also appears in "The Basement" and "The Idol."

Riders Before the Storm

Ray Bradbury passed away in 2012, after having been a part of my life for over twenty years. Every year in elementary school on Halloween, the teacher would roll out the video cart. Back then, monstrous CRTVs were strapped to these dangerously top heavy flimsy carts with a VCR, an alarming number of kids were crushed under those things back in the 80s and 90s, and we would watch "The Halloween Tree" and "Something Wicked This Way Comes." The former, an animated feature, the latter, a traumatizing entry from the Dark Disney era of the 80s.

I absolutely loved that film.

I read his books, and enjoyed his contributions to some of my favorite shows like the "Twilight Zone," such as "Sing the Body Electric." That goes without mentioning, the inspirations he contributed to some of my favorite authors. Safe to say, without Ray

Bradbury, there would be no Stephen King, and with no Stephen King, there would be a lot fewer horror writers, myself included.

Upon hearing of his passing, I was saddened, but also inspired to write this story in his honor. While I could never in a million years manage to copy his almost poetic prose, I feel this story does a decent job of capturing the atmosphere of the film, along with the themes of lamenting lost and self-guilt.

Even as I write this and think of all we owe this great man, I have tears in my eyes.

This one is for you, Ray.

The Balloon

I grew up reading EC comics. I absolutely loved them. They were most famous for their horror comics, "Tales from the Crypt," "Horrors from the Vault," and "Volumes of Terror." They were so amazing. Graphic and gory, and way more adult in theme than my Marvel or DC comics at the time. The stories were great, but theartwork was so...gooshy. They stayed with you. I was thrilled when I read "Salem's Lot" and found out that one of my favorite tales, "Midnight Mess," was also one of Stephen King's, and part of the inspiration for the story. I agree with King, the artwork was excellent. Especially when they tap the poor bastard like a beer keg.

Despite the false moral outrage that killed the comic company, the comics were not all mindless violence and gore. For the most part, the people getting got in them more or less deserved their fate. There actually were some morals. They were usually victims of their own evil deeds or hubris. They were crooked businessmen, criminals, cheating spouses—in short, bad things happening to bad people. So, you never really felt sorry for these people.

Unlike many of my stories where bad things happened to people though no real fault of their own. I think this reflects the randomness of the real world. The idea that bad things can happen to good people frights humanity and is part of why we invented religion. We want to believe in Karma, we want to believe there is a plan, and that bad people will get theirs in the end. Though these days, it feels more like bad people get rewarded for their evil deeds rather than punished. Hard to believe that we all grew up reading comics, and this is how things turned out. All those billionaires, and not one Batman?

In this story, I created a character who is horrible—a vain, selfish, self-involved, unapologetic bitch. I did this so that the reader could feel good for once that a character was getting brutally beaten with the Krama stick. And the threat being something as innocuous as a toy balloon, I find interesting. There is something about taking something we see as an innocent, everyday object and turning it sinister that really is the bread and butter of horror, though some critics think Stephen King has been playing it a bit too fast and loose with that concept for the last thirty years.

Personally, I laughed the whole time I wrote those scenes, but I'm sure that's not a sign of a disturbed mind.

Charlie Wasn't There

I hate prompts.

Some people see them as tools or fun exercises. I see them as a crutch for the terminally unimaginative. I find them extremely limiting. There is something to be said for the inventiveness that comes out of limitations, but this is not it for me. I get boxed in and this happens. The prompt was the title of the story, and it had to be used within a horror story about the ecological damage man has done. This was set up for an anthology some agent was putting together. I made sure to follow all the guidelines and rules to try to get as close as humanly possible to what they were asking for. I could not have hit the mark any closer had I smeared myself in peanut butter and jumped headfirst through their front window.

Imagine my shock when I was told that I completely misunderstood the assignment. I was not shocked at all. This is a well-known trope in the industry. No matter how well an agent fits your work or your work fits what the agent says they want, it's a guaranteed rejection.

The anthology project fell apart completely when it was made public that the agent was rejecting people not because their work didn't fit their prompt and theme, but because the agent was only looking for a "certain type" of author. That being, best-selling/award-winning established household names and expect-

ing them to contribute for the "exposure." The authors who were onboard that had been accepted learned of this, and while I wish I could say they resigned on principal to support lesser-known indie artists, they did so solely citing it was an insult to expect them to do it for exposure.

It felt like a shame to just throw the story away after so much work, and I like the monster in this one. Another Lovecraft inspired entity, in this case, the Shunned house, where a father and son digging in the basement of a supposedly haunted house find the elbow of a colossal beast. The idea that there are ancient monsters and eldritch gods buried beneath our feet is a common theme for Lovecraft, which he used a number of times.

I took this and ran with the idea of a fracking company accidentally awaking such a monster. Not knowing that this would later be used as the plot to the film "Underwater," where a deep-sea mining team accidentally finds a Cthulhu-like creature at the bottom of the sea. Not saying they stole the idea from me, especially not since it's the plot of a "South Park" episode, too.

The thing I liked most about this story is that I didn't bother to actually describe the monster. Another thing that Lovecraft commonly did, such as with the Hounds of Tindalos in his story the "Whisper in the Darkness." The narrator simply describes the monster as so maddening that his brain refuses to see it. He simply sees it as a combination of a blank spot in his vision, and the footprints it leaves in the snow.

In the Valley of the Garden

This is the third and final Lovecraft inspired story where I try to imitate his style. While "Charlie Wasn't There" has Lovecraftian elements and feels a bit like "In the Mountains of Madness," it doesn't try to copy Lovecraft's writing style.

The main thing I was working with for this story was the journal style of writing, similar to Stoker's "Dracula," or King's "Jerusalem's Lot." Two works I was familiar with at the time which used the style. I really wanted to try to capture that historical feel as it were, and trying to push myself to see such an event through the eyes of someone who didn't have thirty years of bad movies as a frame of reference.

Of course, this is one of my earlier works where I was still trying to get a handle on the essence of horror, so I tended to rely on edgy shock value and gore rather than more subtle horror. I still find it a bit lazy and could have done better, but I think it's still a good Lovecraftian story and achieves what I set out to do with it.

It was also far too long for a lit mag submission. While trying to submit to literary magazines, most of which would set word limits on submissions, I figured out how to finally get relatively reliable acceptances. Most of the limitations were due to the fact that paying mags don't really have a lot of money to spend on writers. Many of them are run on shoestring budgets by people doing it for the love of the craft. God bless those people. And Lord knows, none of us write for the money, because there is none. What little money I've received from my writing usually goes right back out for some expense. My first royalty check for "Midnight Falls" was spent getting an oil change for my eighteen-year-old car.

So, what I had to do to get these ungainly stories excepted was to notify the mags that I would accept their payrate up to the maximum word count. Many agreed to this, and I started getting stories published on a more regular basis. You are looking at about ten years of work in this collection.

Of course, the unions will probably be upset about this but, if they don't want people to have to do things like this, they have to start actually helping indie authors.

The Passenger

This is probably the best story in the collection, at least, according to readers, and I can see why. It's fun, classical horror from the 70s/80s era. This very much could've been an episode on "Tales from the Crypt." Sadly, this is another story where an otherwise undeserving character has their life ruined by being in the wrong place at the wrong time. Though still very much in line with the theme of road trips.

The key draw for me was the Road Devil character. I love how enigmatic he is, and that was by design. He owes this to two key

Stephen King villains. As you know, I'm a huge King Fan, and growing up during the 90s, I got to enjoy the wonder and magic that were the Stephen King Miniseries. Realizing that his works were too big to translate into movies well, they opted for breaking them down into hour long shorts they could air each night for a week. Which was a good call following the disastrous attempt at letting Stephen direct "Maximum Overdrive."

While Stephen is a phenomenal writer, an underrated actor, and fairly talented musician, the man cannot direct his way out of a wet paper bag. King ruined what was a pretty compelling short story. But if anyone is going to ruin your work, might as well be you.

The King Miniseries' were amazing. Some of them stinkers, like "The Tommy Knockers" and the "Salem's Lot" remake. Others like "It" and "The Stand" were great. But there was none better than "Storm of the Century." That one was an absolute banger, maybe because it was written to be a TV series.

King adaptations are weird. Most of his short stories don't have enough meat on them to be feature length films, but his novels have far too much subtext to be paired down into a two hour film. The sweet spot are the novellas, like "The Mist" and "Secret Window," which I maintain are some of his best adaptations, as they fix King's well known weak endings.

Out of the miniseries, we got two amazing characters, though. Randal Flagg, played by Jamey Sheridan, and Andre Linoge, played by Colm Feore. These characters owe as much to the actors' talents as King's writing, but they are fascinating characters because of how little we know of them. Throughout "Storm of the Century" and "The Stand," we don't know much about Flagg or Linoge, other than what we see of the violent and charismatic facades they project. By the time these stories are over, we are left with more questions than answers. Who really are they, where do they come from, what are their powers, and are they what they claim to be? One of the biggest theories is that Flagg and Linoge are the same character with ties to the "Dark Tower."

I wanted this same kind of element for my character, and he very much emulates similar vibes to Flagg. The casual, laid back, almost cult leader like Charisma. His friendly demeanor is all but an act hiding a deep dark evil underneath. While from Linoge, he takes a surrealness with his weirdly clean sneakers and possession of knowledge and abilities he should not have.

His flashing of his wolf-like teeth is a nod to Linoge, who does the same in the series, showing that while he looks like a man, it's more of wolf in sheep's clothing kind of deal, and what lies beneath could drive a man to madness.

He also derives his almost random acts of violence and trauma from Norse/Pagan trickster gods. He is puckish in his cruelty and does not spare anyone from his wicked little games, whose rules are known only to him.

The road devil moniker, and I guess you would say concept, comes from the old Robert Johnson folklore of a blues man who meets the devil at the crossroads and sells his soul for musical talent. Though, this road devil is a tad bit more capricious. These are, in fact, a sequel/prequel to this short story called "The Cross Road Blues" in which we see the road devil up to his old tricks, but this time more in line with the folktale. It doesn't appear here due to publication rights having not reverted yet, but maybe in another ten years you will see it.

This was also the first appearance of Trans National, a sort of faceless evil corporation stand-in that I use in a number of stories. It appears as an energy company in "Charlie Wasn't There," and in "The Valley of the Garden" behind the plan to drain the valley. It was inspired by the Dunwich Boring Company from the Fallout video game series that, in turn, owes its inspiration to Lovecraft's "The Dunwich Horror." In the Fallout games, the Dunwich Boring Company had a vaguely sinister mission statement that seems to be digging up Lovecraftian horrors within the game's universe. Trans National does much the same, though it's unclear as to whether this is on purpose or an accidental consequence of corporate greed. We will have to see.

That about wraps it up. Thank you, reader, for coming along with me on this not-so-magical journey. Hopefully these tales have helped you whittle away the long hours and miles you travel, keeping you entertained. Remember, not all who wander are lost, and not all those you travel with can be trusted. But this is where we part ways, my faithful trail hands, for we are at a crossroad of our own. You must go your way, and I must go mine.

Remember to take care, because the roads are dark, dangerous, and deep, and you still have many miles to go before you sleep.

CHECK OUT THESE OTHER THRILLING READS FROM ROWAN PROSE:

John Evans's debut, "Midnight Falls," has received many accolades. He also writes the "Tobias Halson Hunter" urban fantasy series and various short stories. Inspired by greats like Stephen King and Gary Brandner, he loves all things "old school" horror, and often claims his purpose is to give readers a little bit of fun Lovecraftian escapism from the scarier real world. He resides in Kentucky.

www.ingramcontent.com/pod-product-compliance
Lightning Source LLC
LaVergne TN
LVHW040135080526
838202LV00042B/2917